Praise for Debbie Macomber's
bestselling novels from Ballantine Books

Must Love Flowers

"A testament to the power of new beginnings . . . Wise, warm, witty, and charmingly full of hope, this story celebrates the surprising and unexpected ways that family, friendship, and love can lift us up."
—KRISTIN HANNAH,
bestselling author of *The Nightingale*

"Uplifting, warm, and hopeful . . . With her signature charm and wit, Debbie Macomber proves that the best relationships, like the perfect blooms, are always worth the wait. This can't-miss novel is Macomber at the height of her storytelling prowess. I absolutely adored it!"
—KRISTY WOODSON HARVEY, *New York Times* bestselling author of *The Summer of Songbirds*

"Debbie Macomber never fails to deliver an uplifting, heart-warming story. Whether you're just starting out, just starting over, or anything in between, *Must Love Flowers* should be at the top of your summer reading list!"
—BRENDA NOVAK, *New York Times* bestselling author of *Before We Were Strangers*

The Best Is Yet to Come

"Macomber's latest is a wonderful inspirational read that has just enough romance as the characters heal their painful emotional wounds." —*Library Journal*

"This tale of redemption and kindness is a gift to Macomber's many readers and all who love tales of sweet and healing romance." —*Booklist*

"Macomber never disappoints. Tears and laughter abound in this story of loss and healing that will wrap you up and pull you in; readers will finish it in one sitting."
—*Library Journal* (starred review)

"Macomber's story of tragedy and triumph is emotionally engaging from the outset and ends with a satisfying conclusion. Readers will be most taken by the characters, particularly Annie, a heartwarming lead who bolsters the novel."
—*Publishers Weekly*

Any Dream Will Do

"*Any Dream Will Do* is . . . so realistic, it's hard to believe it's fiction through the end. Even then, it's hard to say goodbye to these characters. This standalone novel will make you hope it becomes a Hallmark movie, or gets a sequel. It's an inspiring, hard-to-put-down tale. . . . You need to read it."
—*The Free Lance–Star*

"*Any Dream Will Do* by Debbie Macomber is a study in human tolerance and friendship. Macomber masterfully shows how all people have value." —*Fresh Fiction*

If Not for You

"A heartwarming story of forgiveness and unexpected love."
—*Harlequin Junkie*

"A fun, sweet read." —*Publishers Weekly*

A Girl's Guide to Moving On

"Beloved author Debbie Macomber reaches new heights in this wise and beautiful novel. It's the kind of reading experience that comes along only rarely, bearing the hallmarks of a classic. The timeless wisdom in these pages will stay with you long after the book is closed."
—SUSAN WIGGS, #1 *New York Times* bestselling author of *Starlight on Willow Lake*

"Debbie dazzles! A wonderful story of friendship, forgiveness, and the power of love. I devoured every page!"
—SUSAN MALLERY, #1 *New York Times*
bestselling author of *The Friends We Keep*

Last One Home

"Fans of bestselling author Macomber will not be disappointed by this compelling stand-alone novel." —*Library Journal*

ROSE HARBOR

Sweet Tomorrows

"Macomber fans will leave the Rose Harbor Inn with warm memories of healing, hope, and enduring love."
—*Kirkus Reviews*

"Overflowing with the poignancy, sweetness, conflicts and romance for which Debbie Macomber is famous, *Sweet Tomorrows* captivates from beginning to end." —*Bookreporter*

"Fans will enjoy this final installment of the Rose Harbor series as they see Jo Marie's story finally come to an end."
—*Library Journal*

Silver Linings

"Macomber's homespun storytelling style makes reading an easy venture. . . . She also tosses in some hidden twists and turns that will delight her many longtime fans."
—*Bookreporter*

"Reading Macomber's novels is like being with good friends, talking and sharing joys and sorrows."
—*New York Journal of Books*

Love Letters

"Macomber's mastery of women's fiction is evident in her latest. . . . [She] breathes life into each plotline, carefully intertwining her characters' stories to ensure that none of them overshadow the others. Yet it is her ability to capture different facets of emotion which will entrance fans and newcomers alike." —*Publishers Weekly*

"Romance and a little mystery abound in this third installment of Macomber's series set at Cedar Cove's Rose Harbor Inn. . . . Readers of Robyn Carr and Sherryl Woods will enjoy Macomber's latest, which will have them flipping pages until the end and eagerly anticipating the next installment."
—*Library Journal* (starred review)

"Uplifting . . . a cliffhanger ending for Jo Marie begs for a swift resolution in the next book." —*Kirkus Reviews*

Rose Harbor in Bloom

"[Debbie Macomber] draws in threads of her earlier book in this series, *The Inn at Rose Harbor,* in what is likely to be just as comfortable a place for Macomber fans as for Jo Marie's guests at the inn." —*The Seattle Times*

"Macomber's legions of fans will embrace this cozy, heartwarming read." —*Booklist*

"Readers will find the emotionally impactful storylines and sweet, redemptive character arcs for which the author is famous. Classic Macomber, which will please fans and keep them coming back for more." —*Kirkus Reviews*

"The storybook scenery of lighthouses, cozy bed and breakfast inns dotting the coastline, and seagulls flying above takes readers on personal journeys of first love, lost love and recaptured love [presenting] love in its purest and most personal forms."
—*Bookreporter*

The Inn at Rose Harbor

"Debbie Macomber's Cedar Cove romance novels have a warm, comfy feel to them. Perhaps that's why they've sold millions."
—*USA Today*

"Debbie Macomber has written a charming, cathartic romance full of tasteful passion and good sense. Reading it is a lot like enjoying comfort food, as you know the book will end well and leave you feeling pleasant and content. The tone is warm and serene, and the characters are likeable yet realistic. . . . *The Inn at Rose Harbor* is a wonderful novel that will keep the reader's undivided attention." —*Bookreporter*

"The prolific Macomber introduces a spin-off of sorts from her popular Cedar Cove series, still set in that fictional small town but centered on Jo Marie Rose, a youngish widow who buys and operates the bed and breakfast of the title. This clever premise allows Macomber to craft stories around the B&B's guests, Abby and Josh in this inaugural effort, while using Jo Marie and her ongoing recovery from the death of her husband Paul in Afghanistan as the series' anchor. . . . With her characteristic optimism, Macomber provides fresh starts for both." —*Booklist*

"Emotionally charged romance." —*Kirkus Reviews*

BLOSSOM STREET

Blossom Street Brides

"A wonderful, love-affirming novel . . . an engaging, emotionally fulfilling story that clearly shows why [Macomber] is a peerless storyteller." —*Examiner.com*

"Rewarding . . . Macomber amply delivers her signature engrossing relationship tales, wrapping her readers in warmth as fuzzy and soft as a hand-knitted creation from everyone's favorite yarn shop." —*Bookreporter*

"Fans will happily return to the warm, welcoming sanctuary of Macomber's Blossom Street, catching up with old friends from past Blossom Street books and meeting new ones being welcomed into the fold." —*Kirkus Reviews*

"Macomber's nondenominational-inspirational women's novel, with its large cast of characters, will resonate with fans of the popular series." —*Booklist*

Starting Now

"Macomber understands the often complex nature of a woman's friendships, as well as the emotional language women use with their friends." —*New York Journal of Books*

"There is a reason that legions of Macomber fans ask for more Blossom Street books. They fully engage her readers as her characters discover happiness, purpose, and meaning in life. . . . Macomber's feel-good novel, emphasizing interpersonal relationships and putting people above status and objects, is truly satisfying." —*Booklist* (starred review)

"Macomber's writing and storytelling deliver what she's famous for—a smooth, satisfying tale with characters her fans will cheer for and an arc that is cozy, heartwarming and ends with the expected happily-ever-after." —*Kirkus Reviews*

CHRISTMAS NOVELS

The Christmas Spirit

"Exactly what readers want from a Macomber holiday outing."
—*Publishers Weekly*

"With almost all of Debbie Macomber's novels, the reader is not only given a captivating story, but also a lesson in life."
—*New York Journal of Books*

Dear Santa

"[*Dear Santa*] is a quick and fun tale offering surprises and blessings and an all-around feel-good read."
—*New York Journal of Books*

Jingle All the Way

"[*Jingle All the Way*] will leave readers feeling merry and bright." —*Publishers Weekly*

"This delightful Christmas story can be enjoyed any time of the year." —*New York Journal of Books*

A Mrs. Miracle Christmas

"This sweet, inspirational story . . . had enough dramatic surprises to keep pages turning."
—*Library Journal* (starred review)

"Anyone who enjoys Christmas will appreciate this sparkling snow globe of a story." —*Publishers Weekly*

Alaskan Holiday

"Picture-perfect . . . this charmer will please Macomber fans and newcomers alike." —*Publishers Weekly*

"[A] tender romance lightly brushed with holiday magic."
—*Library Journal*

Merry and Bright

"Heartfelt, cheerful . . . Readers looking for a light and sweet holiday treat will find it here." —*Publishers Weekly*

Twelve Days of Christmas

"Another heartwarming seasonal Macomber tale, which fans will find as bright and cozy as a blazing fire on Christmas Eve." —*Kirkus Reviews*

DEBBIE MACOMBER

That Christmas Magic

Christmas Masquerade
and *The Gift of Christmas*

BALLANTINE BOOKS
NEW YORK

That Christmas Magic is a work of fiction.
Names, characters, places, and incidents are the products of
the author's imagination or are used fictitiously.
Any resemblance to actual events, locales, or persons,
living or dead, is entirely coincidental.

2024 Ballantine Books Mass Market Edition

Christmas Masquerade copyright © 1985 by Debbie Macomber
The Gift of Christmas copyright © 1984 by Debbie Macomber
Excerpt from *A Christmas Duet* by Debbie Macomber
copyright © 2024 by Debbie Macomber

Published in the United States by Ballantine Books,
an imprint of Random House, a division of
Penguin Random House LLC, New York.

BALLANTINE is a registered trademark and the colophon is
a trademark of Penguin Random House LLC.

Christmas Masquerade was originally published in the
United States by Silhouette Romance, New York, in 1985.

The Gift of Christmas was originally published in the
United States by Silhouette Inspirations, New York, in 1984.

This book contains an excerpt from the forthcoming book
A Christmas Duet by Debbie Macomber. This excerpt
has been set for this edition only and may not reflect
the final content of the forthcoming edition.

ISBN 978-0-593-49611-4
Ebook ISBN 978-0-593-49612-1

Cover images: © Dana Hoff/Getty Images (house scene with
christmas trees), © Aaron Foster/Getty Images (sky),
© quavondo/Getty Images (christmas lights in eaves),
© Bulgac/Getty Images (trees in background),
© Yellow Cat/Shutterstock (hat on sled),
© fishgrilll/Shutterstock (stars in sky),
© Evikka/Shutterstock (sled)

Printed in the United States of America

randomhousebooks.com

2 4 6 8 9 7 5 3 1

Ballantine Books mass market edition: October 2024

Dear Friends,

I've always been a Christmas kind of girl. Even as a youngster, the holidays were my favorite time of the year, and they remain so even now. Everything felt magical to me. Some of my most treasured memories are baking cookies with my mother, decorating the tree with tinsel and special ornaments. And, of course opening our presents after midnight mass on Christmas Eve.

It was because of my love for Christmas that it was only natural when I started my publishing career to write about that time of year. The two stories you are about to read were some of the first books I wrote that revolve around the holiday season.

My hope is that you will feel the warmth and peace of the season as you step into this festive world of fiction.

Hearing from my readers is something I've always considered a gift. Your feedback and comments have been the guiding force of my career. You can reach me through all the normal media outlets and my website. Or you can write me at P.O. Box 1458, Port Orchard, WA 98366.

Debbie Macomber

Christmas Masquerade

Prologue

The blast of a jazz saxophone that pierced the night was immediately followed by the jubilant sounds of a dixieland band. A shrieking whistle reverberated through the confusion. Singing, dancing, hooting and laughter surrounded Jo Marie Early as she painstakingly made her way down Tulane Avenue. Attracted by the parade, she'd arrived just in time to watch the flambeaux carriers light a golden arc of bouncing flames from one side of the street to the other. Now she was trapped in the milling mass of humanity when she had every intention of going in the opposite direction. The heavy Mardi Gras crowds hampered her progress to a slow crawl. The observation of the "Fat Tuesday" had commenced two weeks earlier with a series of parades and festive balls. Tonight the celebrating culminated in a frenzy of singing, lively dancing and masqueraders who roamed the brilliant streets.

New Orleans went crazy at this time of year, throwing a city-wide party that attracted a million guests. After twenty-three years, Jo Marie thought she would be accustomed to the maniacal behavior in the city she loved. But how could she criticize when she was a participant herself? Tonight, if she ever made it out of this crowd, she was attending a private party dressed as Florence Nightingale. Not her most original costume idea, but the best she could do on such short notice. Just this morning she'd been in a snowstorm in Minnesota and had arrived back this afternoon to hear the news that her roommate, Kelly Beaumont, was in the hospital for a tonsillectomy. Concerned, Joe Marie had quickly donned one of Kelly's nurse's uniforms so she could go directly to the party after visiting Kelly in the hospital.

With a sigh of abject frustration, Jo Marie realized she was being pushed in the direction opposite the hospital.

"Please, let me through," she called, struggling against the swift current of the merrymaking crowd.

"Which way?" a gravelly, male voice asked in her ear. "Do you want to go this way?" He pointed away from the crowd.

"Yes . . . please."

The voice turned out to be one of three young men who cleared a path for Jo Marie and helped her onto a side street.

Laughing, she turned to find all three were dressed as cavaliers of old. They bowed in gentlemanly fashion, tucking their arms at their waists and sweeping their plumed hats before them.

"The Three Musketeers at your disposal, fair lady."

"Your rescue is most welcome, kind sirs," Jo Marie shouted to be heard above the sound of the boisterous celebration.

"Your destination?"

Rather than try to be heard, Jo Marie pointed toward the hospital.

"Then allow us to escort you," the second offered gallantly.

Jo Marie wasn't sure she should trust three young men wearing red tights. But after all, it was Mardi Gras and the tale was sure to cause Kelly to smile. And that was something her roommate hadn't been doing much of lately.

The three young men formed a protective circle around Jo Marie and led the way down a less crowded side street, weaving in and out of the throng when necessary.

Glancing above to the cast iron balcony railing that marked the outer limits of the French Quarter, Jo Marie realized her heroes were heading for the heart of the partying, apparently more interested in capturing her for themselves than in delivering her to the hospital. "We're headed the wrong way," she shouted.

"This is a short cut," the tallest of the trio explained humorously. "We know of several people this way in need of nursing."

Unwilling to be trapped in their game, Jo Marie broke away from her gallant cavaliers and walked as quickly as her starched white uniform would allow. Dark tendrils of her hair escaped the carefully coiled chignon and framed her small face. Her fingers pushed them aside, uncaring for the moment.

Heavy footsteps behind her assured Jo Marie that the Three Musketeers weren't giving up on her so easily. Increasing her pace, she ran across the street and was within a half block of the hospital parking lot when she collided full speed into a solid object.

Stunned, it took Jo Marie a minute to recover and recognize that whatever she'd hit was warm and lean. Jo Marie raised startled brown eyes to meet the intense gray eyes of the most striking man she had ever seen. His hands reached for her shoulder to steady her.

"Are you hurt?" he asked in a deep voice that was low and resonant, oddly sensuous.

Jo Marie shook her head. "Are you?" There was some quality so mesmerizing about this man that she couldn't move her eyes. Although she was self-consciously staring, Jo Marie was powerless to break eye contact. He wasn't tall—under six feet so that she had only to tip her head back slightly to meet his look. Nor dark. His hair was brown, but a shade no deeper than her own soft chestnut curls. And he wasn't handsome. Not in the urbane sense. Although his look and his clothes spoke of wealth and breeding, Jo Marie knew intuitively that this man worked, played and loved hard. His brow was creased in what looked like a permanent frown and his mouth was a fraction too full.

Not tall, not dark, not handsome, but the embodiment of every fantasy Jo Marie had ever dreamed.

Neither of them moved for a long, drawn-out moment. Jo Marie felt as if she'd turned to stone. All those silly, schoolgirl dreams she'd shelved in the back of her mind as products of a whimsical imagination stood before her. He was the swashbuckling pirate to her captured maiden, Rhett Butler to her Scarlett O'Hara, Heathcliff to her Catherine . . .

"Are you hurt?" He broke into her thoughts. Eyes as gray as a winter sea narrowed with concern.

"No." She assured him with a shake of her head and forced her attention over her shoulder. Her three gallant heroes had discovered another female attraction and had directed their attention elsewhere, no longer interested in following her.

His hands continued to hold her shoulder. "You're a nurse?" he asked softly.

"Florence Nightingale," she corrected with a soft smile.

His finger was under her chin. Lifting her eyes, she saw his softly quizzical gaze. "Have we met?"

"No." It was on the tip of her tongue to tell him that yes they had met once, a long time ago in her romantic daydreams. But he'd probably laugh. Who wouldn't? Jo Marie wasn't a star-struck teenager, but a woman who had long since abandoned the practice of reading fairy tales.

His eyes were intent as they roamed her face, memorizing every detail, seeking something he couldn't define. He seemed as caught up in this moment as she.

"You remind me of a painting I once saw," he said, then blinked, apparently surprised that he'd spoken out loud.

"No one's ever done my portrait," Jo Marie murmured, frozen into immobility by the breathless bewilderment that lingered between them.

His eyes skidded past her briefly to rest on the fun-seeking Musketeers. "You were running from them?"

The spellbinding moment continued.

"Yes."

"Then I rescued you."

Jo Marie confirmed his statement as a large group of merrymakers crossed the street toward them. But she barely noticed. What captured her attention was the way in which this dream man was studying her.

"Every hero deserves a reward," he said.

Jo Marie watched him with uncertainty. "What do you mean?"

"This." The bright light of the streetlamp dimmed as he lowered his head, blocking out the golden rays. His warm mouth settled over hers, holding her prisoner, kissing her with a hunger as deep as the sea.

In the dark recesses of her mind, Jo Marie realized she should pull away. A man she didn't know was kissing her deeply, passionately. And the sensations he aroused were far beyond anything she'd ever felt. A dream that had become reality.

Singing voices surrounded her and before she could recognize the source the kiss was abruptly broken.

The Three Musketeers and a long line of others were doing a gay rendition of the rumba. Before she could protest, before she was even aware of what was happening, Jo Marie was grabbed from behind by the waist and forced to join in the rambunctious song and dance.

Her dark eyes sought the dream man only to discover that he was frantically searching the crowd for her, pushing people aside. Desperately, Jo Marie fought to break free, but couldn't. She called out, but to no avail, her voice drowned out by the song of the others. The long line of singing pranksters turned the corner, forcing Jo Marie to go with them. Her last sight of the dream man was of him pushing his way through the crowd to find her, but by then it was too late. She, too, had lost him.

One

"You've got that look in your eye again," pixie-faced Kelly Beaumont complained. "I swear every time you pick me up at the hospital something strange comes over you."

Jo Marie forced a smile, but her soft mouth trembled with the effort. "You're imagining things."

Kelly's narrowed look denied that, but she said nothing.

If Jo Marie had felt like being honest, she would have recognized the truth of what her friend was saying. Every visit to the hospital produced a deluge of memories. In the months that had passed, she was certain that the meeting with the dream man had blossomed and grown out of proportion in her memory. Every word, every action had been relived a thousand times until her mind had memorized the smallest detail, down to the musky, spicy scent of him. Jo Marie had never told anyone about that night of the Mardi Gras. A couple of times she'd wanted to confide in Kelly, but the words wouldn't come. Late in the evenings after she'd prepared for bed, it was the dream man's face that drifted into her consciousness as she fell asleep. Jo Marie couldn't understand why this man who had invaded her life so briefly would have such an overwhelming effect. And yet those few minutes had lingered all these months. Maybe in every woman's life there was a man who was meant to fulfill her dreams. And, in that brief five-minute interlude during Mardi Gras, Jo Marie had found hers.

". . . Thanksgiving's tomorrow and Christmas is just around the corner." Kelly interrupted Jo Marie's thoughts. The blaring horn of an irritated motorist caused them both to grimace. Whenever possible, they preferred taking the bus, but both wanted an early start on the holiday weekend.

"Where has the year gone?" Jo Marie commented absently. She was paying close attention to the heavy traffic as she merged with the late evening flow that led Interstate 10 through the downtown district. The freeway would deliver them to the two-bedroom apartment they shared.

"I saw Mark today," Kelly said casually.

Something about the way Kelly spoke caused Jo Marie to turn her head. "Oh." It wasn't unnatural that her brother, a resident doctor at Tulane, would run into Kelly. After all, they both worked in the same hospital. "Did World War Three break out?" Jo Marie had never known any two people who could find more things to argue about. After three years, she'd given up trying to figure out why Mark and Kelly couldn't get along. Saying that they rubbed each other the wrong way seemed too trite an explanation. Antagonistic behavior wasn't characteristic of either of them. Kelly was a dedicated nurse and Mark a struggling resident doctor. But when the two were together, the lightning arced between them like a turbulent electrical storm. At one time Jo Marie had thought Kelly and Mark might be interested in each other. But after months of constant bickering she was forced to believe that the only thing between them was her overactive imagination.

"What did Mark have to say?"

Pointedly, Kelly turned her head away and stared out the window. "Oh, the usual."

The low, forced cheerfulness in her roommate's voice didn't fool Jo Marie. Where Kelly was concerned, Mark was merciless. He didn't mean to be cruel or insulting, but he loved to tease Kelly about her family's wealth. Not that money or position was that important to Kelly. "You mean he was kidding you about playing at being a nurse again." That was Mark's favorite crack.

One delicate shoulder jerked in response. "Sometimes I think he must hate me," she whispered, pretending a keen interest in the view outside the car window.

The soft catch in Kelly's voice brought Jo Marie's attention from the freeway to her friend. "Don't mind Mark. He doesn't mean anything by it. He loves to tease. You should hear some of the things he says about my job—you'd think a travel agent did nothing but hand out brochures for the tropics."

Kelly's abrupt nod was unconvincing.

Mentally, Jo Marie decided to have a talk with her big brother. He shouldn't tease Kelly as if she were his sister. Kelly didn't know how to react to it. As the youngest daughter of a large southern candy manufacturer, Kelly had been sheltered and pampered most of her life. Her only brother was years older and apparently the age difference didn't allow for many sibling conflicts. With four brothers, Jo Marie was no stranger to family squabbles and could stand her own against any one of them.

The apartment was a welcome sight after the twenty-minute freeway drive. Jo Marie and Kelly thought of it as their port in the storm. The two-floor apartment building resembled the historic mansion from *Gone With the Wind*. It maintained the flavor of the Old South without the problem of constant repairs typical of many older buildings.

The minute they were in the door, Kelly headed for her room. "If you don't mind I think I'll pack."

"Sure. Go ahead." Carelessly, Jo Marie kicked off her low-heeled shoes. Slouching on the love seat, she leaned her head back and closed her eyes. The strain of the hectic rush hour traffic and the tension of a busy day ebbed away with every relaxing breath.

The sound of running bathwater didn't surprise Jo Marie. Kelly wanted to get an early start. Her family lived in an ultramodern home along Lakeshore Drive. The house bordered Lake Pontchartrain. Jo Marie had been inside the Beaumont home only once. That had been enough for her to realize just how good the candy business was.

Jo Marie was sure that Charles Beaumont may have disapproved of his only daughter moving into an apartment with a "nobody" like her, but once he'd learned that she was the great-great-granddaughter of Jubal Anderson Early, a Confederate Army colonel, he'd sanctioned the move. Sometime during the Civil War, Colonel Early had been instrumental in saving the life of a young Beaumont. Hence, a-hundred-and-some-odd years later, Early was a name to respect.

Humming Christmas music softly to herself, Jo Marie wandered into the kitchen and pulled the orange juice from the refrigerator shelf.

"Want a glass?" She held up the pitcher to Kelly who stepped from the bathroom, dressed in a short terry-cloth robe, with a thick towel securing her bouncy blond curls. One look at her friend and Jo Marie set the ceramic container on the kitchen counter.

"You've been crying." They'd lived together for three years, and apart from one sad, sentimental movie, Jo Marie had never seen Kelly cry.

"No, something's in my eye," she said and sniffled.

"Then why's your nose so red?"

"Maybe I'm catching a cold." She offered the weak explanation and turned sharply toward her room.

Jo Marie's smooth brow narrowed. This was Mark's doing. She was convinced he was the cause of Kelly's uncharacteristic display of emotion.

Something rang untrue about the whole situation between Kelly and Mark. Kelly wasn't a soft, southern belle who fainted at the least provocation. That was another teasing comment Mark enjoyed hurling at her. Kelly was a lady, but no shrinking violet. Jo Marie had witnessed Kelly in action, fighting for her patients and several political causes. The girl didn't back down often. After Thanksgiving, Jo Marie would help Kelly fine-tune a few witty comebacks. As Mark's sister, Jo Marie was well acquainted with her brother's weak spots. The only way to fight fire was with fire she mused humorously. Together, Jo Marie and Kelly would teach Mark a lesson.

"You want me to fix something to eat before you head for your parents?" Jo Marie shouted from the kitchen. She was standing in front of the cupboard, scanning its meager contents. "How does soup and a sandwich sound?"

"Boring," Kelly returned. "I'm not really hungry."

"Eight hours of back-breaking work on the surgical ward and you're not interested in food? Are you having problems with your tonsils again?"

"I had them out, remember?"

Slowly, Jo Marie straightened. Yes, she remembered. All too well. It had been outside the hospital that she'd literally run into the dream man. Unbidden thoughts of him crowded her mind and forcefully she shook her head to free herself of his image.

Jo Marie had fixed herself dinner and was sitting in front of the television watching the evening news by the time Kelly reappeared.

"I'm leaving now."

"Okay." Jo Marie didn't take her eyes off the television. "Have a happy Thanksgiving; don't eat too much turkey and trimmings."

"Don't throw any wild parties while I'm away." That was a small joke between them. Jo Marie rarely dated these days. Not since—Mardi Gras. Kelly couldn't understand this change in her friend and affectionately teased Jo Marie about her sudden lack of an interesting social life.

"Oh, Kelly, before I forget—" Jo Marie gave her a wicked smile "—bring back some pralines, would you? After all, it's the holidays, so we can splurge."

At any other time Kelly would rant that she'd grown up with candy all her life and detested the sugary sweet concoction. Pralines were Jo Marie's weakness, but the candy would rot before Kelly would eat any of it.

"Sure, I'll be happy to," she agreed lifelessly and was gone before Jo Marie realized her friend had slipped away.

Returning her attention to the news, Jo Marie was more determined than ever to have a talk with her brother.

The doorbell chimed at seven. Jo Marie was spreading a bright red polish on her toenails. She grumbled under her breath and screwed on the top of the bottle. But before she could answer the door, her brother strolled into the apartment and flopped down on the sofa that sat at right angles to the matching love seat.

"Come in and make yourself at home," Jo Marie commented dryly.

"I don't suppose you've got anything to eat around here." Dark brown eyes glanced expectantly into the kitchen. All five of the Early children shared the same dusty, dark eyes.

"This isn't a restaurant, you know."

"I know. By the way, where's money bags?"

"Who?" Confused, Jo Marie glanced up from her toes.

"Kelly."

Jo Marie didn't like the reference to Kelly's family wealth, but decided now wasn't the time to comment. Her brother worked long hours and had been out of sorts lately. "She's left for her parents' home already."

A soft snicker followed Jo Marie's announcement.

"Damn it, Mark, I wish you'd lay off Kelly. She's not used to being teased. It really bothers her."

"I'm only joking," Mark defended himself. "Kell knows that."

"I don't think she does. She was crying tonight and I'm sure it's your fault."

"Kelly crying?" He straightened and leaned forward, linking his hands. "But I was only kidding."

"That's the problem. You can't seem to let up on her. You're always putting her down one way or another."

Mark reached for a magazine, but not before Jo Marie saw that his mouth was pinched and hard. "She asks for it."

Rolling her eyes, Jo Marie continued adding the fire-engine-red color to her toes. It wouldn't do any good for her to argue with Mark. Kelly and Mark had to come to an agreement on their own. But that didn't mean Jo Marie couldn't hand Kelly ammunition now and again. Her brother had his vulnerable points, and Jo Marie would just make certain Kelly was aware of them. Then she could sit back and watch the sparks fly.

Busy with her polish, Jo Marie didn't notice for several minutes how quiet her brother had become. When she lifted her gaze to him, she saw that he had a pained, troubled look. His brow was furrowed in thought.

"I lost a child today," he announced tightly. "I couldn't understand it either. Not medically, I don't mean that. Anything can happen. She'd been brought in last week with a ruptured appendix. We knew from the beginning it was going to be touch and go." He paused and breathed in sharply. "But you know, deep down inside I believed she'd make it. She was their only daughter. The apple of her parents' eye. If all the love in that mother's heart couldn't hold back death's hand, then what good is medical science? What good am I?"

Mark had raised these questions before and Jo Marie had no answers. "I don't know," she admitted solemnly and reached out to touch his hand in reassurance. Mark didn't want to hear the pat answers. He couldn't see that now. Not when he felt like he'd failed this little girl and her parents in some obscure way. At times like these, she'd look at her brother who was a strong, committed doctor and see the doubt in his eyes. She had no answers. Sometimes she wasn't even sure she completely understood his questions.

After wiping his hand across his tired face, Mark stood. "I'm on duty tomorrow morning so I probably won't be at the folks' place until late afternoon. Tell Mom I'll try to make it on time. If I can't, the least you can do is to be sure and save a plate for me."

Knowing Mark, he was likely to go without eating until tomorrow if left to his own devices. "Let me fix you something now," Jo Marie offered. From his unnatural pallor, Jo Marie surmised that Mark couldn't even remember when he'd eaten his last decent meal, coffee and a doughnut on the run excluded.

He glanced at his watch. "I haven't got time. Thanks anyway." Before she could object, he was at the door.

Why had he come? Jo Marie wondered absently. He'd done a lot of that lately—stopping in for a few minutes without notice. And it wasn't as if her apartment were close to the hospital. Mark had to go out of his way to visit her. With a bemused shrug, she followed him to the front door and watched as he sped away in that rundown old car he was so fond of driving. As he left, Jo Marie mentally questioned if her instincts had been on target all along and Kelly and Mark did hold some deep affection for each other. Mark hadn't come tonight for any specific reason. His first question had been about Kelly. Only later had he mentioned losing the child.

———

"Jo Marie," her mother called from the kitchen. "Would you mind mashing the potatoes?"

The large family kitchen was bustling with activity. The long white countertop was filled with serving bowls ready to be placed on the linen-covered dining room table. Sweet potato and pecan pies were cooling on the smaller kitchen table and the aroma of spice and turkey filled the house.

"Smells mighty good in here," Franklin Early proclaimed, sniffing appreciatively as he strolled into the kitchen and placed a loving arm around his wife's waist.

"Scat," Jo Marie's mother cried with a dismissive wave of her hand. "I won't have you in here sticking your fingers in the pies and blaming it on the boys. Dinner will be ready in ten minutes."

Mark arrived, red faced and slightly breathless. He kissed his mother on the cheek and, when she wasn't looking, popped a sweet pickle into his mouth. "I hope I'm not too late."

"I'd say you had perfect timing," Jo Marie teased and handed him the electric mixer. "Here, mash these potatoes while I finish setting the table."

"No way, little sister." His mouth was twisted mockingly as he gave her back the appliance. "I'll set the table. No one wants lumpy potatoes."

The three younger boys, all in their teens, sat in front of the television watching a football game. The Early family enjoyed sports, especially football. Jo Marie's mother had despaired long ago that her only daughter would ever grow up properly. Instead of playing with dolls, her toys had been cowboy boots and little green army men. Touch football was as much a part of her life as ballet was for some girls.

With Mark out of the kitchen, Jo Marie's mother turned to her. "Have you been feeling all right lately?"

"Me?" The question caught her off guard. "I'm feeling fine. Why shouldn't I be?"

Ruth Early lifted one shoulder in a delicate shrug. "You've had a look in your eye lately." She turned and leaned her hip against the counter, her head tilted at a thoughtful angle. "The last time I saw that look was in your Aunt Bessie's eye before she was married. Tell me, Jo Marie, are you in love?"

Jo Marie hesitated, not knowing how to explain her feelings for a man she had met so briefly. He was more illusion than reality. Her own private fantasy. Those few moments with the dream man were beyond explaining, even to her own mother.

"No," she answered finally, making busy work by placing the serving spoons in the bowls.

"Is he married? Is that it? Save yourself a lot of grief, Jo Marie, and stay away from him if he is. You understand?"

"Yes," she murmured, her eyes avoiding her mother's. For all she knew he could well be married.

Not until late that night did Jo Marie let herself into her apartment. The day had been full. After the huge family dinner, they'd played cards until Mark trapped Jo Marie into playing a game of touch football for old times' sake. Jo Marie agreed and proved that she hadn't lost her "touch."

The apartment looked large and empty. Kelly stayed with her parents over any major holidays. Kelly's family seemed to feel that Kelly still belonged at home and always would, no matter what her age. Although Kelly was twenty-four, the apartment she shared with Jo Marie was more for convenience sake than any need to separate herself from her family.

With her mother's words echoing in her ear, Jo Marie sauntered into her bedroom and dressed for bed. Friday was a work day for her as it was for both Mark and Kelly. The downtown area of New Orleans would be hectic with Christmas shoppers hoping to pick up their gifts from the multitude of sales.

As a travel agent, Jo Marie didn't have many walk-in customers to deal with, but her phone rang continuously. Several people wanted to book holiday vacations, but there was little available that she could offer. The most popular vacation spots had been booked months in advance. Several times her information was accepted with an irritated grumble as if she were to blame. By the time she stepped off the bus outside her apartment, Jo Marie wasn't in any mood for company.

No sooner had the thought formed than she caught sight of her brother. He was parked in the lot outside the apartment building. Hungry and probably looking for a hot meal, she guessed. He knew that their mother had sent a good portion of the turkey and stuffing home with Jo Marie so Mark's appearance wasn't any real surprise.

"Hi," she said and knocked on his car window. The faraway look in his eyes convinced her that after all these years Mark had finally learned to sleep with his eyes open. He was so engrossed in his thoughts that Jo Marie was forced to tap on his window a second time.

"Paging Dr. Early," she mimicked in a high-pitched hospital voice. "Paging Dr. Mark Early."

Mark turned and stared at her blankly. "Oh, hi." He sat up and climbed out of the car.

"I suppose you want something to eat." Her greeting wasn't the least bit cordial, but she was tired and irritable.

The edge of Mark's mouth curled into a sheepish grin. "If it isn't too much trouble."

"No," she offered him an apologetic smile. "It's just been a rough day and my feet hurt."

"My sister sits in an office all day, files her nails, reads books and then complains that her feet hurt."

Jo Marie was too weary to rise to the bait. "Not even your acid tongue is going to get a rise out of me tonight."

"I know something that will," Mark returned smugly.

"Ha." From force of habit, Jo Marie kicked off her shoes and strolled into the kitchen.

"Wanna bet?"

"I'm not a betting person, especially after playing cards with you yesterday, but if you care to impress me, fire away." Crossing her arms, she leaned against the refrigerator door and waited.

"Kelly's engaged."

Jo Marie slowly shook her head in disbelief. "I didn't think you'd stoop to fabrications."

That familiar angry, hurt look stole into Mark's eyes. "It's true, I heard it from the horse's own mouth."

Lightly shaking her head from side to side to clear her thoughts, Jo Marie still came up with a blank. "But who?" Kelly wasn't going out with anyone seriously.

"Some cousin. Rich, no doubt," Mark said and straddled a kitchen chair. "She's got a diamond as big as a baseball. Must be hard for her to work with a rock that size weighing down her hand."

"A cousin?" New Orleans was full of Beaumonts, but none that Kelly had mentioned in particular. "I can't believe it," Jo Marie gasped. "She'd have said something to me."

"From what I understand, she tried to phone last night, but we were still at the folks' house. Just as well," Mark mumbled under his breath. "I'm not about to toast this engagement. First she plays at being nurse and now she wants to play at being a wife."

Mark's bitterness didn't register past the jolt of surprise that Jo Marie felt. "Kelly engaged," she repeated.

"You don't need to keep saying it," Mark snapped.

"Saying what?" A jubilant Kelly walked in the front door.

"Never mind," Mark said and slowly stood. "It's time for me to be going, I'll talk to you later."

"What about dinner?"

"There's someone I'd like you both to meet," Kelly announced.

Ignoring her, Mark turned to Jo Marie. "I've suddenly lost my appetite."

"Jo Marie, I'd like to introduce you to my fiancé, Andrew Beaumont."

Jo Marie's gaze swung from the frustrated look on her brother's face to an intense pair of gray eyes. There was only one man on earth with eyes the shade of a winter sea. The dream man.

Two

Stunned into speechlessness, Jo Marie struggled to maintain her composure. She took in a deep breath to calm her frantic heartbeat and forced a look of pleasant surprise. Andrew Beaumont apparently didn't even remember her. Jo Marie couldn't see so much as a flicker of recognition in the depth of his eyes. In the last nine months it was unlikely that he had given her more than a passing thought, if she'd been worthy of even that. And yet, she vividly remembered every detail of him, down to the crisp dark hair, the broad, muscular shoulders and faint twist of his mouth.

With an effort that was just short of superhuman, Jo Marie smiled. "Congratulations, you two. But what a surprise."

Kelly hurried across the room and hugged her tightly. "It was to us, too. Look." She held out her hand for Jo Marie to admire the flashing diamond. Mark hadn't been exaggerating. The flawless gem mounted in an antique setting was the largest Jo Marie had ever seen.

"What did I tell you," Mark whispered in her ear.

Confused, Kelly glanced from sister to brother. "Drew and I are celebrating tonight. We'd love it if you came. Both of you."

"No," Jo Marie and Mark declared in unison.

"I'm bushed," Jo Marie begged off.

". . . and tired," Mark finished lamely.

For the first time, Andrew spoke. "We insist." The deep, resonant voice was exactly as Jo Marie remembered. But tonight there was something faintly arrogant in the way he spoke that dared Jo Marie and Mark to put up an argument.

Brother and sister exchanged questioning glances, neither willing to be drawn into the celebration. Each for their own reasons, Jo Marie mused.

"Well—" Mark cleared his throat, clearly ill at ease with the formidable fiancé "—perhaps another time."

"You're Jo Marie's brother?" Andrew asked with a mocking note.

"How'd you know?"

Kelly stuck her arm through Andrew's. "Family resemblance, silly. No one can look at the two of you and not know you're related."

"I can't say the same thing about you two. I thought it was against the law to marry a cousin." Mark didn't bother to disguise his contempt.

"We're distant cousins," Kelly explained brightly. Her eyes looked adoringly into Andrew's and Jo Marie felt her stomach tighten. Jealousy. This sickening feeling in the pit of her stomach was the green-eyed monster. Jo Marie had only experienced brief tastes of the emotion; now it filled her mouth until she thought she would choke on it.

"I . . . had a horribly busy day." Jo Marie sought frantically for an excuse to stay home.

"And I'd have to go home and change," Mark added, looking down over his pale gray cords and sport shirt.

"No, you wouldn't," Kelly contradicted with a provocative smile. "We're going to K-Paul's."

"Sure, and wait in line half the night." A muscle twitched in Mark's jaw.

K-Paul's was a renowned restaurant that was ranked sixth in the world. Famous, but not elegant. The small establishment served creole cooking at its best.

"No," Kelly supplied, and the dip in her voice revealed how much she wanted to share this night with her friends. "Andrew's a friend of Paul's."

Mark looked at Jo Marie and rolled his eyes. "I should have known," he muttered sarcastically.

"What time did you say we'd be there, darling?"

Jo Marie closed her eyes to the sharp flash of pain at the affectionate term Kelly used so freely. These jealous sensations were crazy. She had no right to feel this way. This man . . . Andrew Beaumont, was a blown-up figment of her imagination. The brief moments they shared should have been forgotten long ago. Kelly was her friend. Her best friend. And Kelly deserved every happiness.

With a determined jut to her chin, Jo Marie flashed her roommate a warm smile. "Mark and I would be honored to join you tonight."

"We would?" Mark didn't sound pleased. Irritation rounded his dark eyes and he flashed Jo Marie a look that openly contradicted her agreement. Jo Marie wanted to tell him that he owed Kelly this much for all the teasing he'd given her. In addition, her look pleaded with him to understand how much she needed his support tonight. Saying as much was impossible, but she hoped her eyes conveyed the message.

Jo Marie turned slightly so that she faced the tall figure standing only a few inches from her. "It's generous of you to include us," she murmured, but discovered that she was incapable of meeting Andrew's penetrating gaze.

"Give us a minute to freshen up and we'll be on our way," Kelly's effervescent enthusiasm filled the room. "Come on, Jo Marie."

The two men remained in the compact living room. Jo Marie glanced back to note that Mark looked like a jaguar trapped in an iron cage. When he wasn't pacing, he stood restlessly shifting his weight repeatedly from one foot to the other. His look was weary and there was an uncharacteristic tightness to his mouth that narrowed his eyes.

"What do you think?" Kelly whispered, and gave a long sigh. "Isn't he fantastic? I think I'm the luckiest girl in the world. Of course, we'll have to wait until after the holidays to make our announcement official. But isn't Drew wonderful?"

Jo Marie forced a noncommittal nod. The raw disappointment left an aching void in her heart. Andrew should have been hers. "He's wonderful." The words came out sounding more like a tortured whisper than a compliment.

Kelly paused, lowering the brush. "Jo, are you all right? You sound like you're going to cry."

"Maybe I am." Tears burned for release, but not for the reason Kelly assumed. "It's not every day I lose my best friend."

"But you're not losing me."

Jo Marie's fingers curved around the cold bathroom sink. "But you are planning to get married?"

"Oh yes, we'll make an official announcement in January, but we haven't set a definite date for the wedding."

That surprised Jo Marie. Andrew didn't look like the kind of man who would encourage a long engagement. She would have thought that once he'd made a decision, he'd move on it. But then, she didn't know Andrew Beaumont. Not really.

A glance in the mirror confirmed that her cheeks were pale, her dark eyes haunted with a wounded, perplexed look. A quick application of blush added color to her bloodless face, but there was little she could do to disguise the troubled look in her eyes. She could only pray that no one would notice.

"Ready?" Kelly stood just outside the open door.

Jo Marie's returning smile was frail as she mentally braced herself for the coming ordeal. She paused long enough to dab perfume to the pulse points at the hollow of her neck and at her wrists.

"I, for one, am starved," Kelly announced as they returned to the living room. "And from what I remember of K-Paul's, eating is an experience we won't forget."

Jo Marie was confident that every part of this evening would be indelibly marked in her memory, but not for the reasons Kelly assumed.

Andrew's deep blue Mercedes was parked beside Mark's old clunker. The differences between the two men were as obvious as the vehicles they drove.

Clearly ill at ease, Mark stood on the sidewalk in front of his car. "Why don't Jo Marie and I follow you?"

"Nonsense," Kelly returned, "there's plenty of room in Drew's car for everyone. You know what the traffic is like. We could get separated. I wouldn't want that to happen."

Mark's twisted mouth said that he would have given a week's pay to suddenly disappear. Jo Marie studied her brother carefully from her position in the back seat. His displeasure at being included in this evening's celebration was confusing. There was far more than reluctance in his attitude. He might not get along with Kelly, but she would have thought that Mark would wish Kelly every happiness. But he didn't. Not by the stiff, unnatural behavior she'd witnessed from him tonight.

Mark's attitude didn't change any at the restaurant. Paul, the robust chef, came out from the kitchen and greeted the party himself.

After they'd ordered, the small party sat facing one another in stony silence. Kelly made a couple of attempts to start up the conversation, but her efforts were to no avail. The two men eyed each other, looking as if they were ready to do battle at the slightest provocation.

Several times while they ate their succulent shrimp remoulade, Jo Marie found her gaze drawn to Andrew. In many ways he was exactly as she remembered. In others, he was completely different. His voice was low pitched and had a faint drawl. And he wasn't a talker. His expression was sober almost to the point of being somber, which was unusual for a man celebrating his engagement. Another word that her mind tossed out was disillusioned. Andrew Beaumont looked as though he was disenchanted with life. From everything she'd learned he was wealthy and successful. He owned a land development firm. Delta Development, Inc. had been in the Beaumont family for three generations. According to Kelly, the firm had expanded extensively under Andrew's direction.

But if Jo Marie was paying attention to Andrew, he was nothing more than polite to her. He didn't acknowledge her with anything more than an occasional look. And since she hadn't directed any questions to him, he hadn't spoken either. At least not to her.

Paul's special touch for creole cooking made the meal memorable. And although her thoughts were troubled and her heart perplexed, when the waitress took Jo Marie's plate away she had done justice to the meal. Even Mark, who had sat uncommunicative and sullen through most of the dinner, had left little on his plate.

After K-Paul's, Kelly insisted they visit the French Quarter. The others were not as enthusiastic. After an hour of walking around and sampling some of the best jazz sounds New Orleans had to offer, they returned to the apartment.

"I'll make the coffee," Kelly proposed as they climbed from the luxury car.

Mark made a show of glancing at his watch. "I think I'll skip the chicory," he remarked in a flippant tone. "Tomorrow's a busy day."

"Come on, Mark—" Kelly pouted prettily "—don't be a spoil sport."

Mark's face darkened with a scowl. "If you insist."

"It isn't every day I celebrate my engagement. And, Mark, have you noticed that we haven't fought once all night? That must be some kind of a record."

A poor facsimile of a smile lifted one corner of his mouth. "It must be," he agreed wryly. He lagged behind as they climbed the stairs to the second-story apartment.

Jo Marie knew her brother well enough to know he'd have the coffee and leave as soon as it was polite to do so.

They sat in stilted silence, drinking their coffee.

"Do you two work together?" Andrew directed his question to Jo Marie.

Flustered she raised her palm to her breast. "Me?"

"Yes. Did you and Kelly meet at Tulane Hospital?"

"No, I'm a travel agent. Mark's the one in the family with the brains." She heard the breathlessness in her voice and hoped that he hadn't.

"Don't put yourself down," Kelly objected. "You're no dummy. Did you know that Jo Marie is actively involved in saving our wetlands? She volunteers her time as an office worker for the Land For The Future organization."

"That doesn't require intelligence, only time," Jo Marie murmured self-consciously and congratulated herself for keeping her voice even.

For the first time that evening, Andrew directed his attention to her and smiled. The effect it had on Jo Marie's pulse was devastating. To disguise her reaction, she raised the delicate china cup to her lips and took a tentative sip of the steaming coffee.

"And all these years I thought the LFTF was for little old ladies."

"No." Jo Marie was able to manage only the one word.

"At one time Jo Marie wanted to be a biologist," Kelly supplied.

Andrew arched two thick brows. "What stopped you?"

"Me," Mark cut in defensively. "The schooling she required was extensive and our parents couldn't afford to pay for us both to attend university at the same time. Jo Marie decided to drop out."

"That's not altogether true." Mark was making her sound noble and self-sacrificing. "It wasn't like that. If I'd wanted to continue my schooling there were lots of ways I could have done so."

"And you didn't?" Again Andrew's attention was focused on her.

She moistened her dry lips before continuing. "No. I plan to go back to school someday. Until then I'm staying active in the causes that mean the most to me and to the future of New Orleans."

"Jo Marie's our neighborhood scientist," Kelly added proudly. "She has a science club for children every other Saturday morning. I swear she's a natural with those kids. She's always taking them on hikes and planning field trips for them."

"You must like children." Again Andrew's gaze slid to Jo Marie.

"Yes," she answered self-consciously and lowered her eyes. She was grateful when the topic of conversation drifted to other subjects. When she chanced a look at Andrew, she discovered that his gaze centered on her lips. It took a great deal of restraint not to moisten them. And even more to force the memory of his kiss from her mind.

Once again, Mark made a show of looking at his watch and standing. "The evening's been—" he faltered looking for an adequate description "—interesting. Nice meeting you, Beaumont. Best wishes to you and Florence Nightingale."

The sip of coffee stuck in Jo Marie's throat, causing a moment of intense pain until her muscles relaxed enough to allow her to swallow. Grateful that no one had noticed, Jo Marie set her cup aside and walked with her brother to the front door. "I'll talk to you later," she said in farewell.

Mark wiped a hand across his eyes. He looked more tired than Jo Marie could remember seeing him in a long time. "I've been dying to ask you all night. Isn't Kelly's rich friend the one who filled in the swampland for that housing development you fought so hard against?"

"And lost." Jo Marie groaned inwardly. She had been a staunch supporter of the environmentalists and had helped gather signatures against the project. But to no avail. "Then he's also the one who bought out Rose's," she murmured thoughtfully as a feeling of dread washed over her. Rose's Hotel was in the French Quarter and was one of the landmarks of Louisiana. In addition to being a part of New Orleans' history, the hotel was used to house transients. It was true that Rose's was badly in need of repairs, but Jo Marie hated to see the wonderful old building destroyed in the name of progress. If annihilating the breeding habitat of a hundred different species of birds hadn't troubled Andrew Beaumont, then she doubted that an old hotel in ill-repair would matter to him either.

Rubbing her temple to relieve an unexpected and throbbing headache, Jo Marie nodded. "I remember Kelly saying something about a cousin being responsible for Rose's. But I hadn't put the two together."

"He has," Mark countered disdainfully. "And come up with megabucks. Our little Kelly has reeled in quite a catch, if you like the cold, heartless sort."

Jo Marie's mind immediately rejected that thought. Andrew Beaumont may be the man responsible for several controversial land acquisitions, but he wasn't heartless. Five minutes with him at the Mardi Gras had proven otherwise.

Mark's amused chuckle carried into the living room. "You've got that battle look in your eye. What are you thinking?"

"Nothing," she returned absently. But already her mind was racing furiously. "I'll talk to you tomorrow."

"I'll give you a call," Mark promised and was gone.

When Jo Marie returned to the living room, she found Kelly and Andrew chatting companionably. They paused and glanced at her as she rejoined them.

"You've known each other for a long time, haven't you?" Jo Marie lifted the half-full china cup, making an excuse to linger. She sat on the arm of the love seat, unable to decide if she should stay and speak her mind or repress her tongue.

"We've known each other since childhood." Kelly answered for the pair.

"And Andrew is the distant cousin you said had bought Rose's."

Kelly's sigh was uncomfortable. "I was hoping you wouldn't put two and two together."

"To be honest, I didn't. Mark figured it out."

A frustrated look tightened Kelly's once happy features.

"Will someone kindly tell me what you two are talking about?" Andrew asked.

"Rose's," they chimed in unison.

"Rose's," he repeated slowly and a frown appeared between his gray eyes.

Apparently Andrew Beaumont had so much land one small hotel didn't matter.

"The hotel."

The unexpected sharpness in his voice caused Jo Marie to square her shoulders. "It may seem like a little thing to you."

"Not for what that piece of land cost me," he countered in a hard voice.

"I don't think Drew likes to mix business with pleasure," Kelly warned, but Jo Marie disregarded the well-intended advice.

"But the men living in Rose's will have nowhere to go."

"They're bums."

A sadness filled her at the insensitive way he referred to these men. "Rose's had housed homeless men for twenty years. These men need someplace where they can get a hot meal and can sleep."

"It's a prime location for luxury condominiums," he said cynically.

"But what about the transients? What will become of them?"

"That, Miss Early, is no concern of mine."

Unbelievably Jo Marie felt tears burn behind her eyes. She blinked them back. Andrew Beaumont wasn't the dream man she'd fantasized over all these months. He was cold and cynical. The only love he had in his life was profit. A sadness settled over her with a weight she thought would be crippling.

"I feel very sorry for you, Mr. Beaumont," she said smoothly, belying her turbulent emotions. "You may be very rich, but there's no man poorer than one who has no tolerance for the weakness of others."

Kelly gasped softly and groaned. "I knew this was going to happen."

"Are you always so opinionated, Miss Early?" There was no disguising the icy tones.

"No, but there are times when things are so wrong that I can't remain silent." She turned to Kelly. "I apologize if I've ruined your evening. If you'll excuse me now, I think I'll go to bed. Good night, Mr. Beaumont. May you and Kelly have many years of happiness together." The words nearly stuck in her throat but she managed to get them out before walking from the room.

"If this offends you in any way I won't do it." Jo Marie studied her roommate carefully. The demonstration in front of Rose's had been planned weeks ago. Jo Marie's wooden picket sign felt heavy in her hand. For the first time in her life, her convictions conflicted with her feelings. She didn't want to march against Andrew. It didn't matter what he'd done, but she couldn't stand by and see those poor men turned into the streets, either. Not in the name of progress. Not when progress was at the cost of the less fortunate and the fate of a once lovely hotel.

"This picket line was arranged long before you met Drew."

"That hasn't got anything to do with this. Drew is important to you. I wouldn't want to do something that will place your relationship with him in jeopardy."

"It won't."

Kelly sounded far more confident than Jo Marie felt.

"In fact," she continued, "I doubt that Drew even knows anything about the demonstration. Those things usually do nothing to sway his decision. In fact, I'd say they do more harm than good as far as he's concerned."

Jo Marie had figured that much out herself, but she couldn't stand by doing nothing. Rose's was scheduled to be shut down the following week . . . a short month before Christmas. Jo Marie didn't know how anyone could be so heartless. The hotel was to be torn down a week later and new construction was scheduled to begin right after the first of the year.

Kelly paused at the front door while Jo Marie picked up her picket sign and tossed the long strap of her purse over her shoulder.

"You do understand why I can't join you?" she asked hesitatingly.

"Of course," Jo Marie said and exhaled softly. She'd never expected Kelly to participate. This fight couldn't include her friend without causing bitter feelings.

"Be careful." Her arms wrapped around her waist to chase away a chill, Kelly walked down to the parking lot with Jo Marie.

"Don't worry. This is a peaceful demonstration. The only wounds I intend to get are from carrying this sign. It's heavy."

Cocking her head sideways, Kelly read the sign for the tenth time. SAVE ROSE'S HOTEL. A PIECE OF NEW ORLEANS HISTORY. Kelly chuckled and slowly shook her head. "I should get a picture of you. Drew would get a real kick out of that."

The offer of a picture was a subtle reminder that Drew wouldn't so much as see the sign. He probably wasn't even aware of the protest rally.

Friends of Rose's and several others from the Land For

The Future headquarters were gathered outside the hotel when Jo Marie arrived. Several people who knew Jo Marie raised their hands in welcome.

"Have the television and radio stations been notified?" the organizer asked a tall man Jo Marie didn't recognize.

"I notified them, but most weren't all that interested. I doubt that we'll be given air time."

A feeling of gloom settled over the group. An unexpected cloudburst did little to brighten their mood. Jo Marie hadn't brought her umbrella and was drenched in minutes. A chill caused her teeth to chatter and no matter how hard she tried, she couldn't stop shivering. Uncaring, the rain fell indiscriminately over the small group of protesters.

"You little fool," Mark said when he found her an hour later. "Are you crazy, walking around wet and cold like that?" His voice was a mixture of exasperation and pride.

"I'm making a statement," Jo Marie argued.

"You're right. You're telling the world what a fool you are. Don't you have any better sense than this?"

Jo Marie ignored him, placing one foot in front of the other as she circled the sidewalk in front of Rose's Hotel.

"Do you think Beaumont cares?"

Jo Marie refused to be drawn into his argument. "Instead of arguing with me, why don't you go inside and see what's holding up the coffee?"

"You're going to need more than a hot drink to prevent you from getting pneumonia. Listen to reason for once in your life."

"No!" Emphatically Jo Marie stamped her foot. "This is too important."

"And your health isn't?"

"Not now." The protest group had dwindled down to less than ten. "I'll be all right." She shifted the sign from one shoulder to the other and flexed her stiff fingers. Her back ached from the burden of her message. And with every step the rain water in her shoes squished noisily. "I'm sure we'll be finished in another hour."

"If you aren't, I'm carting you off myself," Mark shouted angrily and returned to his car. He shook his finger at her in warning as he drove past.

True to his word, Mark returned an hour later and followed her back to the apartment.

Jo Marie could hardly drive she was shivering so violently. Her long chestnut hair fell in limp tendrils over her face. Rivulets of cold water ran down her neck and she bit into her bottom lip at the pain caused by gripping the steering wheel. Carrying the sign had formed painful blisters in the palms of her hands. This was one protest rally she wouldn't soon forget.

Mark seemed to blame Andrew Beaumont for the fact that she was cold, wet and miserable. But it wasn't Andrew's fault that it had rained. Not a single forecaster had predicted it would. She'd lived in New Orleans long enough to know she should carry an umbrella with her. Mark was looking for an excuse to dislike Andrew. Any excuse. In her heart, Jo Marie couldn't. No matter what he'd done, there was something deep within her that wouldn't allow any bitterness inside. In some ways she was disillusioned and hurt that her dream man wasn't all she'd thought. But that was as deep as her resentments went.

"Little fool," Mark repeated tenderly as he helped her

out of the car. "Let's get you upstairs and into a hot bath."

"As long as I don't have to listen to you lecture all night," she said, her teeth chattering as she climbed the stairs to the second-story apartment. Although she was thoroughly miserable, there was a spark of humor in her eyes as she opened the door and stepped inside the apartment.

"Jo Marie," Kelly cried in alarm. "Good grief, what happened?"

A light laugh couldn't disguise her shivering. "Haven't you looked out the window lately? It's raining cats and dogs."

"This is your fault, Beaumont," Mark accused harshly and Jo Marie sucked in a surprised breath. In her misery, she hadn't noticed Andrew, who was casually sitting on the love seat.

He rose to a standing position and glared at Mark as if her brother were a mad man. "Explain yourself," he demanded curtly.

Kelly intervened, crossing the room and placing a hand on Andrew's arm. "Jo Marie was marching in that rally I was telling you about."

"In front of Rose's Hotel," Mark added, his fists tightly clenched at his side. He looked as if he wanted to get physical. Consciously, Jo Marie moved closer to her brother's side. Fistfighting was so unlike Mark. He was a healer, not a boxer. One look told Jo Marie that in a physical exchange, Mark would lose.

Andrew's mouth twisted scornfully. "You, my dear Miss Early, are a fool."

Jo Marie dipped her head mockingly. "And you, Mr. Beaumont, are heartless."

"But rich," Mark intervened. "And money goes a long way in making a man attractive. Isn't that right, Kelly?"

Kelly went visibly pale, her blue eyes filling with tears. "That's not true," she cried, her words jerky as she struggled for control.

"You will apologize for that remark, Early." Andrew's low voice held a threat that was undeniable.

Mark knotted and unknotted his fists. "I won't apologize for the truth. If you want to step outside, maybe you'd like to make something of it."

"Mark!" Both Jo Marie and Kelly gasped in shocked disbelief.

Jo Marie moved first. "Get out of here before you cause trouble." Roughly she opened the door and shoved him outside.

"You heard what I said," Mark growled on his way out the door.

"I've never seen Mark behave like that," Jo Marie murmured, her eyes lowered to the carpet where a small pool of water had formed. "I can only apologize." She paused and inhaled deeply. "And, Kelly, I'm sure you know he didn't mean what he said to you. He's upset because of the rally." Her voice was deep with emotion as she excused herself and headed for the bathroom.

A hot bath went a long way toward making her more comfortable. Mercifully, Andrew was gone by the time she had finished. She didn't feel up to another confrontation with him.

———

"Call on line three."

Automatically Jo Marie punched in the button and reached for her phone. "Jo Marie Early, may I help you?"

"You won."

"Mark?" He seldom phoned her at work.

"Did you hear me?" he asked excitedly.

"What did I win?" she asked humoring him.

"Beaumont."

Jo Marie's hand tightened around the receiver. "What do you mean?"

"It just came over the radio. Delta Development, Inc. is donating Rose's Hotel to the city," Mark announced with a short laugh. "Can you believe it?"

"Yes," Jo Marie closed her eyes to the onrush of emotion. Her dream man hadn't let her down. "I can believe it."

Three

"But you must come," Kelly insisted, sitting across from Jo Marie. "It'll be miserable without you."

"Kell, I don't know." Jo Marie looked up from the magazine she was reading and nibbled on her lower lip.

"It's just a Christmas party with a bunch of stuffy people I don't know. You know how uncomfortable I am meeting new people. I hate parties."

"Then why attend?"

"Drew says we must. I'm sure he doesn't enjoy the party scene any more than I do, but he's got to go or offend a lot of business acquaintances."

"But I wasn't included in the invitation," Jo Marie argued. She'd always liked people and usually did well at social functions.

"Of course you were included. Both you and Mark," Kelly insisted. "Drew saw to that."

Thoughtfully, Jo Marie considered her roommate's request. As much as she objected, she really would like to go, if for no more reason than to thank Andrew for his generosity regarding Rose's. Although she'd seen him briefly a couple of times since, the opportunity hadn't presented itself to express her appreciation. The party was one way she could do that. New Orleans was famous for its festive balls and holiday parties. Without Kelly's invitation, Jo Marie doubted that there would ever be the chance for her to attend such an elaborate affair.

"All right," she conceded, "but I doubt that Mark will come." Mark and Andrew hadn't spoken since the last confrontation in the girls' living room. The air had hung heavy between them then and Jo Marie doubted that Andrew's decision regarding Rose's Hotel would change her brother's attitude.

"Leave Mark to me," Kelly said confidently. "Just promise me that you'll be there."

"I'll need a dress." Mentally Jo Marie scanned the contents of her closet and came up with zero. Nothing she owned would be suitable for such an elaborate affair.

"Don't worry, you can borrow something of mine," Kelly offered with a generosity that was innate to her personality.

Jo Marie nearly choked on her laughter. "I'm three inches taller than you." And several pounds heavier, but she preferred not to mention that. Only once before had Jo Marie worn Kelly's clothes. The night she'd met Andrew.

Kelly giggled and the bubbly sound was pleasant to the ears. "I heard miniskirts were coming back into style."

"Perhaps, but I doubt that the fashion will arrive in time for Christmas. Don't worry about me, I'll go out this afternoon and pick up some material for a dress."

"But will you have enough time between now and the party to sew it?" Kelly's blue eyes rounded with doubt.

"I'll make time." Jo Marie was an excellent seamstress. She had her mother to thank for that. Ruth Early had insisted that her only daughter learn to sew. Jo Marie had balked in the beginning. Her interests were anything but domestic. But now, as she had been several times in the past, she was grateful for the skill.

She found a pattern of a three-quarter-length dress with a matching jacket. The simplicity of the design made the outfit all the more appealing. Jo Marie could dress it either up or down, depending on the occasion. The silky, midnight blue material she purchased was perfect for the holiday, and Jo Marie knew that shade to be one of her better colors.

When she returned to the apartment, Kelly was gone. A note propped on the kitchen table explained that she wouldn't be back until dinner time.

After washing, drying, and carefully pressing the material, Jo Marie laid it out on the table for cutting. Intent on her task, she had pulled her hair away from her face and had tied it at the base of her neck with a rubber band. Straight pins were pressed between her lips when the doorbell chimed. The neighborhood children often stopped in for a visit. Usually Jo Marie welcomed their company, but she was busy now and interruptions could result in an irreparable mistake. She toyed with the idea of not answering.

The impatient buzz told her that her company was irritated at being kept waiting.

"Damn, damn, damn," she grumbled beneath her breath as she made her way across the room. Extracting the straight pins from her mouth, she stuck them in the small cushion she wore around her wrist.

"Andrew!" Secretly she thanked God the pins were out of her mouth or she would have swallowed them in her surprise.

"Is Kelly here?"

"No, but come in." Her heart was racing madly as he walked into the room. Nervous fingers tugged the rubber band from her chestnut hair in a futile attempt to look more presentable. She shook her hair free, then wished she'd kept it neatly in place. For days Jo Marie would have welcomed the opportunity to thank Andrew, but she discovered as she followed him into the living room that her tongue was tied and her mouth felt gritty and dry. "I'm glad you're here . . . I wanted to thank you for your decision about Rose's . . . the hotel."

He interrupted her curtly. "My dear Miss Early, don't be misled. My decision wasn't—"

Her hand stopped him. "I know," she said softly. He didn't need to tell her his reasoning. She was already aware it wasn't because of the rally or anything that she'd done or said. "I just wanted to thank you for whatever may have been your reason."

Their eyes met and held from across the room. Countless moments passed in which neither spoke. The air was electric between them and the urge to reach out and touch Andrew was almost overwhelming. The same breathlessness that had attacked her the night of the Mardi Gras returned. Andrew had to remember, he had to. Yet he gave no indication that he did.

Jo Marie broke eye contact first, lowering her gaze to the wool carpet. "I'm not sure where Kelly is, but she said she'd be back by dinner time." Her hand shook as she handed him the note off the kitchen counter.

"Kelly mentioned the party?"

Jo Marie nodded.

"You'll come?"

She nodded her head in agreement. "If I finish sewing

this dress in time." She spoke so he wouldn't think she'd suddenly lost the ability to talk. Never had she been more aware of a man. Her heart was hammering at his nearness. He was so close all she had to do was reach out and touch him. But insurmountable barriers stood between them. At last, after all these months she was alone with her dream man. So many times a similar scene had played in her mind. But Andrew didn't remember her. The realization produced an indescribable ache in her heart. What had been the most profound moment in her life had been nothing to him.

"Would you like to sit down?" she offered, remembering her manners. "There's coffee on if you'd like a cup."

He shook his head. "No, thanks." He ran his hand along the top of the blue cloth that was stretched across the kitchen table. His eyes narrowed and he looked as if his thoughts were a thousand miles away.

"Why don't you buy a dress?"

A smile trembled at the edge of her mouth. To a man who had always had money, buying something as simple as a dress would seem the most logical solution.

"I sew most of my own things," she explained softly, rather than enlightening him with a lecture on economics.

"Did you make this?" His fingers touched the short sleeve of her cotton blouse and brushed against the sensitive skin of her upper arm.

Immediately a warmth spread where his fingers had come into contact with her flesh. Jo Marie's pale cheeks instantly flushed with a crimson flood of color. "Yes," she admitted hoarsely, hating the way her body, her voice, everything about her, was affected by this man.

"You do beautiful work."

She kept her eyes lowered and drew in a steadying breath. "Thank you."

"Next weekend I'll be having a Christmas party at my home for the employees of my company. I would be honored if both you and your brother attended."

Already her heart was racing with excitement; she'd love to visit his home. But seeing where he lived was only an excuse. She'd do anything to see more of him. "I can't speak for Mark," she answered after several moments, feeling guilty for her thoughts.

"But you'll come?"

"I'd be happy to. Thank you." Her only concern was that no one from Delta Development would recognize her as the same woman who was active in the protest against the housing development and in saving Rose's Hotel.

"Good," he said gruffly.

The curve of her mouth softened into a smile. "I'll tell Kelly that you were by. Would you like her to phone you?"

"No, I'll be seeing her later. Goodbye, Jo Marie."

She walked with him to the door, holding onto the knob longer than necessary. "Goodbye, Andrew," she murmured.

Jo Marie leaned against the door and covered her face with both hands. She shouldn't be feeling this eager excitement, this breathless bewilderment, this softness inside at the mere thought of him. Andrew Beaumont was her roommate's fiancé. She had to remember that. But somehow, Jo Marie recognized that her conscience could repeat the information all day, but it would have little effect on her restless heart.

The sewing machine was set up at the table when Kelly walked into the apartment a couple of hours later.

"I'm back," Kelly murmured happily as she hung her sweater in the closet.

"Where'd you go?"

"To see a friend."

Jo Marie thought she detected a note of hesitancy in her roommate's voice and glanced up momentarily from her task. She paused herself, then said, "Andrew was by."

A look of surprise worked its way across Kelly's pixie face. "Really? Did he say what he wanted?"

"Not really. He didn't leave a message." Jo Marie strove for nonchalance, but her fingers shook slightly and she hoped that her friend didn't notice the telltale mannerism.

"You like Drew, don't you?"

For some reason, Jo Marie's mind had always referred to him as Andrew. "Yes." She continued with the mechanics of sewing, but she could feel Kelly's eyes roam over her face as she studied her. Immediately a guilty flush reddened her cheeks. Somehow, some way, Kelly had detected how strongly Jo Marie felt about Andrew.

"I'm glad," Kelly said at last. "I'd like it if you two would fall in . . ." She hesitated before concluding with, "Never mind."

The two words were repeated in her mind like the dwindling sounds of an echo off canyon walls.

The following afternoon, Jo Marie arrived home from work and took a crisp apple from the bottom shelf of the refrigerator. She wanted a snack before pulling out her sewing machine again. Kelly was working late and had phoned her at the office so Jo Marie wouldn't worry.

Holding the apple between her teeth, she lugged the heavy sewing machine out of the bedroom. No sooner had she set the case on top of the table than the doorbell chimed.

Releasing a frustrated sigh, she swallowed the bite of apple.

"Sign here, please." A clipboard was shoved under her nose.

"I beg your pardon," Jo Marie asked.

"I'm making a delivery, lady. Sign here."

"Oh." Maybe Kelly had ordered something without telling her. Quickly, she penned her name along the bottom line.

"Wait here," was the next abrupt instruction.

Shrugging her shoulder, Jo Marie leaned against the doorjamb as the brusque man returned to the brown truck parked below and brought up two large boxes.

"Merry Christmas, Miss Early," he said with a sheepish grin as he handed her the delivery.

"Thank you." The silver box was the trademark of New Orleans' most expensive boutique. Gilded lettering wrote out the name of the proprietor, Madame Renaux Marceau, across the top. Funny, Jo Marie couldn't recall Kelly saying she'd bought something there. But with the party coming, Kelly had apparently opted for the expensive boutique.

Dutifully Jo Marie carried the boxes into Kelly's room and set them on the bed. As she did so the shipping order attached to the smaller box, caught her eye. The statement was addressed to her, not Kelly.

Inhaling a jagged breath, Jo Marie searched the order blank to find out who would be sending her anything.

Her parents could never have afforded something from Madame Renaux Marceau.

The air was sucked from her lungs as Jo Marie discovered Andrew Beaumont's name. She fumbled with the lids, peeled back sheer paper and gasped at the beauty of what lay before her. The full-length blue dress was the same midnight shade as the one she was sewing. But this gown was unlike anything Jo Marie had ever seen. A picture of Christmas, a picture of elegance. She held it up and felt tears prickle the back of her eyes. The bodice was layered with intricate rows of tiny pearls that formed a V at the waist. The gown was breathtakingly beautiful. Never had Jo Marie thought to own anything so perfect or so lovely. The second box contained a matching cape with an ornate display of tiny pearls.

Very carefully, Jo Marie folded the dress and cape and placed them back into the boxes. An ache inside her heart erupted into a broken sob. She wasn't a charity case. Did Andrew assume that because she sewed her own clothes that what she was making for the party would be unpresentable?

The telephone book revealed the information she needed. Following her instincts, Jo Marie grabbed a sweater and rushed out the door. She didn't stop until she pulled up in front of the large brick building with the gold plaque in the front that announced that this was the headquarters for Delta Development, Inc.

A listing of offices in the foyer told her where Andrew's was located. Jo Marie rode the elevator to the third floor. Most of the building was deserted, only a few employees remained. Those that did gave her curious stares, but no one questioned her presence.

The office door that had Andrew's name lettered on it was closed, but that didn't dissuade Jo Marie. His receptionist was placing the cover over her typewriter when Jo Marie barged inside.

"I'd like to see Mr. Beaumont," she demanded in a breathless voice.

The gray-haired receptionist glanced at the boxes under Jo Marie's arms and shook her head. "I'm sorry, but the office is closed for the day."

Jo Marie caught the subtle difference. "I didn't ask about the office. I said I wanted to see Mr. Beaumont." Her voice rose with her frustration.

A connecting door between two rooms opened. "Is there a problem, Mrs. Stewart?"

"I was just telling . . ."

"Jo Marie." Andrew's voice was an odd mixture of surprise and gruffness, yet gentle. His narrowed look centered on the boxes clasped under each arm. "Is there a problem?"

"As a matter of fact there is," she said, fighting to disguise the anger that was building within her to volcanic proportions.

Andrew stepped aside to admit her into his office.

"Will you be needing me further?" Jo Marie heard his secretary ask.

"No, thank you, Mrs. Stewart. I'll see you in the morning."

No sooner had Andrew stepped in the door than Jo Marie whirled on him. The silver boxes from the boutique sat squarely in the middle of Andrew's huge oak desk.

"I think you should understand something right now,

Mr. Beaumont," she began heatedly, not bothering to hold back her annoyance. "I am not Cinderella and you most definitely are not my fairy godfather."

"Would I be amiss to guess that my gift displeases you?"

Jo Marie wanted to scream at him for being so calm. She cut her long nails into her palms in an effort to disguise her irritation. "If I am an embarrassment to you wearing a dress I've sewn myself, then I'll simply not attend your precious party."

He looked shocked.

"And furthermore, I am no one's poor relation."

An angry frown deepened three lines across his wide forehead. "What makes you suggest such stupidity?"

"I may be many things, but stupid isn't one of them."

"A lot of things?" He stood behind his desk and leaned forward, pressing his weight on his palms. "You mean like opinionated, headstrong, and impatient."

"Yes," she cried and shot her index finger into the air. "But not stupid."

The tight grip Andrew held on his temper was visible by the way his mouth was pinched until the grooves stood out tense and white. "Maybe not stupid, but incredibly inane."

Her mouth was trembling and Jo Marie knew that if she didn't get away soon, she'd cry. "Let's not argue over definitions. Stated simply, the gesture of buying me a presentable dress was not appreciated. Not in the least."

"I gathered that much, Miss Early. Now if you'll excuse me, I have a dinner engagement."

"Gladly." She pivoted and stormed across the floor

ready to jerk open the office door. To her dismay, the door stuck and wouldn't open, ruining her haughty exit.

"Allow me," Andrew offered bitterly.

The damn door! It would have to ruin her proud retreat.

By the time she was in the parking lot, most of her anger had dissipated. Second thoughts crowded her mind on the drive back to the apartment. She could have at least been more gracious about it. Second thoughts quickly evolved into constant recriminations so that by the time she walked through the doorway of the apartment, Jo Marie was thoroughly miserable.

"Hi." Kelly was mixing raw hamburger for meatloaf with her hands. "Did the dress arrive?"

Kelly knew! "Dress?"

"Yes. Andrew and I went shopping for you yesterday afternoon and found the most incredibly lovely party dress. It was perfect for you."

Involuntarily, Jo Marie stiffened. "What made you think I needed a dress?"

Kelly's smile was filled with humor. "You were sewing one, weren't you? Drew said that you were really attending this function as a favor to me. And since this is such a busy time of year he didn't want you spending your nights slaving over a sewing machine."

"Oh." A sickening feeling attacked the pit of her stomach.

"Drew can be the most thoughtful person," Kelly commented as she continued to blend the ground meat. Her attention was more on her task than on Jo Marie. "You can understand why it's so easy to love him."

A strangled sound made its way past the tightness in Jo Marie's throat.

"I'm surprised the dress hasn't arrived. Drew gave specific instructions that it was to be delivered today in case any alterations were needed."

"It did come," Jo Marie announced, more miserable than she could ever remember being.

"It did?" Excitement elevated Kelly's voice. "Why didn't you say something? Isn't it the most beautiful dress you've ever seen? You're going to be gorgeous." Kelly's enthusiasm waned as she turned around. "Jo, what's wrong? You look like you're ready to burst into tears."

"That's . . . that's because I am," she managed and covering her face with her hands, she sat on the edge of the sofa and wept.

Kelly's soft laugh only made everything seem worse. "I expected gratitude," Kelly said with a sigh and handed Jo Marie a tissue. "But certainly not tears. You don't cry that often."

Noisily Jo Marie blew her nose. "I . . . I thought I was an embarrassment . . . to you two . . . that . . . you didn't want me . . . at the party . . . because I didn't have . . . the proper clothes . . . and . . ."

"You thought what?" Kelly interrupted, a shocked, hurt look crowding her face. "I can't believe you'd even think anything so crazy."

"That's not all. I . . ." She swallowed. "I took the dress to . . . Andrew's office and practically . . . threw it in his face."

"Oh, Jo Marie." Kelly lowered herself onto the sofa beside her friend. "How could you?"

"I don't know. Maybe it sounds ridiculous, but I really

believed that you and Andrew would be ashamed to be seen with me in an outfit I'd made myself."

"How could you come up with something so dumb? Especially since I've always complimented you on the things you've sewn."

Miserably, Jo Marie bowed her head. "I know."

"You've really done it, but good, my friend. I can just imagine Drew's reaction to your visit." At the thought Kelly's face grew tight. "Now what are you going to do?"

"Nothing. From this moment on I'll be conveniently tucked in my room when he comes for you . . ."

"What about the party?" Kelly's blue eyes were rounded with childlike fright and Jo Marie could only speculate whether it was feigned or real. "It's only two days away."

"I can't go, certainly you can understand that."

"But you've got to come," Kelly returned adamantly. "Mark said he'd go if you were there and I need you both. Everything will be ruined if you back out now."

"Mark's coming?" Jo Marie had a difficult time believing her brother would agree to this party idea. She'd have thought Mark would do anything to avoid another confrontation with Andrew.

"Yes. And it wasn't easy to get him to agree."

"I can imagine," Jo Marie returned dryly.

"Jo Marie, please. Your being there means so much to me. More than you'll ever know. Do this one thing and I promise I won't ask another thing of you as long as I live."

Kelly was serious. Something about this party was terribly important to her. Jo Marie couldn't understand what. In order to attend the party she would need to apologize to Andrew. If it had been her choice she would have waited a week or two before approaching him, giving him the necessary time to cool off. As it was, she'd be forced to do it before the party while tempers continued to run hot. Damn! She should have waited until Kelly was home tonight before jumping to conclusions about the dress. Any half-wit would have known her roommate was involved.

"Well?" Kelly regarded her hopefully.

"I'll go, but first I've got to talk to Andrew and explain."

Kelly released a rush of air, obviously relieved. "Take my advice, don't explain a thing. Just tell him you're sorry."

Jo Marie brushed her dark curls from her forehead. She was in no position to argue. Kelly obviously knew Andrew far better than she. The realization produced a rush of painful regrets. "I'll go to his office first thing tomorrow morning," she said with far more conviction in her voice than what she was feeling.

"You won't regret it," Kelly breathed and squeezed Jo Marie's numb fingers. "I promise you won't."

If that was the case, Jo Marie wanted to know why she regretted it already.

To say that she slept restlessly would be an understatement. By morning, dark shadows had formed under her eyes that even cosmetics couldn't completely disguise. The silky blue dress was finished and hanging from a hook on her closet door. Compared to the lovely creation Andrew had purchased, her simple gown looked drab. Plain. Unsophisticated. Swallowing her pride had always left a bitter aftertaste, and she didn't expect it to be any different today.

"Good luck," Kelly murmured her condolences to Jo Marie on her way out the door.

"Thanks, I'll need that and more." The knot in her stomach grew tighter every minute. Jo Marie didn't know what she was going to say or even where to begin.

Mrs. Stewart, the gray-haired guardian, was at her station when Jo Marie stepped inside Andrew's office.

"Good morning."

The secretary was too well trained to reveal any surprise.

"Would it be possible to talk to Mr. Beaumont for a few minutes?"

"Do you have an appointment?" The older woman flipped through the calendar pages.

"No," Jo Marie tightened her fists. "I'm afraid I don't."

"Mr. Beaumont will be out of the office until this afternoon."

"Oh." Discouragement nearly defeated her. "Could I make an appointment to see him then?"

The paragon of virtue studied the appointment calendar. "I'm afraid not. Mr. Beaumont has meetings scheduled all week. But if you'd like, I could give him a message."

"Yes, please," she returned and scribbled out a note that said she needed to talk to him as soon as it was convenient. Handing the note back to Mrs. Stewart, Jo Marie offered the woman a feeble smile. "Thank you."

"I'll see to it that Mr. Beaumont gets your message," the efficient woman promised.

Jo Marie didn't doubt that the woman would. What she did question was whether Andrew would respond.

By the time Jo Marie readied for bed that evening, she realized that he wouldn't. Now she'd be faced with attending the party with the tension between them so thick it would resemble an English fog.

Mark was the first one to arrive the following evening. Dressed in a pin-stripe suit and a silk tie he looked exceptionally handsome. And Jo Marie didn't mind telling him so.

"Wow." She took a step in retreat and studied him thoughtfully. "Wow," she repeated.

"I could say the same thing. You look terrific."

Self-consciously, Jo Marie smoothed out an imaginary wrinkle from the skirt of her dress. "You're sure?"

"Of course, I am. And I like your hair like that."

Automatically a hand investigated the rhinestone combs that held the bouncy curls away from her face and gave an air of sophistication to her appearance.

"When will money bags be out?" Mark's gaze drifted toward Kelly's bedroom as he took a seat.

"Any minute."

Mark stuck a finger in the collar of his shirt and ran it around his neck. "I can't believe I agreed to this fiasco."

Jo Marie couldn't believe it either. "Why did you?"

Her brother's shrug was filled with self-derision. "I don't know. It seemed to mean so much to Kelly. And to be honest, I guess I owe it to her for all the times I've teased her."

"How do you feel about Beaumont?"

Mark's eyes narrowed fractionally. "I'm trying not to feel anything."

The door opened and Kelly appeared in a red frothy creation that reminded Jo Marie of Christmas and Santa and happy elves. She had seen the dress, but on Kelly the full-length gown came to life. With a lissome grace Jo Marie envied, Kelly sauntered into the room. Mark couldn't take his eyes off her as he slowly rose to a standing position.

"Kelly." He seemed to have difficulty speaking. "You . . . you're lovely."

Kelly's delighted laughter was filled with pleasure. "Don't sound so shocked. You've just never seen me dressed up is all."

For a fleeting moment Jo Marie wondered if Mark had ever really seen her roommate.

The doorbell chimed and three pairs of eyes glared at the front door accusingly. Jo Marie felt her stomach tighten with nervous apprehension. For two days she'd dreaded this moment. Andrew Beaumont had arrived.

Kelly broke away from the small group and answered the door. Jo Marie watched her brother's eyes narrow as Kelly stood on her tiptoes and lightly brushed her lips across Andrew's cheek. The involuntary reaction stirred a multitude of questions in Jo Marie about Mark's attitude toward Kelly. And her own toward Andrew.

When her gaze drifted from her brother, Jo Marie discovered that Andrew had centered his attention on her.

"You look exceedingly lovely, Miss Early."

"Thank you. I'm afraid the dress I should have worn was mistakenly returned." She prayed he understood her message.

"Let's have a drink before we leave," Kelly suggested.

She'd been in the kitchen earlier mixing a concoction of coconut milk, rum, pineapple and several spices.

The cool drink helped relieve some of the tightness in Jo Marie's throat. She sat beside her brother, across from Andrew. The silence in the room was interrupted only by Kelly, who seemed oblivious to the terrible tension. She chattered all the way out to the car.

Again Mark and Jo Marie were relegated to the back seat of Andrew's plush sedan. Jo Marie knew that Mark hated this, but he submitted to the suggestion without comment. Only the stiff way he held himself revealed his discontent. The party was being given by an associate of Andrew's, a builder. The minute Jo Marie heard the name of the firm she recognized it as the one that had worked on the wetlands project.

Mark cast Jo Marie a curious glance and she shook her head indicating that she wouldn't say a word. In some ways, Jo Marie felt that she was fraternizing with the enemy.

Introductions were made and a flurry of names and faces blurred themselves in her mind. Jo Marie recognized several prominent people, and spoke to a few. Mark stayed close by her side and she knew without asking that this whole party scene made him uncomfortable.

In spite of being so adamant about needing her, Kelly was now nowhere to be seen. A half hour later, Jo Marie noticed that Kelly was sitting in a chair against the wall, looking hopelessly lost. She watched amazed as Mark delivered a glass of punch to her and claimed the chair beside her roommate. Kelly brightened immediately and soon the two were smiling and chatting.

Scanning the crowded room, Jo Marie noticed that

Andrew was busy talking to a group of men. The room suddenly felt stuffy. An open glass door that led to a balcony invited her outside and into the cool evening air.

Standing with her gloved hands against the railing, Jo Marie glanced up at the starlit heavens. The night was clear and the black sky was adorned with a thousand glittering stars.

"I received a message that you wanted to speak to me." The husky male voice spoke from behind her.

Jo Marie's heart leaped to her throat and she struggled not to reveal her discomfort. "Yes," she said with a relaxing breath.

Andrew joined her at the wrought-iron railing. His nearness was so overwhelming that Jo Marie closed her eyes to the powerful attraction. Her long fingers tightened their grip.

"I owe you an apology. I sincerely regret jumping to conclusions about the dress. You were only being kind."

An eternity passed before Andrew spoke. "Were you afraid I was going to demand a reward, Florence Nightingale?"

Four

Jo Marie's heart went still as she turned to Andrew with wide, astonished eyes. "You do remember." They'd spent a single, golden moment together so many months ago. Not once since Kelly had introduced Andrew as her fiancé had he given her the slightest inkling that he remembered.

"Did you imagine I could forget?" he asked quietly.

Tightly squeezing her eyes shut, Jo Marie turned back to the railing, her fingers gripping the wrought iron with a strength she didn't know she possessed.

"I came back every day for a month," he continued in a deep, troubled voice. "I thought you were a nurse."

The color ebbed from Jo Marie's face, leaving her pale. She'd looked for him, too. In all the months since the Mardi Gras she'd never stopped looking. Every time she'd left her apartment, she had silently searched through a sea of faces. Although she'd never known his name, she had included him in her thoughts every day since their meeting. He was her dream man, the stranger who had shared those enchanted moments of magic with her.

"It was Mardi Gras," she explained in a quavering voice. "I'd borrowed Kelly's uniform for a party."

Andrew stood beside her and his wintry eyes narrowed. "I should have recognized you then," he said with faint self-derision.

"Recognized me?" Jo Marie didn't understand. In the

short time before they were separated, Andrew had said she reminded him of a painting he'd once seen.

"I should have known you from your picture in the newspaper. You were the girl who so strongly protested the housing development for the wetlands."

"I . . . I didn't know it was your company. I had no idea." A stray tendril of soft chestnut hair fell forward as she bowed her head. "But I can't apologize for demonstrating against something which I believe is very wrong."

"To thine own self be true, Jo Marie Early." He spoke without malice and when their eyes met, she discovered to her amazement that he was smiling.

Jo Marie responded with a smile of her own. "And you were there that night because of Kelly."

"I'd just left her."

"And I was on my way in." Another few minutes and they could have passed each other in the hospital corridor without ever knowing. In some ways Jo Marie wished they had. If she hadn't met Andrew that night, then she could have shared in her friend's joy at the coming marriage. As it was now, Jo Marie was forced to fight back emotions she had no right to feel. Andrew belonged to Kelly and the diamond ring on her finger declared as much.

"And . . . and now you've found Kelly," she stammered, backing away. "I want to wish you both a life filled with much happiness." Afraid of what her expressive eyes would reveal, Jo Marie lowered her lashes, which were dark against her pale cheek. "I should be going inside."

"Jo Marie."

He said her name so softly that for a moment she wasn't sure he'd spoken. "Yes?"

Andrew arched both brows and lightly shook his head. His finger lightly touched her smooth cheek, following the line of her delicate jaw. Briefly his gaze darkened as if this was torture in the purest sense. "Nothing. Enjoy yourself tonight." With that he turned back to the railing.

Jo Marie entered the huge reception room and mingled with those attending the lavish affair. Not once did she allow herself to look over her shoulder toward the balcony. Toward Andrew, her dream man, because he wasn't hers, would never be hers. Her mouth ached with the effort to appear happy. By the time she made it to the punch bowl her smile felt brittle and was decidedly forced. All these months she'd hoped to find the dream man because her heart couldn't forget him. And now that she had, nothing had ever been more difficult. If she didn't learn to curb the strong sensual pull she felt toward him, she could ruin his and Kelly's happiness.

Soft Christmas music filled the room as Jo Marie found a plush velvet chair against the wall and sat down, a friendly observer to the party around her. Forcing herself to relax, her toe tapped lightly against the floor with an innate rhythm. Christmas was her favorite time of year—no, she amended, Mardi Gras was. Her smile became less forced.

"You look like you're having the time of your life," Mark announced casually as he took the seat beside her.

"It is a nice party."

"So you enjoy observing the life-style of the rich and famous." The sarcastic edge to Mark's voice was less sharp than normal.

Taking a sip of punch, Jo Marie nodded. "Who wouldn't?"

"To be honest I'm surprised at how friendly everyone's been," Mark commented sheepishly. "Obviously no one suspects that you and I are two of the less privileged."

"Mark," she admonished sharply. "That's a rotten thing to say."

Her brother had the good grace to look ashamed. "To be truthful, Kelly introduced me to several of her friends and I must admit I couldn't find anything to dislike about them."

"Surprise, surprise." Jo Marie hummed the Christmas music softly to herself. "I suppose the next thing I know, you'll be playing golf with Kelly's father."

Mark snorted derisively. "Hardly."

"What have you got against the Beaumonts anyway? Kelly's a wonderful girl."

"Kelly's the exception," Mark argued and stiffened.

"But you just finished telling me that you liked several of her friends that you were introduced to tonight."

"Yes. Well, that was on short acquaintance."

Standing, Jo Marie set her empty punch glass aside. "I think you've got a problem, brother dearest."

A dark look crowded Mark's face, and his brow was furrowed with a curious frown. "You're right, I do." With an agitated movement he stood and made his way across the room.

Jo Marie mingled, talking with a few women who were planning a charity benefit after the first of the year. When they asked her opinion on an important point, Jo Marie was both surprised and pleased. Although she spent a good portion of the next hour with these older ladies, she drifted away as they moved toward the heart of the party. If Andrew had recognized her as the girl involved in the protest against the wetlands development, others might, too. And she didn't want to do anything that would cause him and Kelly embarrassment.

Kelly, with her blue eyes sparkling like sapphires, rushed up to Jo Marie. "Here you are!" she exclaimed. "Drew and I have been looking for you."

"Is it time to leave?" Jo Marie was more than ready, uncomfortably aware that she could be recognized at any moment.

"No . . . no, we just wanted to be certain some handsome young man didn't cart you away."

"Me?" Jo Marie's soft laugh was filled with incredulity. Few men would pay much attention to her, especially since she'd gone out of her way to remain unobtrusively in the background.

"It's more of a possibility than you realize," Andrew spoke from behind her, his voice a gentle rasp against her ear. "You're very beautiful tonight."

"Don't blush, Jo Marie," Kelly teased. "You really are lovely and if you'd given anyone half a chance, they'd have told you so."

Mark joined them and murmured something to Kelly. As he did so, Andrew turned his head toward Jo Marie and spoke so that the other two couldn't hear him. "Only Florence Nightingale could be more beautiful."

A tingling sensation raced down Jo Marie's spine and she turned so their eyes could meet, surprised that he would say something like that to her with Kelly present. Silently, she pleaded with him not to make this any more difficult for her. Those enchanted moments they had shared were long past and best forgotten for both their sakes.

———

Jo Marie woke to the buzz of the alarm early the next morning. She sat on the side of the bed and raised her arms high above her head and yawned. The day promised to be a busy one. She was scheduled to work in the office that Saturday morning and then catch a bus to LFTF headquarters on the other side of the French Quarter. She was hoping to talk to Jim Rowden, the director and manager of the conservationists' group. Jim had asked for additional volunteers during the Christmas season. And after thoughtful consideration, Jo Marie decided to accept the challenge. Christmas was such a busy time of year that many of the other volunteers wanted time off.

The events of the previous night filled her mind. Lowering her arms, Jo Marie beat back the unexpected rush of sadness that threatened to overcome her. Andrew hadn't understood any of the things she'd tried to tell him last night. Several times she found him watching her, his look brooding and thoughtful as if she'd displeased him. No matter where she went during the course of the evening, when she looked up she found Andrew studying her. Once their eyes had met and held and everyone between them had seemed to disappear. The music had faded and it was as if only the two of them existed in the party-filled crowd. Jo Marie had lowered her gaze first, frightened and angry with them both.

Andrew and Mark had been sullen on the drive home. Mark had left the apartment almost immediately and Jo Marie had fled to the privacy of her room, unwilling to witness Andrew kissing Kelly good night. She couldn't have borne it.

Now, in the light of the new day, she discovered that her feelings for Andrew were growing stronger. She wanted to banish him to a special area of her life, long past. But he wouldn't allow that. It had been in his eyes last night as he studied her. Those moments at the Mardi Gras were not to be forgotten by either of them.

At least when she was at the office, she didn't have to think about Andrew or Kelly or Mark. The phone buzzed continually. And because they were short-staffed on the weekends, Jo Marie hardly had time to think about anything but airline fares, bus routes and train schedules the entire morning.

She replaced the telephone receiver after talking with the Costa Lines about booking a spring Caribbean cruise for a retired couple. Her head was bowed as she filled out the necessary forms. Jo Marie didn't hear Paula Shriver, the only other girl in the office on Saturday, move to her desk.

"Mr. Beaumont's been waiting to talk to you," Paula announced. "Lucky you," she added under her breath as Andrew took the seat beside Jo Marie's desk.

"Hello, Jo Marie."

"Andrew." Her hand clenched the ballpoint pen she was holding. "What can I do for you?"

He crossed his legs and draped an arm over the back of the chair giving the picture of a man completely at ease. "I was hoping you could give me some suggestions for an ideal honeymoon."

"Of course. What did you have in mind?" Inwardly she wanted to shout at him not to do this to her, but she forced herself to smile and look attentive.

"What would you suggest?"

She lowered her gaze. "Kelly's mentioned Hawaii several times. I know that's the only place she'd enjoy visiting."

He dismissed her suggestion with a short shake of his head. "I've been there several times. I was hoping for something less touristy."

"Maybe a cruise then. There are several excellent lines operating in the Caribbean, the Mediterranean or perhaps the inside passage to Alaska along the Canadian west coast."

"No." Again he shook his head. "Where would *you* choose to go on a honeymoon?"

Jo Marie ignored his question, not wanting to answer him. "I have several brochures I can give you that could spark an idea. I'm confident that any one of these places would thrill Kelly." As she pulled out her bottom desk drawer, Jo Marie was acutely conscious of Andrew studying her. She'd tried to come across with a strict business attitude, but her defenses were crumbling.

Reluctantly, he accepted the brochures she gave him. "You didn't answer my question. Shall I ask it again?"

Slowly, Jo Marie shook her head. "I'm not sure I'd want to go anywhere," she explained simply. "Not on my honeymoon. Not when the most beautiful city in the world is at my doorstep. I'd want to spend that time alone with my husband. We could travel later." Briefly their eyes met and held for a long, breathless moment. "But I'm not Kelly, and she's the one you should consider while planning this trip."

Paula stood and turned the sign in the glass door, indicating that the office was no longer open. Andrew's gaze followed her movements. "You're closing."

Jo Marie's nod was filled with relief. She was uncomfortable with Andrew. Being this close to him was a test of her friendship to Kelly. And at this moment, Kelly was losing . . . They both were. "Yes. We're only open during the morning on Saturdays."

He stood and placed the pamphlets on the corner of her desk. "Then let's continue our discussion over lunch."

"Oh, no, really that isn't necessary. We'll be finished in a few minutes and Paula doesn't mind waiting."

"But I have several ideas I want to discuss with you and it could well be an hour or so."

"Perhaps you could return another day."

"Now is the more convenient time for me," he countered smoothly.

Everything within Jo Marie wanted to refuse. Surely he realized how difficult this was for her. He was well aware of her feelings and was deliberately ignoring them.

"Is it so difficult to accept anything from me, Jo Marie?" he asked softly. "Even lunch?"

"All right," she agreed ungraciously, angry with him and angrier with herself. "But only an hour. I've got things to do."

A half smile turned up one corner of his mouth. "As you wish," he said as he escorted her to his Mercedes.

Jo Marie was stiff and uncommunicative as Andrew drove through the thick traffic. He parked on a narrow street outside the French Quarter and came around to her side of the car to open the door for her.

"I have reservations at Chez Lorraine's."

"Chez Lorraine's?" Jo Marie's surprised gaze flew to him. The elegant French restaurant was one of New Orleans' most famous. The food was rumored to be exquisite, and expensive. Jo Marie had always dreamed of dining there, but never had.

"Is it as good as everyone says?" she asked, unable to disguise the excitement in her voice.

"You'll have to judge for yourself," he answered, smiling down on her.

Once inside, they were seated almost immediately and handed huge oblong menus featuring a wide variety of French cuisine. Not having sampled several of the more traditional French dishes, Jo Marie toyed with the idea of ordering the calf's sweetbread.

"What would you like?" Andrew prompted after several minutes.

"I don't know. It all sounds so good." Closing the menu she set it aside and lightly shook her head. "I think you may regret having brought me here when I'm so hungry." She'd skipped breakfast, and discovered now that she was famished.

Andrew didn't look up from his menu. "Where you're concerned, there's very little I regret." As if he'd made a casual comment about the weather, he continued. "Have you decided?"

"Yes . . . yes," she managed, fighting down the dizzying effect of his words. "I think I'll try the salmon, but I don't think I should try the French pronunciation."

"Don't worry, I'll order for you."

As if by intuition, the waiter reappeared when they were ready to place their order. "The lady would like *les mouilles à la creme de saumon fumé*, and I'll have *le canard de rouen braise*."

With a nod of approval the red-jacketed waiter departed.

Self-consciously, Jo Marie smoothed out the linen napkin on her lap. "I'm impressed," she murmured, studying the old world French provincial decor of the room. "It's everything I thought it would be."

The meal was fabulous. After a few awkward moments Jo Marie was amazed that she could talk as freely to Andrew. She discovered he was a good listener and she enjoyed telling him about her family.

"So you were the only girl."

"It had its advantages. I play a mean game of touch football."

"I hope you'll play with me someday. I've always enjoyed a rousing game of touch football."

The fork was raised halfway to her mouth and Jo Marie paused, her heart beating double time. "I . . . I only play with my brothers."

Andrew chuckled. "Speaking of your family, I find it difficult to tell that you and Mark are related. Oh, I can see the family resemblance, but Mark's a serious young man. Does he ever laugh?"

Not lately, Jo Marie mused, but she didn't admit as much. "He works hard, long hours. Mark's come a long way through medical school." She hated making excuses for her brother. "He doesn't mean to be rude."

Andrew accepted the apology with a wry grin. "The chip on his shoulder's as big as a California redwood. What's he got against wealth and position?"

"I don't know," she answered honestly. "He teases Kelly unmercifully about her family. I think Kelly's money makes him feel insecure. There's no reason for it; Kelly's never done anything to give him that attitude. I never have understood it."

Pushing her clean plate aside, Jo Marie couldn't recall when she'd enjoyed a meal more—except the dinner they'd shared at K-Paul's the night Kelly and Andrew had announced their engagement. Some of the contentment faded from her eyes. Numbly, she folded her hands in her lap. Being here with Andrew, sharing this meal, laughing and talking with him wasn't right. Kelly should be the one sitting across the table from him. Jo Marie had no right to enjoy his company this way. Not when he was engaged to her best friend. Pointedly, she glanced at her watch.

"What's wrong?"

"Nothing." She shook her head slightly, avoiding his eyes, knowing his look had the ability to penetrate her soul.

"Would you care for some dessert?"

Placing her hand on her stomach, she declined with a smile. "I couldn't," she declared, but her gaze fell with regret on the large table display of delicate French pastries.

The waiter reappeared and a flurry of French flew over her head. Like everything else Andrew did, his French was flawless.

Almost immediately the waiter returned with a plate covered with samples of several desserts, which he set in front of Jo Marie.

"Andrew," she objected, sighing his name, "I'll get fat."

"I saw you eyeing those goodies. Indulge. You deserve it."

"But I don't. I can't possibly eat all that."

"You can afford to put on a few pounds." His voice deepened as his gaze skimmed her lithe form.

"Are you suggesting I'm skinny?"

"My, my," he said, slowly shaking his head from side to side. "You do like to argue. Here, give me the plate. I'll be the one to indulge."

"Not on your life," she countered laughingly, and dipped her fork into the thin slice of chocolate cheesecake. After sampling three of the scrumptious desserts, Jo Marie pushed her plate aside. "Thank you, Andrew," she murmured as her fingers toyed with the starched, linen napkin. "I enjoyed the meal and . . . and the company, but we can't do this again." Her eyes were riveted to the tabletop.

"Jo Marie—"

"No. Let me finish," she interrupted on a rushed breath. "It . . . it would be so easy . . . to hurt Kelly and I won't do that. I can't. Please, don't make this so difficult for me." With every word her voice grew weaker and shakier. It shouldn't be this hard, her heart cried, but it was. Every womanly instinct was reaching out to him until she wanted to cry with it.

"Indulge me, Jo Marie," he said tenderly. "It's my birthday and there's no one else I'd rather share it with."

No one else . . . his words reverberated through her mind. They were on treacherous ground and Jo Marie felt herself sinking fast.

"Happy birthday," she whispered.

"Thank you."

They stood and Andrew cupped her elbow, leading her to the street.

"Would you like me to drop you off at the apartment?"

Andrew asked several minutes later as they walked toward his parked car.

"No. I'm on my way to the LFTF headquarters." She stuck both hands deep within her sweater pockets.

"Land For The Future?"

She nodded. "They need extra volunteers during the Christmas season."

His wide brow knitted with a deep frown. "As I recall, that building is in a bad part of town. Is it safe for you to—"

"Perfectly safe." She took a step in retreat. "Thank you again for lunch. I hope you have a wonderful birthday," she called just before turning and hurrying along the narrow sidewalk.

Jo Marie's pace was brisk as she kept one eye on the darkening sky. Angry gray thunderclouds were rolling in and a cloud burst was imminent. Everything looked as if it was against her. With the sky the color of Andrew's eyes, it seemed as though he was watching her every move. Fleetingly she wondered if she'd ever escape him . . . and worse, if she'd ever want to.

The LFTF headquarters were near the docks. Andrew's apprehensions were well founded. This was a high crime area. Jo Marie planned her arrival and departure times in daylight.

"Can I help you?" The stocky man with crisp ebony hair spoke from behind the desk. There was a speculative arch to his bushy brows as he regarded her.

"Hello." She extended her hand. "I'm Jo Marie Early. You're Jim Rowden, aren't you?" Jim had recently arrived from the Boston area and was taking over the manager's position of the nonprofit organization.

Jim stepped around the large oak desk. "Yes, I remember now. You marched in the demonstration, didn't you?"

"Yes, I was there."

"One of the few who stuck it out in the rain, as I recall."

"My brother insisted that it wasn't out of any sense of purpose, but from a pure streak of stubbornness." Laughter riddled her voice. "I'm back because you mentioned needing extra volunteers this month."

"Do you type?"

"Reasonably well. I'm a travel agent."

"Don't worry, I won't give you a time test."

Jo Marie laughed. "I appreciate that more than you know."

The majority of the afternoon was spent typing personal replies to letters the group had received after the demonstration in front of Rose's. In addition, the group had been spurred on by their success, and was planning other campaigns for future projects. At four-thirty, Jo Marie slipped the cover over the typewriter and placed the letters on Jim's desk for his signature.

"If you could come three times a week," Jim asked, "it would be greatly appreciated."

She left forty minutes later feeling assured that she was doing the right thing by offering her time. Lending a hand at Christmas seemed such a small thing to do. Admittedly, her motives weren't pure. If she could keep herself occupied, she wouldn't have to deal with her feelings for Andrew.

A lot of her major Christmas shopping was completed, but on her way to the bus stop, Jo Marie stopped in at a used-book store. Although she fought it all afternoon, her thoughts had been continually on Andrew. Today was his special day and she desperately wanted to give him something that would relay her feelings. Her heart was filled with gratitude. Without him, she may never have known that sometimes dreams can come true and that fairy tales aren't always for the young.

She found the book she was seeking. A large leather-bound volume of the history of New Orleans. Few cities had a more romantic background. Included in the book were hundreds of rare photographs of the city's architecture, courtyards, patios, ironwork and cemeteries. He'd love the book as much as she. Jo Marie had come by for weeks, paying a little bit each pay day. Not only was this book rare, but extremely expensive. Because the proprietor knew Jo Marie, he had made special arrangements for her to have this volume. But Jo Marie couldn't think of anything else Andrew would cherish more. She wrote out a check for the balance and realized that she would probably be short on cash by the end of the month, but that seemed a small sacrifice.

Clenching the book to her breast, Jo Marie hurried home. She had no right to be giving Andrew gifts, but this was more for her sake than his. It was her thank-you for all that he'd given her.

The torrential downpour assaulted the pavement just as Jo Marie stepped off the bus. Breathlessly, while holding the paper-wrapped leather volume to her stomach, she ran to the apartment and inserted her key into the dead bolt. Once again she had barely escaped a thorough drenching.

Hanging her Irish knit cardigan in the hall closet, Jo Marie kicked off her shoes and slid her feet into fuzzy, worn slippers.

Kelly should arrive any minute and Jo Marie rehearsed what she was going to say to Kelly. She had to have some kind of explanation to be giving her friend's fiancé a birthday present. Her thoughts came back empty as she paced the floor, wringing her hands. It was important that Kelly understand, but finding a plausible reason without revealing herself was difficult. Jo Marie didn't want any ill feelings between them.

When her roommate hadn't returned from the hospital by six, Jo Marie made herself a light meal and turned on the evening news. Kelly usually phoned if she was going to be late. Not having heard from her friend caused Jo Marie to wonder. Maybe Andrew had picked her up after work and had taken her out to dinner. It was, after all, his birthday; celebrating with his fiancé would only be natural. Unbidden, a surge of resentment rose within her and caused a lump of painful hoarseness to tighten her throat. Mentally she gave herself a hard shake. *Stop it,* her mind shouted. *You have no right to feel these things. Andrew belongs to Kelly, not you.*

A mixture of pain and confusion moved across her smooth brow when the doorbell chimed. It was probably Mark, but for the first time in recent memory, Jo Marie wasn't up to a sparring match with her older brother. Tonight she wanted to be left to her own thoughts.

But it wasn't Mark.

"Andrew." Quickly she lowered her gaze, praying he couldn't read her startled expression.

"Is Kelly ready?" he asked as he stepped inside the entryway. "We're having dinner with my mother."

"She isn't home from work yet. If you'd like I could call the hospital and see what's holding her up." So they were going out tonight. Jo Marie successfully managed to rein in her feelings of jealousy, having dealt with them earlier.

"No need, I'm early. If you don't mind, I'll just wait."

"Please, sit down." Self-consciously she gestured toward the love seat. "I'm sure Kelly will be here any minute."

Impeccably dressed in a charcoal-gray suit that emphasized the width of his muscular shoulders, Andrew took a seat.

With her hands linked in front of her, Jo Marie fought for control of her hammering heart. "Would you like a cup of coffee?"

"Please."

Relieved to be out of the living room, Jo Marie hurried into the kitchen and brought down a cup and saucer. Spending part of the afternoon with Andrew was difficult enough. But being alone in the apartment with him was impossible. The tension between them was unbearable as it was. But to be separated by only a thin wall was much worse. She yearned to touch him. To hold him in her arms. To feel again, just this once, his mouth over hers. She had to know if what had happened all those months ago was real.

"Jo Marie," Andrew spoke softly from behind her.

Her pounding heart leaped to her throat. Had he read her thoughts and come to her? Her fingers dug unmercifully into the kitchen countertop. Nothing would induce her to turn around.

"What's this?" he questioned softly.

A glance over her shoulder revealed Andrew holding the book she'd purchased earlier. Her hand shook as she poured the coffee. "It's a book about the early history of New Orleans. I found it in a used-book store and . . ." Her voice wobbled as badly as her hand.

"There was a card on top of it that was addressed to me."

Jo Marie set the glass coffeepot down. "Yes . . . I knew you'd love it and I wanted you to have it as a birthday present." She stopped just before admitting that she wanted him to remember her. "I also heard on the news tonight that . . . that Rose's Hotel is undergoing some expensive and badly needed repairs, thanks to you." Slowly she turned, keeping her hands behind her. "I realize there isn't anything that I could ever buy for you that you couldn't purchase a hundred times over. But I thought this book might be the one thing I could give you . . ." She let her voice fade in midsentence.

A slow faint smile touched his mouth as he opened the card and read her inscription. "To Andrew, in appreciation for everything." Respectfully he opened the book, then laid it aside. "Everything, Jo Marie?"

"For your generosity toward the hotel, and your thoughtfulness in giving me the party dress and . . ."

"The Mardi Gras?" He inched his way toward her.

Jo Marie could feel the color seep up her neck and tinge her cheeks. "Yes, that too." She wouldn't deny how special those few moments had been to her. Nor could she deny the hunger in his hard gaze as he concentrated on her lips. Amazed, Jo Marie watched as Andrew's gray eyes darkened to the shade of a stormy Arctic sea.

No pretense existed between them now, only a shared hunger that could no longer be repressed. A surge of intense longing seared through her so that when Andrew drew her into his embrace she gave a small cry and went willingly.

"Haven't you ever wondered if what we shared that night was real?" he breathed the question into her hair.

"Yes, a thousand times since, I've wondered." She gloried in the feel of his muscular body pressing against the length of hers. Freely her hands roamed his back. His index finger under her chin lifted her face and her heart soared at the look in his eyes.

"Jo Marie," he whispered achingly and his thumb leisurely caressed the full curve of her mouth.

Her soft lips trembled in anticipation. Slowly, deliberately, Andrew lowered his head as his mouth sought hers. Her eyelids drifted closed and her arms reached up and clung to him. The kiss was one of hunger and demand as his mouth feasted on hers.

The feel of him, the touch, the taste of his lips filled her senses until Jo Marie felt his muscles strain as he brought her to him, riveting her soft form to him so tightly that she could no longer breathe. Not that she cared.

Gradually the kiss mellowed and the intensity eased until he buried his face in the gentle slope of her neck. "It was real," he whispered huskily. "Oh, my sweet Florence Nightingale, it was even better than I remembered."

"I was afraid it would be." Tears burned her eyes and she gave a sad little laugh. Life was filled with ironies and finding Andrew now was the most painful.

Tenderly he reached up and wiped the moisture from her face. "I shouldn't have let this happen."

"It wasn't your fault." Jo Marie felt she had to accept part of the blame. She'd wanted him to kiss her so badly. "I . . . I won't let it happen again." If one of them had to be strong, then it would be her. After years of friendship with Kelly she owed her roommate her loyalty.

Reluctantly they broke apart, but his hands rested on either side of her neck as though he couldn't bear to let her go completely. "Thank you for the book," he said in a raw voice. "I'll treasure it always."

The sound of the front door opening caused Jo Marie's eyes to widen with a rush of guilt. Kelly would take one look at her and realize what had happened. Hot color blazed in her cheeks.

"Jo Marie!" Kelly's eager voice vibrated through the apartment.

Andrew stepped out of the kitchen, granting Jo Marie precious seconds to compose herself.

"Oh, heavens, you're here already, Drew. I'm sorry I'm so late. But I've got so much to tell you."

With her hand covering her mouth to smother the sound of her tears, Jo Marie leaned against the kitchen counter, suddenly needing its support.

Five

"Are you all right?" Andrew stepped back into the kitchen and brushed his hand over his temples. He resembled a man driven to the end of his endurance, standing with one foot in heaven and the other in hell. His fingers were clenched at his side as if he couldn't decide if he should haul her back into his arms or leave her alone. But the tortured look in his eyes told Jo Marie how difficult it was not to hold and reassure her.

"I'm fine." Her voice was eggshell fragile. "Just leave. Please. I don't want Kelly to see me." Not like this, with tears streaming down her pale cheeks and her eyes full of confusion. One glance at Jo Marie and the astute Kelly would know exactly what had happened.

"I'll get her out of here as soon as she changes clothes," Andrew whispered urgently, his stormy gray eyes pleading with hers. "I didn't mean for this to happen."

"I know." With an agitated brush of her hand she dismissed him. "Please, just go."

"I'll talk to you tomorrow."

"No." Dark emotion flickered across her face. She didn't want to see him. Everything about today had been wrong. She should have avoided Andrew, feeling as she did. But in some ways, Jo Marie realized that the kiss had been inevitable. Those brief magical moments at the Mardi Gras demanded an exploration of the sensation they'd shared. Both had hoped to dismiss that February night as whimsy—a result of the craziness of the season. Instead, they had discovered how real it had been. From now on, Jo Marie vowed, she would shun Andrew. Her only defense was to avoid him completely.

"I'm sorry to keep you waiting." Kelly's happy voice drifted in from the other room. "Do I look okay?"

"You're lovely as always."

Jo Marie hoped that Kelly wouldn't catch the detached note in Andrew's gruff voice.

"You'll never guess who I spent the last hour talking to."

"Perhaps you could tell me on the way to Mother's?" Andrew responded dryly.

"Drew." Some of the enthusiasm drained from Kelly's happy voice. "Are you feeling ill? You're quite pale."

"I'm fine."

"Maybe we should cancel this dinner. Really, I wouldn't mind."

"There's no reason to disappoint my mother."

"Drew?" Kelly seemed hesitant.

"Are you ready?" His firm voice brooked no disagreement.

"But I wanted to talk to Jo Marie."

"You can call her after dinner," Andrew responded shortly, his voice fading as they moved toward the entryway.

The door clicked a minute later and Jo Marie's fingers loosened their death grip against the counter. Weakly, she wiped a hand over her face and eyes. Andrew and Kelly were engaged to be married. Tonight was his birthday and he was taking Kelly to dine with his family. And Jo

Marie had been stealing a kiss from him in the kitchen. Self-reproach grew in her breast with every breath until she wanted to scream and lash out with it.

Maybe she could have justified her actions if Kelly hadn't been so excited and happy. Her roommate had come into the apartment bursting with enthusiasm for life, eager to see and talk to Andrew.

The evening seemed interminable and Jo Marie had a terrible time falling asleep, tossing and turning long past the time Kelly returned. Finally at the darkest part of the night, she flipped on the bedside lamp and threw aside the blankets. Pouring herself a glass of milk, Jo Marie leaned against the kitchen counter and drank it with small sips, her thoughts deep and dark. She couldn't ask Kelly to forgive her for what had happened without hurting her roommate and perhaps ruining their friendship. The only person there was to confront and condemn was herself.

Once she returned to bed, Jo Marie lay on her back, her head clasped in her hands. Moon shadows fluttered against the bare walls like the flickering scenes of a silent movie.

Unhappy beyond words, Jo Marie avoided her roommate, kept busy and occupied her time with other friends. But she was never at peace and always conscious that her thoughts never strayed from Kelly and Andrew. The episode with Andrew wouldn't happen again. She had to be strong.

Jo Marie didn't see her roommate until the following Monday morning. They met in the kitchen where Jo Marie was pouring herself a small glass of grapefruit juice.

"Morning." Jo Marie's stiff smile was only slightly forced.

"Howdy, stranger. I've missed you the past couple of days."

Jo Marie's hand tightened around the juice glass as she silently prayed Kelly wouldn't ask her about Saturday night. Her roommate must have known Jo Marie was in the apartment, otherwise Andrew wouldn't have been inside.

"I've missed you," Kelly continued. "It seems we hardly have time to talk anymore. And now that you're going to be doing volunteer work for the foundation, we'll have even less time together. You're spreading yourself too thin."

"There's always something going on this time of year." A chill seemed to settle around the area of Jo Marie's heart and she avoided her friend's look.

"I know, that's why I'm looking forward to this weekend and the party for Drew's company. By the way, he suggested that both of us stay the night on Saturday."

"Spend the night?" Jo Marie repeated like a recording and inhaled a shaky breath. That was the last thing she wanted.

"It makes sense, don't you think? We can lay awake until dawn the way we used to and talk all night." A distant look came over Kelly as she buttered the hot toast and poured herself a cup of coffee. "Drew's going to have enough to worry about without dragging us back and forth. From what I understand, he goes all out for his company's Christmas party."

Hoping to hide her discomfort, Jo Marie rinsed out her glass and deposited it in the dishwasher, but a gnawing sensation attacked the pit of her stomach. Although she'd promised Kelly she would attend the lavish affair, she had to find a way of excusing herself without arousing suspicion. "I've been thinking about Andrew's party and honestly feel I shouldn't go—"

"Don't say it. You're going!" Kelly interrupted hastily. "There's no way I'd go without you. You're my best friend, Jo Marie Early, and as such I want you with me. Besides, you know how I hate these things."

"But as Drew's wife you'll be expected to attend a lot of these functions. I won't always be around."

A secret smile stole over her friend's pert face. "I know, that's why it's so important that you're there now."

"You didn't seem to need me Friday night."

Round blue eyes flashed Jo Marie a look of disbelief. "Are you crazy? I would have been embarrassingly uncomfortable without you."

It seemed to Jo Marie that Mark had spent nearly as much time with Kelly as she had. In fact, her brother had spent most of the evening with Kelly at his side. It was Mark whom Kelly really wanted, not her. But convincing her roommate of that was a different matter. Jo Marie doubted that Kelly had even admitted as much to herself.

"I'll think about going," Jo Marie promised. "But I can't honestly see that my being there or not would do any good."

"You've got to come," Kelly muttered, looking around unhappily. "I'd be miserable meeting and talking to all those people on my own." Silently, Kelly's bottomless blue eyes pleaded with Jo Marie. "I promise never to ask anything from you again. Say you'll come. Oh, please, Jo Marie, do this one last thing for me."

An awkward silence stretched between them and a feeling of dread settled over Jo Marie. Kelly seemed so genuinely distraught that it wasn't in Jo Marie's heart to refuse her. As Kelly had pointedly reminded her, she was Kelly's best friend. "All right, all right," she agreed reluctantly. "But I don't like it."

"You won't be sorry, I promise." A mischievous gleam lightened Kelly's features.

Jo Marie mumbled disdainfully under her breath as she moved out of the kitchen. Pausing at the closet, she took her trusted cardigan from the hanger. "Say, Kell, don't forget this is the week I'm flying to Mazatlán." Jo Marie was scheduled to take a familiarization tour of the Mexican resort town. She'd be flying with ten other travel agents from the city and staying at the Riviera Del Sol's expense. The luxury hotel was sponsoring the group in hopes of having the agents book their facilities for their clients. Jo Marie usually took the "fam" tours only once or twice a year. This one had been planned months before and she mused that it couldn't have come at a better time. Escaping from Andrew and Kelly was just the thing she needed. By the time she returned, she prayed, her life could be back to normal.

"This is the week?" Kelly stuck her head around the kitchen doorway. "Already?"

"You can still drive me to the airport, can't you?"

"Sure," Kelly answered absently. "But if I can't, Drew will."

Jo Marie's heart throbbed painfully. "No," she returned forcefully.

"He doesn't mind."

But I do, Jo Marie's heart cried as she fumbled with

the buttons of her sweater. If Kelly wasn't home when it came time to leave for the airport, she would either call Mark or take a cab.

"I'm sure Drew wouldn't mind," Kelly repeated.

"I'll be late tonight," she answered, ignoring her friend's offer. She couldn't understand why Kelly would want her to spend time with Andrew. But so many things didn't make sense lately. Without a backward glance, Jo Marie went out the front door.

Joining several others at the bus stop outside the apartment building en route to the office, Jo Marie fought down feelings of guilt. She'd honestly thought she could get out of attending the party with Kelly. But there was little to be done, short of offending her friend. These constant recriminations regarding Kelly and Andrew were disrupting her neatly ordered life, and Jo Marie hated it.

Two of the other girls were in the office by the time Jo Marie arrived.

"There's a message for you," Paula announced. "I think it was the same guy who stopped in Saturday morning. You know, I'm beginning to think you've been holding out on me. Where'd you ever meet a hunk like that?"

"He's engaged," she quipped, seeking a light tone.

"He is?" Paula rolled her office chair over to Jo Marie's desk and handed her the pink slip. "You could have fooled me. He looked on the prowl, if you want my opinion. In fact, he was eyeing you like a starving man looking at a cream puff."

"Paula!" Jo Marie tried to toss off her co-worker's observation with a forced laugh. "He's engaged to my roommate."

Paula lifted one shoulder in a half shrug and scooted

the chair back to her desk. "If you say so." But both her tone and her look were disbelieving.

Jo Marie read the message, which listed Andrew's office number and asked that she call him at her earliest convenience. Crumbling up the pink slip, she tossed it in the green metal wastebasket beside her desk. She might be attending this party, but it was under duress. And as far as Andrew was concerned, she had every intention of avoiding him.

Rather than rush back to the apartment after work, Jo Marie had dinner in a small café near her office. From there she walked to the Land For The Future headquarters.

She was embarrassingly early when she arrived outside of the office door. The foundation's headquarters were on the second floor of an older brick building in a bad part of town. Jo Marie decided to arrive earlier than she'd planned rather than kill time by walking around outside. From the time she'd left the travel agency, she'd wandered around with little else to do. Her greatest fear was that Andrew would be waiting for her at the apartment. She hadn't returned his call and he'd want to know why.

Jim Rowden, the office manager and spokesman, was busy on the telephone when Jo Marie arrived. Quietly she slipped into the chair at the desk opposite him and glanced over the letters and other notices that needed to be typed. As she pulled the cover from the top of the typewriter, Jo Marie noticed a shadowy movement from the other side of the milky white glass inset of the office door.

She stood to investigate and found a dark-haired man with a worn felt hat that fit loosely on top of his head. His clothes were ragged and the faint odor of cheap wine permeated the air. He was curling up in the doorway of an office nearest theirs.

His eyes met hers briefly and he tugged his thin sweater around his shoulders. "Are you going to throw me out of here?" The words were issued in subtle challenge.

Jo Marie teetered with indecision. If she did tell him to leave he'd either spend the night shivering in the cold or find another open building. On the other hand if she were to give him money, she was confident it wouldn't be a bed he'd spend it on.

"Well?" he challenged again.

"I won't say anything," she answered finally. "Just go down to the end of the hall so no one else will find you."

He gave her a look of mild surprise, stood and gathered his coat before turning and ambling down the long hall in an uneven gait. Jo Marie waited until he was curled up in another doorway. It was difficult to see that he was there without looking for him. A soft smile of satisfaction stole across her face as she closed the door and returned to her desk.

Jim replaced the receiver and smiled a welcome at Jo Marie. "How'd you like to attend a lecture with me tonight?"

"I'd like it fine," she agreed eagerly.

Jim's lecture was to a group of concerned city businessmen. He relayed the facts about the dangers of thoughtless and haphazard land development. He presented his case in a simple, straightforward fashion without emotionalism or sensationalism. In addition, he confidently answered their questions, defining the difference between building for the future and preserving a link with the past. Jo Marie was impressed and from the looks on the faces of his audience, the businessmen had been equally affected.

"I'll walk you to the bus stop," Jim told her hours later after they'd returned from the meeting. "I don't like the idea of you waiting at the bus stop alone. I'll go with you."

Jo Marie hadn't been that thrilled with the prospect herself. "Thanks, I'd appreciate that."

Jim's hand cupped her elbow as they leisurely strolled down the narrow street, chatting as they went. Jim's voice was drawling and smooth and Jo Marie mused that she could listen to him all night. The lamplight illuminated little in the descending fog and would have created an eerie feeling if Jim hadn't been at her side. But walking with him, she barely noticed the weather and instead found herself laughing at his subtle humor.

"How'd you ever get into this business?" she queried. Jim Rowden was an intelligent, warm human being who would be a success in any field he chose to pursue. He could be making twice and three times the money in the business world that he collected from the foundation.

At first introduction, Jim wasn't the kind of man who would bowl women over with his striking good looks or his suave manners. But he was a rare, dedicated man of conscience. Jo Marie had never known anyone like him and admired him greatly.

"I'm fairly new with the foundation," he admitted, "and it certainly wasn't what I'd been expecting to do with my life, especially since I struggled through college for a degree in biology. Afterward I went to work for the state, but this job gives me the opportunity to work first-hand with saving some of the—well, you heard my speech."

"Yes, I did, and it was wonderful."

"You're good for my ego, Jo Marie. I hope you'll stick around."

Jo Marie's eyes glanced up the street, wondering how long they'd have to wait for a bus. She didn't want their discussion to end. As she did, a flash of midnight blue captured her attention and her heart dropped to her knees as the Mercedes pulled to a stop alongside the curb in front of them.

Andrew practically leaped from the driver's side. "Just what do you think you're doing?" The harsh anger in his voice shocked her.

"I beg your pardon?" Jim answered on Jo Marie's behalf, taking a step forward.

Andrew ignored Jim, his eyes cold and piercing as he glanced over her. "I've spent the good part of an hour looking for you."

"Why?" Jo Marie demanded, tilting her chin in an act of defiance. "What business is it of yours where I am or who I'm with?"

"I'm making it my business."

"Is there a problem here, Jo Marie?" Jim questioned as he stepped forward.

"None whatsoever," she responded dryly and crossed her arms in front of her.

"Kelly's worried sick," Andrew hissed. "Now I suggest you get in the car and let me take you home before . . ." He let the rest of what he was saying die. He paused for several tense moments and exhaled a sharp breath. "I apologize, I had no right to come at you like that." He closed the car door and moved around the front of the Mercedes. "I'm Andrew Beaumont," he introduced himself and extended his hand to Jim.

"From Delta Development?" Jim's eyes widened appreciatively. "Jim Rowden. I've been wanting to meet you so that I could thank you personally for what you did for Rose's Hotel."

"I'm pleased I could help."

When Andrew decided to put on the charm it was like falling into a jar of pure honey, Jo Marie thought. She didn't know of a man, woman or child who couldn't be swayed by his beguiling showmanship. Having been under his spell in the past made it all the more recognizable now. But somehow, she realized, this was different. Andrew hadn't been acting the night of the Mardi Gras, she was convinced of that.

"Jo Marie was late coming home and luckily I remembered her saying something about volunteering for the foundation. Kelly asked that I come and get her. We were understandably worried about her taking the bus alone at this time of night."

"I'll admit I was a bit concerned myself," Jim returned, taking a step closer to Jo Marie. "That's why I'm here."

As Andrew opened the passenger's side of the car, Jo Marie turned her head to meet his gaze, her eyes fiery as she slid into the plush velvet seat.

"I'll see you Friday," she said to Jim.

"Enjoy Mexico," he responded and waved before turning and walking back toward the office building. A fine mist filled the evening air and Jim pulled up his collar as he hurried along the sidewalk.

Andrew didn't say a word as he turned the key in the

ignition, checked the rearview mirror and pulled back onto the street.

"You didn't return my call." He stopped at a red light and the full force of his magnetic gray eyes was turned on her.

"No," she answered in a whisper, struggling not to reveal how easily he could affect her.

"Can't you see how important it is that we talk?"

"No." She wanted to shout the word. When their eyes met, Jo Marie was startled to find that only a few inches separated them. Andrew's look was centered on her mouth and with a determined effort she averted her gaze and stared out the side window. "I don't want to talk to you." Her fingers fumbled with the clasp of her purse in nervous agitation. "There's nothing more we can say." She hated the husky emotion-filled way her voice sounded.

"Jo Marie." He said her name so softly that she wasn't entirely sure he'd spoken.

She turned back to him, knowing she should pull away from the hypnotic darkness of his eyes, but doing so was impossible.

"You'll come to my party?"

She wanted to explain her decision to attend—she hadn't wanted to go—but one glance at Andrew said that he understood. Words were unnecessary.

"It's going to be difficult for us both for a while."

He seemed to imply things would grow easier with time. Jo Marie sincerely doubted that they ever would.

"You'll come?" he prompted softly.

Slowly she nodded. Jo Marie hadn't realized how tense she was until she exhaled and felt some of the coiled tightness leave her body. "Yes, I'll . . . be at the party." Her breathy stammer spoke volumes.

"And wear the dress I gave you?"

She ended up nodding again, her tongue unable to form words.

"I've dreamed of you walking into my arms wearing that dress," he added on a husky tremor, then shook his head as if he regretted having spoken.

Being alone with him in the close confines of the car was torture. Her once restless fingers lay limp in her lap. Jo Marie didn't know how she was going to avoid Andrew when Kelly seemed to be constantly throwing them together. But she must for her own peace of mind . . . she must.

All too quickly the brief respite of her trip to Mazatlán was over. Saturday arrived and Kelly and Jo Marie were brought to Andrew's home, which was a faithful reproduction of an antebellum mansion.

The dress he'd purchased was hanging in the closet of the bedroom she was to share with Kelly. Her friend threw herself across the canopy bed and exhaled on a happy sigh.

"Isn't this place something?"

Jo Marie didn't answer for a moment, her gaze falling on the dress that hung alone in the closet. "It's magnificent." There was little else that would describe this palace. The house was a three-story structure with huge white pillars and dark shutters. It faced the Mississippi River and had a huge garden in the back. Jo Marie learned that it was his mother who took an avid interest in the wide variety of flowers that grew in abundance there.

The rooms were large, their walls adorned with paintings and works of art. If Jo Marie was ever to doubt Andrew's wealth and position, his home would prove to be a constant reminder.

"Drew built it himself," Kelly explained with a proud lilt to her voice. "I don't mean he pounded in every nail, but he was here every day while it was being constructed. It took months."

"I can imagine." And no expense had been spared from the look of things.

"I suppose we should think about getting ready," Kelly continued. "I don't mind telling you that I've had a queasy stomach all day dreading this thing."

Kelly had! Jo Marie nearly laughed aloud. This party had haunted her all week. Even Mazatlán hadn't been far enough away to dispel the feeling of dread.

Jo Marie could hear the music drifting in from the reception hall by the time she had put on the finishing touches of her makeup. Kelly had already joined Andrew. A quick survey in the full-length mirror assured her that the beautiful gown was the most elegant thing she would ever own. The reflection that came back to her of a tall, regal woman was barely recognizable as herself. The dark crown of curls was styled on top of her head with a few stray tendrils curling about her ears. A lone strand of pearls graced her neck.

Self-consciously she moved from the room, closing the door. From the top of the winding stairway, she looked down on a milling crowd of arriving guests. Holding in her breath, she placed her gloved hand on the polished bannister, exhaled, and made her descent. Keeping her eyes on her feet for fear of tripping, Jo Marie was surprised when she glanced down to find Andrew waiting for her at the bottom of the staircase.

As he gave her his hand, their eyes met and held in a tender exchange. "You're beautiful."

The deep husky tone in his voice took her breath away and Jo Marie could do nothing more than smile in return.

Taking her hand, Andrew tucked it securely in the crook of his elbow and led her into the room where the other guests were mingling. Everyone was meeting for drinks in the huge living room and once the party was complete they would be moving up to the ballroom on the third floor. The evening was to culminate in a midnight buffet.

With Andrew holding her close by his side, Jo Marie had little option but to follow where he led. Moving from one end of the room to the other, he introduced her to so many people that her head swam trying to remember their names. Fortunately, Kelly and Andrew's engagement hadn't been officially announced and Jo Marie wasn't forced to make repeated explanations. Nonetheless, she was uncomfortable with the way he was linking the two of them together.

"Where's Kelly?" Jo Marie asked under her breath. "She should be the one with you. Not me."

"Kelly's with Mark on the other side of the room."

Jo Marie faltered in midstep and Andrew's hold tightened as he dropped his arm and slipped it around her slim waist. "With Mark?" She couldn't imagine her brother attending this party. Not feeling the way he did about Andrew.

Not until they were upstairs and the music was playing did Jo Marie have an opportunity to talk to her brother. He was sitting against the wall in a high-backed mahogany chair with a velvet cushion. Kelly was at his side. Jo Marie couldn't recall a time she'd seen her brother dress so formally or look more handsome. He'd had his hair trimmed and was clean shaven. She'd never dreamed she'd see Mark in a tuxedo.

"Hello, Mark."

Her brother looked up, guilt etched on his face. "Jo Marie." Briefly he exchanged looks with Kelly and stood, offering Jo Marie his seat.

"Thanks," she said as she sat and slipped the high-heeled sandals from her toes. "My feet could use a few moments' rest."

"You certainly haven't lacked for partners," Kelly observed happily. "You're a hit, Jo Marie. Even Mark was saying he couldn't believe you were his sister."

"I've never seen you look more attractive," Mark added. "But then I bet you didn't buy that dress out of petty cash either."

If there was a note of censure in her brother's voice, Jo Marie didn't hear it. "No." Absently her hand smoothed the silk skirt. "It was a gift from Andrew . . . and Kelly." Hastily she added her roommate's name. "I must admit though, I'm surprised to see you here."

"Andrew extended the invitation personally," Mark replied, holding his back ramrod stiff as he stared straight ahead.

Not understanding, Jo Marie glanced at her roommate. "Mark came for me," Kelly explained, her voice soft and vulnerable. "Because I . . . because I wanted him here."

"We're both here for you, Kelly," Jo Marie reminded her and punctuated her comment by arching her brows.

"I know, and I love you both for it."

"Would you care to dance?" Mark held out his hand to Kelly, taking her into his arms when they reached the boundary of the dance floor as if he never wanted to let her go.

Confused, Jo Marie watched their progress. Kelly was engaged to be married to Andrew, yet she was gazing into Mark's eyes as if he were her knight in shining armor who had come to slay dragons on her behalf. When she'd come upon them, they'd acted as if she had intruded on their very private party.

Jo Marie saw Andrew approach her, his brows lowered as if something had displeased him. His strides were quick and decisive as he wove his way through the throng of guests.

"I've been looking for you. In fact, I was beginning to wonder if I'd ever get a chance to dance with you." The pitch of his voice suggested that she'd been deliberately avoiding him. And she had.

Jo Marie couldn't bring herself to meet his gaze, afraid of what he could read in her eyes. All night she'd been pretending it was Andrew who was holding her and yet she'd known she wouldn't be satisfied until he did.

"I believe this dance is mine," he said, presenting her with his hand.

Peering up at him, a smile came and she paused to slip the strap of her high heel over her ankle before standing.

Once on the dance floor, his arms tightened around

her waist, bringing her so close that there wasn't a hair's space between them. He held her securely as if challenging her to move. Jo Marie discovered that she couldn't. This inexplicable feeling was beyond argument. With her hands resting on his muscular shoulders, she leaned her head against his broad chest and sighed her contentment.

She spoke first. "It's a wonderful party."

"You're more comfortable now, aren't you?" His fingers moved up and down her back in a leisurely exercise, drugging her with his firm caress against her bare skin.

"What do you mean?" She wasn't sure she understood his question and slowly lifted her gaze.

"Last week, you stayed on the outskirts of the crowd afraid of joining in or being yourself."

"Last week I was terrified that someone would recognize me as the one who had once demonstrated against you. I didn't want to do anything that would embarrass you," she explained dryly. Her cheek was pressed against his starched shirt and she thrilled to the uneven thump of his heart.

"And this week?"

"Tonight anyone who looked at us would know that we've long since resolved our differences."

She sensed more than felt Andrew's soft touch. The moment was quickly becoming too intimate. Using her hands for leverage, Jo Marie straightened, creating a space between them. "Does it bother you to have my brother dance with Kelly?"

Andrew looked back at her blankly. "No. Should it?"

"She's your fiancée." To the best of Jo Marie's knowledge, Andrew hadn't said more than a few words to Kelly all evening.

A cloud of emotion darkened his face. "She's wearing my ring."

"And . . . and you care for her."

Andrew's hold tightened painfully around her waist. "Yes, I care for Kelly. We've always been close." His eyes darkened to the color of burnt silver. "Perhaps too close."

The applause was polite when the dance number finished.

Jo Marie couldn't escape fast enough. She made an excuse and headed for the powder room. Andrew wasn't pleased and it showed in the grim set of his mouth, but he didn't try to stop her. Things weren't right. Mark shouldn't be sitting like an avenging angel at Kelly's side and Andrew should at least show some sign of jealousy.

When she returned to the ballroom, Andrew was busy and Jo Marie decided to sort through her thoughts in the fresh night air. A curtained glass door that led to the balcony was open, and unnoticed she slipped silently into the dark. A flash of white captured her attention and Jo Marie realized she wasn't alone. Inadvertently, she had invaded the private world of two young lovers. With their arms wrapped around each other they were locked in a passionate embrace. Smiling softly to herself, she turned to escape as silently as she'd come. But something stopped her. A sickening knot tightened her stomach.

The couple so passionately embracing were Kelly and Mark.

Six

Jo Marie woke just as dawn broke over a cloudless horizon. Standing at the bedroom window, she pressed her palms against the sill and surveyed the beauty of the landscape before her. Turning, she glanced at Kelly's sleeping figure. Her hands fell limply to her side as her face darkened with uncertainty. Last night while they'd prepared for bed, Jo Marie had been determined to confront her friend with the kiss she'd unintentionally witnessed. But when they'd turned out the lights, Kelly had chatted happily about the success of the party and what a good time she'd had. And Jo Marie had lost her nerve. What Mark and Kelly did wasn't any of her business, she mused. In addition, she had no right to judge her brother and her friend when she and Andrew had done the same thing.

The memory of Andrew's kiss produced a breathlessness, and surrendering to the feeling, Jo Marie closed her eyes. The infinitely sweet touch of his mouth seemed to have branded her. Her fingers shook as she raised them to the gentle curve of her lips. Jo Marie doubted that she would ever feel the same overpowering rush of sensation at another man's touch. Andrew was special, her dream man. Whole lifetimes could pass and she'd never find anyone she'd love more. The powerful ache in her heart drove her to the closet where a change of clothes was hanging.

Dawn's light was creeping up the stairs, awaking a

sleeping world, when Jo Marie softly clicked the bedroom door closed. Her overnight bag was clenched tightly in her hand. She hated to sneak out, but the thought of facing everyone over the breakfast table was more than she could bear. Andrew and Kelly needed to be alone. Time together was something they hadn't had much of lately. This morning would be the perfect opportunity for them to sit down and discuss their coming marriage. Jo Marie would only be an intruder.

Moving so softly that no one was likely to hear her, Jo Marie crept down the stairs to the wide entry hall. She was tiptoeing toward the front door when a voice behind her interrupted her quiet departure.

"What do you think you're doing?"

Releasing a tiny, startled cry, Jo Marie dropped the suitcase and held her hand to her breast.

"Andrew, you've frightened me to death."

"Just what are you up to?"

"I'm . . . I'm leaving."

"That's fairly easy to ascertain. What I want to know is why." His angry gaze locked with hers, refusing to allow her to turn away.

"I thought you and Kelly should spend some time together and . . . and I wanted to be gone this morning before everyone woke." Regret crept into her voice. Maybe sneaking out like this wasn't such a fabulous idea, after all.

He stared at her in the dim light as if he could examine her soul with his penetrating gaze. When he spoke again, his tone was lighter. "And just how did you expect to get to town. Walk?"

"Exactly."

"But it's miles."

"All the more reason to get an early start," she reasoned.

Andrew studied her as though he couldn't believe what he was hearing. "Is running away so important that you would sneak out of here like a cat burglar and not tell anyone where you're headed?"

How quickly her plan had backfired. By trying to leave unobtrusively she'd only managed to offend Andrew when she had every reason to thank him. "I didn't mean to be rude, although I can see now that I have been. I suppose this makes me look like an ungrateful house guest."

His answer was to narrow his eyes fractionally.

"I want you to know I left a note that explained where I was going to both you and Kelly. It's on the nightstand."

"And what did you say?"

"That I enjoyed the party immensely and that I've never felt more beautiful in any dress."

A brief troubled look stole over Andrew's face. "Once," he murmured absently. "Only once have you been more lovely." There was an unexpectedly gentle quality to his voice.

Her eyelashes fluttered closed. Andrew was reminding her of that February night. He too hadn't been able to forget the Mardi Gras. After all this time, after everything that had transpired since, neither of them could forget. The spell was as potent today as it had been those many months ago.

"Is that coffee I smell?" The question sought an invitation to linger with Andrew. Her original intent had been to escape so that Kelly could have the opportunity to spend this time alone with him. Instead, Jo Marie was seeking it herself. To sit in the early light of dawn and savor a few solitary minutes alone with Andrew was too tempting to ignore.

"Come and I'll get you a cup." Andrew led her toward the back of the house and his den. The room held a faint scent of leather and tobacco that mingled with the aroma of musk and spice.

Three walls were lined with leather-bound books that reached from the floor to the ceiling. Two wing chairs were angled in front of a large fireplace.

"Go ahead and sit down. I'll be back in a moment with the coffee."

A contented smile brightened Jo Marie's eyes as she sat and noticed the leather volume she'd given him lying open on the ottoman. Apparently he'd been reading it when he heard the noise at the front of the house and had left to investigate.

Andrew returned and carefully handed her the steaming earthenware mug. His eyes followed her gaze, which rested on the open book. "I've been reading it. This is a wonderful book. Where did you ever find something like this?"

"I've known about it for a long time, but there were only a few volumes available. I located this one about three months ago in a used-book store."

"It's very special to me because of the woman who bought it for me."

"No." Jo Marie's eyes widened as she lightly tossed her head from side to side. "Don't let that be the reason. Appreciate the book for all the interesting details it gives of New Orleans' colorful past. Or admire the pictures of the city architects' skill. But don't treasure it because of me."

Andrew looked for a moment as if he wanted to argue, but she spoke again.

"When you read this book ten, maybe twenty, years from now, I'll only be someone who briefly passed through your life. I imagine you'll have trouble remembering what I looked like."

"You'll never be anyone who flits in and out of my life."

He said it with such intensity that Jo Marie's fingers tightened around the thick handle of the mug. "All right," she agreed with a shaky laugh. "I'll admit I barged into your peaceful existence long before Kelly introduced us but—"

"But," Andrew interrupted on a short laugh, "it seems we were destined to meet. Do you honestly believe that either of us will ever forget that night?" A faint smile touched his eyes as he regarded her steadily.

Jo Marie knew that she never would. Andrew was her dream man. It had been far more than mere fate that had brought them together, something almost spiritual.

"No," she answered softly. "I'll never forget."

Regret moved across his features, creasing his wide brow and pinching his mouth. "Nor will I forget," he murmured in a husky voice that sounded very much like a vow.

The air between them was electric. For months she'd thought of Andrew as the dream man. But coming to know him these past weeks had proven that he wasn't an apparition, but real. Human, vulnerable, proud, intelligent, generous—and everything that she had ever hoped to find in a man. She lowered her gaze and studied the dark depths of the steaming coffee. Andrew might be everything she had ever wanted in a man, but Kelly wore his ring and her roommate's stake on him was far more tangible than her own romantic dreams.

Taking an exaggerated drink of her coffee, Jo Marie carefully set aside the rose-colored mug and stood. "I really should be leaving."

"Please stay," Andrew requested. "Just sit with me a few minutes longer. It's been in this room that I've sat and thought about you so often. I'd always hoped that someday you would join me here."

Jo Marie dipped her head, her heart singing with the beauty of his words. She'd fantasized about him too. Since their meeting, her mind had conjured up his image so often that it wouldn't hurt to steal a few more moments of innocent happiness. Kelly would have him for a lifetime. Jo Marie had only today.

"I'll stay," she agreed and her voice throbbed with the excited beat of her heart.

"And when the times comes, I'll drive you back to the city."

She nodded her acceptance and finished her coffee. "It's so peaceful in here. It feels like all I need to do is lean my head back, close my eyes and I'll be asleep."

"Go ahead," he urged in a whispered tone.

A smile touched her radiant features. She didn't want to fall asleep and miss these precious moments alone with him. "No." She shook her head. "Tell me about yourself. I want to know everything."

His returning smile was wry. "I'd hate to bore you."

"Bore me!" Her small laugh was incredulous. "There's no chance of that."

"All right, but lay back and close your eyes and let me start by telling you that I had a good childhood with parents who deeply loved each other."

As he requested, Jo Marie rested her head against the cushion and closed her eyes. "My parents are wonderful too."

"But being raised in an ideal family has its drawbacks," Andrew continued in a low, soothing voice. "When it came time for me to think about a wife and starting a family there was always a fear in the back of my mind that I would never find the happiness my parents shared. My father wasn't an easy man to love. And I won't be either."

In her mind, Jo Marie took exception to that, but she said nothing. The room was warm, and slipping off her shoes, she tucked her nylon-covered feet under her. Andrew continued speaking, his voice droning on as she tilted her head back.

"When I reached thirty without finding a wife, I became skeptical about the women I was meeting. There were some who never saw past the dollar signs and others who were interested only in themselves. I wanted a woman who could be soft and yielding, but one who wasn't afraid to fight for what she believes, even if it meant standing up against tough opposition. I wanted someone who would share my joys and divide my worries. A woman as beautiful on the inside as any outward beauty she may possess."

"Kelly's like that." The words nearly stuck in Jo Marie's throat. Kelly was everything Andrew was describing and more. As painful as it was to admit, Jo Marie under-

stood why Andrew had asked her roommate to marry
him. In addition to her fine personal qualities, Kelly had
money of her own and Andrew need never think that she
was marrying him for any financial gains.

"Yes, Kelly's like that." There was a doleful timbre to
his voice that caused Jo Marie to open her eyes.

Fleetingly she wondered if Andrew had seen Mark and
Kelly kissing on the terrace last night. If he had created
the picture of a perfect woman in his mind, then finding
Kelly in Mark's arms could destroy him. No matter how
uncomfortable it became, Jo Marie realized she was going
to have to confront Mark about his behavior. Having
thoughtfully analyzed the situation, Jo Marie believed it
would be far better for her to talk to her brother. She
could speak more freely with him. It may be the hardest
thing she'd ever do, but after listening to Andrew, Jo
Marie realized that she must talk to Mark. The happiness
of too many people was at stake.

Deciding to change the subject, Jo Marie shifted her
position in the supple leather chair and looked to Andrew. "Kelly told me that you built the house yourself."

Grim amusement was carved in his features. "Yes, the
work began on it this spring."

"Then you've only been living in it a few months?"

"Yes. The construction on the house kept me from
going insane." He held her look, revealing nothing of his
thoughts.

"Going insane?" Jo Marie didn't understand.

"You see, for a short time last February, only a matter
of moments really, I felt my search for the right woman
was over. And in those few, scant moments I thought I
had met that special someone I could love for all time."

Jo Marie's heart was pounding so fast and loud that she wondered why it didn't burst right out of her chest. The thickening in her throat made swallowing painful. Each breath became labored as she turned her face away, unable to meet Andrew's gaze.

"But after those few minutes, I lost her," Andrew continued. "Ironically, I'd searched a lifetime for that special woman, and within a matter of minutes, she was gone. God knows I tried to find her again. For a month I went back to the spot where I'd last seen her and waited. When it seemed that all was lost I discovered I couldn't get the memory of her out of my mind. I even hired a detective to find her for me. For months he checked every hospital in the city, searching for her. But you see, at the time I thought she was a nurse."

Jo Marie felt moisture gathering in the corner of her eyes. Never had she believed that Andrew had looked for her to the extent that he hired someone.

"For a time I was convinced I was going insane. This woman, whose name I didn't even know, filled my every waking moment and haunted my sleep. Building the house was something I've always wanted to do. It helped fill the time until I could find her again. Every room was constructed with her in mind."

Andrew was explaining that he'd built the house for her. Jo Marie had thought she'd be uncomfortable in such a magnificent home. But she'd immediately felt welcome in the walls. Little had she dreamed the reason why.

"Sometimes," Jo Marie began awkwardly, "people build things up in their minds and when they're confronted with reality they're inevitably disappointed." Andrew was making her out to be wearing angel's wings. So much time had passed that he no longer saw her as flesh and bone, but a wonderful fantasy his mind had created.

"Not this time," he countered smoothly.

"I wondered where I'd find the two of you." A sleepy-eyed Kelly stood poised in the doorway of the den. There wasn't any censure in her voice, only her usual morning brightness. "Isn't it a marvelous morning? The sun's up and there's a bright new day just waiting for us."

Self-consciously, Jo Marie unwound her feet from beneath her and reached for her shoes. "What time is it?"

"A quarter to eight." Andrew supplied the information.

Jo Marie was amazed to realize that she'd spent the better part of two hours talking to him. But it would be time she'd treasure all her life.

"If you have no objections," Kelly murmured and paused to take a wide yawn, "I thought I'd go to the hospital this morning. There's a special . . . patient I'd like to stop in and visit."

A patient or Mark, Jo Marie wanted to ask. Her brother had mentioned last night that he was going to be on duty in the morning. Jo Marie turned to Andrew, waiting for a reaction from him. Surely he would say or do something to stop her. Kelly was his fiancée and both of them seemed to be regarding their commitment to each other lightly.

"No problem." Andrew spoke at last. "In fact I thought I'd go into the city myself this morning. It is a beautiful day and there's no better way to spend a portion of it than in the most beautiful city in the world. You don't mind if I tag along with you, do you, Jo Marie?"

Half of her wanted to cry out in exaltation. If there

was anything she wished to give of herself to Andrew it was her love of New Orleans. But at the same time she wanted to shake both Andrew and Kelly for the careless attitude they had toward their relationship.

"I'd like you to come." Jo Marie spoke finally, answering Andrew.

It didn't take Kelly more than a few moments to pack her things and be ready to leave. In her rush, she'd obviously missed the two sealed envelopes Jo Marie had left propped against the lamp on Kelly's nightstand. Or if she had discovered them, Kelly chose not to mention it. Not that it mattered, Jo Marie decided as Andrew started the car. But Kelly's actions revealed what a rush she was in to see Mark. If it was Mark that she was indeed seeing. Confused emotions flooded Jo Marie's face, pinching lines around her nose and mouth. She could feel Andrew's caressing gaze as they drove toward the hospital.

"Is something troubling you?" Andrew questioned after they'd dropped Kelly off in front of Tulane Hospital. Amid protests from Jo Marie, Kelly had assured them that she would find her own way home. Standing on the sidewalk, she'd given Jo Marie a happy wave, before turning and walking toward the double glass doors that led to the lobby of the hospital.

"I think Kelly's going to see Mark," Jo Marie ventured in a short, rueful voice.

"I think she is too."

Jo Marie sat up sharply. "And that doesn't bother you?"

"Should it?" Andrew gave her a bemused look.

"Yes," she said and nodded emphatically. She would

never have believed that Andrew could be so blind. "Yes, it should make you furious."

He turned and smiled briefly. "But it doesn't. Now tell me where you'd like to eat breakfast. Brennan's?"

Jo Marie felt trapped in a labyrinth in which no route made sense and from which she could see no escape. She was thoroughly confused by the actions of the three people she loved.

"I don't understand any of this," she cried in frustration. "You should be livid that Kelly and Mark are together."

A furrow of absent concentration darkened Andrew's brow as he drove. Briefly he glanced in her direction. "The time will come when you do understand," he explained cryptically.

Rubbing the side of her neck in agitation, Jo Marie studied Andrew as he drove. His answer made no sense, but little about anyone's behavior this last month had made sense. She hadn't pictured herself as being obtuse, but obviously she was.

Breakfast at Brennan's was a treat known throughout the south. The restaurant was built in the classic Vieux Carre style complete with courtyard. Because they didn't have a reservation, they were put on a waiting list and told it would be another hour before there would be a table available. Andrew eyed Jo Marie, who nodded eagerly. For all she'd heard, the breakfast was worth the wait.

Taking her hand in his, they strolled down the quiet streets that comprised the French Quarter. Most of the stores were closed, the streets deserted.

"I was reading just this morning that the French established New Orleans in 1718. The Spanish took over the

3,000 French inhabitants in 1762, although there were so few Spaniards that barely anyone noticed until 1768. The French Quarter is like a city within a city."

Jo Marie smiled contentedly and looped her hand through his arm. "You mean to tell me that it takes a birthday present for you to know about your own fair city?"

Andrew chuckled and drew her closer by circling his arm around her shoulders. "Are you always snobbish or is this act for my benefit?"

They strolled for what seemed far longer than a mere hour, visiting Jackson Square and feeding the pigeons. Strolling back, with Andrew at her side, Jo Marie felt she would never be closer to heaven. Never would she want for anything more than today, this minute, with this man. Jo Marie felt tears mist her dusty eyes. A tremulous smile touched her mouth. Andrew was here with her. Within a short time he would be married to Kelly and she must accept that, but for now, he was hers.

The meal was everything they'd been promised. Ham, soft breads fresh from the bakery, eggs and a fabulous chicory coffee. A couple of times Jo Marie found herself glancing at Andrew. His expression revealed little and she wondered if he regretted having decided to spend this time with her. She prayed that wasn't the case.

When they stood to leave, Andrew reached for her hand and smiled down on her with shining gray eyes.

Jo Marie's heart throbbed with love. The radiant light of her happiness shone through when Andrew's arm slipped naturally around her shoulder as if branding her with his seal of protection.

"I enjoy being with you," he said and she couldn't doubt the sincerity in his voice. "You're the kind of woman who would be as much at ease at a formal ball as you would fishing from the riverside with rolled-up jeans."

"I'm not Huck Finn," she teased.

"No," he smiled, joining in her game. "Just my Florence Nightingale, the woman who has haunted me for the last nine months."

Self-consciously, Jo Marie eased the strap of her leather purse over her shoulder. "It's always been my belief that dreams have a way of fading, especially when faced with the bright light of the sun and reality."

"Normally, I'd agree with you," Andrew responded thoughtfully, "but not this time. There are moments so rare in one's life that recognizing what they are can sometimes be doubted. Of you, of that night, of us, I have no doubts."

"None?" Jo Marie barely recognized her own voice.

"None," he confirmed.

If that were so, then why did Kelly continue to wear his ring? How could he look at her with so much emotion and then ask another woman to share his life?

The ride to Jo Marie's apartment was accomplished in a companionable silence. Andrew pulled into the parking space and turned off the ignition. Jo Marie's gaze centered on the dashboard. Silently she'd hoped that he wouldn't come inside with her. The atmosphere when they were alone was volatile. And with everything that Andrew had told her this morning, Jo Marie doubted that she'd have the strength to stay out of his arms if he reached for her.

"I can see myself inside." Gallantly, she made an effort to avoid temptation.

"Nonsense," Andrew returned, and opening the car door, he removed her overnight case from the back seat.

Jo Marie opened her side and climbed out, not waiting for him to come around. A feeling of doom settled around her heart.

Her hand was steady as she inserted the key into the apartment lock, but that was the only thing that was. Her knees felt like rubber as the door swung open and she stepped inside the room, standing in the entryway. The drapes were pulled, blocking out the sunlight, making the apartment's surroundings all the more intimate.

"I have so much to thank you for," she began and nervously tugged a strand of dark hair behind her ear. "A simple thank-you seems like so little." She hoped Andrew understood that she didn't want him to come any farther into the apartment.

The door clicked closed and her heart sank. "Where would you like me to put your suitcase?"

Determined not to make this situation any worse for them, Jo Marie didn't move. "Just leave it here."

A smoldering light of amused anger burned in his eyes as he set the suitcase down. "There's no help for this," he whispered as his hand slid slowly, almost unwillingly along the back of her waist. "Be angry with me later."

Any protests died the moment his mouth met hers in a demanding kiss. An immediate answering hunger seared through her veins, melting all resistance until she was molded against the solid wall of his chest. His caressing fingers explored the curve of her neck and shoulders and his mouth followed, blazing a trail that led back to her waiting lips.

Jo Marie rotated her head, giving him access to any

part of her face that his hungry mouth desired. She offered no protest when his hands sought the fullness of her breast, then sighed with the way her body responded to the gentleness of his fingers. He kissed her expertly, his mobile mouth moving insistently over hers, teasing her with light, biting nips that made her yearn for more and more. Then he'd change his tactics and kiss her with a hungry demand. Lost in a mindless haze, she clung to him as the tears filled her eyes and ran unheeded down her cheeks. Everything she feared was happening. And worse, she was powerless to stop him. Her throat felt dry and scratchy and she uttered a soft sob in effort to abate the flow of emotion.

Andrew went still. He cupped her face in his hands and examined her tear-streaked cheeks. His troubled expression swam in and out of her vision.

"Jo Marie," he whispered, his voice tortured. "Don't cry, darling, please don't cry." With an infinite tenderness he kissed away each tear and when he reached her trembling mouth, the taste of salt was on his lips. A series of long, drugging kisses only confused her more. It didn't seem possible she could want him so much and yet that it should be so wrong.

"Please." With every ounce of strength she possessed Jo Marie broke from his embrace. "I promised myself this wouldn't happen again," she whispered feeling miserable. Standing with her back to him, her hands cradled her waist to ward off a sudden chill.

Gently he pressed his hand to her shoulder and Jo Marie couldn't bring herself to brush it away. Even his touch had the power to disarm her.

"Jo Marie." His husky tone betrayed the depths of his turmoil. "Listen to me."

"No, what good would it do?" she asked on a quavering sob. "You're engaged to be married to my best friend. I can't help the way I feel about you. What I feel, what you feel, is wrong as long as Kelly's wearing your ring." With a determined effort she turned to face him, tears blurring her sad eyes. "It would be better if we didn't see each other again . . . at least until you're sure of what you want . . . or who you want."

Andrew jerked his hand through his hair. "You're right. I've got to get this mess straightened out."

"Promise me, Andrew, please promise me that you won't make an effort to see me until you know in your own mind what you want. I can't take much more of this." She wiped the moisture from her cheekbones with the tips of her fingers. "When I get up in the morning I want to look at myself in the mirror. I don't want to hate myself."

Andrew's mouth tightened with grim displeasure. He looked as if he wanted to argue. Tense moments passed before he slowly shook his head. "You deserve to be treated so much better than this. Someday, my love, you'll understand. Just trust me for now."

"I'm only asking one thing of you," she said unable to meet his gaze. "Don't touch me or make an effort to see me as long as Kelly's wearing your ring. It's not fair to any one of us." Her lashes fell to veil the hurt in her eyes. Andrew couldn't help but know that she was in love with him. She would have staked her life that her feelings were returned full measure. Fresh tears misted her eyes.

"I don't want to leave you like this."

"I'll be all right," she murmured miserably. "There's nothing that I can do. Everything rests with you, Andrew. Everything."

Dejected, he nodded and added a promise. "I'll take care of it today."

Again Jo Marie wiped the wetness from her face and forced a smile, but the effort was almost more than she could bear.

The door clicked, indicating that Andrew had gone and Jo Marie released a long sigh of pent-up emotion. Her reflection in the bathroom mirror showed that her lips were parted and trembling from the hungry possession of his mouth. Her eyes had darkened from the strength of her physical response.

Andrew had asked that she trust him and she would, with all her heart. He loved her, she was sure of it. He wouldn't have hired a detective to find her or built a huge home with her in mind if he didn't feel something strong toward her. Nor could he have held her and kissed her the way he had today without loving and needing her.

While she unpacked the small overnight bag a sense of peace came over her. Andrew would explain everything to Kelly, and she needn't worry. Kelly's interests seemed to be centered more on Mark lately, and maybe . . . just maybe, she wouldn't be hurt or upset and would accept that neither Andrew nor Jo Marie had planned for this to happen.

Time hung heavily on her hands and Jo Marie toyed with the idea of visiting her parents. But her mother knew her so well that she'd take one look at Jo Marie and want to know what was bothering her daughter. And today Jo Marie wasn't up to explanations.

A flip of the radio dial and Christmas music drifted into the room, surrounding her with its message of peace and love. Humming the words softly to herself, Jo Marie felt infinitely better. Everything was going to be fine, she felt confident.

A thick Sunday paper held her attention for the better part of an hour, but at the slightest noise, Jo Marie's attention wandered from the printed page and she glanced up expecting Kelly. One look at her friend would be enough to tell Jo Marie everything she needed to know.

Setting the paper aside, Jo Marie felt her nerves tingle with expectancy. She felt weighted with a terrible guilt. Kelly obviously loved Andrew enough to agree to be his wife, but she showed all the signs of falling in love with Mark. Kelly wasn't the kind of girl who would purposely hurt or lead a man on. She was too sensitive for that. And to add to the complications were Andrew and Jo Marie who had discovered each other again just when they had given up all hope. Jo Marie loved Andrew, but she wouldn't find her own happiness at her friend's expense. But Andrew was going to ask for his ring back, Jo Marie was sure of it. He'd said he'd clear things up today.

The door opened and inhaling a calming breath, Jo Marie stood.

Kelly came into the apartment, her face lowered as her gaze avoided her friend's.

"Hi," Jo Marie ventured hesitantly.

Kelly's face was red and blotchy; tears glistened in her eyes.

"Is something wrong?" Her voice faltered slightly.

"Drew and I had a fight, that's all." Kelly raised her hand to push back her hair and as she did so the engagement ring Andrew had given her sparkled in the sunlight.

Jo Marie felt the knot tighten in her stomach. Andrew had made his decision.

Seven

Somehow Jo Marie made it through the following days. She didn't see Andrew and made excuses to avoid Kelly. Her efforts consisted of trying to get through each day. Once she left the office, she often went to the LFTF headquarters, spending long hours helping Jim. Their friendship had grown. Jim helped her laugh when it would have been so easy to cry. A couple of times they had coffee together and talked. But Jim did most of the talking. This pain was so all-consuming that Jo Marie felt like a newly fallen leaf tossed at will by a fickle wind.

Jim asked her to accompany him on another speaking engagement which Jo Marie did willingly. The talk was on a stretch of wetlands Jim wanted preserved and it had been well received. Silently, Jo Marie mocked herself for not being attracted to someone as wonderful as Jim Rowden. He was everything a woman could want. In addition, she was convinced that he was interested in her. But it was Andrew who continued to fill her thoughts, Andrew who haunted her dreams, Andrew whose soft whisper she heard in the wind.

Lost in the meandering trail of her musing, Jo Marie didn't hear Jim's words as they sauntered into the empty office. Her blank look prompted him to repeat himself. "I thought it went rather well tonight, didn't you?" he asked, grinning boyishly. He brushed the hair from his forehead and pulled out the chair opposite hers.

"Yes," Jo Marie agreed with an absent shake of her head. "It did go well. You're a wonderful speaker." She could feel Jim's gaze watching her and in an effort to avoid any questions, she stood and reached for her purse. "I'd better think about getting home."

"Want some company while you walk to the bus stop?"

"I brought the car tonight." She almost wished she was taking the bus. Jim was a friendly face in a world that had taken on ragged, pain-filled edges.

Kelly had been somber and sullen all week. Half the time she looked as if she were ready to burst into tears at the slightest provocation. Until this last week, Jo Marie had always viewed her roommate as an emotionally strong woman, but recently Jo Marie wondered if she really knew Kelly. Although her friend didn't enjoy large parties, she'd never known Kelly to be intimidated by them. Lately, Kelly had been playing the role of a damsel in distress to the hilt.

Mark had stopped by the apartment only once and he'd resembled a volcano about to explode. He'd left after fifteen minutes of pacing the living-room carpet when Kelly didn't show.

And Andrew—yes, Andrew—by heaven's grace she'd been able to avoid a confrontation with him. She'd seen him only once in the last five days and the look in his eyes had seared her heart. He desperately wanted to talk to her. The tormented message was clear in his eyes, but she'd gently shaken her head, indicating that she intended to hold him to his word.

"Something's bothering you, Jo Marie. Do you want

to talk about it?" Dimples edged into Jim's round face. Funny how she'd never noticed them before tonight.

Sadness touched the depths of her eyes and she gently shook her head. "Thanks, but no. Not tonight."

"Venturing a guess, I'd say it had something to do with Mr. Delta Development."

"Oh?" Clenching her purse under her arm, Jo Marie feigned ignorance. "What makes you say that?"

Jim shook his head. "A number of things." He rose and tucked both hands in his pants pockets. "Let me walk you to your car. The least I can do is see that you get safely outside."

"The weather's been exceptionally cold lately, hasn't it?"

Jim's smile was inviting as he turned the lock in the office door. "Avoiding my questions, aren't you?"

"Yes." Jo Marie couldn't see any reason to lie.

"When you're ready to talk, I'll be happy to listen." Tucking the keys in his pocket, Jim reached for Jo Marie's hand, placing it at his elbow and patting it gently.

"Thanks, I'll remember that."

"Tell me something more about you," Jo Marie queried in a blatant effort to change the subject. Briefly Jim looked at her, his expression thoughtful.

They ventured onto the sidewalk. The full moon was out, its silver rays clearing a path in the night as they strolled toward her car.

"I'm afraid I'd bore you. Most everything you already know. I've only been with the foundation a month."

"LFTF needs people like you, dedicated, passionate, caring."

"I wasn't the one who gave permission for a transient to sleep in a doorway."

Jo Marie softly sucked in her breath. "How'd you know?"

"He came back the second night looking for a handout. The guy knew a soft touch when he saw one."

"What happened?"

Jim shrugged his shoulder and Jo Marie stopped walking in mid-stride. "You gave him some money!" she declared righteously. "And you call me a soft touch."

"As a matter of fact, I didn't. We both knew what he'd spend it on."

"So what did you do?"

"Took him to dinner."

A gentle smile stole across her features at the picture that must have made. Jim dressed impeccably in his business suit and the alcoholic in tattered, ragged clothes.

"It's sad to think about." Slowly, Jo Marie shook her head.

"I got in touch with a friend of mine from a mission. He came for him afterward so that he'll have a place to sleep at least. To witness, close at hand like that, a man wasting his life is far worse to me than . . ." he paused and held her gaze for a long moment, looking deep into her brown eyes. Then he smiled faintly and shook his head. "Sorry, I didn't mean to get so serious."

"You weren't," Jo Marie replied, taking the car keys from her purse. "I'll be back Monday and maybe we could have a cup of coffee."

The deep blue eyes brightened perceptively. "I'd like that and listen, maybe we could have dinner one night soon."

Jo Marie nodded, revealing that she'd enjoy that as well. Jim was her friend and she doubted that her feelings would ever go beyond that, but the way she felt lately, she needed someone to lift her from the doldrums of self-pity.

The drive home was accomplished in a matter of minutes. Standing outside her apartment building, Jo Marie heaved a steadying breath. She dreaded walking into her own home—what a sad commentary on her life! Tonight, she promised herself, she'd make an effort to clear the air between herself and Kelly. Not knowing what Andrew had said to her roommate about his feelings for her, if anything, or the details of the argument, had put Jo Marie in a precarious position. The air between Jo Marie and her best friend was like the stillness before an electrical storm. The problem was that Jo Marie didn't know what to say to Kelly or how to go about making things right.

She made a quick survey of the cars in the parking lot to assure herself that Andrew wasn't inside. Relieved, she tucked her hands inside the pockets of her cardigan and hoped to give a nonchalant appearance when she walked through the front door.

Kelly glanced up from the book she was reading when Jo Marie walked inside. The red, puffy eyes were a testimony of tears, but Kelly didn't explain and Jo Marie didn't pry.

"I hope there's something left over from dinner," she began on a forced note of cheerfulness. "I'm starved."

"I didn't fix anything," Kelly explained in an ominously quiet voice. "In fact I think I'm coming down with something. I've got a terrible stomachache."

Jo Marie had to bite her lip to keep from shouting that

she knew what was wrong with the both of them. Their lives were beginning to resemble a three-ring circus. Where once Jo Marie and Kelly had been best friends, now they rarely spoke.

"What I think I'll do is take a long, leisurely bath and go to bed."

Jo Marie nodded, thinking Kelly's sudden urge for a hot soak was just an excuse to leave the room and avoid the problems that faced them.

While Kelly ran her bathwater, Jo Marie searched through the fridge looking for something appetizing. Normally this was the time of the year that she had to watch her weight. This Christmas she'd probably end up losing a few pounds.

The radio was playing a series of spirited Christmas carols and Jo Marie started humming along. She took out bread and cheese slices from the fridge. The cupboard offered a can of tomato soup.

By the time Kelly came out of the bathroom, Jo Marie had set two places at the table and was pouring hot soup into deep bowls.

"Dinner is served," she called.

Kelly surveyed the table and gave her friend a weak, trembling smile. "I appreciate the effort, but I'm really not up to eating."

Exhaling a dejected sigh, Jo Marie turned to her friend. "How long are we going to continue pretending like this? We need to talk, Kell."

"Not tonight, please, not tonight."

The doorbell rang and a stricken look came over Kelly's pale features. "I don't want to see anyone," she announced and hurried into the bedroom, leaving Jo Marie to deal with whoever was calling.

Resentment burned in her dark eyes as Jo Marie crossed the room. If it was Andrew, she would simply explain that Kelly was ill and not invite him inside.

"Merry Christmas." A tired-looking Mark greeted Jo Marie sarcastically from the other side of the door.

"Hi." Jo Marie watched him carefully. Her brother looked terrible. Tiny lines etched about his eyes revealed lack of sleep. He looked as though he was suffering from both mental and physical exhaustion.

"Is Kelly around?" He walked into the living room, sat on the sofa and leaned forward, roughly rubbing his hands across his face as if that would keep him awake.

"No, she's gone to bed. I don't think she's feeling well."

Briefly, Mark stared at the closed bedroom door and as he did, his shoulder hunched in a gesture of defeat.

"How about something to eat? You look like you haven't had a decent meal in days."

"I haven't." He moved lackadaisically to the kitchen and pulled out a chair.

Lifting the steaming bowls of soup from the counter, Jo Marie brought them to the table and sat opposite her brother.

As Mark took the soup spoon, his tired eyes held a distant, unhappy look. Kelly's eyes had revealed the same light of despair. "We had an argument," he murmured.

"You and Kell?"

"I said some terrible things to her." He braced his elbow against the table and pinched the bridge of his nose. "I don't know what made me do it. The whole time

I was shouting at her I felt as if it was some stranger doing this. I know it sounds crazy but it was almost as if I were standing outside myself watching, and hating myself for what I was doing."

"Was the fight over something important?"

Defensively, Mark straightened. "Yeah, but that's between Kelly and me." He attacked the toasted cheese sandwich with a vengeance.

"You're in love with Kelly, aren't you?" Jo Marie had yet to touch her meal, more concerned about what was happening between her brother and her best friend than about her soup and sandwich.

Mark hesitated thoughtfully and a faint grimness closed off his expression. "In love with Kelly? I am?"

"You obviously care for her."

"I care for my cat, too," he returned coldly and his expression hardened. "She's got what she wants—money. Just look at who she's marrying. It isn't enough that she's wealthy in her own right. No, she sets her sights on J. Paul Getty."

Jo Marie's chin trembled in a supreme effort not to reveal her reaction to his words. "You know Kelly better than that." Averting her gaze, Jo Marie struggled to hold back the emotion that tightly constricted her throat.

"Does either one of us really know Kelly?" Mark's voice was taut as a hunter's bow. Cynicism drove deep grooved lines around his nose and mouth. "Did she tell you that she and Drew have set their wedding date?" Mark's voice dipped with contempt.

A pain seared all the way through Jo Marie's soul. "No, she didn't say." With her gaze lowered, she struggled to keep her hands from shaking.

"Apparently they're going to make it official after the first of the year. They're planning on a spring wedding."

"How . . . nice." Jo Marie nearly choked on the words.

"Well, all I can say is that those two deserve each other." He tossed the melted cheese sandwich back on the plate and stood. "I guess I'm not very hungry, after all."

Jo Marie rose with him and glanced at the table. Neither one of them had done more than shred their sandwiches and stir their soup. "Neither am I," she said, and swallowed at the tightness gripping her throat.

Standing in the living room, Mark stared for a second time at the closed bedroom door.

"I'll tell Kelly you were by." For a second it seemed that Mark hadn't heard.

"No," he murmured after a long moment. "Maybe it's best to leave things as they are. Good night, sis, thanks for dinner." Resembling a man carrying the weight of the world on his shoulders, Mark left.

Leaning against the front door, Jo Marie released a bitter, pain-filled sigh and turned the dead bolt. Tears burned for release. So Andrew and Kelly were going to make a public announcement of their engagement after Christmas. It shouldn't shock her. Kelly had told her from the beginning that they were. The wedding plans were already in the making. Wiping the salty dampness from her cheek, Jo Marie bit into the tender skin inside her cheek to hold back a sob.

"There's a call for you on line one," Paula called to Jo Marie from her desk.

"Thanks." With an efficiency born of years of experience, Jo Marie punched in the telephone tab and lifted the receiver to her ear. "This is Jo Marie Early, may I help you?"

"Jo Marie, this is Jim. I hope you don't mind me calling you at work."

"No problem."

"Good. Listen, you, ah, mentioned something the other night about us having coffee together and I said something about having dinner."

If she hadn't known any better, Jo Marie would have guessed that Jim was uneasy. He was a gentle man with enough sensitivity to campaign for the future. His hesitancy surprised her now. "I remember."

"How would you feel about this Wednesday?" he continued. "We could make a night of it."

Jo Marie didn't need to think it over. "I'd like that very much." After Mark's revelation, she'd realized the best thing to do was to put the past and Andrew behind her and build a new life for herself.

"Good." Jim sounded pleased. "We can go Wednesday night . . . or would you prefer Friday?"

"Wednesday's fine." Jo Marie doubted that she could ever feel again the deep, passionate attraction she'd experienced with Andrew, but Jim's appeal wasn't built on fantasy.

"I'll see you then. Goodbye, Jo Marie."

"Goodbye, Jim, and thanks."

The mental uplifting of their short conversation was enough to see Jo Marie through a hectic afternoon. An airline lost her customer's reservations and the tickets didn't arrive in time. In addition the phone rang repeatedly.

By the time she walked into the apartment, her feet hurt and there was a nagging ache in the small of her back.

"I thought I heard you." Kelly sauntered into the kitchen and stood in the doorway dressed in a robe and slippers.

"How are you feeling?"

She lifted one shoulder in a weak shrug. "Better."

"You stayed home?" Kelly had still been in bed when Jo Marie left for work. Apparently her friend had phoned in sick.

"Yeah." She moved into the living room and sat on the sofa.

"Mark was by last night." Jo Marie mentioned the fact casually, waiting for a response from her roommate. Kelly didn't give her one. "He said that the two of you had a big fight," she continued.

"That's all we do anymore—argue."

"I don't know what he said to you, but he felt bad about it afterward."

A sad glimmer touched Kelly's eyes and her mouth formed a brittle line that Jo Marie supposed was meant to be a smile. "I know he didn't mean it. He's exhausted. I swear he's trying to work himself to death."

Now that her friend mentioned it, Jo Marie realized that she hadn't seen much of her brother lately. It used to be that he had an excuse to show up two or three times a week. Except for last night, he had been to the apartment only twice since Thanksgiving.

"I don't think he's eaten a decent meal in days," Kelly

continued. "He's such a good doctor, Jo Marie, because he cares so much about his patients. Even the ones he knows he's going to lose. I'm a nurse, I've seen the way the other doctors close themselves off from any emotional involvement. But Mark's there, always giving." Her voice shook uncontrollably and she paused to bite into her lip until she regained her composure. "I wanted to talk to him the other night, and do you know where I found him? In pediatrics holding a little boy who's suffering with terminal cancer. He was rocking this child, holding him in his arms and telling him the pain wouldn't last too much longer. From the hallway, I heard Mark talk about heaven and how there wouldn't be any pain for him there. Mark's a wonderful man and wonderful doctor."

And he loves you so much it's tearing him apart, Jo Marie added silently.

"Yesterday he was frustrated and angry and he took it out on me. I'm not going to lie and say it didn't hurt. For a time I was devastated, but I'm over that now."

"But you didn't go to work today." They both knew why she'd chosen to stay home.

"No, I felt Mark and I needed a day away from each other."

"That's probably a good idea." There was so much she wanted to say to Kelly, but everything sounded so inadequate. At least they were talking, which was a major improvement over the previous five days.

The teakettle whistled sharply and Jo Marie returned to the kitchen bringing them both back a steaming cup of hot coffee.

"Thanks." Kelly's eyes brightened.

"Would you like me to talk to Mark?" Jo Marie's offer

was sincere, but she wasn't exactly sure what she'd say. And in some ways it could make matters worse.

"No. We'll sort this out on our own."

The doorbell chimed and the two exchanged glances. "I'm not expecting anyone," Kelly murmured and glanced down self-consciously at her attire. "In fact I'd rather not be seen, so if you don't mind I'll vanish inside my room."

The last person Jo Marie expected to find on the other side of the door was Andrew. The welcome died in her eyes as their gazes met and clashed. Jo Marie quickly lowered hers. Her throat went dry and a rush of emotion brought a flood of color to her suddenly pale cheeks. A tense air of silence surrounded them. Andrew raised his hand as though he wanted to reach out and touch her. Instead he clenched his fist and lowered it to his side, apparently having changed his mind.

"Is Kelly ready?" he asked after a breathless moment. Jo Marie didn't move, her body blocking the front door, refusing him admittance.

She stared up at him blankly. "Ready?" she repeated.

"Yes, we're attending the opera tonight. Bizet's *Carmen*," he added as if in an afterthought.

"Oh, dear." Jo Marie's eyes widened. Kelly had obviously forgotten their date. The tickets for the elaborate opera had been sold out for weeks. Her roommate would have to go. "Come in, I'll check with Kelly."

"Andrew's here," Jo Marie announced and leaned against the wooden door inside the bedroom, her hands folded behind her.

"Drew?"

"Andrew to me, Drew to you," she responded cattily. "You have a date to see *Carmen*."

Kelly's hand flew to her forehead. "Oh, my goodness, I completely forgot."

"What are you going to do?"

"Explain, what else is there to do?" she snapped.

Jo Marie followed her friend into the living room. Andrew's gray eyes widened at the sight of Kelly dressed in her robe and slippers.

"You're ill?"

"Actually, I'm feeling better. Drew, I apologize, I completely forgot about tonight."

As Andrew glanced at his gold wristwatch, a frown marred his handsome face.

"Kelly can shower and dress in a matter of a few minutes," Jo Marie said sharply, guessing what Kelly was about to suggest.

"I couldn't possibly be ready in forty-five minutes," she denied. "There's only one thing to do. Jo Marie, you'll have to go in my place."

Andrew's level gaze crossed the width of the room to capture Jo Marie's. Little emotion was revealed in the impassive male features, but his gray eyes glinted with challenge.

"I can't." Her voice was level with hard determination.

"Why not?" Two sets of eyes studied her.

"I'm . . ." Her mind searched wildly for an excuse. "I'm baking cookies for the Science Club. We're meeting Saturday and this will be our last time before Christmas."

"I thought you worked Saturdays," Andrew cut in sharply.

"Every other Saturday." Calmly she met his gaze. Over the past couple of weeks, Kelly had purposely brought Jo Marie and Andrew together, but Jo Marie wouldn't fall prey to that game any longer. She'd made an agreement with him and refused to back down. As long as he was engaged to another woman she wouldn't . . . couldn't be with him. "I won't go," she explained in a steady voice which belied the inner turmoil that churned her stomach.

"There's plenty of time before the opening curtain if you'd care to change your mind."

Kelly tossed Jo Marie an odd look. "It looks like I'll have to go," she said with an exaggerated sigh. "I'll be as fast as I can." Kelly rushed back inside the bedroom leaving Jo Marie and Andrew separated by only a few feet.

"How have you been?" he asked, his eyes devouring her.

"Fine," she responded on a stiff note. The lie was only a little one. The width of the room stood between them, but it might as well have been whole light-years.

Bowing her head, she stared at the pattern in the carpet. When she suggested Kelly hurry and dress, she hadn't counted on being left alone with Andrew. "If you'll excuse me, I'll get started on those cookies."

To her dismay Andrew followed her into the kitchen.

"What are my chances of getting a cup of coffee?" He sounded pleased with himself, his smile was smug.

Wordlessly Jo Marie stood on her tiptoes and brought down a mug from the cupboard. She poured in the dark granules, stirred in hot water and walked past him to carry the mug into the living room. All the while her mind was screaming with him to leave her alone.

Andrew picked up the mug and followed her back into the kitchen. "I've wanted to talk to you for days."

"You agreed."

"Jo Marie, believe me, talking to Kelly isn't as easy as it seems. There are some things I'm not at liberty to explain that would resolve this whole mess."

"I'll just bet there are." The bitter taste of anger filled her mouth.

"Can't you trust me?" The words were barely audible and for an instant Jo Marie wasn't certain he'd spoken.

Everything within her yearned to reach out to him and be assured that the glorious times they'd shared had been as real for him as they'd been for her. Desperately she wanted to turn and tell him that she would trust him with her life, but not her heart. She couldn't, not when Kelly was wearing his engagement ring.

"Jo Marie." A faint pleading quality entered his voice. "I know how all this looks. At least give me a chance to explain. Have dinner with me tomorrow. I swear I won't so much as touch you. I'll leave everything up to you. Place. Time. You name it."

"No." Frantically she shook her head, her voice throbbing with the desire to do as he asked. "I can't."

"Jo Marie." He took a step toward her, then another, until he was so close his husky voice breathed against her dark hair.

Forcing herself into action, Jo Marie whirled around and backed out of the kitchen. "Don't talk to me like that. I realized last week that whatever you feel for Kelly is stronger than any love you have for me. I've tried to accept that as best I can."

Andrew's knuckles were clenched so tightly that they went white. He looked like an innocent man facing a firing squad, his eyes resigned, the line of his jaw tense, anger and disbelief etched in every rugged mark of his face.

"Just be patient, that's all I'm asking. In due time you'll understand everything."

"Will you stop?" she demanded angrily. "You're talking in puzzles and I've always hated those. All I know is that there are four people who—"

"I guess this will have to do," Kelly interrupted as she walked into the room. She had showered, dressed and dried her hair in record time.

Jo Marie swallowed the taste of jealousy as she watched the dark, troubled look dissolve from Andrew's eyes. "You look great," was all she could manage.

"We won't be too late," Kelly said on her way out.

"Don't worry," Jo Marie murmured and breathed in a sharp breath. "I won't be up; I'm exhausted."

Who was she trying to kid? Not until the key turned in the front door lock five hours later did Jo Marie so much as yawn. As much as she hated herself for being so weak, the entire time Kelly had been with Andrew, Jo Marie had been utterly miserable.

The dinner date with Jim the next evening was the only bright spot in a day that stretched out like an empty void. She dressed carefully and applied her makeup with extra care, hoping to camouflage the effects of a sleepless night.

"Don't fix dinner for me, I've got a date," was all she said to Kelly on her way out the door to the office.

As she knew it would, being with Jim was like stumbling upon an oasis in the middle of a sand-tossed desert. He made her laugh, teasing her affectionately. His humor was subtle and light and just the antidote for a broken heart. She'd known from the moment they'd met that she was going to like Jim Rowden. With him she could relax and be herself. And not once did she have to look over her shoulder.

"Are you going to tell me what's been troubling you?" he probed gently over their dessert.

"What? And cry all over my lime-chiffon pie?"

Jim's returning smile was one of understanding and encouragement. Again she noted the twin dimples that formed in his cheeks. "Whenever you're ready, I'm available to listen."

"Thanks." She shook her head, fighting back an unexpected swell of emotion. "Now what's this surprise you've been taunting me with most of the evening?" she questioned, averting the subject from herself.

"It's about the wetlands we've been crusading for during the last month. Well, I talked to a state senator today and he's going to introduce a bill that would make the land into a state park." Lacing his hands together, Jim leaned toward the linen-covered table. "From everything he's heard, George claims from there it should be a piece of cake."

"Jim, that's wonderful." This was his first success and he beamed with pride over the accomplishment.

"Of course, nothing's definite yet, and I'm not even sure I should have told you, but you've heard me give two speeches on the wetlands and I wanted you to know."

"I'm honored that you did."

He acknowledged her statement with a short nod. "I should know better than to get my hopes up like this, but George—my friend—sounded so confident."

"Then you should be too. We both should."

Jim reached for her hand and squeezed it gently. "It would be very easy to share things with you, Jo Marie. You're quite a woman."

Flattery had always made her uncomfortable, but Jim sounded so sincere. It cost her a great deal of effort to simply smile and murmur her thanks.

Jim's arm rested across her shoulder as they walked back toward the office. He held open her car door for her and paused before lightly brushing his mouth over hers. The kiss was both gentle and reassuring. But it wasn't Andrew's kiss and Jim hadn't the power to evoke the same passionate response Andrew seemed to draw so easily from her.

On the ride home, Jo Marie silently berated herself for continuing to compare the two men. It was unfair to them both to even think in that mode.

The apartment was unlocked when Jo Marie let herself inside. She was hanging up her sweater-coat when she noticed Andrew. He was standing in the middle of the living room carpet, regarding her with stone cold eyes.

One glance and Jo Marie realized that she'd never seen a man look so angry.

"It's about time you got home." His eyes were flashing gray fire.

"What right is it of yours to demand what time I get in?"

"I have every right." His voice was like a whip lashing out at her. "I suppose you think you're playing a game. Every time I go out with Kelly, you'll pay me back by dating Jim?"

Stunned into speechlessness, Jo Marie felt her voice die in her throat.

"And if you insist on letting him kiss you the least you can do is look for someplace more private than the street." The white line about his mouth became more pronounced as his eyes filled with bitter contempt. "You surprise me, Jo Marie, I thought you had more class than that."

Eight

"How dare you . . . how dare you say such things to me!" Jo Marie's quavering voice became breathless with rage. Her eyes were dark and stormy as she turned around and jerked the front door open.

"What do you expect me to believe?" Andrew rammed his hand through his hair, ruffling the dark hair that grew at his temple.

"I expected a lot of things from you, but not that you'd follow me or spy on me. And then . . . then to have the audacity to confront and insult me." The fury in her faded to be replaced with a deep, emotional pain that pierced her heart.

Andrew's face was bloodless as he walked past her and out the door. As soon as he was through the portal, she slammed it closed with a sweeping arc of her hand.

Jo Marie was so furious that the room wasn't large enough to contain her anger. Her shoulders rose and sagged with her every breath. At one time Andrew had been her dream man. Quickly she was learning to separate the fantasy from the reality.

Pacing the carpet helped relieve some of the terrible tension building within her. Andrew's behavior was nothing short of odious. She should hate him for saying those kinds of things to her. Tears burned for release, but deep, concentrated breaths held them at bay. Andrew Beaumont wasn't worth the emotion. Staring sightlessly at the ceiling, her damp lashes pressed against her cheek.

The sound of the doorbell caused her to whirl around. Andrew. She'd stake a week's salary on the fact. In an act of defiance, she folded her arms across her waist and stared determinedly at the closed door. He could rot in the rain before she'd open that door.

Again the chimes rang in short, staccato raps. "Come on, Jo Marie, answer the damn door."

"No," she shouted from the other side.

"Fine, we'll carry on a conversation by shouting at each other. That should amuse your neighbors."

"Go away." Jo Marie was too upset to talk things out. Andrew had hurt her with his actions and words.

"Jo Marie." The appealing quality in his voice couldn't be ignored. "Please, open the door. All I want is to apologize."

Hating herself for being so weak, Jo Marie turned the lock and threw open the solid wood door. "You have one minute."

"I think I went a little crazy when I saw Jim kiss you," he said pacing the area in front of the door. "Jo Marie, promise me that you won't see him again. I don't think I can stand the thought of any man touching you."

"This is supposed to be an apology?" she asked sarcastically. "Get this, Mr. Beaumont," she said, fighting to keep from shouting at him as her finger punctuated the air. "You have no right to dictate anything to me."

His tight features darkened. "I can make your life miserable."

"And you think you haven't already?" she cried. "Just leave me alone. I don't need your threats. I don't want to see you again. Ever." To her horror, her voice cracked. Shaking her head, unable to talk any longer, she shut the door and clicked the lock.

Almost immediately the doorbell chimed, followed by continued knocking. Neither of them were in any mood to discuss things rationally. And perhaps it was better all the way around to simply leave things as they were. It hurt, more than Jo Marie wanted to admit, but she'd recover. She'd go on with her life and put Andrew, the dream man and all of it behind her.

Without glancing over her shoulder, she ignored the sound and moved into her bedroom.

The restaurant was crowded, the luncheon crowd filling it to capacity. With Christmas only a few days away the rush of last-minute shoppers filled the downtown area and flowed into the restaurants at lunch time.

Seeing Mark come through the doors, Jo Marie raised her hand and waved in an effort to attract her brother's attention. He looked less fatigued than the last time she'd seen him. A brief smile momentarily brightened his eyes, but faded quickly.

"I must admit this is a surprise," Jo Marie said as her brother slid into the upholstered booth opposite her. "I can't remember the last time we met for lunch."

"I can't remember either." Mark picked up the menu, decided and closed it after only a minute.

"That was quick."

"I haven't got a lot of time."

Same old Mark, always in a rush, hurrying from one

place to another. "You called me, remember?" she taunted softly.

"Yeah, I remember." His gaze was focused on the paper napkin which he proceeded to fold into an intricate pattern. "This is going to sound a little crazy so promise me you won't laugh."

The edge of her mouth was already twitching. "I promise."

"I want you to attend the hospital Christmas party with me Saturday night."

"Me?"

"I don't have time to go out looking for a date and I don't think I can get out of it without offending half the staff."

In the past three weeks, Jo Marie had endured enough parties to last her a lifetime. "I guess I could go."

"Don't sound so enthusiastic."

"I'm beginning to feel the same way about parties as you do."

"I doubt that," he said forcefully and shredded the napkin in half.

The waitress came for their order and delivered steaming mugs of coffee almost immediately afterward.

Jo Marie lifted her own napkin, toying with the pressed paper edge. "Will Kelly and . . . Drew be there?"

"I doubt it. Why should they? There won't be any ballroom dancing or a midnight buffet. It's a pot luck. Can you picture old 'money bags' sitting on a folding chair and balancing a paper plate on her lap? No. Kelly goes more for the two-hundred-dollar-a-place-setting affairs."

Jo Marie opened her mouth to argue, but decided it

would do little good. Discussing Andrew—Drew, her mind corrected—or Kelly with Mark would be pointless.

"I suppose Kelly's told you?"

"Told me what?" Jo Marie glanced up curious and half-afraid. The last time Mark had relayed any information about Drew and Kelly it had been that they were going to publicly announce their engagement.

"She's given her two-week notice."

"No," Jo Marie gasped. "She wouldn't do that. Kelly loves nursing; she's a natural." Even more surprising was the fact that Kelly hadn't said a word to Jo Marie about leaving Tulane Hospital.

"I imagine with the wedding plans and all that she's decided to take any early retirement. Who can blame her, right?"

But it sounded very much like Mark was doing exactly that. His mouth was tight and his dark eyes were filled with something akin to pain. What a mess this Christmas was turning out to be.

"Let's not talk about Kelly or Drew or anyone for the moment, okay. It's Christmas next week." She forced a bit of yuletide cheer into her voice.

"Right," Mark returned with a short sigh. "It's almost Christmas." But for all the enthusiasm in his voice he could have been discussing German measles.

Their soup and sandwiches arrived and they ate in strained silence. "Well, are you coming or not?" Mark asked, pushing his empty plate aside.

"I guess." No need to force any enthusiasm into her voice. They both felt the same way about the party.

"Thanks, sis."

"Just consider it your Christmas present."

Mark reached for the white slip the waitress had placed on their table, examining it. "And consider this lunch yours," he announced and scooted from his seat. "See you Saturday night."

"Mark said you've given the hospital your two-week notice?" Jo Marie confronted her roommate first thing that evening.

"Yes," Kelly replied lifelessly.

"I suppose the wedding will fill your time from now on."

"The wedding?" Kelly gave her an absent look. "No," she shook her head and an aura of dejected defeat hung over her, dulling her responses. "I've got my application in at a couple of other hospitals."

"So you're going to continue working after you're married."

For a moment it didn't look as if Kelly had heard her. "Kell?" Jo Marie prompted.

"I'd hoped to."

Berating herself for caring how Kelly and Andrew lived their lives, Jo Marie picked up the evening paper and pretended an interest in the front page. But if Kelly had asked her so much as what the headline read she couldn't have answered.

Saturday night Jo Marie dressed in the blue dress that she'd sewn after Thanksgiving. It fit her well and revealed a subtle grace in her movements. Although she took extra time with her hair and cosmetics, her heart wasn't up to attending the party.

Jo Marie had casually draped a lace shawl over her

shoulder when the front door opened and Kelly entered with Andrew at her side.

"You're going out," Kelly announced, stopping abruptly inside the living room. "You . . . you didn't say anything."

Jo Marie could feel Andrew's gaze scorching her in a slow, heated perusal, but she didn't look his way. "Yes, I'm going out; don't wait up for me."

"Drew and I have plans too."

Reaching for her evening bag, Jo Marie's mouth curved slightly upward in a poor imitation of a smile. "Have a good time."

Kelly said something more, but Jo Marie was already out the door, grateful to have escaped without another confrontation with Andrew.

Mark had given her the address of the party and asked that she meet him there. He didn't give any particular reason he couldn't pick her up. He didn't need an excuse. It was obvious he wanted to avoid Kelly.

She located the house without a problem and was greeted by loud music and a smoke-filled room. Making her way between the dancing couples, Jo Marie delivered the salad she had prepared on her brother's behalf to the kitchen. After exchanging pleasantries with the guests in the kitchen, Jo Marie went back to the main room to search for Mark.

For all the noisy commotion the party was an orderly one and Jo Marie spotted her brother almost immediately. He was sitting on the opposite side of the room talking to a group of other young men, who she assumed were fellow doctors. Making her way across the carpet, she was waylaid once by a nurse friend of Kelly's that she'd met a couple of times. They chatted for a few minutes about the weather.

"I suppose you've heard that Kelly's given her notice," Julie Frazier said with a hint of impatience. "It's a shame, if you ask me."

"I agree," Jo Marie murmured.

"Sometimes I'd like to knock those two over the head." Julie motioned toward Mark with the slight tilt of her head. "Your brother's one stubborn male."

"You don't need to tell me. I'm his sister."

"You know," Julie said and glanced down at the cold drink she was holding in her hand. "After Kelly had her tonsils out I could have sworn those two were headed for the altar. No one was more surprised than me when Kell turns up engaged to this mystery character."

"What do you mean about Kelly and Mark?" Kelly's tonsils had come out months ago during the Mardi Gras. No matter how much time passed, it wasn't likely that Jo Marie would forget that.

"Kelly was miserable—adult tonsillectomies are seldom painless—anyway, Kelly didn't want anyone around, not even her family. Mark was the only one who could get close to her. He spent hours with her, coaxing her to eat, spoon-feeding her. He even read her to sleep and then curled up in the chair beside her bed so he'd be there when she woke."

Jo Marie stared back in open disbelief. "Mark did that?" All these months Mark had been in love with Kelly and he hadn't said a word. Her gaze sought him now and she groaned inwardly at her own stupidity. For months she'd been so caught up in the fantasy of those few precious moments with Andrew that she'd been blind to what was right in front of her own eyes.

"Well, speaking of our friend, look who's just arrived."

Jo Marie's gaze turned toward the front door just as Kelly and Andrew came inside. From across the length of the room, her eyes clashed with Andrew's. She watched as the hard line of his mouth relaxed and he smiled. The effect on her was devastating; her heart somersaulted and color rushed up her neck, invading her face. These were all the emotions she had struggled against from the beginning. She hated herself for being so vulnerable when it came to this one man. She didn't want to feel any of these emotions toward him.

"Excuse me—" Julie interrupted Jo Marie's musings "—there's someone I wanted to see."

"Sure." Mentally, Jo Marie shook herself and joined Mark, knowing she would be safe at his side.

"Did you see who just arrived?" Jo Marie whispered in her brother's ear.

Mark's dusty dark eyes studied Kelly's arrival and Jo Marie witnessed an unconscious softening in his gaze. Kelly did look lovely tonight, and begrudgingly Jo Marie admitted that Andrew and Kelly were the most striking couple in the room. They belonged together—both were people of wealth and position. Two of a kind.

"I'm surprised that she came," Mark admitted slowly and turned his back to the pair. "But she's got as much right to be here as anyone."

"Of course she does."

One of Mark's friends appointed himself as disc jockey and put on another series of records for slow dancing. Jo Marie and Mark stood against the wall and watched as several couples began dancing on the makeshift dance floor. When Andrew turned Kelly into his arms, Jo Marie diverted her gaze to another section of the room, unable to look at them without being affected.

"You don't want to dance, do you?" Mark mumbled indifferently.

"With you?"

"No, I'd get one of my friends to do the honors. It's bad enough having to invite my sister to a party. I'm not about to dance with you, too."

Jo Marie couldn't prevent a short laugh. "You really know how to sweet-talk a woman don't you, brother dearest?"

"I try," he murmured and his eyes narrowed on Kelly whose arms were draped around Andrew's neck as she whispered in his ear. "But obviously not hard enough," he finished.

Standing on the outskirts of the dancing couples made Jo Marie uncomfortable. "I think I'll see what I can do to help in the kitchen," she said as an excuse to leave.

Julie Frazier was there, placing cold cuts on a round platter with the precision of a mathematician.

"Can I help?" Jo Marie offered, looking around for something that needed to be done.

Julie turned and smiled her appreciation. "Sure. Would you put the serving spoons in the salads and set them out on the dining room table?"

"Glad to." She located the spoons in the silverware drawer and carried out a large glass bowl of potato salad. The Formica table was covered with a vinyl cloth decorated with green holly and red berries.

"And now ladies and gentlemen——" the disc jockey demanded the attention of the room "——this next number is a ladies' choice."

With her back to the table, Jo Marie watched as Kelly whispered something to Andrew. To her surprise, he nodded and stepped aside as Kelly made her way to the other side of the room. Her destination was clear—Kelly was heading directly to Mark. Jo Marie's pulse fluttered wildly. If Mark said or did anything cruel to her friend, Jo Marie would never forgive him.

Her heart was in her eyes as Kelly tentatively tapped Mark on the shoulder. Engrossed in a conversation, Mark apparently wasn't aware he was being touched. Kelly tried again and Mark turned, surprise rounding his eyes when he saw her roommate.

Jo Marie was far enough to the side so that she couldn't be seen by Mark and Kelly, but close enough to hear their conversation.

"May I have this dance?" Kelly questioned, her voice firm and low.

"I thought it was the man's prerogative to ask." The edge of Mark's mouth curled up sarcastically. "And if you've noticed, I haven't asked."

"This number is ladies' choice."

Mark tensed visibly as he glared across the room, eyeing Andrew. "And what about Rockefeller over there?"

Slowly, Kelly shook her head, her inviting gaze resting on Mark. "I'm asking you. Don't turn me down, Mark, not tonight. I'll be leaving the hospital in a little while and then you'll never be bothered with me again."

Jo Marie doubted that her brother could have refused Kelly anything in that moment. Wordlessly he approached the dance floor and took Kelly in his arms. A slow ballad was playing and the soft, melodic sounds of Billy Joel filled the room. Kelly fit her body to Mark's. Her arms slid around his neck as she pressed her temple against his jaw. Mark reacted to the contact by closing his eyes and inhaling as his eyes drifted closed. His hold, which had been loose, tightened as he knotted his hands at the small of Kelly's back, arching her body closer.

For the first time that night, her brother looked completely at ease. Kelly belonged with Mark. Jo Marie had been wrong to think that Andrew and Kelly were meant for each other. They weren't, and their engagement didn't make sense.

Her eyes sought out the subject of her thoughts. Andrew was leaning against the wall only a few feet from her. His eyes locked with hers, refusing to release her. He wanted her to come to him. She couldn't. His gaze seemed to drink her in as it had the night of the Mardi Gras. She could almost feel him reaching out to her, imploring her to come, urging her to cross the room so he could take her in his arms.

With unconscious thought Jo Marie took one step forward and stopped. No. Being with Andrew would only cause her more pain. With a determined effort she lightly shook her head, effectively breaking the spell. Her heart was beating so hard that breathing was difficult. Her steps were marked with decision as she returned to the kitchen.

A sliding glass door led to a lighted patio. A need to escape for a few moments overtook her and silently she slipped past the others and escaped into the darkness of the night.

A chill ran up her arms and she rubbed her hands over her forearms in an effort to warm her blood. The stars were out in a dazzling display and Jo Marie tilted her face toward the heavens, gazing at the lovely sight.

Jo Marie stiffened as she felt more than heard someone join her. She didn't need to turn around to realize that it was Andrew.

He came and stood beside her, but he made no effort to speak, instead focusing his attention on the dark sky.

Whole eternities seemed to pass before Andrew spoke. "I came to ask your forgiveness."

All the pain of his accusation burned in her breast. "You hurt me," she said on a breathless note after a long pause.

"I know, my love, I know." Slowly he removed his suit jacket and with extraordinary concern, draped it over her shoulders, taking care not to touch her.

"I'd give anything to have those thoughtless words back. Seeing Jim take you in his arms was like waving a red flag in front of an angry bull. I lashed out at you, when it was circumstances that were at fault."

Something about the way he spoke, the emotion that coated his words, the regret that filled his voice made her feel that her heart was ready to burst right out of her breast. She didn't want to look at him, but somehow it was impossible to keep her eyes away. With an infinite tenderness, he brushed a stray curl from her cheek.

"Can you forgive me?"

"Oh, Andrew." She felt herself weakening.

"I'd go on my knees if it would help."

The tears felt locked in her throat. "No, that isn't necessary."

He relaxed as if a great burden had been lifted from his shoulders. "Thank you."

Neither moved, wanting to prolong this tender moment. When Andrew spoke it was like the whisper of a gentle breeze and she had to strain to hear him.

"When I first came out here you looked like a blue sapphire silhouetted in the moonlight. And I was thinking that if it were in my power, I'd weave golden moonbeams into your hair."

"Have you always been so poetic?"

His mouth curved upward in a slow, sensuous smile. "No." His eyes were filled with an undisguised hunger as he studied her. Ever so slowly, he raised his hand and placed it at the side of her neck.

The tender touch of his fingers against her soft skin caused a tingling sensation to race down her spine. The feeling was akin to pain. Jo Marie loved this man as she would never love again and he was promised to another woman.

"Jo Marie," he whispered and his warm breath fanned her mouth. "There's mistletoe here. Let me kiss you."

There wasn't, of course, but Jo Marie was unable to pull away. She nodded her acquiescence. "One last time." She hadn't meant to verbalize her thoughts.

He brought her into his arms and she moistened her lips anticipating the hungry exploration of his mouth over hers. But she was to be disappointed. Andrew's lips lightly moved over hers like the gentle brush of the spring sun on a hungry earth. Gradually the kiss deepened as he worked his way from one corner of her mouth to another—again like the earth long starved from summer's absence.

"I always knew it would be like this for us, Florence Nightingale," he whispered against her hair. "Even when I couldn't find you, I felt a part of myself would never be the same."

"I did too. I nearly gave up dating."

"I thought I'd go crazy. You were so close all these months and yet I couldn't find you."

"But you did." Pressing her hands against the strong cushion of his chest she created a space between them. "And now it's too late."

Andrew's eyes darkened as he seemed to struggle within himself. "Jo Marie." A thick frown marred his face.

"Shh." She pressed her fingertips against his lips. "Don't try to explain. I understand and I've accepted it. For a long time it hurt so much that I didn't think I'd be able to bear it. But I can and I will."

His hand circled her wrist and he closed his eyes before kissing the tips of her fingers. "There's so much I want to explain and can't."

"I know." With his arm holding her close, Jo Marie felt a deep sense of peace surround her. "I'd never be the kind of wife you need. Your position demands a woman with culture and class. I'm proud to be an Early and proud of my family, but I'm not right for you."

The grip on her wrist tightened. "Is that what you think?" The frustrated anger in his voice was barely suppressed. "Do you honestly believe that?"

"Yes," she answered him boldly. "I'm at peace within myself. I have no regrets. You've touched my heart and a part of me will never be the same. How can I regret having loved you? It's not within me."

He dropped her hand and turned from her, his look a mixture of angry torment. "You honestly think I should marry Kelly."

It would devastate Mark, but her brother would need to find his own peace. "Or someone like her." She removed his suit jacket from her shoulders and handed it back to him, taking care to avoid touching him. "Thank you," she whispered with a small catch to her soft voice. Unable to resist any longer, she raised her hand and traced his jaw. Very lightly, she brushed her mouth over his. "Goodbye, Andrew."

He reached out his hand in an effort to stop her, but she slipped past him. It took her only a moment to collect her shawl. Within a matter of minutes, she was out the front door and on her way back to the apartment. Mark would never miss her.

Jo Marie spent Sunday with her family, returning late that evening when she was assured Kelly was asleep. Lying in bed, studying the darkness around her, Jo Marie realized that she'd said her final goodbye to Andrew. Continuing to see him would only make it difficult for them both. Avoiding him had never succeeded, not when she yearned for every opportunity to be with him. The best solution would be to leave completely. Kelly would be moving out soon and Jo Marie couldn't afford to pay the rent on her own. The excuse would be a convenient one although Kelly was sure to recognize it for what it was.

After work Monday afternoon, before she headed for the LFTF office, Jo Marie stopped off at the hospital, hoping to talk to Mark. With luck, she might be able to convince her brother to let her move in with him. But only until she could find another apartment and another roommate.

Julie Frazier, the nurse who worked with both Kelly and Mark, was at the nurses' station on the surgical floor when Jo Marie arrived.

"Hi," she greeted cheerfully. "I don't suppose you know where Mark is?"

Julie glanced up from a chart she was reading. "He's in the doctors' lounge having a cup of coffee."

"Great. I'll talk to you later." With her shoes making clicking sounds against the polished floor, Jo Marie mused that her timing couldn't have been more perfect. Now all she needed was to find her brother in a good mood.

The doctors' lounge was at the end of the hall and was divided into two sections. The front part contained a sofa and a couple of chairs. A small kitchen area was behind that. The sound of Mark's and Kelly's voices stopped Jo Marie just inside the lounge.

"You can leave," Mark was saying in a tight, pained voice. "Believe me I have no intention of crying on your shoulder."

"I didn't come here for that," Kelly argued softly.

Jo Marie hesitated, unsure of what she should do. She didn't want to interrupt their conversation, which seemed intense, nor did she wish to intentionally stay and listen in either.

"That case with the Randolph girl is still bothering you, isn't it?" Kelly demanded.

"No, I did everything I could. You know that."

"But it wasn't enough, was it?"

Jo Marie had to bite her tongue not to interrupt Kelly. It wasn't like her roommate to be unnecessarily cruel. Jo Marie vividly recalled her brother's doubts after the young child's death. It had been just before Thanksgiving and Mark had agonized that he had lost her.

"No," Mark shouted, "it wasn't enough."

"And now you're going to lose the Rickard boy." Kelly's voice softened perceptively.

Fleetingly Jo Marie wondered if this child was the one Kelly had mentioned who was dying of cancer.

"I've known that from the first." Mark's tone contained the steel edge of anger.

"Yes, but it hasn't gotten any easier, has it?"

"Listen, Kelly, I know what you're trying to do, but it isn't going to work."

"Mark," Kelly murmured his name on a sigh, "sometimes you are so blind."

"Maybe it's because I feel so inadequate. Maybe it's because I'm haunted with the fact that there might have been something more I could have done."

"But there isn't, don't you see?" Kelly's voice had softened as if her pain was Mark's. "Now won't you tell me what's really bothering you?"

"Maybe it's because I don't like the odds with Tommy. His endless struggle against pain. The deck was stacked against him from the beginning and now he hasn't got a bettor's edge. In the end, death will win."

"And you'll have lost, and every loss is a personal one."

Jo Marie didn't feel that she could eavesdrop any longer. Silently she slipped from the room.

The conversation between Mark and Kelly played back in her mind as she drove toward the office and Jim.

Mark would have serious problems as a doctor unless he came to terms with these feelings. Kelly had recognized that and had set personal relationships aside to help Mark settle these doubts within himself. He'd been angry with her and would probably continue to be until he fully understood what she was doing.

Luckily Jo Marie found a parking space within sight of the office. With Christmas just a few days away the area had become more crowded and finding parking was almost impossible.

Her thoughts were heavy as she climbed from the passenger's side and locked her door. Just as she turned to look both ways before crossing the street she caught a glimpse of the dark blue Mercedes. A cold chill raced up her spine. Andrew was inside talking to Jim.

Nine

"Is everything all right?" Wearily Jo Marie eyed Jim, looking for a telltale mannerism that would reveal the reason for Andrew's visit. She'd avoided bumping into him by waiting in a small antiques shop across the street from the foundation. After he'd gone, she sauntered around for several additional minutes to be certain he was out of the neighborhood. Once assured it was safe, she crossed the street to the foundation's office.

"Should anything be wrong?" Jim lifted two thick brows in question.

"You tell me. I saw Andrew Beaumont's car parked outside."

"Ah, yes." Jim paused and smiled fleetingly. "And that concerns you?"

"No." She shook her head determinedly. "All right, yes!" She wasn't going to be able to fool Jim, who was an excellent judge of human nature.

A smile worked its way across his round face. "He came to meet the rest of the staff at my invitation. The LFTF Foundation is deeply indebted to your friend."

"My friend?"

Jim chuckled. "Neither one of you has been successful at hiding your feelings. Yes, my dear, sweet Jo Marie, *your* friend."

Any argument died on her tongue.

"Would you care for a cup of coffee?" Jim asked, walking across the room and filling a Styrofoam cup for her.

Jo Marie smiled her appreciation as he handed it to her and sat on the edge of her desk, crossing his arms. "Beaumont and I had quite a discussion."

"And?" Jo Marie didn't bother to disguise her curiosity.

The phone rang before Jim could answer her. Jim reached for it and spent the next ten minutes in conversation. Jo Marie did her best to keep occupied, but her thoughts were doing a crazy tailspin. Andrew was here on business. She wouldn't believe it.

"Well?" Jo Marie questioned the minute Jim replaced the receiver.

His expression was empty for a moment. "Are we back to Beaumont again?"

"I don't mean to pry," Jo Marie said with a rueful smile, "but I'd really like to know why he was here."

Jim was just as straightforward. "Are you in love with him?"

Miserably, Jo Marie nodded. "A lot of good it's done either of us. Did he mention me?"

A wry grin twisted Jim's mouth. "Not directly, but he wanted to know my intentions."

"He didn't!" Jo Marie was aghast at such audacity.

Chuckling, Jim shook his head. "No, he came to ask me about the foundation and pick up some of our literature. He's a good man, Jo Marie."

She studied the top of the desk and typewriter keys. "I know."

"He didn't mention you directly, but I think he would have liked to. I had the feeling he was frustrated and concerned about you working here so many nights, especially in this neighborhood."

"He needn't worry, you escort me to my car or wait at the bus stop until the bus arrives."

Jim made busy work with his hands. "I had the impression that Beaumont is deeply in love with you. If anything happened to you while under my protection, he wouldn't take it lightly."

Even hours later when Jo Marie stepped into the apartment the echo of Jim's words hadn't faded. Andrew was concerned for her safety and was deeply in love with her. But it was all so useless that she refused to be comforted.

Kelly was sitting up, a blanket wrapped around her legs and torso as she paid close attention to a television Christmas special.

"Hi, how'd it go tonight?" Kelly greeted, briefly glancing from the screen.

Her roommate looked pale and slightly drawn, but Jo Marie attributed that to the conversation she'd overheard between her brother and her roommate. She wanted to ask how everything was at the hospital, but doubted that she could adequately disguise her interest.

"Tonight . . . oh, everything went as it usually does . . . fine."

"Good." Kelly's answer was absentminded, her look pinched.

"Are you feeling all right, Kell?"

Softly, she shook her head. "I've got another stomachache."

"Fever?"

"None to speak of. I think I might be coming down with the flu."

Tilting her head to one side, Jo Marie mused that Kelly had been unnaturally pale lately. But again she had attributed that to painfully tense times they'd all been through in the past few weeks.

"You know, one advantage of having a brother in the medical profession is that he's willing to make house calls."

Kelly glanced her way, then turned back to the television. "No, it's nothing to call Mark about."

But Kelly didn't sound as convincing as Jo Marie would have liked. With a shrug, she went into the kitchen and poured herself a glass of milk.

"Want one?" She raised her glass to Kelly for inspection.

"No thanks," Kelly murmured and unsuccessfully tried to disguise a wince. "In fact, I think I'll head for bed. I'll be fine in the morning, so don't worry about me."

But Jo Marie couldn't help doing just that. Little things about Kelly hadn't made sense in a long time—like staying home because of an argument with Mark. Kelly wasn't a shy, fledgling nurse. She'd stood her ground with Mark more than once. Even her behavior at the Christmas parties had been peculiar. Nor was Kelly a shrinking violet, yet she'd behaved like one. Obviously it was all an act. But her reasons remained unclear.

In the morning, Kelly announced that she was going to take a day of sick leave. Jo Marie studied her friend with worried eyes. Twice during the morning she phoned to see how Kelly was doing.

"Fine," Kelly answered impatiently the second time.

"Listen, I'd probably be able to get some decent rest if I didn't have to get up and answer the phone every fifteen minutes."

In spite of her friend's testiness, Jo Marie chuckled. "I'll try to restrain myself for the rest of the day."

"That would be greatly appreciated."

"Do you want me to bring you something back for dinner?"

"No," she answered emphatically. "Food sounds awful."

Mark breezed into the office around noon, surprising Jo Marie. Sitting on the corner of her desk, he dangled one foot as she finished a telephone conversation.

"Business must be slow if you've got time to be dropping in here," she said, replacing the receiver.

"I come to take you to lunch and you're complaining?"

"You've come to ask about Kelly?" She wouldn't hedge. The time for playing games had long passed.

"Oh?" Briefly he arched a brow in question. "Is that so?"

"She's got the flu. There, I just saved you the price of lunch." Jo Marie couldn't disguise her irritation.

"You didn't save me the price of anything," Mark returned lazily. "I was going to let you treat."

Unable to remain angry with her brother for long, Jo Marie joined him in a nearby café a few minutes later, but neither of them mentioned Kelly again. By unspoken agreement, Kelly, Andrew, and Kelly's unexpected resignation were never mentioned.

Jo Marie's minestrone soup and turkey sandwich arrived and she unwrapped the silverware from the paper napkin. "How would you feel about a roommate for a while?" Jo Marie broached the subject tentatively.

"Male or female?" Dusky dark eyes so like her own twinkled with mischief.

"This may surprise you—female."

Mark laid his sandwich aside. "I'll admit my interest has been piqued."

"You may not be as keen once you find out that it's me."

"You?"

"Well I'm going to have to find someplace else to move sooner or later and—"

"And you're interested in the sooner," he interrupted.

"Yes." She wouldn't mention her reasons, but Mark was astute enough to figure it out for himself.

Peeling open his sandwich, Mark removed a thin slice of tomato and set it on the beige plate. "As long as you do the laundry, clean, and do all the cooking I won't object."

A smile hovered at the edges of her mouth. "Your generosity overwhelms me, brother dearest."

"Let me know when you're ready and I'll help you cart your things over."

"Thanks, Mark."

Briefly he looked up from his meal and grinned. "What are big brothers for?"

Andrew's car was in the apartment parking lot when Jo Marie stepped off the bus that evening after work. The darkening sky convinced her that waiting outside for him to leave would likely result in a drenching. Putting aside her fears, she squared her shoulders and tucked her hands deep within her pockets. When Kelly was home she usually didn't keep the door locked so Jo Marie was surprised to discover that it was. While digging through her purse, she was even more surprised to hear loud voices from the other side of the door.

"This has to stop," Andrew was arguing. "And soon."

"I know," Kelly cried softly. "And I agree. I don't want to ruin anyone's life."

"Three days."

"All right—just until Friday."

Jo Marie made unnecessary noise as she came through the door. "I'm home," she announced as she stepped into the living room. Kelly was dressed in her robe and slippers, slouched on the sofa. Andrew had apparently been pacing the carpet. She could feel his gaze seek her out. But she managed to avoid it, diverting her attention instead to the picture on the wall behind him. "If you'll excuse me I think I'll take a hot shower."

"Friday," Andrew repeated in a low, impatient tone.

"Thank you, Drew," Kelly murmured and sighed softly.

Kelly was in the same position on the sofa when Jo Marie returned, having showered and changed clothes. "How are you feeling?"

"Not good."

For Kelly to admit to as much meant that she'd had a miserable day. "Is there anything I can do?"

Limply, Kelly laid her head back against the back of the couch and closed her eyes. "No, I'm fine. But this is the worst case of stomach flu I can ever remember."

"You're sure it's the flu?"

Slowly Kelly opened her eyes. "I'm the nurse here."

"Yes, your majesty." With a dramatic twist to her chin, Jo Marie bowed in mock servitude. "Now would you like me to fix you something for dinner?"

"No."

"How about something cool to drink?"

Kelly nodded, but her look wasn't enthusiastic. "Fine."

As the evening progressed, Jo Marie studied her friend carefully. It could be just a bad case of the stomach flu, but Jo Marie couldn't help but be concerned. Kelly had always been so healthy and full of life. When a long series of cramps doubled Kelly over in pain, Jo Marie reached for the phone.

"Mark, can you come over?" She tried to keep the urgency from her voice.

"What's up?"

"It's Kelly. She's sick." Jo Marie attempted to keep her voice low enough so her roommate wouldn't hear. "She keeps insisting it's the flu, but I don't know. She's in a lot of pain for a simple intestinal virus."

Mark didn't hesitate. "I'll be right there."

Ten minutes later he was at the door. He didn't bother to knock, letting himself in. "Where's the patient?"

"Jo Marie." Kelly's round eyes tossed her a look of burning resentment. "You called Mark?"

"Guilty as charged, but I wouldn't have if I didn't think it was necessary."

Tears blurred the blue gaze. "I wish you hadn't," she murmured dejectedly. "It's just the flu."

"Let me be the judge of that." Mark spoke in a crisp professional tone, kneeling at her side. He opened the small black bag and took out the stethoscope.

Not knowing what else to do, Jo Marie hovered at his side for instructions. "Should I boil water or something?"

"Call Drew," Kelly insisted. "He at least won't overreact to a simple case of the flu."

Mark's mouth went taut, but he didn't rise to the intended gibe.

Reluctantly Jo Marie did as she was asked. Andrew answered on the third ring. "Beaumont here."

"Andrew, this is—"

"Jo Marie," he finished for her, his voice carrying a soft rush of pleasure.

"Hi," she began awkwardly and bit into the corner of her bottom lip. "Mark's here. Kelly's not feeling well and I think she may have something serious. She wanted to know if you could come over."

"I'll be there in ten minutes." He didn't take a breath's hesitation.

As it was, he arrived in eight and probably set several speed records in the process. Jo Marie answered his hard knock. "What's wrong with Kelly? She seemed fine this afternoon." He directed his question to Mark.

"I'd like to take Kelly over to the hospital for a couple of tests."

Jo Marie noted the way her brother's jaw had tightened as if being in the same room with Andrew was a test of his endurance. Dislike exuded from every pore.

"No," Kelly protested emphatically. "It's just the stomach flu."

"With the amount of tenderness in the cecum?" Mark argued, shaking his head slowly from side to side in a mocking gesture.

"Mark's the doctor," Andrew inserted and Jo Marie could have kissed him for being the voice of reason in a room where little evidence of it existed.

"You think it's my appendix?" Kelly said with shocked disbelief.

"It isn't going to hurt to run a couple of tests," Mark countered, again avoiding answering a direct question.

"Why should you care?" Kelly's soft voice wavered uncontrollably. "After yesterday I would have thought . . ."

"After yesterday," Mark cut in sharply, "I realized that you were right and that I owe you an apology." His eyes looked directly into Kelly's and the softness Jo Marie had witnessed in his gaze at the hospital Christmas party returned. He reached for Kelly's hand, folding it in his own. "Will you accept my apology? What you said yesterday made a lot of sense, but at the time I was angry at the world and took it out on you. Forgive me?"

With a trembling smile, Kelly nodded. "Yes, of course I do."

The look they shared was both poignant and tender, causing Jo Marie to feel like an intruder. Briefly, she wondered what Andrew was thinking.

"If it does turn out that I need surgery would you be the one to do it for me?"

Immediately Mark lowered his gaze. "No."

His stark response was cutting and Kelly flinched. "There's no one else I'd trust as much as you."

"I said I wouldn't." Mark pulled the stethoscope from his neck and placed it inside his bag.

"Instead of fighting about it now, why don't we see what happens?" Jo Marie attempted to reason. "There's no need to argue."

"There's every reason," Andrew intervened. "Tell us, Mark, why wouldn't you be Kelly's surgeon if she needed one?"

Jo Marie stared at Andrew, her dark eyes filled with irritation. Backing Mark into a corner wouldn't help the situation. She wanted to step forward and defend her brother, but Andrew stopped her with an abrupt motion of his hand, apparently having read her intent.

"Who I choose as my patients is my business." Mark's tone was dipped in acid.

"Isn't Kelly one of your patients?" Andrew questioned calmly. "You did hurry over here when you heard she was sick."

Coming to a standing position, Mark ignored the question and the man. "Maybe you'd like to change clothes." He directed his comment to Kelly.

Shaking her head she said, "No, I'm not going anywhere."

"Those tests are important." Mark's control on his anger was a fragile thread. "You're going to the hospital."

Again, Kelly shook her head. "No, I'm not."

"You're being unreasonable." Standing with his feet braced apart, Mark looked as if he was willing to take her to the hospital by force if necessary.

"Why not make an agreement," Andrew suggested with cool-headed resolve. "Kelly will agree to the tests, if you agree to be her doctor."

Tiredly, Mark rubbed a hand over his jaw and chin. "I can't do that."

"Why not?" Kelly implored.

"Yes, Mark, why not?" Andrew taunted.

Her brother's mouth thinned grimly as he turned aside and clenched his fists. "Because it isn't good practice to work on the people you're involved with emotionally."

The corners of Kelly's mouth lifted in a sad smile. "We're not emotionally involved. You've gone out of your way to prove that to me. If you have any emotion for me it would be hate."

Mark's face went white and it looked for an instant as if Kelly had physically struck him. "Hate you?" he repeated incredulously. "Maybe," he replied in brutal honesty. "You're able to bring out every other emotion in me. I've taken out a lot of anger on you recently. Most of which you didn't deserve and I apologize for that." He paused and ran a hand through his hair, mussing it. "No, Kelly," he corrected, "I can't hate you. It would be impossible when I love you so much," he announced with an impassive expression and pivoted sharply.

A tense silence engulfed the room until Kelly let out a small cry. "You love me? All these months you've put me through this torment and you love me?" She threw back the blanket and stood, placing her hands defiantly on her hips.

"A lot of good it did me." Mark's angry gaze crossed the width of the room to hold hers. "You're engaged to Daddy Warbucks over there so what good would it do to let you know?"

Jo Marie couldn't believe what she was hearing and gave a nervous glance to Andrew. Casually standing to the side of the room, he didn't look the least disturbed by what was happening. If anything, his features were relaxed as if he were greatly relieved.

"And if you cared for me then why didn't you say something before now?" Kelly challenged.

Calmly he met her fiery gaze. "Because he's got money, you've got money. Tell me what can I offer you that could even come close to the things he can give you."

"And you relate love and happiness with things?" Her

low words were scathing. "Let me tell you exactly what you can offer me, Mark Jubal Early. You have it in your power to give me the things that matter most in my life: your love, your friendship, your respect. And . . . and . . . if you turn around and walk out that door, by heaven I'll never forgive you."

"I have no intention of leaving," Mark snapped in return. "But I can't very well ask you to marry me when you're wearing another man's ring."

"Fine." Without hesitating Kelly slipped Andrew's diamond from her ring finger and handed it back to him. Lightly she brushed her mouth over his cheeks. "Thanks, Drew."

His hands cupped her shoulders as he kissed her back. "Much happiness, Kelly," he whispered.

Brother and sister observed the scene with open-mouthed astonishment.

Turning, Kelly moved to Mark's side. "Now," she breathed in happily, "if that was a proposal, I accept."

Mark was apparently too stunned to answer.

"Don't tell me you've already changed your mind?" Kelly muttered.

"No, I haven't changed my mind. What about the hospital tests?" he managed finally, his voice slightly raw as his eyes devoured her.

"Give me a minute to change." Kelly left the room and the three were left standing, Jo Marie and Mark staring blankly at each other. Everything was happening so fast that it was like a dream with dark shades of unreality.

Kelly reappeared and Mark tucked her arm in his. "We should be back in an hour," Mark murmured, but he only had eyes for the pert-faced woman on his arm. Kelly's gaze was filled with a happy radiance that brought tears of shared happiness to Jo Marie's eyes.

"Take your time and call if you need us," Andrew said as the happy couple walked toward the door.

Jo Marie doubted that either Kelly or Mark heard him. When she turned her attention to Andrew she discovered that he was already walking toward her. With eager strides he eliminated the distance separating them.

"As I recall, our agreement was that I wouldn't try to see you or contact you again while Kelly wore my engagement ring."

Her dark eyes smiled happily into his. "That's right."

"Then let's be rid of this thing once and for all." He led her into the kitchen where he carelessly tossed the diamond ring into the garbage.

Jo Marie gasped. Andrew was literally throwing away thousands of dollars. The diamond was the largest she had ever seen.

"The ring is as phony as the engagement."

Still unable to comprehend what he was saying, she shook her head to clear her thoughts. "What?"

"The engagement isn't any more real than that so-called diamond."

"Why?" Reason had escaped her completely.

His hands brought Jo Marie into the loving circle of his arms. "By Thanksgiving I'd given up every hope of ever finding you again. I'd convinced myself that those golden moments were just a figment of my imagination and that some quirk of fate had brought us together, only to pull us apart."

It seemed the most natural thing in the world to have his arms around her. Her eyes had filled with moisture so that his features swam in and out of her vision. "I'd given up hope of finding you, too," she admitted in an achingly soft voice. "But I couldn't stop thinking about you."

Tenderly he kissed her, briefly tasting the sweetness of her lips. As if it was difficult to stop, he drew in an uneven breath and rubbed his jaw over the top of her head, mussing her hair. "I saw Kelly at her parents' house over the Thanksgiving holiday and she was miserable. We've always been close for second cousins and we had a long talk. She told me that she'd been in love with Mark for months. The worst part was that she was convinced that he shared her feelings, but his pride was holding him back. Apparently your brother has some strange ideas about wealth and position."

"He's learning," Jo Marie murmured, still caught in the rapture of being in Andrew's arms. "Give him time." She said this knowing that Kelly was willing to devote the rest of her life to Mark.

"I told Kelly she should give him a little competition and if someone showed an interested in her, then Mark would step forward. But apparently she'd already tried that."

"My brother can be as stubborn as ten men."

"I'm afraid I walked into this phony engagement with my eyes wide open. I said that if Mark was worth his salt, he wouldn't stand by and let her marry another man. If he loved her, really loved her, he'd step in."

"But he nearly didn't."

"No," Andrew admitted. "I was wrong. Mark loved Kelly enough to sacrifice his own desires to give her what he thought she needed. I realized that the night of my Christmas party. By that time I was getting desperate. I'd found you and every minute of this engagement was agony. In desperation, I tried to talk to Mark. But that didn't work. He assumed I was warning him off Kelly and told me to make her happy or I'd pay the consequences."

The irony of the situation was almost comical. "You were already suffering the consequences. Why didn't you say something? Why didn't you explain?"

"Oh, love, if you'd been anyone but Mark's sister I would have." Again his mouth sought hers as if he couldn't get enough of her kisses. "Here I was trapped in the worst set of circumstances I've ever imagined. The woman who had haunted me for months was within my grasp and I was caught in a steel web."

"I love you, Andrew. I've loved you from the moment you held me all those months ago. I knew then that you were meant to be someone special in my life."

"This has taught me the most valuable lesson of my life." He arched her close. So close it was impossible to breath normally. "I'll never let you out of my arms again. I'm yours for life, Jo Marie, whether you want me or not. I've had to trust against every instinct that you would wait for me. Dear Lord, I had visions of you falling in love with Jim Rowden, and the worst part was I couldn't blame you if you did. I can only imagine what kind of man you thought me."

Lovingly, Jo Marie spread kisses over his face. "It's going to take me a lifetime to tell you."

"Oh, love." His grip tightened against the back of her waist, arching her closer until it was almost painful to breathe. Not that Jo Marie cared. Andrew was holding her and had promised never to let her go again.

"I knew something was wrong with you and Kelly

from the beginning," she murmured between soft, exploring kisses. Jo Marie couldn't have helped but notice.

"I've learned so much from this," Andrew confessed. "I think I was going slowly mad. I want more than to share my life with you, Jo Marie. I want to see our children in your arms. I want to grow old with you at my side."

"Oh, Andrew." Her arms locked around his neck and the tears of happiness streamed down her face.

"I love you, Florence Nightingale."

"And you, Andrew Beaumont, will always be my dream man."

"Forever?" His look was skeptical.

She lifted her mouth to his. "For all eternity," she whispered in promise.

"An ulcer?" Jo Marie shook her head slowly.

"Well, with all the stress I was under in the past few weeks, it's little wonder," Kelly defended herself.

The four sat in the living room sipping hot cocoa. Kelly was obediently drinking plain heated milk and hating it. But her eyes were warm and happy as they rested on Mark who was beside her with an arm draped over her shoulders.

"I've felt terrible about all this, Jo Marie," Kelly continued. "Guilt is a horrible companion. I didn't know exactly what was going on with you and Andrew. But he let it be known that he was in love with you and wanted this masquerade over quickly."

"You felt guilty?" Mark snorted. "How do you think I felt kissing another man's fiancée?"

"About the same way Jo Marie and I felt," Andrew returned with a chuckle.

"You know, Beaumont. Now that you're marrying my sister, I don't think you're such a bad character after all."

"That's encouraging."

"I certainly hope you get along since you're both going to be standing at the altar at the same time."

Three pairs of blank eyes stared at Kelly. "Double wedding, silly. It makes sense, doesn't it? The four of us have been through a lot together. It's only fitting we start our new lives at the same time."

"But soon," Mark said emphatically. "Sometime in January."

Everything was moving so fast, Jo Marie barely had time to assimilate the fact that Andrew loved her and she was going to share his life.

"Why not?" she agreed with a small laugh. "We've yet to do anything else conventionally."

Her eyes met Andrew's. They'd come a long way, all four of them, but they'd stuck it out through the doubts and the hurts. Now their whole lives stretched before them filled with promise.

The Gift of Christmas

One

Ashley Robbins clenched her hands together as she sat in a plush velvet chair ten stories up in a Seattle high-rise. The cashier's check to Cooper Masters was in her purse. Rather than mail him the money, Ashley had impulsively decided to deliver it herself.

People moved about her, in and out of doors, as she thoughtfully watched their actions. Curious glances darted her way. She had never been one to blend into the background. Over the years she'd wondered if it was the striking ash-blond hair that attracted attention, or her outrageous choice of clothes. Today, however, since she was meeting Cooper, she'd dressed conservatively. Never shy, she was a hit in the classroom, using techniques that had others shaking their heads in wonder. But no one doubted that she was the most popular teacher at John Knox Christian High School. Cooper had made that possible. No one knew he had loaned her the money to complete her studies. Not even Claudia, her best friend and Cooper's niece.

Ashley and Cooper were the godparents to John, Claudia's older boy. Being linked to Cooper had pleased Ashley more than her friend suspected. She'd been secretly in love with him since she was sixteen. It amazed her that no one had guessed during those ten years, least of all Cooper.

"Mr. Masters will see you now," his receptionist informed her.

Ashley smiled her appreciation and followed the attractive woman through the heavy oak door.

"Ashley." Cooper stood and strode to the front of his desk. "What a pleasant surprise."

"Hello, Cooper." He'd changed over the last six months since she'd seen him. Streaks of silver ran through his hair, and tiny lines fanned out from his eyes. But it would take more than years to disguise his strongly marked features. He wasn't a compellingly handsome man, not in the traditional sense, but seeing him again stirred familiar feelings of admiration and appreciation for all he'd done for her.

"Sit down, please." He indicated a chair not unlike the one she'd recently vacated. "What can I do for you? Any problems?"

She responded with a slight shake of her head. He had always been generous with her. Deep down, she doubted that there was anything she couldn't ask of this man, although she didn't expect any more favors, and he was probably aware of that.

"Everything's fine." She didn't meet his eyes as she opened the clasp of her purse and took out the check. "I wanted to personally give you this." Extending her arm, she handed him the check. "I owe you so much, it seemed almost rude to put it in the mail." The satisfaction of paying off the loan was secondary to the opportunity of seeing Cooper again. If she'd been honest with herself, she would have admitted she was hungry for the sight of him. After all these months she'd been looking for an excuse.

He glanced at the check and seemed to notice the

amount. Two dark brows arched with surprise. "This satisfies the loan," he said thoughtfully. Half turning, he placed the check in the center of the large wooden desk. "Your mother tells me you've taken a second job?" The intonation in his voice made the statement a question.

"You see her more often than I do," she said in an attempt to evade the question. Her mother had been the Masters' cook and housekeeper from the time Ashley was a child.

He regarded her steadily, and although she could read no emotion in his eyes, she felt his irritation. "Was it necessary to pay this off as quickly as possible?"

"Fast? I've owed you this money for over four years." She laughed lightly. Someone had once told her that her laugh was one of the most appealing things about her. Sweet, gentle, melodic. She chanced a look at Cooper, whose cool dark eyes revealed nothing.

"I didn't care if you ever paid me back. I certainly didn't expect you'd half kill yourself to return it."

The displeasure in his voice surprised her. Taken aback, she watched as he stalked to the far corner of the office, putting as much distance between them as possible. Was it pride that had driven her to pay him back as quickly as possible? Maybe, but she doubted it. The loan to finish her schooling had been the answer to long, difficult prayers. From the time she'd been accepted into the University of Washington, she had attended on faith. Faith that God would supply the money for books and tuition. Faith that if God wanted her to obtain her teaching degree, then He would meet her needs. And He had. In the beginning things had worked well. She roomed with Claudia and managed two part-time jobs. But when

Claudia and Seth got married, she was forced to find other accommodations, which quickly drained her funds. Cooper's offer had been completely unexpected. The loan had come at a time when she'd been hopeless and had been preparing to withdraw from classes. They'd never discussed terms, but surely he'd known she intended to repay him.

A tentative smile brushed her lips. She'd thought he would be pleased. His reaction amazed her. She attempted to keep her voice level as she assured him, "It was the honorable thing to do."

"But it wasn't necessary," he answered, turning back to her.

Again she experienced the familiar twinge of awareness that only Cooper Masters was capable of stirring within her.

"It was for me," she countered quickly.

"It wasn't necessary," he repeated in a flat tone.

Ashley released a slow breath. "We could go on like this all day. I didn't mean to offend you, I only came here today because I wanted to show my appreciation."

He stared back at her, then slowly nodded. "I understand."

Silence stretched between them.

"Have you heard from Claudia and Seth?" he asked after a while.

Ashley smiled. They had so little in common that whenever they were together the conversation invariably centered around Claudia and their godson. "The last I heard she said something about coming down for Christmas."

"I hope they do." His intercom buzzed, and he leaned over and pressed a button on the phone. "Yes, Gloria?"

"Mr. Benson is here."

"Thank you."

Taking her cue, Ashley stood. "I won't keep you." Her fingers brushed her wool skirt. She'd been hoping he would notice the new outfit and comment. He hadn't. "Thank you again. I guess you know that I wouldn't have been able to finish school without your help."

"I was wondering . . ." Cooper moved to her side, his look slightly uneasy, as if he was unsure of himself. "I mean, I can understand if you'd rather not."

"Rather not what?" She couldn't remember him ever acting with anything but supreme confidence. In control of himself and every situation.

"Have dinner with me. A small celebration for paying off the loan."

"I'd like that very much. Anytime." Her heart soared at the suggestion; she wasn't sure how she managed to keep her voice level.

"Tonight at seven?"

"Wonderful. Should I wear something . . . formal?" It wouldn't hurt to ask, and he hadn't mentioned where he intended they dine.

"Dress comfortably."

"Great."

An hour later Ashley's heart still refused to beat at a normal pace. This was the first time Cooper had asked her out or given any indication he would like to see her socially. The man was difficult to understand, always had been. Even Claudia didn't fully know him; she saw him as dignified, predictable and overly concerned with respectability. In some ways he was, but through the years Ashley had seen past that facade. He might be refined, and sometimes overly proper, but he was a man who'd been forced to take on heavy responsibility at an early age. There had been little time for fun or frivolity in his life. Ashley wanted to be the one to change that. She loved him. Her mother claimed that opposites attract, and after meeting Cooper, Ashley had never doubted the truth of that statement.

Ashley chose to wear her finest designer jeans, knowing she looked good. At five foot nine, she was all legs. Her pink sweatshirt contained a starburst of sequins that extended to the ends of the full-length sleeves. Her hair was styled in a casual perm, and soft curls reached her shoulders. Her perfume was a fragrance Cooper had given her the previous Christmas. Although not imaginative, the gift had pleased her immeasurably, even though he hadn't given it to her personally, but to her mother, who'd passed it on. When she'd phoned to thank him, his response had been clipped and vaguely ill-at-ease. Politely, he'd assured her that it was his duty, since they were John's godparents. He'd also told her he'd sent the same fragrance to Claudia. Ashley had hung up the phone feeling deflated. The next time she'd seen him had been in June, when her mother had gone to the hospital for surgery. Cooper had come for a visit at the same time Ashley had arrived. Standing on opposite sides of the bed, her sleeping mother between them, Ashley had hungrily drunk in the sight of him. Their short conversation had been carried on in hushed tones, and after a while they hadn't spoken at all. Afterward he'd had coffee out of a machine, and she'd sipped fruit juice as they sat talking in the waiting area at the end of the corridor. She hadn't seen him again until today.

Over the months she had dated several men, and she'd recently been seeing Dennis Webb, another teacher, on a steady basis. But no one had ever attracted her the way Cooper did. Whenever a pensive mood overtook her, she recognized how pointless that attraction was. Whole universes stretched between them, both social and economic. For Ashley, loving Cooper Masters was as impossible as understanding income tax forms.

The doorbell chimed precisely at seven. Claudia had claimed that she could set her watch by Cooper. If he said seven, he would arrive exactly at seven.

A sense of panic filled Ashley as she glanced at her wristwatch. It couldn't possibly be that time already, could it? With one red cowboy boot on and the other lying on the carpet, she looked around frantically. The laundry still hadn't been put away. Quickly she hobbled across the floor and shoved the basket full of folded clean clothes into the entryway closet, then closed the door with her back as she conducted a sweeping inspection of the apartment. Expelling a calming sigh, she forced herself to smile casually as she opened the door.

He greeted her with a warm look, that gradually faded as he handed her a florist's box.

To Cooper, apparently informal meant a three-piece suit and flowers. Glancing down at her jeans and sweatshirt, one cowboy boot on, the other missing, she smiled weakly and felt wretched. "Thank you." She took the small white box. "Sit down, please." Hurrying ahead of him, she fluffed up the pillows at the end of the sofa, then hugged one to her stomach. "I'm running a little late tonight. If you'll give me a few minutes I'll change clothes."

"You look fine just the way you are," he murmured, glancing at his watch.

What he was really saying, she realized, was that they would be late for their reservation if she took the time to change clothes. After glancing down at the hot pink sweatshirt, she raised her gaze to meet his. "You're sure? It'll only take a minute."

His nod seemed determined. Self-conscious, embarrassed and angry with herself, Ashley sat at the opposite end of the sofa and slipped her foot into the other boot. After tucking in her denim pant leg, she sat up and reached for the florist's box. A lovely white orchid was nestled in a bed of sheer green paper. A gasp of pleasure escaped her.

"Oh, Cooper," she murmured, feeling close to tears. No one had ever given her an orchid. "Thank you."

"Since I didn't know the color of your dress . . ." He paused to correct himself, ". . . your outfit . . . this seemed appropriate." He remained standing, studying her. "It's the type women wear on their wrist."

As Ashley lifted the orchid from the box, its gentle fragrance drifted pleasantly to her. "I'm always having to thank you, Cooper. You've been very good to me."

He dismissed her appreciation with a hard shake of his head. "Nonsense."

She knew that further discussion would only embarrass them both. Standing, she glanced at the closet door, knowing nothing would induce her to open it and expose her folded underwear to Cooper. "I'll get my purse and we can go."

"You might want to wear a coat," he suggested. "I heard something about the possibility of snow over the radio this afternoon."

"Yes, of course." If he remained standing exactly as he was, she might be able to open the door just enough to slip her hand in and jerk her faux fur jacket off the hanger. Somehow she managed it. Turning, she noted that Cooper was regarding her curiously. Rather than fabricate a wild excuse about why she couldn't open the closet all the way, she decided to say nothing.

He took the coat from her grasp, holding it open for her to slip her arms into the sleeves. It seemed as if his hands lingered longer than necessary on her shoulders, but it could have been her imagination. He had never been one to display affection openly.

"Where are we going?" she asked, and her voice trembled slightly, affected by even the most impersonal touch.

"I chose an Italian restaurant not far from here. I hope that suits you."

"Sounds delicious. I love Italian food." Her tastes in food were wide and varied, but it wouldn't have mattered. If he had suggested hot dogs, she would have been thrilled. The idea of Cooper eating anything with his fingers produced a quivering smile. If he noticed it, he said nothing.

Cooper parked outside the small, family-owned restaurant and came around to her side of the car, opening the door for her. It was apparent when they were seated that he had never been there before. The thought flashed through her mind that he didn't want to be seen with her where he might be recognized. But she quickly dismissed the idea. If he didn't want to be with her, then he wouldn't have asked her out. Those thoughts were unworthy of Cooper, who had always been good to her.

"Is everything all right?" As he stared across the table at her, a frown drew his brows together.

"Yes, of course." She looked down at her menu, guiltily forcing a smile on her face. "I wonder how long it'll be before we know if Claudia will be coming for Christmas," she said, hoping to resume the even flow of conversation.

"Time's getting close. I imagine we'll know soon."

Thanksgiving was the following weekend, but Christmas displays were already up in stores; some had shown up as early as Halloween. Doubtless Seth and Claudia would let them know by the end of next week. The prospect of sharing the holiday with her friend—and therefore Cooper—produced a glow of happiness inside Ashley.

The waiter took their order, then promptly delivered their fresh green salads.

"It's been exceptionally chilly for this time of the year," Cooper commented, lifting his fork, his gaze centered on his plate.

Ashley thought it was a sad commentary that their only common ground consisted of Claudia and the weather. "Yes, it has." She looked up to note that a veiled look had come over his features. Perhaps he was thinking the same thing.

The conversation during dinner seemed stiff and strained to her. Cooper asked her about school and politely inquired if she liked teaching. In return she asked him about the business supply operation he owned and was surprised to learn how much it had grown over the past few years. The knowledge should have pleased her, but instead it only served to remind her that he was a rich man and she was still struggling financially.

When they stepped out of the restaurant, she was pleased to discover that it was snowing.

"Oh, Cooper, look!" she cried with delight. "I love it when it snows. Let's go for a walk." She couldn't keep the excitement out of her voice. "There's something magical about walking in the falling snow."

"Are you sure that's what you want?" He glanced at the thin layer of white powder that covered the ground, then he looked up, his expression odd as his eyes searched hers.

"I'd forgotten, you'll have to drive back in this stuff. Maybe it wouldn't be such a good idea," she commented, unable to hide her disappointment.

His hand cupped her elbow, bringing her near, and when she slipped on the slick sidewalk he quickly placed his arm around her waist, preventing her from falling. He left his arm there, holding her protectively close to his side. Her spirits soared at being linked this way with Cooper.

"Where would you like to walk?" An indiscernible expression clouded his eyes.

"There's a marina a couple of blocks from here, and I love to watch the snow fall on the water, but if you'd rather not, I understand."

"By all means, let's go to the marina." The smile he gave her was the first genuine one she'd witnessed the entire evening.

"Doesn't this make you want to sing?" she asked, and

started to hum "White Christmas" even before he could answer.

"No," he said, and chuckled. "It makes me want to sit in front of a roaring fireplace with a warm drink."

She clucked and pressed her lips together to keep from laughing.

"What was that all about?"

"What?" she asked, feigning ignorance.

"That silly little noise you just made."

"If you must know, I don't think you've done anything impulsive or daring in your entire life, Cooper Masters." She said it all in one giant breath, then watched as a shocked look came over his face.

"Of course I have," he insisted righteously.

"Then I dare you to do something right now."

"What?" He looked unsure.

"Make a snowball and throw it at me," she demanded. Breaking from his hold, she ran a few steps ahead of him. "Bet you can't do it," she taunted, and waved her hands at him.

With marked determination, Cooper stuffed his hands inside his coat pockets. "This is silly."

"It's supposed to be crazy, remember?" she chided him softly.

"But it's not right for a man to throw snowballs at a woman."

"Will this make things easier for you?" she shouted, bending over to scoop up a handful of snow. With an accuracy that astonished her, she threw a snowball that hit him directly in the middle of his chest. If she was surprised, the horrified look on Cooper's face sent her into peals of laughter. Losing her balance on the ice-slickened sidewalk, she went sprawling to the cement with an un-dignified plop.

"That's what you get for hurling snow at courteous gentlemen," Cooper called once he was sure she wasn't hurt. As he advanced toward her, he shifted a tightly packed snowball from one hand to the other.

"Cooper, you wouldn't—would you?" She gave him her most defenseless look, batting her eyelashes. "Here, help me up." She extended a hand to him, which he ignored.

A wicked gleam flashed from the dark depths of his eyes. "I thought you said I never did anything crazy or daring?"

"You wouldn't!" Her voice trembled with laughter as she struggled to stand up.

"You're right, I wouldn't," he murmured, dropping the snowball and reaching for her. Surprise rocked her as he pulled her into his arms. He hesitated momentarily, as if expecting her to protest. When she didn't, he gently brushed the hair from her temple and just as softly pressed his mouth over hers. The kiss should have been tender, but the moment their lips met it became hungry and needy. The effect was jarring, as if a bolt of awareness were flashing through them. They broke apart, shocked and breathless. The oxygen was trapped in her lungs, making it impossible to breathe.

"Did I hurt you?" he asked, his voice thick with concern.

A shake of her head was all she could manage. "Cooper?" Her voice was a mere whisper. "Would you mind doing that again?"

"Now?"

She nodded.

"Here?"

Again she nodded.

He pulled her back into his embrace, his eyes drinking deeply from hers. This time the kiss was gentle, as if he, too, needed to test these sensations. Lost in the swirling awareness, Ashley felt as if he had touched the deep inner part of her being. For years she had dreamed of this moment, wondered what effect his touch would have on her. Now she knew. She felt a free-flowing happiness steal over her. He had taken her heart and touched her spirit. When he entwined his fingers in the curling length of her hair, she pressed her head against his shoulder and breathed in deeply. A soft smile lifted her lips at the sound of his furiously pounding heart.

"This is crazy," he murmured hoarsely.

"No," she swiftly countered. "This is wonderful."

Carefully he relaxed his hold, easing her from his embrace. His features were unnaturally pale as he smoothed the hair at the side of his head with an impatient movement. "I'm too old for you." His mouth had thinned, and his look was remote.

Her bubble of happy contentment burst; he regretted kissing her. What had been so wonderful for her was a source of embarrassment for him. "I dared you to do something impulsive, remember?" she said with forced gaiety. "It doesn't mean anything. I've been kissed before. It happens all the time."

"I'm sure it does," he replied stiffly. His gaze moved pointedly to his watch. "I think it would be best if I took you home now. Perhaps we could see the marina another time."

"Sure."

His touch was impersonal as they strolled purpose-fully back toward the restaurant parking lot. To hide her discomfort, Ashley began to hum Christmas music again.

"Rushing the season a bit, aren't you?"

She concentrated on moving one foot in front of the other. "I suppose. But the snow makes it feel like Christmas. Christ wouldn't mind if we celebrated His birth every day of the year."

"The shopping malls would love it if we did," he remarked cynically.

"You're speaking of the commercial aspect of the holiday, I'm talking about the spiritual one."

Cooper didn't comment. In fact, neither one of them spoke until he pulled up to the curb in front of her apartment building.

"Would you like to come in and warm up? It would only take a minute to heat up some cocoa." Although the offer was sincere, she knew he wouldn't accept.

"Perhaps another time."

There wouldn't be another time. He wouldn't ask her out again; the whole evening had been a fiasco. Cooper Masters was a powerful, influential man, whereas she was a high school English Lit teacher.

"You'll let me know if you hear anything from Seth and Claudia?"

"Of course."

He came around to her side of the car, opening the door. "You don't need to walk me all the way to my door," she mumbled miserably.

"There's every need." Although his voice was level,

she could tell he was determined to live up to what he felt a gentleman should be.

She didn't argue when he took the keys out of her hand and opened the door of her first-floor apartment for her. "Thank you," she murmured. "The evening was . . ."

"Crazy," he finished for her.

Wonderful, her mind insisted in return. Afraid of what her eyes would reveal, she lowered her head and her blond curls fell forward, wreathing her face. "Crazy," she repeated.

A finger placed under her chin lifted her eyes to his. His were dark and unreadable, hers soft and shining. Slowly his hand moved to caress the soft, smooth skin of her cheek. The gentle caress sent the blood pulsing through her veins, flushing her face with telltale color.

"If ever you're in trouble or need someone, I want you to contact me."

Although he had never verbally said as much, she had always been aware that she could go to him if ever she needed help.

"I will." Her voice sounded irritatingly weak.

"I want you to promise me." He unbuttoned his coat pocket and took out a business card. Using the door as a support, he wrote down a phone number. "You can reach me here any time of the day."

"I'm not going to trouble you with—"

"Promise me, Ashley."

He was so serious, his look demanding. "Okay," she agreed, accepting the card. "But why?"

A long moment passed before he answered her. "I have a vested interest in you," he said, and shrugged, the indifferent gesture contradicting his words. "Besides, I'd hate to have anything happen to Johnny's godmother."

"Nothing's going to happen to me."

"In case it does, I want you to know I'll always be there."

The business card seemed to sear her hand. In his own way, Cooper cared about her. "Thank you." Impulsively, she raised two fingers to her lips, then brushed them across his mouth. His hand stopped hers, gripping her wrist; his look branded her. Slowly he lowered his mouth to hers in a gentle, sweet kiss.

"Good night, Ashley."

"Good night." Standing in the open doorway, she watched until he drove into the dark night. A solitary figure illuminated by the falling snow.

Expelling her breath in a long quivering sigh, she tucked the card in her purse. Why did she have to love Cooper Masters? Why couldn't she feel for Webb what she did for Cooper? Webb was nice and almost as unpredictable as she was. Maybe that was why they got along so well. Yet it was Cooper who occupied her thoughts. Cooper who made her heart sing. Cooper who filled her dreams. The time had come to wake up and face reality. She was at the age when she should start thinking about marriage and a family, because she definitely wanted children. Cooper wasn't going to be interested in someone like her. He might care about her, even feel some affection for her, but she wasn't the type of woman he would ever ask to be his wife.

Troubled and confused, Ashley made herself a cup of cocoa and sat on the sofa, her feet tucked under the cushion next to her. Things had been so easy for her friends, even Claudia. They met someone, fell in love, got married and started a family. Maybe God had decided He didn't want her to marry. The thought seemed intolerable, but she had learned long ago not to second-guess her heavenly Father. She'd given Him her life, her will, even Cooper's safekeeping. Now she had to learn to trust.

She rinsed out the cup, placed it in the kitchen sink and turned out the lights. Her eyes fell on her purse, hanging on the closet doorknob. She wondered if the day might come when she would need to use the card, not that she intended to.

That same thought ran through her mind several days later when the police officer directed her to the phone. She didn't want to contact Cooper, so she'd tried phoning her family first, hoping she would catch her father at home. But there had been no answer.

"Is there anyone else, miss?" the tall, uniformed man asked.

"Yes," she answered tightly, opening her purse and taking out the card. Her fingers actually trembled as she dialed the number.

"Cooper Masters."

As she suspected, he'd given her his private cell number. "Oh, hi . . . it's Ashley."

"Ashley." His voice carried clearly over the line. "What's wrong?"

"It isn't an emergency or anything," she began, feeling incredibly silly. "I mean, I don't think they'll keep me."

"Ashley," he heaved her name on an angry sigh. "What's going on?"

"It's a long story."

"All right, tell me where you are. I'll come to you, and then we'll straighten everything out."

She hesitated, swallowing past the lump forming in her throat. "I'm in jail."

Two

"Jail!" Cooper's voice boomed over the line. "I'll be there in ten minutes."

"But, Cooper, Kent's a good thirty minutes from downtown Seattle."

"Kent?" The anger in his voice was barely controlled.

"If you're going to get so mad . . ." Ashley let the rest of the sentence fade, realizing that the phone line had already been disconnected.

Casting a glance at the police officer beside her, she gave him a wary smile. "A friend's coming."

A smile quivered at one corner of the older man's mouth. "I heard." Looking away, he asked, "Would you like a cup of coffee while you wait?"

"No thanks."

Ashley heard Cooper's voice several minutes before she saw him. By the time he was brought into the area where she was waiting, there wasn't a person in the entire police station who hadn't heard him. She had always known him to be a calm, discreet person. That he would react this way to a minor misunderstanding shocked her. Although . . . a lot of things about Cooper had surprised her lately. She was standing, her face devoid of color, when he was escorted into the room.

"Can you tell me what's going on here?" he demanded.

His look did little to encourage confidences; she swallowed tightly and waved her hand helplessly. "Well, apparently someone took the license plate off Milligan."

"Who the heck . . . ?" He paused and took a deep, calming breath. "Who's Milligan?"

"Not who," she corrected, "but what. Milligan's my moped. I parked it outside the Mexican restaurant where I work odd hours, and someone apparently took off with my license plate."

"That isn't any reason to arrest you!" he shouted.

"They haven't arrested me!" she yelled in return, and was humiliated when her voice cracked and wavered. "And if you won't quit shouting at me, then you can just leave."

Raking his fingers roughly through his hair, Cooper stalked to the other side of the room. His mouth was tightly pinched, and he said nothing for several long moments. "All right, let's try this again," he replied in a deceivingly soft tone. "Start at the beginning, and tell me everything."

"There's not much to tell. Someone took the license plate, and since I don't have the registration on me, the police need some evidence that I own the bike. I haven't been arrested or anything. In fact, they've been very nice." In nervous reaction she looped a long strand of curly hair around her ear. "All I need for you to do is go to my apartment and bring back the registration for Milligan. Then I'll be free to leave." She opened her purse and took out her key ring, then extracted the key to the apartment. "Here," she said, handing it to him. "The registration's in the kitchen, in the silverware drawer, stuck under the aluminum foil. I keep all my important papers there."

If he thought her record storage system was a bit unusual, he said nothing.

"There's a lawyer on his way here, I'll leave word at the front desk for him." Without another word, he turned and left the room.

Within twenty minutes she heard him talking to the officer who had offered her the coffee. A few moments later they both entered the waiting area.

"You're free to go," the policeman explained. "Although I'm afraid we can't let you drive the moped until you have a new license plate."

Before she could protest Cooper inserted, "No need to worry. I've already made arrangements for the bike to be picked up." He turned and directed his words to Ashley. "It'll be delivered to your place sometime tomorrow afternoon."

Rather than argue, Ashley mutely agreed.

"If you're ready, I'll take you home," Cooper said.

Shoving her knit cap onto her head, she stood and swung her backpack over her shoulder, then gave the kind officer a polite smile. She wasn't pleased with the way things were working out. If she didn't have Milligan, she would have to take a series of busses to and from work, with a long trek between stops. Surely something could be done to enable her to ride her moped until she could replace the plate. One look from Cooper discouraged her from asking.

His hand cupped her elbow as they walked to the parking lot. Her attention was centered on the scenery outside the car window as they crossed the Green River and connected with the freeway. Wordlessly, he took the first exit and a couple of minutes later pulled into the parking lot to her apartment building.

He turned off the engine, then called his office. "Gloria, cancel the rest of my appointments for today," he said stiffly, his voice clipped and abrupt. Without waiting for a confirmation, he promptly ended the call, and then turned to Ashley. "Invite me in for coffee."

Her heart lodged someplace near her throat. "Yes, of course." She didn't wait for him to come around to her side of the car and let herself out. He gave her a disapproving look as they met in front of the vehicle. He opened the apartment door and returned the key to her. She placed it back on the key ring and took off her jacket, carelessly tossing it across the top of the sofa. He removed his black overcoat and neatly folded it over the back of the chair opposite the sofa.

"I'll put on the coffee." She moved into the kitchen, pouring water into the small, five-cup pot. She could hear Cooper agitatedly pacing the floor behind her.

"Why are you so angry with me?" she asked. She couldn't look at him, not when he was so obviously furious with her. "I couldn't help it if someone stole my license plate. I never should have phoned you, I'm sorry I did."

"I'm not mad at you," he stormed. "I'm angry that you were put through that ordeal, that you were treated like a criminal, that . . ." He left the rest unsaid.

"It's not the policeman's fault. He was only doing his job," she tried to explain, still not facing him. Her fingers trembled as she added the grounds to the pot, placed the lid on top and set it to brew.

A large masculine hand landed on her shoulder, and

she had to fight not to lay her cheek on it. A subtle pressure turned her around. With both hands behind her, she gripped the oven door for support. Slowly she raised her eyes to meet his. She was surprised at the tenderness she saw in the dark depths of his gaze, which seemed to be centered on her mouth. Nervously she moistened her dry lips with the tip of her tongue. She hadn't meant to be provocative, but when Cooper softly groaned she realized what she'd done. When he reached for her, she went willingly into his embrace.

He held her against him, breathing in deeply as he buried his face in the curve of her neck. His hands roamed her back, arching her as close as humanly possible. Ashley molded herself to him, savoring the light scent of musk and man; she longed for him to kiss her. She silently pleaded with him to throw common sense to the wind and crush his mouth over hers. Just being held by him was more happiness than she'd ever hoped to experience. Happiness and torment all rolled into one. An embrace, a light caress, a longing look, could never satisfy her, not when she wanted so much more. Gently he kissed the crown of her head and released her. She wanted to cry with disappointment.

The coffee had begun to perk, and to disguise her emotions, Ashley turned and reached for two cups, waiting for the pot to finish before pouring.

While she dealt with the coffee, Cooper sat in the living room waiting for her. He stood when she entered, taking one cup from her hand.

"I'm sorry, Ashley," he said, his eyes probing hers.

He didn't need to elaborate. He was sorry for his anger, sorry he'd overreacted in the police station, but mostly he regretted throwing aside his self-control and taking her in his arms.

Unable to verbally acknowledge his apology she simply shook her head, letting him know that she understood what he was saying.

"So you work at a Mexican restaurant?" he asked, after taking a sip from the steaming cup.

She wasn't fooled by the veiled interest. He'd commented on the fact she'd taken a second job once before, and he hadn't been pleased then.

"I only work odd hours, less now that I've paid off the loan," she answered, her finger making lazy loops around the rim of her cup.

He pinched his mouth tightly shut, and she recognized that he was biting back words. She wondered how he managed in business confrontations when she found him so easy to read.

Taking another sip of coffee, he stood and moved into the kitchen to put the half-full cup into the sink. "I should go."

She followed his movements. "I haven't thanked you. I . . . I don't know what I would have done if you hadn't come."

Her appreciation seemed to embarrass him, because his mouth thinned. He lifted his coat off the back of the chair. "I said I wanted you to call me if you needed help. I'm glad you did."

She walked him to the door. "How'd you get to Kent so fast?" Asking him questions helped delay the time when he would leave.

"I was already in the car when you phoned. It was simply a matter of heading in the right direction."

"Oh," she said in a small voice. "I apologize if I inconvenienced you."

"You didn't," he returned gruffly. His eyes met hers then, and again she found herself drowning in those dark depths.

Clenching her hands at her sides, she gave him a falsely cheerful smile. "Thanks again, Cooper. God go with you."

He turned. "And you," he murmured, surprising her.

"Have a nice Thanksgiving."

"I'm sure I will. Are you spending the day with your family?"

"Yes, Mom's making her famous turkey stuffing, and Jeff and his wife, Marsha, are coming." Jeff was her younger brother. John, the youngest Robbins, was working in Spokane and had decided not to make the long drive over the Cascade Mountains in uncertain weather.

Cooper didn't elaborate on his own plans for the holiday, and she didn't ask. "Goodbye, and thanks again."

"Goodbye, Ashley."

As she watched him walk away, she had the strongest desire to blow him a kiss. Immediately she quelled the impulse, but she couldn't help feeling disappointed and frustrated. Closing the front door, she leaned against it and breathed in deeply. She was filling her head with fanciful dreams if she dared to hope Cooper would ever come to love her. Wasting her time and her life. But her heart refused to listen.

As Cooper promised, her moped was delivered safely to her apartment the following afternoon. Webb drove her home from school, and once she dropped off her things, he took her to the Department of Motor Vehicles, where she applied for new license plates. Granted a temporary plate, she was relieved to learn she could now ride Milligan. The moped might not be much, but it got her where she needed to go in the most economical way.

Webb was tall and thin, his facial features almost gaunt, but he was one of the nicest people Ashley had ever known. When he dropped her off at her apartment, she invited him inside. He accepted with a smile.

"Got plans for the weekend?" he asked over a cup of cocoa.

She shrugged. "Not really. I wanted to do some Christmas shopping, but I dread fighting the crowds."

"Want to go skiing Saturday afternoon? I understand the slopes are open."

"I didn't know you skied?" Ashley questioned, her eyes twinkling.

"I don't," Webb confirmed. "I thought you'd teach me."

"Forget that, buddy. You can take lessons like everyone else, then we'll talk about skiing," she said with a laugh. "You could invite me to dinner instead," she suggested hopefully.

"Fine, what are you cooking?"

"Leftovers."

"I'll bring the egg nog," he said with a sly grin.

"Honestly, Webb, how do you do it?" she asked, laughing.

"Do what?"

"Invite me out to dinner, and I end up cooking?"

"It's all in the wrist, all in the wrist," he told her, flexing his hand, looking smug.

Thinking about their conversation later, she couldn't help laughing. Webb was a fun person, but what she felt for Cooper was exciting and intense and couldn't compare with the friendship she shared with her co-worker.

With Cooper she felt vulnerable in a way that couldn't be explained. But then she was in love with Cooper Masters, and that was simply pointless.

Disturbed by her thoughts, she went to change clothes. As part of her preparation for the coming holidays and the extra calories she would consume, she had started to work out. Following the instructions on the DVD she'd purchased, she practiced a routine that used Christian music for an aerobic dancercise program. Dressed in purple satin shorts, pink leg-warmers and a gray T-shirt, she placed her hands on her hips in the middle of the living room and waited for the warm-up instructions. Just as she completed the first round of exercises, the doorbell rang.

She paused, and with her breath deep and ragged, she turned off the player and checked the peephole in the door. She wasn't expecting anyone. To her horror, she saw it was Cooper.

The doorbell buzzed again, and for a fleeting second she was tempted to let him think she wasn't home, but overriding her embarrassment at having him see her dressed in shorts and a T-shirt was her desire to know why he'd come.

"Hello," she said as she opened the door.

He walked into the apartment, his brow marred by a

puzzled frown as he glanced at her. "Maybe I should come back later."

"Nonsense," she mumbled, dismissing the suggestion. She grabbed a towel to wipe the perspiration from her face. "I was just doing some aerobics. Care to join me?"

"No thanks." The corners of his mouth formed deep grooves as he suppressed a smile. "But don't let me stop you."

His attempt at humor amazed her. It was the first time she could remember him bantering with her—or anyone. "I think I'll skip the rest of the program," she said and laughed.

"Is that coffee I smell?" he asked as he sat on the edge of the sofa.

"No, cocoa. Want some? If you want coffee, though, it'd only take me a minute to brew a pot."

He shook his head.

Looping the towel around her neck, she sat cross-legged opposite him. Her face was glowing and red from the exertion, and she noted the way Cooper couldn't keep his eyes off her. Her heart was pounding fiercely, but she wasn't sure if it was the effects of seeing him again or the aerobics.

For a long moment silence filled the room. "Did you get Madigan back?" he eventually asked.

"Milligan," she corrected.

"How'd you happen to name a moped Milligan?"

"It was the salesman's name. We went out a couple of times afterward, and I couldn't think of the bike without thinking of Milligan, so I started calling it by his name."

Cooper's mouth narrowed slightly. "What do you do when it rains?"

"Wear rain gear," she returned casually. "It's a bit of a hassle, but I don't mind." Why was he so curious about Milligan? Certainly he'd known—or at least known of—someone who rode a moped before now?

"They're not the safest thing around, are they?"

"I suppose not, but I'm careful." This line of questioning was beginning to rankle. "Why all the curiosity?"

Leaning forward, he rested his elbows on his knees, then quickly shifted position, placing his ankle across one knee as if to give a casual impression. "The more I thought about you riding that moped, the more concerned I became. In checking statistics I discovered—"

"Statistics?" she interrupted him. "Honestly, Cooper, I'm perfectly safe."

He closed his eyes for a moment in apparent frustration, then opened them again. "I knew this wasn't going to be easy. You're as stubborn as Claudia," he said, and expelled his breath slowly. "I'm going to worry about you riding around on that silly bit of chrome and rubber."

"I've had Milligan for almost two years," she inserted, feeling the color drain from her face.

"Ashley," he said, his gaze lingering on her. "I want you to accept these and promise me you'll use them." He took a set of keys from his pocket and held them out to her.

"What are they?" Her voice trembled slightly.

"The keys to a new car. If you don't like the color we can—"

"The keys to a new car?" she echoed in shocked disbelief. "You don't honestly expect me to accept that, do you?"

"No," he acknowledged with a heavy sigh, "knowing

you, I didn't think you would. If you insist on paying me—"

"Paying you!" she cried, leaping to her feet. "I just cleared one loan—I'm not about to take on another." Her arms cradling her waist, she paced the floor directly in front of him. "Don't you realize how many enchiladas I had to serve to pay off the last loan? I can't understand you. I can't understand why you'd do something like this."

He inhaled deeply, his look full of trepidation. "I don't want you riding around on a stupid moped and getting yourself killed."

"You know, Cooper, you're beginning to sound like my father. I don't need another parent. I'm a capable twenty-six-year-old woman, not a half-wit teenager. What I ride to work is my prerogative."

"I'm only trying to . . ."

"I know what you're trying to do," she stormed. "Run my life! I have to admit, I was fooled." Her hand flew to her face and she wiped a thin layer of moisture from her brow. "You gave me your phone number and told me to call, but you didn't tell me there were strings attached."

"You're overreacting!" Although he appeared outwardly calm, she knew he was as unsettled as she was. Bright red color was creeping up his neck, but she doubted that he would vent his emotions in front of her.

"I'm not overreacting!" she exclaimed at fever pitch. "You think that because I phoned you, it gives you the right to step into my life. Keep the car, because I assure you I don't need it."

"As you wish," he murmured, his voice tight and controlled. Standing, he returned the keys to his pocket, his expression a stoic mask. "If you'll excuse me, I have an appointment."

"I hope the car isn't in the apartment parking lot, because the manager will have it towed away." The minute the words were out, she regretted having said them.

"It's not," he assured her coldly. Brushing past her, he let himself out, leaving her feeling deflated and depressed. The nerve of the man . . . He seemed to think . . . Her thoughts faded as she felt a hard knot form in her stomach. Now she'd done it, really done it.

"Happy Thanksgiving, Mom." Ashley laid the freshly baked pie on the kitchen countertop and leaned over to kiss her mother on the cheek.

"Hello, sweetheart." Sarah Robbins placed an arm around Ashley's waist and hugged her close. "I'm glad you're early, dear, would you mind peeling the potatoes?"

"Sure, Mom," she agreed, pulling open the kitchen drawer and taking out the peeler. Ashley had hoped for some time to talk to her mother privately. "How's work?" she asked in what she hoped was a casual tone. "Is Mr. Masters cracking the whip?" Her mother would have thought it disrespectful if she'd called Cooper anything but Mr. Masters, but the formal title nearly stuck in her throat.

"Oh, hardly." Sarah wiped the back of her hand across her apron. "He's always been wonderful to work for. I must say, he certainly loves those nephews of his. There are pictures of John and Scott all over that house, and I swear the only reason he moved out of the condominium was so those boys would have a decent yard to play in when they came to visit. That's all he ever talks about." Opening the oven door, she pulled out the rack to baste the turkey with a giblet broth simmering on the top of the stove. "Have you heard from Claudia and Seth?"

Ashley was chewing on a stalk of celery, and she waited until she'd swallowed before answering. "We chat all the time. I'm hoping she'll be here for Christmas."

"That'll please Mr. Masters. I think he needs a bit of cheering up. He's been in the blackest mood the last couple of days."

"He has?" She hoped to disguise her attentiveness. Her family, especially her mother, wouldn't approve of her interest in Cooper. Her feelings for her mother's employer had never been discussed, but she had sensed her mother's subtle disapproval of even their shared role as godparents more than once. In some ways Sarah Robbins and Cooper Masters were a lot alike. Her mother would view it as inappropriate for Ashley to be interested in an important man like Cooper.

"Did you cook a turkey for him this year?"

"No, he said he'd fix himself something, said he didn't want me fussing, when I had a family to tend to," she said on a soft sigh. "He really is the nicest man."

"I think he's wonderful," Ashley agreed absently, without thinking, and colored slightly when she turned to find her mother staring at her with questioning eyes. She was saved from answering any embarrassing questions by her sister-in-law, Marsha, who breezed through the door full of the joy of the season. She was grateful that she and her mother were never alone after that, and soon the meal was on the table.

Everything was delicious, as all her mother's cooking

was. As they sat around the table, Ashley's father asked the blessing, then opened the Bible to Psalms and read several praises aloud. After a moment's silence he asked each family member to verbally state one of the blessings they were most thankful for this year. Tears shimmered in Marsha's eyes as she announced that she and Jeff were going to have a baby. The news brought shouts of delight from Ashley's parents. When it came to her turn she thanked God for the rich Christian heritage she had received from her parents and also that she was going to be an aunt at last.

Later, as she helped with the dishes, Ashley's thoughts again drifted to Cooper. Here she was, with a loving family surrounding her, and he was probably alone in his large house. No, she told herself, most likely he was sharing the day with friends or business associates. But she wasn't convinced.

Hounded by constant self-recrimination since their last meeting, she had berated her quick temper a hundred times. He had only been concerned about her safety, and she'd acted as if he'd accosted her.

"Mom," she said and swallowed tightly. "Would you mind if I took a plate of food over to a friend who has to spend the day alone?"

"Of course not, dear, but why didn't you say something earlier? You could have invited them to dinner."

"I wish I'd thought of it," she said.

When she was all set with a large cooler overflowing with turkey and all the extras, Ashley's father loaned her the family car.

Her heartbeat raced frantically as she pulled into Cooper's driveway in the exclusive Redondo area of south Seattle. She wouldn't blame him if he closed the door on her. He'd purchased the house with the surrounding two acres of prime view property shortly after Claudia had given birth to John. Ashley had never seen the house although her mother had told her about it several times.

Now the large, two-story brick structure loomed before her, elegant and impressive. Adjusting her red beret, she rang the doorbell and waited. Several minutes passed before Cooper answered. He wore a suit, and she couldn't recall ever seeing him look more distinguished.

"Happy Thanksgiving, Cooper," she said with a trembling smile. If he didn't invite her inside, she was afraid she would burst into tears and humiliate them both.

"Ashley." He sounded shocked to see her. "Come in. For heaven's sake you didn't ride that deathtrap moped over here, did you?"

"No." She smiled and cast a glance over her shoulder to the older model car parked in the driveway. "Dad loaned me his car."

"Come in, it's cold, and it looks like rain," he offered again. He held out his hand, gesturing her inside.

Ashley didn't need a second invitation. "Here." She handed him the cooler. "I didn't know if you . . ." She hesitated. "Mom sent this along." Might as well jump in with both feet. Being underhanded about anything went against her inherent streak of honesty, but if her mother questioned her later, she would explain then.

Cooper took the cooler into the kitchen. She followed close behind, awestruck by every nook of the impressive home. The kitchen was a study in polished chrome and marble. It looked as clean as a hospital, yet welcoming. That was her mother's gift, she realized.

"Let me fix you something to drink. Coffee okay?" His eyes pinned hers, and she nodded.

After he poured her a mug, she followed him into a room with a fireplace and book-lined walls. His den, she decided. Two dark leather chairs with matching ottomans sat obliquely in front of the fireplace. He took her hat and red wool coat, hung them in a closet and motioned for her to sit in the chair opposite him.

Centering her attention on the steaming coffee, Ashley paused before speaking again. "I came to apologize."

A movement out of the corner of her eye attracted her gaze, and she watched as Cooper relaxed against the back of the chair.

"Apologize? Whatever for?" he asked.

Her head shot up, and she swallowed the bitter taste in her mouth. He wasn't going to make this easy for her. "I was unforgivably rude the other day, and I have no excuse. You were being thoughtful, and . . ."

He didn't allow her to finish. Instead he gestured with his hand, dismissing her regret. "Nonsense."

Scooting to the very edge of her cushion, she inhaled a quivering breath. "Will you please stop waving at me as though you find my apology amusing?" she said, fighting to keep a grip on her rising irritation. She bolted to her feet and walked to the far side of the room, pretending to examine his collection of books while struggling to keep her composure. Without turning around she mumbled miserably, "I'm sorry, I didn't mean that."

His soft chuckle sounded remarkably close, and when she turned she discovered that only a few inches separated them.

"Oh, Cooper." Her eyes drank in the heady sight of

him. "I've felt wretched all week. Please forgive me for the way I acted the other day."

"Have you decided to accept my offer?" The laughter drained from his eyes.

Sadly she shook her head. "Please understand why I can't."

He raked his hands through his hair, ruining the well-groomed effect.

Ashley's finger itched to smooth down the sides, to follow the proud line of his jaw, to touch him. Of its own volition her hand rose halfway to his face before she realized what she was doing.

Their eyes holding one another, Cooper captured her hand and held her motionless. Even his touch had the power to shoot sparks of awareness up her spine. When he raised her fingers to his mouth, his lips gently caressed her knuckles. Trapped in a whirlpool of sensation, she swayed toward him.

Her movement seemed to snap something within him, and he roughly pulled her into his embrace.

"Cooper." His name was a bittersweet sigh that was muffled as his mouth crushed hers. His hold was so tight that for a moment it was difficult to breathe, not that it mattered when she was in his arms.

Automatically, she raised her hands and linked them behind his neck as their mouths strained against one another. It was as if they couldn't get close enough, couldn't give enough. Ashley's lithe frame was flooded with a warm excitement, a glowing happiness that stole over her. A soft, whispering sigh escaped as he moved his face against her hair, brushing against her like a cat seeking contentment.

"Why is it you bring out the—"

The phone interrupted him, the sharp ringing shattering the tender moment. With a low, protesting groan he kissed the tip of her nose and moved across the room to answer the insistent call.

Ashley watched him, her heart swelling with pride and love. Their eyes met, and she noticed a warm light she had never seen in him before.

"Yes," he answered abruptly, then stiffened. "Claudia, this is a surprise."

Three

"Wonderful." Cooper continued speaking into the receiver, his eyes avoiding Ashley's. "Of course you're welcome, you know that. Plan to stay as long as you like."

The conversation lasted several more minutes, but it didn't take Ashley long to realize that Cooper wasn't going to let her friend know she was with him. She couldn't help wondering if she was a source of embarrassment to him. How could he hold her and kiss her one minute, then pretend that she wasn't even there with him the next? The promise of happiness she had savored so briefly in his arms left a bitter aftertaste. He must have sensed her confusion, because he turned away as the conversation with Claudia continued and kept his back to her until it ended a few minutes later.

"That was Claudia and Seth," he told her unnecessarily. "He's got a conference coming up in Seattle the second week of December. They've decided to fly down for that, then stay for the holidays."

He sounded so genuinely pleased that Ashley quickly quelled the spark of hurt. She didn't know why he'd chosen to ignore her, but she was going to put it out of her mind, and she certainly wouldn't ask.

"That's great."

"It is, isn't it?" He moved back to her side, gently easing her into his arms. "This is going to be a wonderful

Christmas," he murmured against the softness of her hair.

His voice was like that of an eager child, and it rang a chord of compassion within her. He had taken over his brother's business when he was barely into his twenties. Over the years he had built up the supply operation that extended into ten western states. Claudia had once told her that his goal was to have the business go nationwide. But at what price? she wondered. His health? His personal life? What drove a man like Cooper Masters? she wondered. Could it be the desire for wealth? He was already richer than anyone she knew. Recognition? Yet he was careful to keep a low profile, and from what her mother and Claudia told her, he seemed to jealously guard his privacy. The man was a mystery she might never understand, a puzzle she might never solve.

What did it matter, as long as he held her like this? she asked herself. Her arms around his waist, she laid her head against his solid, muscular chest. The steady beat of his heart sounded in her ear, and she smiled with contentment.

"I feel like doing something crazy," he said, and tipped his head back, laughter dancing in his eyes. "Usually that means taking you in my arms and kissing you like there's no tomorrow."

"I'm game." The urge to wrap her arms around his neck and abandon her pride was almost overwhelming. *What pride?* her mind echoed. That had been lost long ago where Cooper was concerned.

"Let's go for a walk," he suggested.

Ashley stifled a protest. "It's raining," she warned. A torrential downpour would have been a more accurate description of the turn the weather had taken. She moistened her lips. For once she would have been content to sit in front of the fireplace.

"I'll get us an umbrella," he said, a smile softening the sharp, angular lines of his face.

When he returned, he'd changed clothes and shoes, and was wearing a dark overcoat. A black umbrella dangled from his forearm.

"Ready?" he asked, regarding her expectantly.

He took her red beret and matching wool coat from the closet. He held the coat open for her to slip her arms into the silk-lined sleeves. As he pulled the coat to her shoulders, he paused to gently kiss the slim column of her neck from behind. The tiny kiss shot a tingling awareness over her skin, and she sighed.

"Doesn't this make you want to sing?" he teased as they stepped outside. Rain pelted the earth in an angry outburst.

"No." She laughed. "It makes me want to sit in front of a warm fireplace and drink something warm."

Cooper tipped back his head and howled with laughter. She was only echoing his words to her the night it had snowed. It hadn't been that funny. She watched him sheepishly, trying to recall a time she had ever heard him really laugh.

One arm tucked around her waist, he brought her close to his side. "Why is it when I'm with you I want to laugh and sing and behave totally irrationally?"

Wrapping her arm around his waist, she looked up into his sparkling eyes. "I seem to bring out that quality in a lot of people."

He chuckled and opened the umbrella, which protected them from the worst of the downpour. He led her along a cement walkway that meandered around the property, finally ending at a chain-link fence that was built at the top of a bluff that fell sharply into Puget Sound. The night view was spectacular. Ashley could only imagine how much more beautiful it would be during the day. An array of distant lights illuminated the sky and cast their reflective glow into the dark waters of the Sound.

"That must be Vashon Island," she said without realizing she had spoken out loud.

"Yes, and over there's Commencement Bay in Tacoma." He pointed to another section of lights. But his gaze wasn't on the city. Instead she felt it lingering, gently caressing her. When she turned her head, their eyes locked and time came to a screeching halt. Later she wouldn't remember who moved first. But suddenly she was tightly held in his arms, the umbrella carelessly tossed aside as they wrapped one another in a feverish embrace. The kiss that followed was the most beautiful she had ever received, filled with some unnameable emotion, deep, tender, sweet and all-consuming.

Rain bombarded them, drenching her hair until it hung in wet ringlets. He looked down at her, his breathing uneven and hoarse. Gently he smiled, wiping the moisture from her face. With a laugh, he tugged her hand, and together they ran back to the safety and warmth of the house.

It was the memory of his kiss and that night that sustained Ashley through the long, silent days that followed.

Every night she hurried home from work hoping Cooper would contact her in some way. Each day led to bitter disillusionment. When her mother phoned Wednesday afternoon, Ashley already knew what she was going to say.

"Mr. Masters thanked me for the Thanksgiving dinner you brought him. Why didn't you say he was the friend you were going to see?" Her tone hinted of disapproval.

"Because I knew what you would have said if I did," Ashley countered honestly.

"I had no idea you've been seeing Mr. Masters."

"We've only gone out once."

A short, stilted silence followed. "He's too old for you, dear. He's forty, you know."

Closing her eyes, Ashley successfully controlled the desire to argue. "I don't think you need to worry, Mother," she said soothingly. "I doubt that I'll be seeing him again."

"I just don't want to see you get hurt," her mother added on a gentler note.

"I know you don't."

They chatted for a few minutes longer and ended the conversation on a happy note, talking about Marsha and the coming baby, her mother's first grandchild.

Replacing the phone, Ashley released a long, slow breath. Cooper's image returned to trouble her again. Everything about him only served as a confirmation of her mother's unspoken warning. He wore expensively tailored suits, his hair was professionally styled and he seemed to be stamped with an unmistakable look of refinement. Something she would never have. And he was almost fourteen years older than she was, but why should that bother him or her parents when it had never mattered to her? At least she didn't need an explanation for why he hadn't contacted her. After talking to her mother, he had undoubtedly been reminded of their differences. Once again he would shut himself off from her, and who knew how long it would be before she could break through the thick wall of his pride?

Sunday morning during church the pastor lit the first candle of the Advent wreath. Ashley listened attentively as the man of God explained that the first candle represented prophecy. Then he read Scripture from the Old Testament that foretold the birth of a Savior.

Ashley left church feeling more uplifted than she had the entire week. How could she be depressed and miserable at the happiest time of the year? Claudia, Seth and the boys were coming, and Cooper wouldn't be able to avoid seeing her. Perhaps then she could find a way to prove that their obvious differences weren't all that significant.

An email from Claudia was waiting for her after work Monday afternoon. It read:

Ashley,

I'm sorry it's taken me so long to write. I can't believe how busy my boys manage to keep me. I've got some wonderful news! No, I'm not pregnant again, although I don't think Seth would mind. Cooper, either, for that matter. He's surprised both of us the way he loves the boys. The good news is that we'll be arriving at Sea/Tac Airport, Saturday, December 12th at 10 A.M. and plan to stay with Cooper through to the first of the year. That first week Seth will be involved in a series of meetings,

*but the remainder of the time will be the vacation
we didn't get the chance to take this summer.*

*I can't tell you how excited I am to be seeing
you again. I've missed you so much. You've always
been closer to me than any sister. You'll hardly
recognize John. At three, he's taller than most
four-year-olds, but then what can we expect, with
Seth being almost six-six? There's so much I want
to tell you that it seems impossible to put in an
email or speak about over the phone. Promise to
block out the holidays on your calendar, because
I'm dying to see you again. The Lord's been good
to me, and I have so much to tell you.*

*Scotty just woke from his nap and he never has
been one to wake in a happy mood. Take care. I'm
counting the days until the 12th.*

*Love,
Claudia, Seth, John and Scott*

Ashley read the message several times. Of course,
Claudia didn't realize that she already knew they were
coming. Again the hurt washed over her that Cooper had
pretended she wasn't there when Claudia had phoned on
Thanksgiving Day.

She circled the day on her calendar and stepped back
wistfully. When Scott had been born that spring, Cooper
had flown up to Nome to spend time with Claudia, Seth
and John. Ashley had yet to see the newest Lessinger.
Cooper had said it earlier, and now Ashley added her own
affirmation. This was going to be the most wonderful
Christmas yet.

———

Ashley's alarm buzzed early the morning of the twelfth. She groaned defiantly until she remembered that she would have to hurry and shower if she was going to meet Claudia's plane as she intended.

A little while later, wearing jeans and a red cable-knit sweater, she tucked her pant legs into her boots. Thank goodness it wasn't raining.

She parked Milligan in the multistory circular parking garage, then hurried down to baggage claim, her heels clicking against the tiled surface.

Cooper was already waiting when she arrived. He didn't notice her, and for a moment she enjoyed just watching him. He looked fresh and vital. It hardly seemed like more than two weeks since she'd last seen him, and yet they'd been the longest weeks of her life.

The morning sunlight filtered unrestrained through the large plate-glass windows, glinting on his dark hair. He was tall and broad shouldered. Seeing him again allowed all her pent-up feelings to spill over. It took more restraint than she cared to admit not to run into his arms. Instead she adjusted her purse strap over her shoulder, stuffed her hands in her pockets and approached him with a dignified air.

"Good morning, Cooper." She gave him a bright smile, although the muscles at the corners of her mouth trembled with the effort. "It's a beautiful day, isn't it?"

If he was surprised to see her, he hid the shock well.

"Ashley," he said, and stood. "Did you bring Madigan with you?" Concern laced his voice.

"Milligan," she corrected and laughed. "You never give up, do you?"

"Not if I can help it." He seemed to struggle with himself for a moment. "How have you been?"

"Sick," she lied unmercifully. "I was in the hospital for several days, doctors said I could have died. But I'm fine now. How about you?" she asked with a flippant air.

"Don't taunt me, Ashley," he warned thickly.

She was deliberately provoking him, but she didn't care. "For all you know it could be true. It's been more than two weeks since I've heard from you."

Turning his gaze to the window, he stood stiffly, watching the sky. "It seems longer," he murmured so low she had to strain to hear.

"Why?" she challenged, standing directly beside him, her own gaze cast toward the heavens.

"How's Webber?" He answered her question with one of his own.

"Webber?" she repeated, her face twisted into a puzzled frown. "You mean Webb?"

"Whoever." He shrugged.

"How do you know about Webb? Oh, wait. Mom." She answered her own question before he had the chance. "Webb and I are friends, nothing more." So this was the way her mother had handled the situation. For a moment fiery resentment burned in her eyes. She loved her mother, but there were times when Sarah Robbins's actions incensed her.

"Your mother mentioned that you and he see a lot of one another." His words were spoken without emotion, as if the subject bored him.

"Friends often do," she returned defensively. "But then, I doubt you'd know that."

She could feel the anger exude from him as he bristled.

"I'm sorry," she whispered, her tone contrite. "I didn't mean that the way it sounded." When she turned her head to look at him, she saw the cold fury leave his eyes. She placed her hand gently on his forearm, drawing his attention to her. "I don't want to argue. Seth and Claudia will know something's wrong, we won't be able to hide it."

He placed his hand on top of hers and squeezed it momentarily. "I don't want to argue, either," he finished. "According to the notice board, their flight has landed."

Ashley's heart fluttered with excitement. "Cooper," she mouthed softly. "My school is having a Christmas party next weekend. Would you . . ." Her tongue stumbled over the words. "I mean, could you . . . would you consider going with me?"

His shocked look cut through her hopes. "Next weekend?"

"The nineteenth . . . it's a Friday night. A dinner party, I don't think it'll be all that formal, just a faculty get-together. It's the last day of school, and the dinner is a small celebration."

"Will you be wearing your red cowboy boots?"

"No, I was going to borrow Dad's fishing rubbers," she shot back, then immediately relented. "All right, for you, I'll wear a dress, pantyhose, the whole bit."

Unbuttoning his coat, Cooper took out his cell phone from inside his suit pocket. He punched a few buttons. A frown brought thick brows together. "It seems I've already got plans that night."

Disappointment settled over Ashley. Somehow she'd known he wouldn't accept, that he would find an excuse not to attend.

"I understand," she murmured, but her voice wobbled dangerously.

The silence between them lasted until she saw Claudia, Seth and the boys descending the escalator. As soon as they reached the bottom John broke loose from his father's hand and ran into Cooper's waiting arms.

"Uncle Coop, Uncle Coop!" he cried with childish delight and looped his arms around Cooper's neck. John didn't seem to remember Ashley at first until she offered him a bright smile. "Auntie Ash?" he questioned, holding out his arms to her.

She held out her own arms, and Cooper handed the boy to her. Immediately John spread moist kisses over her cheek. When she glanced over she noticed that Seth and Cooper were enthusiastically shaking hands.

"Ashley," Claudia chimed happily. "I didn't know whether you'd make it to the airport or not. I love your hair."

"So does Webb," she laughed, and had the satisfaction of seeing Cooper's eyes narrow angrily. "And this little angel must be Scott." With John's legs wrapped around her waist, Ashley leaned over to examine the eight-month-old baby in Claudia's arms. "And I bet John's a wonderful big brother, aren't you, John?"

The boy's head bobbed up and down. Both of the Lessinger boys had Seth's dark looks, but their eyes were as blue as a cloudless sky. Claudia's eyes.

Ashley didn't get a chance to talk to her friend until later that afternoon. Both boys were down for a nap, Seth and Cooper were concentrating on a game of chess in Cooper's den, while Ashley and Claudia sat enjoying the view from a bay window in the formal dining room.

"I can't get over how good you look," Claudia said, blowing into a steaming coffee mug. "Your hair really is great."

"The easiest style I've ever had." Ashley ran her fingers through the bouncing curls and shook her head, and her blond locks fell naturally into place.

"Do you see much of Cooper?" Claudia delivered the question with deceptive casualness.

"Hardly at all," Ashley replied truthfully. "Why do you ask?"

"I don't know. You two were giving one another odd looks at the airport. I could tell he wasn't pleased with your riding that moped. I thought maybe something was going on between the two of you."

Ashley dismissed Claudia's words with a short shake of her hand. "I'm sure you're mistaken. Can you imagine Cooper Masters being interested in anyone like me?"

"In some ways I can," Claudia insisted. "You two balance one another. He takes everything so seriously, while you finagle your way in and out of anything. I know one thing," she said. "He thinks very highly of you. He has for years."

"You're kidding!"

"I'm not. I don't know that he would have been as happy about me marrying Seth if it hadn't been for you."

"Nonsense," Ashley countered quickly. "I knew you and Seth were right for one another from the first moment I saw you with him. I don't know of any couple who belong together more than you two. And it shows, Claudia, it shows. Your face is radiant. That kind of inner happiness only comes with the deep love of a man."

Claudia's face flushed with color. "I know it sounds crazy, but I'm more in love with Seth now than when I married him four years ago. I never thought that would be possible. I don't understand how I could have doubted our love and that God wanted us together. My priorities are so different now."

"What about your degree? Do you think you'll ever go back to school?"

"I don't know. Maybe someday, but my life is so full now with the boys I can't imagine squeezing another thing in. I wouldn't want to. John and Scott need me. I suppose when they're older and in school full-time I might think about finishing my doctorate, but that's years down the road. I do know that Seth will do whatever he can to help me if I decide to go ahead and get my degree." Pausing, she took another drink from her mug. "What about you? Any man in your life?"

"Several," Ashley teased, without looking at her friend. "None I'm serious about, though."

"What about Webb? You've written about him."

Before Ashley could assure Claudia her relationship with Webb didn't extend beyond a convenient friendship, a dark shadow fell into the room, diverting their attention to the two men who had just entered.

Seth's smile rested on his wife as he crossed the room and placed a loving arm across her shoulders. Cooper remained framed in the archway.

"As usual, Cooper beat the socks off me. I don't know why I bother to play. I can't recall ever beating him."

"What about you, Claudia?" Cooper asked. "You used to play a mean, if a bit unorthodox, game of chess."

Standing, Claudia looped her arm around her husband's waist. "Not me, I'm too tired to concentrate. If everyone will excuse me, I think I'll join the boys and take a nap."

Clenching her mug with both hands, Ashley stood. "I'd better rev up Milligan and get home before the weather—"

"No," Claudia interrupted. "You play Cooper, Ash. You always were a better chess player than me."

Ashley threw a speculative glance toward Cooper, awaiting his reaction. He arched his thick brows in challenge. "Would you care for a game, Miss Robbins?" he asked formally.

Wickedly fluttering her eyelashes, she placed both hands over her heart. "Just what are you suggesting, Mr. Masters?"

Claudia giggled. "You know, suddenly I'm not the least bit tired."

"Yes, you are," Seth murmured, tightening his grip on his wife's waist. "You and I are going to rest and leave these two to a game of chess."

Claudia didn't object when Seth led her from the room.

"Shall we?" Cooper asked, long strides carrying him to her side. He extended his elbow, and when Ashley placed her arm in his, he gave her a curt nod.

The thought of playing chess with Cooper was an opportunity too good to miss. She was an excellent player and had been the assistant coach for the school's team the year before.

The two leather chairs were pushed opposite one another with a mahogany table standing between. An inlaid board with ivory figures sat atop the table.

"I would like to suggest a friendly wager." The words were offered as a clear challenge.

"Just what are you suggesting?" she asked.

"I'm saying that if I win the match, then you'll accept the new car."

"Honestly, Cooper, you don't give up, do you?"

"Accept the car without any obligation to reimburse me," he continued undaunted, "plus the promise that you'll faithfully drive it to and from work daily."

"And just what do I get if *I* win?" she countered.

"That's up to you."

She released a weary sigh. "I don't think you can give me what I want," she mumbled, lowering her gaze to her hands, laced tightly together in her lap.

"I think I can."

"All right," she added, straightening slightly. "If I win, you must promise never to speak derogatorily of Milligan again, or in any way insinuate that riding my moped is unsafe." He opened and closed his mouth in mute protest. "And in addition I would ask that a generous donation be made to the school's scholarship fund. Agreed?" She could tell he wasn't pleased.

"Agreed." The teasing light left his eyes as he viewed the chess board with a serious look. Taking both a black and a white pawn, he placed them behind his back, then extended his clenched fists for her to choose.

She mumbled a silent prayer, knowing she would have the advantage if she were lucky enough to pick white. Lightly, she tapped his right hand.

Cooper relaxed his fist and revealed the white pawn.

Her spirits soared. He would now be on the defensive.

Neither spoke as they positioned the pieces on the board. A strained, tense air filled the den, and the only sound was the occasional crackle from the fireplace.

Her first move was a standard opening, pawn to king four, which he countered with an identical play. She immediately responded with a gambit, pawn to king's bishop four.

It didn't take her long to impress him with her ability. A smug smile lightly brushed her mouth as she viewed his shock as she gained momentum and dominated the game.

Bending forward, he rubbed a hand across his forehead and then his eyes. Ashley was forced to restrain another smile when he glanced up at her.

"Claudia was right, you *are* a good player."

"Thank you," she responded, hoping to hide the pleasure his acknowledgment gave her.

He made his next move, and she paused to study the board.

"Claudia was right about something else, too," he said softly.

"What's that?" she asked absently, pinching her bottom lip between her thumb and index finger, her concentration centered on the chess board.

"I don't think I've ever told you what an attractive woman you are."

His husky tone seemed to reach out and wrap itself around her. "What'd you say?" Her concentration faltered, and she lifted her gaze to his.

His eyes were narrowed on her mouth. "I said you're beautiful."

The current of awareness between them was so strong that she would gladly have surrendered the game right then and there. She felt close to Cooper, closer than she had to any other person. They had so little in common, and yet they shared the most basic, the strongest, emotion of all. If he had moved or in any way indicated that he wanted her, she would have tossed the chess game aside and wrapped herself in his arms. As it was, her will to win, the determination to prove herself, was quickly lost in the power of his gaze.

"It's your move."

Her eyes darkened with anger as she seethed inwardly. He was playing another game with her, a psychological game in which he had proved to be the clear winner with the first move. Using the attraction she felt for him, he'd hope to derail her concentration. His game read Cooper one, Ashley zilch.

She jumped to her feet and jogged around the room. Pausing to take a series of deep breaths, she took in his cynical look with amusement.

"I hate to appear ignorant here, but just what are you doing?"

"What does it look like?" she countered sarcastically.

"Either you're training for the Olympics or you're sorely testing my limited patience."

"Guess again," she returned impudently, beginning a series of jumping jacks.

"I thought we were playing chess, not twenty questions."

Hands resting challengingly on her hips, she paused and tossed him a brazen glare. "It was either vent my anger physically or punch you out, Cooper Masters."

"Punch me out?" he echoed in disbelief. "What did I do?"

"You know, so don't try to deny it." The anger had dissipated from her blue eyes as she returned to her chair and resumed her study of the board. As the blood pounded in her ears, she knew she'd made a mistake the minute she lifted her hand from the pawn. But would Cooper recognize her error and gain the advantage?

"Cooper?" she whispered.

"Hmm," he answered absently.

"Do you remember the last time I was here?"

He lifted his gaze to hers. "I'm not likely to forget it. After the cold I caught, I coughed for a week."

"Sometimes doing something crazy and irrational has a price." She leaned forward, her chin supported by the palm of her hand.

"Not this time, Ashley Robbins," he gloated, making the one move that would cost her the game. "Check."

Four

Ashley stared at the chess board with a sense of unreality. There was only one move she could make, and she knew what would happen when she took it.

"Checkmate."

She stared at him for a long moment, unable to speak or move. Cooper stood and crossed the room to a huge oak desk that dominated one corner. She watched as he opened a drawer and took out some papers. When he returned to her side, he gave her the car keys.

Her hand was shaking so badly she nearly dropped them.

"This is the registration," he told her, handing her a piece of paper. "After what happened not so long ago, I suggest you keep it in the glove compartment."

Unable to respond with anything more than a nod, she avoided his eyes, which were sure to be sparkling with triumph.

"These are the insurance forms, made out in your name. I believe there's a space for you to sign at the bottom of the policy." He pointed to the large "X" marking the spot, then handed her a pen.

Mutely Ashley complied, but her signature was barely recognizable. She returned the pen.

"I believe that's everything."

"No," she protested, unable to recognize the thin, high voice as her own. "I insist upon paying for the car."

"That wasn't part of our agreement."

"Nonetheless, I insist." She had to struggle to speak clearly.

"No, Ashley," he insisted, "the car is yours."

"But I can't accept something so valuable, not over a silly chess game." She raised her eyes to meet his. Their gazes held, his proud and determined, hers wary and unsure. A muscle moved convulsively at the side of his jaw, and she realized she had lost.

"The car is a gift from me to you. There isn't any way on this earth that I'll accept payment. You were aware of the terms before you agreed to the game."

A painful lump filled her throat, and when she spoke her voice was hoarse. "You have so much," she murmured, her voice cracking. "Must you take my pride, too?" Tears shimmered in the clear depths of her eyes. Wordlessly she left the den, took her coat and walked out the front door. Without a backward glance she climbed aboard Milligan and rode home.

Her mood hadn't improved the next morning as she dressed for church. The sky was dark and threatening, mirroring her temper. How could she love someone as headstrong and narrow minded as Cooper Masters? No wonder his business had grown and prospered over the years. He was ruthless, determined and obstinate.

After tucking her Bible into her backpack, she stepped outside to lock her apartment door. A patch of red in the parking lot caught her attention and she noted that a shiny new car was parked beside Milligan in front of her apartment. As she seethed inwardly, it took great restraint not to vent her anger by kicking the gleaming new car.

The first drops of rain fell lazily to the ground. Even God seemed to be on Cooper's side, she thought, as she heaved a troubled sigh. Either she had to change into her rain gear or drive the car. She chose the latter. Pulling out of the parking lot, she was forced to admit the car handled like a dream. Ashley was prepared to hate the car, but it didn't even take the full five miles to church for her to acknowledge she was going to love this car. Just as much as she loved the man who had given it to her.

As the Sunday School teacher for the three-year-olds, she was excited that John Lessinger would be in her class.

Claudia dropped him off at the classroom, Scotty resting on her hip, the diaper bag dangling from her arm.

"Morning." Ashley beamed warmly. "How's Johnny?" She directed her attention to the small boy who hid behind Claudia's skirts.

"He's playing shy today," Claudia warned.

"I don't blame him," Ashley whispered in return. "A lot's happened in the last couple of days."

"I'll drop Scotty off at the nursery and come back to see how John does."

"He'll be fine," Ashley assured her. "Did you see the playdough, Johnny?" she asked, directing his attention to the low table where several other children were busy playing. "Come over here and I'll introduce you to some of my friends."

John's look was unsure, and he glanced over his shoulder at his retreating mother. His lower lip began to quiver as tears welled in his blue eyes. Kneeling down to his level,

Ashley placed her hands on his small shoulders. "Johnny, it's Auntie Ash. You remember me, don't you? There's nothing to frighten you here. Come over and meet Joseph and Matthew. You can tell them all about Alaska."

John was playing nicely with the other children when Claudia returned. She sighed in relief. "Now I can relax," she whispered. "I don't know what it is about men and Sunday mornings, but it takes Seth twice as long as me to get ready. Then I'm left to carry Scott, steer John, haul the diaper bag, the Bibles and my purse, while Seth can't manage anything more than his car keys."

Ashley stifled a giggle. She allowed the children to play for several more minutes, chatting with Claudia, who insisted on staying for the first part of Sunday School to be sure John was really all right.

Ashley gathered the children in a circle and had them sit on the patch of carpet in the middle of the floor. As she sat cross-legged on the floor with them, one of the shyer children came over and seated herself in Ashley's lap. "I'm glad we're all together, together, together," the little girl sang in a sweet, melodious voice. "Because Jesus is here, and teacher's here, and—"

"Cooper's here," Claudia chimed in softly.

The song died on the girl's lips as everyone looked over at the tall, compelling figure standing in the open door. His attention was centered on Ashley and the little girl in her lap. For a moment he seemed to go pale, and the muscles in his jaw jerked, and Ashley wondered what she had done now to anger him. Without a word, he pivoted and left the room.

"I'd better see what he wanted," Claudia said, following him out of the room.

Ashley didn't see either of them again until it was time for the morning worship service. The four adults sat together, Claudia between her and Cooper. A hundred questions whirled in her mind. How had Claudia gotten Cooper to attend church? It wasn't all that long ago that he had scoffed at her friend's newfound faith. She wondered if Seth had some influence on Cooper's decision to attend church. More than likely John had said something, and Cooper had been unable to refuse.

Just as the pastor stepped in front of the congregation to light the third candle of the Advent wreath, a loud cry came from the nursery.

Claudia emitted a low groan. "Scotty." She leaned over and whispered to Ashley, "I wasn't sure I'd be able to leave him this long." She stood and made her way out of the pew. Cooper closed the space separating them.

Never had Ashley been more aware of a man's presence. As his thigh lightly touched hers, she closed her eyes at the potency of the contact. Nervously she scooted away, putting some space between them. When he turned and looked at her an unfamiliar quality had entered his eyes. He smiled, one of those rare smiles that came from his heart and nearly stopped hers. Its overwhelming force left her exposed and completely vulnerable. Undoubtedly he would be able to read the effect he had on her and know her thoughts. Quickly turning her face away, she squeezed her eyes closed, and then the pastor, the service, everything, everyone, was lost as Cooper closed his hand firmly over hers.

In all the years she had loved Cooper, Ashley had never dared to dream that he would sit beside her in church or share her strong faith. The intense sensations of having him near touched her so dramatically that for a moment she was sure her heart would burst with unrestrained happiness.

His grip remained tight and firm until Claudia returned to the pew and sat beside Seth. Immediately Cooper released Ashley's hand. The happiness that had filled her so briefly was gone. He seemed content to hold her hand only as long as no one knew. The minute someone came, he let her go.

Once again she was forcefully reminded of the huge differences that separated them. He was a corporate manager, a powerful, wealthy man. She was a financially struggling schoolteacher. In some ways she was certain he cared for her, but not enough to admit it openly. She sometimes feared she was an embarrassment to him, a fear that had dogged her from the beginning.

"Did you win the Irish Sweepstakes?" Webb asked Ashley as she pulled into the school parking lot and climbed out of the shining new car.

"No," she said and sighed unhappily. "I lost a chess game."

He gave her a funny look. "Let me make certain I've got this straight. You *lost* the chess game and won the car?"

"You got it."

Rubbing the side of his chin with one hand, he stared at her with confused eyes. "I know there's logic in this someplace, but for the moment it's escaped me."

"I wouldn't doubt it," she said, and nodded a friendly

greeting to the school secretary as she walked through the door.

"What would you have gotten if you'd *won?*" Webb asked as he followed on her heels.

"Milligan and my pride."

"That's another one of those answers that seems to have gone right over my head." He waved his hand over the top of his blond head in illustration. Confusion clouded his eyes. "All I really want to know is whether this person likes chess and plays often? It wouldn't be hard for me to lose. I don't even like the game."

"You wouldn't want to play this person," she mumbled under her breath, heading toward the faculty room.

"Don't be hasty, Ashley," he countered quickly. "Let me be the judge of that."

Tossing him a look she usually reserved for rowdy students was enough to quell his curiosity.

"We're going to the Christmas party Friday night, aren't we?" he asked, steering clear of the former topic of discussion.

Releasing a slow breath, Ashley cupped a coffee mug with both hands. Her enthusiasm for the party had disappeared with Cooper's excuse not to attend. Probably because she believed that the previous appointment he claimed to have was merely a pretext to avoid refusing her outright.

"I don't know, I have a friend visiting from Alaska," she said before sipping. "We may be doing something that night."

"Sure, no problem," he said with a smile. "Let me know if you change your mind."

No pleading, no hesitation, no regrets. The least he

could do was show some remorse over her missing the party. As she watched him saunter out of the faculty room, she threw imaginary daggers at his back. Unhappy and more than a little depressed, she finished her coffee and went to her homeroom.

"Is there something drastically wrong with me?" Ashley asked Claudia later that afternoon. She'd stopped by after school for a short visit with Claudia and the boys before Cooper returned from his office.

When Claudia looked up from bouncing Scotty on her knee, her eyes showed surprise. "Heavens, no. What makes you ask?"

"I mean, you'd tell me if I had bad breath or something, wouldn't you?"

"You know me well enough to answer that."

As Johnny weaved a toy truck around the chair legs, then pushed it under the table to the far side of the room, Ashley's eyes followed the movement of her godson. Lowering her face, she took a deep breath, afraid she might do something stupid like cry. "I want to get married and have children. I'm twenty-six and not getting any younger."

"I'm sure there are plenty of men out there who'd be interested. Only yesterday Seth was saying how pretty you've gotten. Surely there's someone—"

"That's just it," Ashley interrupted, knowing she couldn't mention Cooper. "There isn't, and I found a gray hair the other day. I'm getting scared."

"You and Cooper both. Have you noticed how he's getting gray along his sideburns? It really makes him look distinguished, doesn't it?"

Ashley agreed with a smile, but her eyes refused to meet her friend's, afraid she wouldn't be able to disguise her feelings for Cooper.

"Oh, before I forget, Seth and I have been invited to a dinner party this Friday night, and we were wondering if you could watch the boys. If you have plans just say so, because I think your mother might be able to do it."

Some devilish impulse made her ask, "What about Cooper?"

"He's got some appointment he can't get out of."

For a startled second the oxygen seemed trapped in Ashley's lungs. He had been telling the truth. He *did* have an appointment. In that brief second the sun took on a brighter intensity; it was as if the birds began to chirp.

"I'd love to stay with John and Scott," she returned enthusiastically. "We'll have a wonderful time, won't we, boys?" Neither one looked especially pleased. Glancing at her watch, Ashley quickly stood. "I've gotta scoot, I'll see you Friday. What time do you want me?"

"Is six too early? I'll try to get the boys fed and dressed."

"Don't do that," Ashley admonished with a laugh. "It'll be good practice for me. I need to learn all this motherhood stuff, you know."

"Don't rush off," Claudia said. "Cooper will be home any minute."

"I can't stay. Tell him I said hello—no, don't," she added abruptly. He might have been telling the truth about being busy Friday night, but it didn't lessen the hurt of his rejection. "Mid-year reports go home this Friday, and I want to get a head start."

Claudia regarded her quizzically as she walked her to

the door. "Thanks again for Friday. I don't like to leave the boys with strangers. It's bad enough for them to be away from home."

"Happy to help," Ashley said sincerely. Giving a tiny wave to both boys, she smiled when Scotty raised his chubby hand to her. Johnny ran to the front window to look out, and Ashley played peek-a-boo with him. The small head had just bobbed out from behind the drapes when Cooper spoke from behind her.

"Hello, Ashley."

She stiffened at the sound of his voice, her heartbeat racing double time. Last Sunday at church had been the last time she'd seen him.

"Hello." Her voice was devoid of any warmth or welcome. He looked dignified in his suit and silk tie. Childishly she was upset at him all the more for it.

"Is something the matter?" he asked in a quiet voice.

"No," she answered, her gaze stern and unyielding. "I'm just surprised that you'd taint your image by being seen with me."

"What are you talking about?"

"If you don't know, then I'm not going to tell you."

His gaze narrowed. "What's wrong? Obviously something's troubling you."

"The man's a genius," she replied flippantly. "Now, if you'll excuse me, I'll be on my way."

Cooper's eyes contained a hard gleam she had never seen. His hand shot out and gripped her upper arm. "Tell me what's going on in that unpredictable mind of yours."

Defiance flared from her as she stared pointedly at his hand until he relaxed his hold. Breaking free, she took a few steps in retreat, creating the breathing space she needed to vent her frustration. "I'll have you know, Cooper Masters, I'm not the least bit ashamed of who or what I am. My mother may be your housekeeper, but she has served you well all these years. My father's a skilled sheet metal worker, and I'm proud of them both. I don't have a thing to be ashamed about. Not in front of you or anyone." Having finished her tirade, she avoided looking at him and walked straight to her car.

She never made it. A strong hand on her shoulder swung her around, pinning her against the side of the car. "What are you implying?" The tone of his voice made Ashley shudder. His nostrils flared with barely restrained fury.

Tears shimmered in her eyes until his face was swimming before her. She bit her bottom lip. Suddenly she could feel the anger drain out of him.

"What's the matter with us?" he demanded hoarsely, then expelled an impatient breath.

"Everything!" she cried, her voice trembling. "Everything," she repeated. When she struggled, he released her and didn't try to stop her again. He stepped back as she climbed inside the car, revved the engine and drove away.

If Ashley was miserable then, it was nothing compared to the way she felt later. To soothe away her emotional turmoil and frustration, she filled the bathtub with hot water and bubble bath, and soaked in it until the water became tepid. In an attempt to pray, she tried the conversational approach that had come so naturally to her in the past, but even that was impossible in her present state of mind.

Sleep was a long time coming that night. She couldn't

seem to find a comfortable position, and when she did drift off she found herself trapped in a dream of hopelessness. Waking early the next morning, she rose before the alarm sounded, put on the coffee and sat in the dark, shadow-filled room waiting for the first light.

Lackadaisically, she reached for her devotional and discovered the suggested reading for the day was the famous love chapter in First Corinthians, Chapter Thirteen. *Love is very patient and kind,* verse four stated.

Had she been patient? Ten years seemed a long time to her, and that was how long it had been since she first realized she'd loved Cooper. Since the tender age of sixteen. Glancing back to her Bible, she continued reading. *Love doesn't demand its own way. It isn't irritable or touchy. It doesn't hold grudges and will hardly notice when others do wrong. . . . If you love someone you will always believe in him, always expect the best of him and always stand your ground in defending him.*

Closing her Bible, Ashley released an uneven breath. It looked as though she had a long way to go to achieve the standards God had set.

When it came time for her to pray, she got down on her knees, meditating first on the words she had read. Ever since Sunday she'd expected the worst from Cooper, thought the worst of him. She'd wanted to explain how hurt she was, but it sounded so petty to accuse him of being ashamed of her because he'd quit holding her hand. In voicing her thoughts, the whole incident sounded ludicrous. It seemed she was building things in her own mind because she was insecure. The same thoughts had come to her the night he'd taken her to the Italian restaurant, and the night Claudia had phoned from Alaska. She'd never thought of herself as someone with low self-esteem before Cooper.

"Oh, ye of little faith," she said aloud. *No*, her heart countered, *ye of little love*.

Ashley hummed cheerfully as she pulled into the school parking lot. She was proud of the fact that she had worked things out in her own mind—with God's help, of course. The next time she saw Cooper, she would apologize for her behavior and ask that they start again. Poor man, he wouldn't know what to think. One minute she was ranting and raving, and the next she was apologizing.

Today was a special day for her Senior Literature class. They'd been reading and studying the Western classic *The Oxbow Incident* by Walter Van Tilburg Clark. As part of her preparation for their final exam, Ashley dressed up as one of the characters in the book. Portraying the part as believably as possible, she was usually able to draw out heated discussions and points that might otherwise have been glossed over.

Today she was dressing as Donald Martin, one of the three men accused of cattle rustling in the powerful narrative. This was always Ashley's favorite part of the quarter, and her classroom antics were well known.

Her afternoon students were buzzing with speculation when the bell rang. She waited until everyone was seated before she came through the door to be greeted by laughter and cheers. She was wearing a ten-gallon hat. Her cowboy boots had silver spurs, and her long, slim legs were disguised by leather chaps. Two toy six-shooters were holstered at her hips. With her hair tucked under the hat, she'd made a token attempt toward realism by smearing dirt over her creamy smooth cheeks and pasting a long black mustache across her upper lip.

The class loved it, and immediate speculation arose about what character she was portraying.

"I'm here today to talk about mob justice," she began, sitting on the corner of her desk and dangling one foot over the edge.

"She's Gil," one of the boys in the back row called out.

"Good guess, David," she said, pointing to him. "But I'm no drifter. I own my own spread at Pike's Hole. Me and the missus are building up our herd."

"It's Mex," someone else shouted.

"No way," Diana Crosby corrected. "Mex wasn't married."

"Good girl, Diana." She twirled both six-shooters around a couple of times and by pure luck happened to place them in the holsters right side up. When her class applauded she bowed, her hat falling off her head. As she bent to pick it up she noticed a face staring at her from the small glass portion of the class door. The face was lovingly familiar. Cooper.

"If you'll excuse me a minute, I have to check my horse," she said, quickly making up a pretense to escape into the hallway.

"What are you doing here?" she demanded in a low tone.

A smile danced in his eyes as he attempted to hide his grin by rubbing his thumb across the angular line of his jaw. "Butch Cassidy, I presume."

"Cooper, I'm in the middle of class," she muttered with an exaggerated sigh, both hands gripping his arms.

"But I'm so glad to see you. I feel terrible about the way I acted yesterday. I was wrong, terribly wrong."

The laughter faded from his features as he regarded her seriously. "I had no idea the dinner party meant so much to you."

"What dinner party?" He was talking in riddles.

"The one you asked me to attend with you. I assumed that was what upset you yesterday."

She shook her head in wry dismay. "No . . . that wasn't it."

"Then what was?"

Casting an apprehensive glare over her shoulder, she turned pleading eyes to him. "I can't talk now."

He rubbed a weary hand over his face. "Ashley, I rearranged my schedule. I'll be happy to take you to the school Christmas party."

She groaned softly. "But I can't go now."

"What do you mean, you can't go?" His dark, steely eyes narrowed.

He didn't need to say another word for her to know how much it had inconvenienced him to readjust his schedule.

"Cooper, I'm sorry, but I . . ."

"Invited someone else," he finished for her, his eyes as cold as a blast of arctic wind. "That Webber fellow, I imagine."

"I haven't got time to stand in the hall and argue with you. My class is waiting."

"And so, I imagine, is Webber."

Fury blazed in her eyes as she slashed him a cutting look. "You do that on purpose."

"Do what?" His voice was barely civil.

"Call Webb 'Webber,' the same way you call Milligan 'Madigan.' I find the whole denial thing rather childish," she snapped resentfully. By now she was too incensed to care if she was making sense.

"I find that statement unworthy of comment."

"You would." She spun away and stalked back into the classroom, restraining the impulse to slam the door.

Claudia was dressed in a mauve-colored chiffon evening gown that was a stunning complement to her auburn hair and cream coloring. Seth, too, looked remarkably attractive in his suit and tie.

"Okay, I showed you where everything is in the bedroom, and here's the phone number of the restaurant." Claudia laid the pad near the phone in the kitchen. "I've left a baby bottle in the refrigerator, but I've already nursed Scotty, so he probably won't need it."

"Okay," Ashley said, following Claudia out of the kitchen.

"Both boys are dressed for bed, and don't let either of them stay up past eight-thirty. You may need to rock Scotty to sleep."

"No problem, I got my degree in rocking chair." Checking her reflection in the hallway mirror, Claudia tucked a stray hair back into her coiled French coiffure. "You didn't happen to have an argument with Cooper, did you?" The question came out of the blue.

Ashley could feel the blood rush from her face, then just as quickly flood back. "What makes you ask?"

"Seth and I have hardly seen him the last couple of

days, and he's been in the foulest mood. It's not like him to behave like this. I can't understand it."

"What makes you think I have anything to do with it?" she asked, doing her best to conceal her reaction.

"I know it sounds crazy, and I wouldn't want to offend you, Ash, but I still think something's stirring between you two. I may be an old married fuddy-duddy, but I recognize the looks he's been giving you. What I can't understand is why the two of you work so hard at hiding it. As far as I'm concerned, you're perfect for one another."

"Ha," Ashley said harshly. "We can't spend two minutes together lately without going for each other's jugular."

Seth took Claudia's wrap from the hall closet and placed it over her shoulders. "Sounds like the way it was with us a few times, doesn't it, honey?" he asked, and tenderly kissed the creamy smooth slope of Claudia's neck.

"Call if you have any problems, won't you?" Claudia said, suddenly sounding worried. "Scotty will cry the first few minutes after we've left, but he should quiet down in a little bit, so don't panic."

"I never panic," Ashley assured her with a cheeky grin.

True to his mother's word, Scott gave a hearty cry the minute the door was closed.

"It's all right. Look, here's your teddy."

Scotty took the stuffed animal, threw it across the room and cried all the louder.

Ten minutes passed and nothing seemed to calm his frantic cries. Even John looked as if he was ready to give way and start howling.

"Come on, sweetie, not you, too."

"I want my mommy."

"Let's pretend I'm your mommy," Ashley offered, "and then you can tell me how to make Scotty happy."

"Will you hold me like my mommy?" Johnny asked, a tear running down his pale face.

"Sure, join the crowd," Ashley laughed, lifting him so that she had a baby on each hip. Johnny cried in small whimpering sounds and Scott in large howling sobs.

Pacing the floor, she glanced up to find Cooper standing in the entryway watching her, a stunned look on his face.

Five

"Look, Johnny, Scott," Ashley said cheerfully. "Uncle Cooper's here."

Both boys cried harder. Scotty buried his face in her neck, his stubby hands tangled in her blond hair. When he pulled a long strand, she cried out involuntarily, "Ouch."

The small protest spurred Cooper into action. He hung his overcoat in the hall closet and entered the living room, taking John from Ashley.

"What's the matter, fella?" he asked in a reassuring tone.

"I want my mommy!" John wailed.

"They went out for the evening," Ashley explained, both hands supporting Scott as she paced the floor, making cooing sounds in his ear. But nothing seemed to comfort the baby, who continued to cry pitifully.

"What about Webber and your party?" Cooper asked stiffly.

"I tried to tell you that I wasn't going," she explained, and breathed in deeply. "I didn't say a thing about attending the party with Webb. You assumed I was."

"Are you telling me the reason you didn't go tonight is because you'd promised to baby-sit John and Scotty?"

Ashley silently confirmed the statement with a weak nod. His dark eyes narrowed with self-directed anger.

"Why do you put up with me?" he asked.

She didn't get the opportunity to answer, because Scotty began bellowing even louder.

A troubled frown broke across Cooper's expression. "Is he sick? I've never heard him cry like that."

"No, just unhappy. Claudia said she'd left a bottle for him. Maybe we should heat it up."

All four moved into the kitchen. With Scotty balanced on her hip, Ashley took the baby bottle out of the refrigerator. "It needs to be heated." She held it out to him.

"If you say so," he said, shrugging his broad shoulders. "How does your mommy do it?" he asked Johnny, who seemed more secure now that his uncle had arrived.

"She nurses Scotty."

Slowly Cooper's dark eyes met hers, amusement flickering across his face. She giggled, and soon they were both laughing. Scotty cried all the harder, clinging to Ashley.

The humor broke the terrible tension that had existed between them for days.

Cooper smiled warmly into her eyes, trying to hold back his laughter. He walked across the room and took a large pan out of the bottom cupboard, then filled it with hot water. "I don't want to chance the microwave. What if I melt the bottle? It's plastic, after all." By the time he'd set the pan on the stove and turned on the burner, he'd regained his composure.

Ashley placed the baby bottle in the water. "Is it supposed to float?"

"I don't know." He shook his head briefly, the look in his eyes unbelievably tender.

"Oh well, we'll experiment, won't we, boys?"

"What's an experiment?" Johnny asked. He was sitting on top of the counter, his short legs dangling over the edge.

"It's a process by which we examine the validity of a hypothesis and determine the nature of something as yet unknown."

"Cooper . . ." Ashley laughed at the way the three-year-old's mouth and eyes rounded as he tried to understand what Cooper was saying. "Honestly! Let me explain." She turned to Johnny. "An experiment is trying something you've never done before."

"Oh!" Johnny's clouded expression brightened, and he eagerly shook his head. "Mommy does that a lot with dinner."

"That's right." Ashley beamed.

"Smart aleck," Cooper whispered under his breath, his gaze lingering on her for a heart-stopping moment.

Ashley found herself drowning in the dark depths of his eyes and quickly averted her head. The water in the pan was coming to a boil, the baby bottle tossing back and forth in the bubbling liquid.

"It must be ready by now," she commented as she turned off the burner.

Cooper went out to the back porch and returned with a huge pair of barbeque tongs. He quickly lifted the bottle from the hot water, setting it upright on the counter.

"Nicely done," she commented, and waited a few minutes before testing the milk's temperature. Once she was sure it wouldn't burn Scotty's tender mouth, she led the way into the living room.

Remembering what Claudia had said about rocking the baby, Ashley sat in the polished wooden rocker and gently tipped back and forth. Scotty reached for the bottle and held it himself, sucking greedily. Her eyes filled with tenderness. She brushed the fine hair from his face and cupped his ear. The room was blissfully silent as John and Cooper sat across from her.

Johnny crawled into Cooper's lap and handed him a book that he wanted read. Cooper complied, his voice and face expressive as he turned page after page, reading quietly.

Ashley found her attention drawn again and again to the man and the young boy. A surge of love filled her, so strong and overpowering that tears formed in her eyes. Hurriedly she looked away, batting her eyelashes to forestall the moisture.

Losing interest in the bottle, Scotty began chewing the nipple and watching Ashley. His round eyes held a fascinated expression as he studied her hair and reached out to grab her blond curls.

Carefully, she brushed her hair back. As she did her eyes met Cooper's. His gaze had centered on her mouth with a disturbing intensity. The power he had over her produced an aching tightness in her throat.

"You'll make a good mother someday." His voice was low and husky.

"I was just thinking the same thing about you," she murmured, then realized what she'd said and hastened to correct herself. "I mean a good father."

"I know what you meant."

"Uncle Cooper." Johnny tugged at Cooper's arm. "You're supposed to be reading."

"So I am," he agreed in a lazy drawl. "So I am."

Finished now, Scotty tossed the bottle aside, then struggled to sit up. "I know I should burp him," Ashley said, "but I'm not sure of the best way to hold him." Cooper stood. "Claudia left a baby book lying around here somewhere. Maybe it would be best to look it up."

The small party moved into Cooper's den. Ashley carried Scotty on her hip. He didn't make a sound, having apparently become accustomed to her, and that pleased her.

Cooper found the book and set it on his desk, flipping the pages. As soon as Ashley bent over next to him to read a paragraph, Scotty burped loudly.

"Well I guess that answers that, doesn't it?" she said, laughing.

"Uncle Coop, can I have a piggyback ride?" Johnny climbed onto the chair and held out his hands entreatingly.

Cooper looked unsure for a moment but agreed with a good-natured nod. "Okay, partner."

Johnny climbed onto Cooper's back, looped his legs around his uncle's waist and clung tightly with his chubby arms. "Gitty-up, horsey," he commanded happily.

Cooper grinned. "How come this is called a piggyback ride and you say 'Gitty-up, horsey'?"

Johnny chuckled. "It's an experiment."

"He's got you there." Ashley flashed him a cheeky grin.

Cooper mumbled something unintelligible and trotted into the next room.

Ashley followed, enjoying the sight of Cooper looking so relaxed. Scotty clapped his hands gleefully, and Ashley trotted after the others.

After a moment Cooper paused. "I smell something."

"Not . . ." She didn't finish.

"I think it must be."

Three pairs of eyes centered on the baby. Dramatically, Johnny plugged his nose. "Scotty has a messy diaper," he announced with the formality of a judge.

"Well, he's still a baby, and they're expected to do that sort of thing. Isn't that right, Scotty?"

Unconcerned, Scotty cooed happily, chewing on his pajama sleeve.

"Claudia showed me where everything is, this shouldn't take long."

"Ashley." Cooper stopped her, his face tight. "I think I should probably be the one to change him."

"You? Why? Are you saying it's the proper thing to do, since he's a boy?"

"I'm saying it's not a lot of fun and I've done it before, so . . ."

Unsuccessfully disguising a grateful smile, she handed him the baby. Scotty protested loudly as Cooper supported him with his hands under the baby's armpits, holding him as far away as possible.

"Call me if you need help."

Johnny led the way up the stairs, the large wooden steps almost more than he could manage. Cooper glanced down, his brow marred by a frown, then followed his nephew down the hall.

Ashley waited at the foot of the stairs, one shoe positioned on the bottom step, in case Cooper called.

"Auntie Ash." Johnny came running down the wide hallway and stopped at the top of the stairs. "Uncle Cooper says he needs you."

A tiny smile formed lines at the edges of her mouth. Somehow the words sounded exceedingly beautiful. She yearned to hear them from Cooper himself, though not exactly in this context.

She entered the bedroom and saw that his frown had deepened. He extended a hand to stop her as she entered the nursery. "I need a washcloth or something . . . you can give it to John."

Ashley ran the water in the bathroom sink until it was warm and soaked the washcloth in it. After wringing out most of the moisture, she handed it to Johnny, who ran full speed into the bedroom.

Loitering outside the room, Ashley impatiently stuck her head inside the door. "Cooper, this is silly."

"I'm almost finished," he mumbled. "This was just a little . . . more than I'm used to dealing with." His expensive silk tie was loosened, and the long sleeves of his crisp business shirt had been rolled up to his elbows.

Ashley watched from the doorway, highly amused.

"Voilà," he said, pleased with himself, as he stood Scotty up on the table.

Ashley dissolved into fits of laughter. The disposable diaper stuck out at odd angles in every direction. Had he really done this before, or had he just been trying to spare her an unpleasant task? As she was giggling, the diaper began to slide down Scotty's legs, stopping at knee level. She laughed so hard that her shoulders shook.

"Here, let me try," she insisted after a moment, swallowing her amusement as best she could.

Cooper looked almost grateful when she took the baby and laid him back onto the changing table. She did the best she could, but her efforts weren't much better than Cooper's. He was kind enough not to comment.

When she had finished, she paused to look around the

room for the first time. Claudia had told her about the bedroom Cooper had decorated for the boys, but she hadn't had a chance to take it all in earlier. Now she could stand back and marvel. The walls were painted blue, with cotton candy clouds floating past and a huge multicolored rainbow with a pot of gold.

Johnny, who had apparently noticed her appreciation, tugged at her hand. "Come look."

Obligingly, Ashley followed.

He closed the door, and flipped the light switch, casting the room into darkness. "See," he said, pointing to the ceiling.

Ashley looked up and noticed a hundred glittering stars illuminated on the huge ceiling. What had been an attractive, whimsical room with the light on became a land of fantasy with the light off.

"It's great," she murmured, her voice slightly thick. Over and over again Claudia had commented on how much Cooper loved the boys. Ashley had seen it herself. He wasn't lofty or untouchable when he was with John and Scott. His affinity for children showed he could be human and vulnerable. He was so warm and loving with the boys that it was all she could do to keep from running into his arms.

Cooper made a show of checking his wristwatch. "Isn't it about time for you boys to go to bed?"

"Can I wear your watch again?" Johnny asked eagerly.

Cooper didn't hesitate, slipping the gold band from his wrist and placing it on his godson's arm.

Ashley couldn't help but wonder at the ease with which Cooper relinquished a timepiece that must have cost thousands of dollars.

Scotty cried when she placed him in the crib. She stayed for several minutes, attempting to comfort him, but to no avail. She would just get him to lie down and tuck him under the blanket when he would pull himself upright, hold onto the bars and look at her with those pleading blue eyes. She couldn't refuse, and finally gave in and lifted him out of the crib.

"Claudia said something about rocking him to sleep."

"No problem," Cooper said with a sly grin. He left and returned a minute later with the wooden rocker from downstairs.

"Will you pray with me, Uncle Cooper?" Johnny— who was also still wide awake—requested, kneeling at his bedside.

Cooper joined the little boy on the plush navy blue carpet.

For the second time that night Ashley was emotionally stirred by the sight of this man with a child.

"God bless Mommy, Daddy and Scotty," John prayed, his head bowed reverently, his small hands folded. "And God bless Uncle Cooper, Auntie Ash and all the angels. And I love You, Jesus, and amen."

"Amen," Cooper echoed softly.

Scotty had his eyes closed as he lay securely in Ashley's arms. Gently she stood to lay him in the crib, but both eyes flew open anxiously and he struggled to sit up. With a short sigh of acquiescence, she sat back down and began to rock again. Content, Scotty watched her, but with every minute his eyes closed a little more. She wouldn't make the mistake of getting up too early a second time. Gently, she brushed the wisps of hair from his brow.

Cooper was sitting on the mattress beside Johnny, who was playing with the wristwatch, his gaze fixed on the lighted digits. Cooper pushed a variety of buttons, which delighted the boy. After a few minutes, Cooper tucked Johnny between the sheets and leaned over to kiss his brow.

"Night, night, Auntie Ash," Johnny whispered.

She blew him a kiss. Johnny pretended to catch it, then tucked his stuffed animal under his arm and rolled over.

The moment was serene and peaceful. Finally sure that Scotty was asleep, she stood and gently put him into the crib. Cooper came to stand at her side, a hand cupping her shoulder as they looked down on the sleeping baby.

Neither spoke, afraid of destroying the tranquility. When they finally stepped back, he removed his hand. Immediately, Ashley missed the warmth of his touch as they headed back downstairs.

He paused at the bottom of the stairs, a step ahead of her. He turned, halting her descent.

"Ashley," he whispered on a soft trembling breath, his look dark and troubled.

A tremor ran through her at the perplexing expression she saw in his eyes. Spontaneously she slipped her arms around his neck without even being aware of what she was doing.

"Ashley," he repeated, the husky sound a gentle caress. He crushed her to him, his arms hugging her waist as his lips sought hers. The kiss was like it had always been between them. That jolt of awareness so strong it seemed to catch them both off guard. When his mouth broke from hers, she could hear his labored breathing and the heavy thud of his heart.

He loosened his hold, bringing his hands up to her neck, weaving long fingers through her hair. His lips soothed her chin and temple, and she gloried in the tingling sensations that spread through her. She continued to lean against him, needing his support, because her legs felt weak and wobbly.

"I'm sorry about the party tonight," he murmured, and she couldn't doubt the sincerity in his voice.

"No, I'm the one who should be sorry. I said so many terrible things to you." Tipping her head back so she could gaze into his impassioned eyes, she spoke again. "I'm amazed you put up with me." Lovingly, she traced the proud line of his jaw; a finger paused to investigate the tiny cleft in his chin. Unable to resist, she kissed him there and loved the sound of his groan.

"Ashley," he warned, "please, it's hard enough keeping my hands off you."

"It is? Really? Oh, Cooper, really?"

"Yes, so don't tease."

"I think that's the nicest thing you've ever said to me."

His hand curved around her waist as he brought her down the last step. "Have you eaten dinner?"

"No, I didn't have time. You?"

"I'm starved. Maybe we can dig up something in the kitchen."

She couldn't see why they needed to look for anything. Her mother did the cooking for him, and there were bound to be leftovers. "Mom—"

"I gave her the rest of the month off," he explained before she could finish.

"Well, in that case, I vote for pizza."

"Pizza?" He glanced at her, aghast.

"All right, you choose." She placed an arm around him and smiled deeply into his dark eyes.

"Let's look." Together they rounded the corner that led to the kitchen. He checked the refrigerator and turned, shaking his head. "I don't know how we'd manage to make pizza from any of this."

"Not make," she corrected. "Order. All we need to do is phone and wait for the delivery guy."

"Amazing." He tilted his head at an inquiring angle. "Is this something you and this Webber fellow do often?" A denial rose automatically to her lips, but she successfully swallowed it back. "Sometimes. And his name is Dennis Webb."

The corner of his mouth lifted in a half smile. "Sorry." But he didn't look the least bit repentant.

"Do you want me to order?"

He straightened and leaned against the kitchen counter. "Sure, whatever you want."

"Canadian bacon, pineapple and olives."

His dark eyes widened questioningly, but he nodded his agreement.

She couldn't help laughing. "It tastes great, trust me."

"I'm afraid I'll have to."

She used the phone in the kitchen. Cooper regarded her suspiciously when she punched in the number without looking it up in the directory.

"You know the number by heart? Just how often do you do this?"

"I'm good with numbers."

After placing their order, she turned and smiled seductively. "Shall we play a game of chess while we're waiting?"

His look was faintly mocking. "I have a feeling I'd better not."

"Why?" she asked, batting her long lashes.

"If I say yes, then no wagers," he insisted.

"You take all the fun out of it," she said, and feigned a pout. "But I'll manage to whip you anyway."

He chuckled and took her hand, leading them into his den.

While she set up the game board, Cooper lit the logs in the fireplace. Within minutes flickering shadows played across the walls.

His eyes were serious as he sat down opposite her. As before, each move was measured and thought-filled. At mid-game the advantage was Ashley's. Then the doorbell chimed, interrupting their concentration.

Cooper answered and returned with a huge flat box, his look slightly abashed. "You ordered enough for a family of five," he chastised her.

"You said you were hungry," she argued, not lifting her gaze from the game. Her eyes brightened as she moved and captured his knight, lifting it from the board.

"How'd you do that?" His expression turned serious as he set the pizza on the hearth to keep warm. "I don't want to stop now. We can eat later."

"I'm hungry," she insisted slyly.

He waved her away with the flick of his hand, his attention centered on the board. "You go ahead and eat, then."

She left the room and returned a minute later with a plate and napkin, sitting on the floor in front of the fire.

The aroma of melted cheese and Canadian bacon filled the room when she lifted the lid. "Yum, this is delicious," she said after swallowing her first bite.

A frown drove three wide creases into his brow as he glanced up. "You're eating in here," he said, as if noticing her for the first time.

"I'm not supposed to?" Color invaded her face until her cheeks felt hot. She was always doing something she shouldn't where Cooper was concerned. Her actions had probably shocked him. No doubt he had never in his entire life eaten any place but on a table with a linen cloth. Pizza on the floor made her look childish and gauche.

His expression softened. "It's fine, I'm sure. It's just that I never have."

"Oh." She felt ridiculously close to tears and bowed her head. The pizza suddenly tasted like glue. She closed the lid, then set her plate aside. "The carpet is probably worth a fortune. I wouldn't want to ruin it," she said with total sincerity.

He put a finger under her chin and raised her eyes to his. "Shh," he whispered, and gently laid his mouth over hers.

His kiss had been unexpected, catching her off guard, but quickly she became a willing victim.

"You're right," Cooper murmured, then chuckled. "The pizza does taste good." He lowered himself onto the floor beside her and helped himself to a piece. "Delicious," he agreed, his eyes smiling.

"Can I have a taste?" she asked, a faint smile curving her mouth.

He held out the triangular wedge. She leaned forward and carefully took a bite.

"Thank you," she told him seriously.

With slow, deliberate movements, he placed the pizza box, plates and napkins aside, and reached for her.

Ashley moved willingly into his arms. Sliding her hands around his neck, she raised her face, eager for his attention. Her mouth was trembling in anticipation when he claimed it. A feeling of warmth wove its way through her and seemed to touch Cooper as the kiss deepened.

Somewhere, a long way in the distance, a bell began to chime. Fleetingly, she wondered why it had taken so long to hear bells when Cooper kissed her.

Abruptly, he broke away, grumbling something unintelligible. He briefly touched his mouth to her cheek before he stood and answered the phone.

Six

"It's Claudia," Cooper said, holding out the receiver.

Ashley stood, her movements awkward as the lingering effects of Cooper's kiss continued to stir her senses. "Hello."

"Ash, I'm sorry," Claudia began. "I didn't know Cooper was going to show up. Is everything okay?"

"Wonderful."

"You two aren't arguing, are you?"

"Quite the contrary," Ashley murmured, closing her eyes as Cooper cupped her cheek with his hand. A kaleidoscope of emotions rippled through her.

"Are the boys down?" Claudia inquired.

"The boys?" Ashley jerked her eyes open and straightened. "Yes, they're both asleep."

"Seth and I may be several hours yet. If everything's peaceful, then don't feel like you need to stay. I'm sure Cooper can handle things if the boys wake up. But they probably won't."

"Okay," she agreed. "I'll talk to you later. Don't worry about anything."

The sound of Claudia's soft laugh came over the line. "I don't think I need to. Take care."

"Bye," Ashley said, and replaced the phone. "That was Claudia checking on the boys," she explained unnecessarily.

"I thought it might be," he said, and nuzzled the top of her head. "Let's finish our dinner," he suggested, taking her by the hand and leading her back to the fireplace.

They ate in contented silence. His look was thoughtful as he paused once to ask, "Do you pray?"

The question was completely unexpected.

"Yes," she responded simply. "What makes you ask?"

He shrugged indifferently, and she had the impression he was far more interested than he wanted to admit. "This is the first time I've eaten pizza on the floor with a beautiful woman."

"Beautiful woman?" she teased. "Where?"

His eyes were more serious than she had ever seen them. "You," he answered, and looked away. The steady tone of his voice revealed how sincere he was.

"There are a lot of things I haven't done in my life. Prayer is one of them. Tonight when Johnny had me get down on my knees with him . . ." He let the rest of what he was going to say fade. "It felt right." He glanced back at her. "Do you kneel down, too, or is that just something for children?"

"I do on occasion, but it certainly isn't necessary."

Cooper straightened, leaning back against the ottoman. "How do you pray?"

Ashley was surprised by the directness of his question. "Whole books have been written on the subject. I don't know if I'm qualified to answer."

"I didn't ask about anyone else, only you," he countered.

"Well," she began, unsure on how best to answer him. "I don't know that anyone else does it like me."

"I've noted on several occasions that you're a free

spirit," he muttered, doing his best to hide his amusement. "Okay, let's go at this from a different angle. When do you pray?"

Answering questions was easier for her. "Mostly in the morning, but any time throughout the day. I pray for little things, parking places at the grocery store, and before I pay bills, and over the mail, and also for the big ones, like everyone in my life staying healthy and happy."

"Why mostly in the morning?" He regarded her steadily.

"That's when I do my devotions," she explained patiently.

"What are devotions?"

"Bible reading and praying," she told him. "My private time with the Lord. My day goes better when I've had a chance to discuss things with Jesus."

"You talk to Him as if He were a regular person?"

"He is," she said, more forcefully than she intended.

He paused and appeared to consider her words thoughtfully. "Do you speak to Him conversationally, then?"

"Yes and no."

"You don't like talking about this, do you?"

"It isn't that," she tried to explain, a soft catch in her voice. "If I tell you . . . I guess I'm afraid you'll think it's silly."

"I won't." The wealth of tenderness in his voice assured her he wouldn't.

"Usually I set aside a formal time for reading my Bible, other devotional books and praying. After I do my Bible reading, I get down on my knees, close my eyes and picture myself on a beautiful beach." She glanced up hesitantly, and Cooper nodded. The warmth in his look seemed to caress her, and she continued. "The scene is perfectly set in my mind. The waves are crashing against the sandy shore and easing back into the sea. I envision the tiny bubbles popping against the sand as the water ebbs out. This is where I meet Christ."

"Does He talk to you?"

"Not with words." She looked away uneasily. "I don't know how to explain this part. I know He hears me, and I know He answers my prayers. I see the evidence of that every day. But as for Him verbally speaking to me, I'd have to say no, though I hear His voice in other ways."

"I don't understand."

"I'm not sure I can explain, I just *do*."

Cooper seemed to accept that. "Then all you do is talk. You make it sound too easy." He seemed unsure, and she hastened to arrest his doubts.

"No, I spend part of the time thanking Him or . . . praising Him would be a better description, I guess. Another part is spent going over the previous day and asking His forgiveness for any wrongs I've done."

"That shouldn't take a lot of time," he teased.

"Longer than I care to admit," she informed him sheepishly and mentally added that the time had increased since she'd been seeing Cooper. "I also keep a list of requests that I pray about regularly and go down each one."

"Am I on your list?" The question was asked so softly that she wasn't sure he'd even spoken.

"Yes," she answered. "I pray for you every day," she admitted, her voice gaining intensity. She didn't add that all the people she loved were on her list. To avoid other questions she continued speaking. "For a while I wrote out my prayers. That was years ago, and it became a journal of God's faithfulness. But I can't write as fast as I think, so I found that often I'd lose my train of thought. But I've saved those journals and sometimes read over them. When I do, I'm amazed again at God's goodness to me."

A baby's frantic cry broke into their conversation. "Scotty," Ashley said, bounding to her feet. "I'll go see what's wrong."

Scotty was standing in the crib, holding onto the sides. His crying grew louder and more desperate as she hurried into the room.

"What's wrong, Scotty?" she asked soothingly. Soft light from the hallway illuminated the dark recess of the bedroom. She lifted him out of the crib and hugged him close. Checking his diaper, she noted that he didn't seem to be wet. Probably he'd been frightened by a nightmare. Settling him in her arms, she sat in the rocking chair and rocked until she was sure he was back to sleep. With a kiss on the top of his head, she placed him back in his crib.

Cooper was waiting for her at the bottom of the stairs.

"He's asleep again," she whispered.

"I made coffee, would you like a cup?"

She smiled her appreciation. He curved an arm around her narrow waist, bringing her close to his side as he led her back into the den. A silver tea service was set on his desk. She saw that the remains of their dinner had been cleared away, along with their chess game. Biting into her bottom lip to contain her amusement, she decided not to comment on what a neat-freak he was.

He poured the steaming liquid into the china cups,

then offered her one. Her hand shook momentarily as she accepted it. Dainty pieces of delicate china made her nervous, and she would have much preferred a ceramic mug.

"This set is lovely," she said, holding the cup in one hand. Tiny pink rosebuds, faded with age, decorated the teacup. She balanced the matching saucer in the palm of her other hand.

"It was my grandmother's," he said proudly. "There are only a few of the original pieces left."

"Oh." Her index finger tightened around the porcelain handle. In her nervousness, her hand wobbled and the boiling hot coffee sloshed over the side onto her hand and her lap, immediately soaking through her thin corduroy jeans. With a gasp of pain, she jumped to her feet. The saucer flew out of her lap and smashed against the leg of the desk, shattering into a thousand pieces.

"Ashley, are you all right?" Cooper bounded to his feet beside her.

Stunned, she couldn't move, her eyes fixed on the broken china as despair filled her. "I'm so sorry," she mumbled. Her voice cracked, and she swallowed past the huge lump building in her throat.

"Forget the china," he said, and took the teacup out of her hand. "It doesn't matter, none of it matters."

"It does matter!" she cried, her voice wobbling uncontrollably. "It matters very much."

"You've got to get that hand in ice water. What about your leg? Is it badly burned?" He tugged at her elbow, almost dragging her into the kitchen. He brought her to the sink and stuck her hand under the cold water. She looked down to see an angry red patch on the back of her left hand, where the coffee had spilled. Funny, she didn't feel any pain. Nothing. Only a horrible deep regret.

"Cooper, please, listen to me. I'm so sorry . . . your grandmother's china is ruined because of me."

"Keep that hand under the water," he said, ignoring her words. Then he went to get ice from the automatic dispenser on the refrigerator door.

Ashley looked away rather than face him. She heard the water splash as he dumped the ice into the sink.

"What about your leg?" he demanded.

"It's fine." She tilted her chin upward and closed her eyes to forestall the tears. The burns didn't hurt; if anything, her hand was growing numb with cold. How could she have been so stupid? His grandmother's china . . . only a few pieces left. His earlier words echoed in her ears until they were nearly deafening.

"Ashley," he whispered, a hand on her shoulder. "Are you all right? You've gone pale. Is the pain very bad? Should I take you to a doctor?"

Talking was impossible, because her throat felt raw and painful, so she shook her head. "Your grandmother's china," she said at last, her voice barely above a tortured whisper.

"Would you quit acting like it's some great tragedy? You've been burned, and that's far more important than some stupid china."

"Do you know what my mother uses for fancy dinners?" she asked in a hoarse voice, then didn't wait for him to answer. "Dishes she picked up at the grocery store. With every ten dollar purchase she could buy another plate at a discount price."

"What has that go to do with anything?" he demanded irritably.

"Nothing. Everything. I swear I'll replace the saucer. I'll contact an antique dealer, I promise . . ."

"Ashley, stop." His firm hands squeezed her shoulders. "Stop right now. I don't care about a stupid saucer. But I do care about you." His grip tightened. "The saucer means nothing. Nothing," he repeated. "Do you understand?"

Her throat muscles had constricted so that she couldn't speak. Miserably, she hung her head, and her soft curls fell forward, wreathing her face.

She started to tremble, and with a muted groan Cooper hauled her into his arms.

"Honey, it doesn't matter. Please believe me when I tell you that."

She held onto him hard, because only the warmth of his touch was capable of easing the cold that pierced her heart. A lone tear squeezed past her lashes. She loved Cooper Masters so much it had become a physical pain. Never before had she realized how wrong she was for him. He needed someone who . . .

She wasn't allowed to complete the thought as Cooper's hand touched her face, turning her to meet his gaze. Her tortured eyes tried to avoid him, but he held her steady.

"Ashley, look at me." He sounded gruff, impatient.

But she was determined, and she shook herself loose, then swayed against him, her fingers spread against his shirt. He found her lips and kissed her with a desperation she hadn't experienced from him. It was as if he needed to confirm what he was saying, to comfort her, reassure her.

She knew she shouldn't accept any of it. But one minute in Cooper's arms and it didn't matter. All she could do was feel.

His hands roamed her back as he buried his face in the hair at the side of her face. "Let's sit down."

He took her into the living room and set her down in the soft comfort of the large sofa. Next he opened the drapes and revealed the same view of Puget Sound that they'd enjoyed on Thanksgiving Day, when they'd walked on his property in the rain.

Hands in his pockets, he paused to admire the beauty. "Sometimes in the evening I sit here, staring into the sky, counting the stars." He spoke absently, standing at the far corner of the window, gazing into the still night. "Looking at all that magnificence makes me feel small and very insignificant. One man, alone." His back was to her. "It's times like this that make me regret not having a wife and family. I've worked hard, and what do I have to show for it? An expensive home and no one to share it with." He stopped and turned, their eyes meeting. For a breathless moment they stared at one another. Then he dropped his gaze and turned slowly back to the window.

Confused for a moment, she watched as he turned away from her, as if trying to block her out of his mind. His action troubled her. He stood alone, across the room, a solitary figure silhouetted against the night. What was he telling her? She didn't understand, but she did realize that he had revealed a part of himself others didn't see.

Unfolding her long legs from the sofa, she joined him at the window. Standing at his side, she slipped an arm around his waist as if she'd done it a thousand times.

He smiled at her then, and she couldn't remember ever

seeing anything transform a face more. His dark eyes seemed to spark with something she couldn't define. Happiness? Contentment? Pleasure? His smile widened as he looped his arm over her shoulders, and then he brushed her temple with a light kiss.

"Do you have your Christmas tree up yet?"

"No," she whispered, afraid talking normally would destroy the wonderful mood. "I thought I'd put it up tomorrow."

"Would you like some help?"

The offer shocked her. "I'd . . . I'd love some."

"What time?"

"Probably afternoon." Her sigh was filled with a sense of dread. "I've got to get some shopping done. There are only a few days left, and I've hardly started."

"Me, either, and I still need to get something for the boys."

"I'm afraid I haven't had the chance to shop. The last days of school were so hectic. I hate leaving everything to the last minute like this."

"Why don't we make a day of it?" he suggested. "I'll pick you up, say around ten. We can do the shopping, go for lunch and decorate your tree afterward."

"That sounds wonderful. I'd like that. I'd like it very much."

"And, Ashley . . ." Cooper said, looking away uncomfortably.

"Yes?"

"I was thinking about buying myself a pair of cowboy boots and wanted to ask your advice about the best place to go."

"I know just the store, in the Pavilion near Southcenter. But be warned, they're expensive." As soon as the words were out, she regretted them. Cooper didn't need to worry about money.

He chuckled and gave her a tiny squeeze. "I wish other people were as reluctant to spend my money."

"We'll see how reluctant I am tomorrow," she murmured with a small laugh.

Seven

Ashley changed clothes three times before the doorbell chimed, announcing Cooper's arrival. Her final choice had been a soft gray wool skirt and a white bouclé-knit sweater. The outfit, with knee-high black leather boots, was one she usually reserved for church, but she wanted everything to be perfect for Cooper.

A warm smile lit up her face as she opened the door. "Morning, you're right on . . ." She didn't finish; the words died on her lips. Cooper in jeans! Levis so new and stiff they looked as if they would stand up on their own. Her lashes fluttered downward to disguise her shock.

"Morning. You look as beautiful as ever."

"Thank you," she whispered, somewhat bewildered. "Do you want a cup of coffee or something before we go?"

"No, I think we'd better get started before the crowds get too bad."

She lounged back in her seat, content to let him drive. He flipped a switch, and immediately the interior was filled with classical music. She savored the gentle sounds of the string section and glanced up, surprised when the music abruptly changed to a top forty station.

"Why'd you do that?" she asked, her blue gaze sweeping toward him, searching his profile.

"I thought this would probably be more to your liking." His gaze remained on the freeway, the traffic surprisingly heavy for early morning.

"It's not," she murmured, a little of her earlier happiness dissipating with the thought that Cooper assumed she preferred more popular music to the classics. *But don't you?* her mind countered.

They took the exit for Southcenter, a huge shopping complex south of Seattle, but didn't stop there. The area's largest toy store was situated nearby, and they had decided earlier that it would be the best place to start.

The parking lot was already full, so Cooper had to drive around a couple of times before locating a spot at the far end.

His hand cupped her elbow as they hurried inside. Only a few shopping carts were left, and she glanced around, doing her best to squelch a growing sense of panic. The store had barely opened, and already there was hardly room to move through the aisles.

"My goodness," she murmured impatiently. They were forced to wait to move past the throng of shoppers entering the first aisle. "Do you want to come back later?" she asked, glancing at him anxiously.

"I don't think it's going to get any better," he muttered darkly.

"I don't think it will, either. Maybe we should decide now what we want to buy the boys. That would at least streamline the process. We're going together, aren't we?" At Cooper's questioning glance, she added, "I mean, we'll split the cost."

"I'll pay," he insisted.

"Cooper," she groaned. "Either we divide the cost or forget it."

His mouth thinned slightly. "All right, I should know better. You and that pride of yours."

He looked as if he wanted to add something more, but the crowd moved, and she pushed the cart forward.

"Okay, what should we get Johnny?" Her eyes followed the floor-to-ceiling display of computer games. On the other side of the aisle were more traditional games and puzzles.

"I've thought of something perfect," Cooper announced proudly. "I'm sure you'll agree."

"What?"

"A computer chess game. I saw one advertised the other day."

"He's too young for that," Ashley declared. She hated to stifle Cooper's enthusiasm, but Johnny wasn't interested in chess.

"He's not," Cooper shot back. "I've been teaching him a few moves. It's the perfect gift—educational, too."

"Good," she said emphatically. "Then you get him that, but I want to buy him something he'll enjoy."

Cooper's soft chuckle caught her unaware. "What's so funny?" she asked.

"You." He paused and looked around before lightly kissing her cheek. "I can't think of a thing in the world that you and I will ever agree on. Our tastes are too different." His gaze seemed to be fixed on her softly parted lips. "Do men often have to restrain themselves from kissing you?"

A happy light shimmered from her deep blue eyes. "Hundreds," she teased. Immediately she realized it had been the wrong thing to say. She could almost visualize the wall that was going up between them.

He straightened and pretended an interest in one of the displays.

"Cooper," she whispered, and laid her hand across his forearm. "That was a dumb joke."

"I imagine it was closer to the truth than you realize."

"Oh, hardly," she denied with a light laugh.

An hour and a half later, their packages stored in the booth beside them, Ashley exhaled a long sigh.

"Coffee," Cooper told the waitress, who quickly returned and filled their mugs.

"I can't remember a time when I needed this more," Ashley murmured and took an appreciative sip.

"Me, either. Could you believe that checkout line?"

"But Johnny's going to love his fire truck and hat."

"And his computer chess game."

"Of course," she agreed, grinning.

"At least we agreed on Scotty's gift. That wasn't so difficult, was it?"

Ashley's gaze skipped from Cooper to the stuffed animal beside him, and she burst into peals of laughter. "Oh, Cooper, if only your friends could see you now with that gorilla next to you."

"Yes, I guess that would be cause for amusement."

Digging through her purse, Ashley brought out her Bible, flipping through the worn pages.

"What are you doing now?" he asked in a hushed whisper.

"Don't worry, I'm not going to stand on the seat and start a crusade. I want to find something."

"What?"

"A verse." She paused, a finger marking the place. "Here it is. First Peter 1:4."

"Honestly, you've got to be the only woman in the world who whips out her Bible in a restaurant."

Unaffected by his teasing tone, she laid the book open on the tabletop, turned it sideways and pointed to the passage she wanted him to read. "After what we just went through, I decided I wanted to be sure heaven has reserved seating. It does, look." Aloud she read a portion of the text. "'To obtain an inheritance which is reserved in heaven for you.'"

A hint of a smile quivered at the edges of his mouth. "You're serious, aren't you?"

"Sure I am. I've seen pictures of riots that looked more organized than that mess we were in."

He laughed loudly then, attracting the curious glances of others. "Ashley Robbins, I find you delightful."

Pleased, she beamed and placed the small Bible back inside her purse.

"Where do you want to go next?" he asked as he glanced at his wristwatch.

"Do you need to be back for something?"

He raised his eyes to meet hers. "No," he said, and shook his head to emphasize his denial.

"If you feel like you could brave the madding crowd a second time, we could tackle the mall."

He looked unsure for a moment. She couldn't blame him. The thought of facing thousands of last-minute shoppers wasn't an appealing one, but she did still have gifts to buy—and he wanted those boots.

"Sure, why not?" he agreed.

Ashley could think of forty thousand hectic reasons

why not, but she didn't voice a single one, content simply being with Cooper.

"However, I hope you don't object if we store Tarzan's friend in the trunk of the car," he added, and glanced wryly at the stuffed animal.

The crowds at the mall proved to be even worse than the toy store, but a couple of hours later, their arms loaded with packages, they finally retreated to the car.

Even Cooper, who was normally so calm and reserved, looked a bit ashen after fighting the chaos. They hadn't even stopped for lunch, eating caramel apples instead as they walked from one end of the mall to the other.

"Do you think Claudia will like the necklace?" he asked as he joined her in the front seat and inserted the key into the ignition.

"Of course." Ashley had picked out the turquoise necklace and knew her friend would love it, but he was still skeptical. "Trust me."

"There's something about that phrase that makes me nervous."

"But you didn't buy two. Now I'm curious," she ventured, not paying attention to what he'd said.

"Two? Two what?"

"Necklaces." She gave him an impatient look. Sometimes they seemed to be speaking at complete cross purposes.

"Do you think Claudia would want two?" He gave her a curious glance.

"Of course not," she said with a sigh. "But you always buy me the same thing as Claudia." She didn't add that it had been perfume for the past three Christmases.

"Not this year."

"Really?" Her interest piqued, she asked, "What are you getting me?"

"Like John and Scott, you'll have to wait until Christmas morning."

She was more pleased than she dared show. Not that she would be forced to wait until Christmas, but that she'd moved beyond the same safe category as Claudia. It thrilled her to know that their relationship had evolved to the point that he wanted to get her something different this year.

Cooper played with the radio until he found some Christmas music.

Again Ashley could feel the comforting music float around her, soothing her tattered nerves. "Doesn't that make you want to sing?"

"Every time you say that we have a storm," he complained.

"Killjoy," she muttered under her breath.

A large hand reached over and squeezed hers. "Ready to decorate the tree?"

"More than ready," she agreed. Much of her shopping remained to be done, but she'd promised Claudia that they would head out early Monday morning so there would be plenty of time to finish.

The remainder of the short drive to her apartment was accomplished in a companionable silence. Her mind wandered to the first time Cooper had asked her to dinner after she'd paid off the loan. At the time she would have doubted she could ever sit at his side without being nervous. Now she felt relaxed, content.

Although nothing had ever been openly stated, their relationship had come a long way in the past couple of months. She could only pray that this budding rapport would continue after Claudia, Seth and the boys returned to Alaska.

Ever the gentleman, Cooper took the apartment key away from her and unlocked the door. Men didn't usually do that sort of thing for her, but then again, she probably wouldn't have let anyone but Cooper.

"I put the tree on the lanai until it was time to decorate," she told him, and took his coat, hanging it with hers in the closet. When she turned around Cooper was helping himself to a handful of popcorn.

"I wouldn't eat that if I were you, it's a week old."

He dropped the kernels back into the bowl and wrinkled his nose.

"Quit giving me funny looks like I'm a terrible housekeeper. You're supposed to leave the popcorn out to get stale. It strings easier that way."

"Strings?"

"For the tree."

"Of course, for the tree," he echoed.

She had the uneasy sensation that he didn't know what she meant. Lightly, she shrugged her shoulders. He would learn soon enough.

"Are you hungry?" she asked on her way into the kitchen. "I can make us pastrami sandwiches with dill pickles and potato chips."

"That sounds good, except I'll have my potato chips on the side."

"Cute," she murmured, sticking her head around the corner.

"With you I never know," he complained with a full smile.

While she made lunch, Cooper brought the Christmas tree inside. Since it was already in the stand, all he had to do was find a place to set it in the living room. When he'd finished he joined her in the compact kitchen.

Working contentedly with her back to him, she hummed softly and cut thin slices of pickle.

"You can have one of the chocolates I bought if you like," she told him, as she spread a thick layer of mustard across the bread.

"I thought you said chocolates weren't meant to be shared."

She laughed softly. "I was only teasing."

"Ashley . . ."

Just the way he spoke her name caused her to pause and turn around.

"I think we should do this before we eat."

"Do what?" Her heart was chugging like a locomotive at the look he was giving her.

"This." He took the knife out of her hand and laid it on the counter. His gaze centered on her mouth.

She gave a soft welcoming moan as his lips fit over hers. All day she'd yearned for his touch. It was torture to be so close to him and maintain the friendly facade, when in her heart all she wanted was to be held and loved by him.

When he dragged his mouth from hers, she knew he felt as unsatisfied as she did. Kissing was quickly becoming insufficient to satisfy either of them. His hands roamed possessively over her back, arching her closer. Again his mouth dipped to drink from the sweetness of hers. With a shuddering breath he released her.

Sensation after sensation swirled through her. These feelings he stirred within her were what God had intended her to feel toward the man she loved, and she couldn't doubt the rightness of them. But what was *he* feeling? Certainly he wasn't immune to all this.

His smile was gentle when he asked, "Did you say something about lunch?"

"Lunch," she repeated like a robot, then lightly shook her head, irritated that she was reacting like a lovesick teenager. No, she mused, Cooper couldn't help but be aware of the powerful physical attraction between them. He was simply much more in control of himself than she was.

A few minutes later she carried their meal into the living room on a tray. He was sorting through her ornaments and looked up. A frown was creasing his brow.

"What's wrong?" she asked, setting their plates on the coffee table and glancing over at him.

"There's something written across these glass ornaments."

"I know," she answered simply.

"But what is it and why?"

A soft smile touched her mouth as she lifted half of her sandwich and prepared to take the first bite. "Remember how I mentioned that I dated the man who sold me Milligan a couple of times?"

"I remember."

The tightness in his voice sent her searching gaze to him a second time. "Unfortunately, Jim was decidedly not a Christian. We saw one another a couple of times in December, and he couldn't understand why I didn't want to do certain things."

"What things?" Cooper's tone had taken on an arctic chill.

"It doesn't matter," she said, and smiled, dismissing his curiosity. The past was over, and she didn't want to review it with him. "But one thing I *am* grateful for is the fact Jim told me the Christmas tree is a pagan custom. He found it interesting that I professed this deep faith in Christ yet chose to allow a pagan ritual to desecrate my home." She set the sandwich aside and knelt beside Cooper on the carpet. "You know, he's right. I was shocked, so I decided to make my Christmas tree Christ centered."

"But how?"

"It wasn't that difficult. The tree is an evergreen, constant, never changing, just as my faith in Christ is meant to be. And Christ died upon a tree. The lights were the easiest part. Jesus asks that each one of us be the light of the world. But when it came to the ornaments, I had to be a little inventive, so I took glitter glue—"

"Glitter glue?" he interrupted.

"Glue that has glitter already in it. It's much easier to write out the fruits of the Holy Spirit that way."

"Hold on, you've lost me."

"Here." She stood and retrieved her Bible from the oak end table. Flipping the pages, she located the verses she wanted. "Paul wrote in his epistle to the Galatians about the fruits of the Christian life."

"Love, joy, peace," he read from each of the pink glass ornaments. "I get it now."

"Exactly," she stated excitedly.

"Clever girl." His thick brows arched expressively.

"Thank you."

"I'm very curious now about how you tie in the popcorn."

"Yes, well . . ." Frantically, her mind searched for a plausible reason. She hadn't thought about the decorative strings she added each year.

"I've got it," he said. "White and spotless like the Christ child."

"Very good," she congratulated him.

There was a disconcerted look in his eyes as they met hers. "Your commitment to Christ is important to you, isn't it?"

"Vital," she confirmed. "One's relationship with God is a personal thing. But Christ is the most important person in my life. He has been for several years."

"You stopped seeing Madigan because he didn't have the same belief system as you."

"More or less. In some ways we hit it off immediately. I liked Jim, I still do. But our relationship was headed for a dead end, so I cut it off before either one of us got serious."

"Because he didn't believe the same way as you? Isn't that narrow minded?"

"To me it isn't, and that wasn't the only reason. Cooper . . ." She paused and held her breath when she saw his troubled look. "Why all the questions? Do you think I'm wrong in the way I believe?"

"It doesn't matter what I think."

"Of course, it matters." *Because you do,* she added silently.

He rose and walked to the far side of the room. "I don't believe the same way you do. Oh, I acknowledge there's a God. I couldn't look at the heavens and examine our world and not believe in a Supreme Being. I accept that Christ was born, but I never have understood salvation, justification and all the rest of it. Everyone talks about the free gift, but—"

A loud knock on her door interrupted him.

She glanced at him and shrugged. She wasn't expecting anyone. She got to her feet, crossed the room and checked the peephole.

"It's Webb," she told Cooper before opening the door.

"Hello, Sweet Thing. How's your day been?" He sauntered into the room whistling "White Christmas" and paused long enough to brush his lips across her cheek. The song died on his lips when he spotted Cooper.

"Webb," Ashley said stiffly, folding her hands tightly together in front of her. "This is Cooper Masters. I believe I've mentioned him."

She watched as the two men exchanged handshakes. "Cooper, this is Dennis Webb."

Ashley wanted to shout at her friend. Webb couldn't have picked a worse time to pop in for one of his spontaneous visits.

"No, I can't say that I recall you mentioning him," Webb announced as he glanced back to Ashley.

She seethed silently and somehow managed a weak smile.

"I can't say the same about you," Cooper muttered in the stiff, formal tone she'd come to hate.

"Would you like to sit down, Webb?" She motioned toward the sofa and glared at him, desperately hoping he would get the message and leave.

"Thanks." He plopped down on the couch and crossed

his legs. "You missed a great party last night. Hardly seemed right without you there, Ash. Next time I won't take no for an answer."

Cooper lowered himself onto the far end of the sofa. His back remained rigid.

"I'll make coffee," Ashley volunteered as she left the room, thinking the atmosphere back there was so thick she could taste it.

"I'll see if I can help in the kitchen," she heard Webb say, and a second later he was at her side.

"Who is this guy?" he hissed.

"What do you mean?" she demanded in a hushed whisper, then didn't wait for an answer. "He's my best friend's uncle, and what do you mean I've never mentioned him? I talk about him all the time."

"You haven't," Webb insisted. "Unless he's the one you played chess with and lost?"

"That's him." Her fingers refused to work properly, and coffee grounds spilled across the counter. "Darn, darn, darn."

"I don't care who he is, if he calls me Webber one more time, I'm going to punch him."

"Webb," she expelled her breath and noticed that Cooper was watching her intently from the doorway. She stopped talking and forced a beguiling smile onto her face. Her teeth were clenched so tight her jaw hurt. "Can't you see it's not a good time?" she hissed beneath her breath.

"Are you saying you want me to leave?"

"Yes." She nearly shouted the one word.

Cooper stepped closer. "Is everything all right, Ashley?" he asked in a formal tone, but his burning gaze was focused on Webb.

The look was searing. She had never seen such disapproval illuminated so clearly on anyone's features. Cooper's mouth was pinched, his eyes narrowed. For a crazy second she wanted to laugh. The two men were eyeing one another like bears who had encroached on each other's territory.

"I'm fine. Webb was just saying that he has to go."

"I do?" he said. "Oh, yes, I guess I do." He walked out of the kitchen with Ashley on his heels. "I'll talk to you soon," he told her, his gaze full of meaning.

"Right." She held open the door for him. "Sorry you have to leave so soon."

The look Webb gave her nearly sent her into peals of laughter. "I'll phone you soon," she promised.

"Nice meeting you, Cooper," Webb said graciously. "Now that I recall, Ash *has* mentioned you. I understand you play a mean game of chess."

"I play," Cooper admitted with a look of indifference.

"I dabble in the game myself," Webb said, tossing Ashley a teasing glance.

"See you later, Webb," she said firmly, and closed the door. The lock clicked shut, and she paused, her eyes closed, and released a long, slow breath.

"Nice fellow, Webber," Cooper said from behind her.

"He's a friend." She had to be certain Cooper understood that her relationship with Webb didn't go any further than that of congenial co-workers.

"I imagine he's the kind of Christian who fits right into that cozy picture you have built in your mind." His tone was almost harsh.

Ashley did her best to ignore it. "Webb's a wonderful Christian man."

"You probably should marry someone like him," he stated with a sharp edge. His gaze narrowed on her. It wasn't difficult to tell that he was angry, but she didn't know why.

"You're upset, aren't you?" she asked, confronting him. Her back was against the door, her hands clenched at her side.

Cooper's long strides carried him to the far side of the room. He tried to ram his hands in his pockets, apparently forgetting he was wearing jeans. That seemed to irritate him all the more.

"We never did eat our lunch," she said shakily.

He glared at the thick sandwich and then back to her. "I'm not hungry."

"Let's decorate the tree, then." She hugged her middle to ward off the cold she felt beginning to surround her. Cooper was freezing her out, and she didn't know what to say or do to prevent him from doing that.

He stared at her blankly, as if he hadn't heard a word she'd said. Helplessly, she watched as he opened the closet door and took out his coat.

"Cooper?" she whispered, but he didn't hesitate, slipping his arms into the sleeves and starting on the buttons.

She was still standing in front of the door, and she decided she wouldn't move, wouldn't let him walk out as if she wasn't there. What had happened? Everything had been so beautiful last night and today, and now, for no apparent reason, he was pushing her away. She felt as if their relationship had taken a giant step backward.

His drawn expression didn't alter as he came to stand

directly in front of her. His hand brushed a blond curl off her face and lingered a second to trace a finger across her cheek.

"You really should marry someone like Webber."

"No." The sound was barely audible. "I won't." How could she marry Webb when she loved Cooper?

"Funny how we never seem to do the things we should," he muttered cryptically.

"Cooper?" Her voice throbbed with a feeling she couldn't identify. Agony? Need? Desperation? "What's wrong?" she tried again.

"Other than the fact you and I are as different as night and day?"

"We've always been different, why should it matter now?"

"I don't know," he told her honestly.

"I had a wonderful time today," she whispered, and hung her head to avoid his searching look. Her lashes fluttered wearily. She knew she was losing, but not why. "I don't want it to end like this. I didn't know Webb was coming."

"It isn't Webber," Cooper admitted harshly. "It's everything." An ominous silence followed his announcement. "I like to pretend with you."

"Pretend?" She lifted her gaze, uncertain of what he was admitting.

"You're warm and alive, and you make me yearn for things that were never meant to be."

"Now you're talking in riddles. And I hate riddles, because I can never understand them. I don't understand *you*."

"No," he murmured, and rubbed a hand across his face. "I don't suppose that's possible."

Ashley didn't know what directed her, perhaps instinct. Of their own volition her arms slipped around his neck. At first he held himself stiff and unyielding against her, but she refused to be deterred. Her exploring fingers toyed with the dark hair at the back of his head. She applied a gentle pressure, urging his mouth to hers. His resistance grew stronger, forcing her to stand on her tiptoes and mold herself to him. Gradually, she eased her mouth over his.

He didn't want her kiss, but she could feel the part of him that unwillingly reached out to her.

Abruptly he broke the contact and pulled himself away. Both hands cupped her face, tilting it up at an angle. A smoldering light of something she couldn't decipher burned in his eyes.

"Ashley." The husky tone of his voice betrayed his desire, yet she marveled at his control.

"Hmm?" she answered with a contented whisper.

"Next time I start acting like a jerk, promise me you'll bring me out of my ill temper just like this."

She gave a glad cry and kissed him again. "I promise," she said after a long while.

Eight

"Was Cooper with you Saturday?" Claudia asked as she laid the menu aside.

Most of Monday morning and half the afternoon had been spent finishing up their Christmas shopping. For the past two hours Ashley had dragged Claudia to every antiques store she could find.

Her index finger made a lazy circle around the rim of her water glass. "What makes you ask?" A peculiar pain knotted her stomach. It happened every time she suspected Cooper didn't want anyone to know they were seeing one another. She had spent the entire day with him. After decorating the tree they'd gone out to dinner and a movie. It was midnight before he kissed her good night. Yet he hadn't told Claudia anything.

"What makes me ask?" Claudia repeated incredulously. "You mean besides the fact that he mysteriously disappeared for the entire day? Then he saunters in about midnight with a sheepish look. Gets up early Sunday morning whistling. Cooper. Whistling. He even went to church with us again, which surprised both Seth and me."

"What makes you think I had anything to do with it?"

"What is it with you two? You'd think you were ashamed to be seen with one another."

"You're being ridiculous."

"I'm not. Look at how elusive you're being. Were you or were you not with Cooper Saturday?"

"Yes, I was with him."

"Just part of the time?"

"No," she admitted and breathed in heavily. "All day."

"Ash?" Claudia hesitated as if searching for the right words. "I know you're probably going to say this is none of my business, but I've never seen you act like this."

"Act like what?" she returned defensively.

"All our lives you were the fearless one. There didn't seem to be anything you weren't willing to try. I've never seen you so reticent."

Ashley shrugged one shoulder slightly.

"You're in love with Cooper, aren't you?"

A small smile played over Ashley's mouth. "Yes." It felt good to finally verbalize her feelings. "Very much."

Claudia's eyes glinted with an inner glow of happiness. "Who would ever have guessed you'd fall in love with Cooper?"

"I don't know. Probably no one."

"Has he told you he loves you yet?" Claudia asked, obviously doing her best to contain her excitement.

"No, but then I'm not exactly an 'uptown girl,' am I?" The words slipped out more flippantly than she'd intended.

"Ashley," Claudia snapped, "I can't believe you'd say something like that. You're closer to me than any sister could ever—"

"It's not you," Ashley interrupted, lowering her gaze to her half-full water glass. "Cooper's ashamed to be seen with me."

"That's pure nonsense," Claudia insisted.

"I wish it was," Ashley said in a serious tone.

Any additional discussion was interrupted by the waitress, who arrived to take their order.

"Promise me one thing," Claudia asked as soon as the woman was gone, her eyes pleading.

"What?"

"That you won't drag me to any more antiques shops. Cooper doesn't care about that saucer, so I don't see why you should."

"But I do," Ashley said forcefully. "I'm going to replace it if I have to look for the rest of my life."

"Honestly, Ash, it's not that big a deal. Cooper would feel terrible if he knew the trouble you're putting yourself through."

"Don't you dare tell him."

Their Cobb salads arrived, and the flow of conversation came to a halt as they began to eat.

"You're planning to come with us Wednesday, aren't you?" Claudia asked, looking up from her salad.

"Is that the day you're taking the boys to Seattle Center Enchanted Forest?" Every Christmas the Food Circus inside the Center created a fantasyland for young children. The large open area was filled with tall trees and a train that enthralled the youngsters. Clowns performed and handed out balloons. "That's Christmas Eve day."

"Brilliant deduction," Claudia teased. "Cooper's going," she added, as if Ashley needed an inducement.

Ashley's blond curls bounced as she laughed. "I'd be excited about it even if Cooper wasn't coming along. We're going to have a wonderful time. The boys will love it."

"Cooper's been asking Seth a lot of questions," Claudia announced unexpectedly.

"Questions? About what?"

"The Bible." Claudia placed her fork beside her plate. "They spent almost the entire afternoon on Sunday discussing things. When I talked to Seth about it later, he told me that he felt inadequate because some of Cooper's questions were so complicated. Personally, I don't know where Cooper stands with the Lord, but he seems to be having a difficult time with some of the basic concepts." She paused, then added, "He can't seem to accept that salvation is not something we can earn with donations or good works."

"I can understand that," Ashley defended him. "Cooper has worked hard all his life. Nothing's been free. I can see that the concept would be more difficult for him to accept than for others."

Claudia lounged back, a smile twinkling in her eyes. "You really *do* love him, don't you?"

"I'll tell you something else that'll shock you." Ashley nervously smoothed her pant leg. "I've loved him from the time I was sixteen. It's just been . . . harder to hide lately."

Claudia's expression softened knowingly. "I think I guessed how you felt almost as soon as I saw the two of you together at the airport when Seth and I arrived with the boys. And then, when I thought back, I realized how long it had been going on, at least for you."

"How did you know?" Ashley's eyes narrowed thoughtfully.

"From the time we were teens, it was you who defended Cooper when he did something to irritate me. You were always ready to leap to his defense."

"Was I so obvious?"

"Not at all," Claudia assured her. "Now, are you ready for something else?" She didn't wait for a response. "Cooper's been in love with you since before I married Seth."

"That I don't believe," Ashley argued. She picked up her fork and put it back down twice before finally setting it aside.

"Think about it," Claudia challenged, a determined lift to her chin. "Seth asked me to marry him, and I was so undecided. I knew I loved him, but moving to Alaska, leaving school and all my dreams of becoming a doctor, made the decision difficult. You were telling me to follow my heart, and at the same time Cooper was unconditionally opposed to the whole idea."

"I remember how miserable you were."

"I was more than miserable. I was at the airport wanting to die, I loved him so much, yet I felt it would never work for Seth and me. You told me if I loved him to go after him." Her blue eyes glimmered with the memory, and a soft smile played at the corners of her mouth. "Still, I was undecided, and I looked to Cooper, wanting him to make up my mind for me. It's funny how clearly I can recall that scene now. Cooper glanced from me to you. At the time I didn't recognize the look in his eyes, but I do now. After so many bitter arguments, Cooper looked at you and told me the decision was mine."

"I think you've blown the whole thing out of proportion." Ashley felt safer in denying what her friend thought than placing any faith in it.

"Don't you see?" Claudia persisted. "Cooper changed

his mind because, for the first time in his life, he knew what it was to be in love with someone."

"I wish it were true," Ashley murmured sadly, "but if he felt that way four years ago, why didn't he make an effort to go out with me?"

A wayward lock of auburn hair fell across Claudia's cheek. "Knowing Cooper, that isn't so difficult to understand."

"I wish I could believe it, I really do."

Claudia reached across the small table and squeezed Ashley's forearm. "I've been waiting four years to give you the kind of advice you gave me. Go for him, Ash. Cooper needs you."

Ashley's eyes were filled with determination. "I have no intention of letting him go."

Claudia's laugh was almost musical. "In some ways I almost pity my uncle."

Ashley was sitting on the floor with Scott on her lap when Johnny crawled in beside him. "Can we play a game, Auntie Ash?"

Ashley looked into his round blue eyes, unsure. She'd told Claudia she'd watch the boys while her friends wrapped Christmas presents, and she didn't want to get Johnny all wound up.

"What kind of game?"

"Horsey. Uncle Cooper let me ride him, and Scotty and Daddy were the other horsey."

The picture that flashed into her mind produced a warm smile. "But I wouldn't be a good horse for both you *and* Scotty," she told him gently.

A disappointed look clouded his expressive face, but he accepted her decision. "Can you read?" he asked next, and handed her a book.

"Sure." With her natural flair for theatrics, she began to read from the *Bible Story Book*.

"How many days until Jesus's birthday?" Johnny asked when she'd finished.

"Only a few now. Are you excited to open all your presents?"

Eagerly he shook his head. "If Jesus hadn't been born, would we have Christmas?" He cocked his head at a curious angle so he could look at her.

"No. We wouldn't have any churches or Sunday School, either."

"What else wouldn't we have?"

"If Jesus hadn't come, our world would be a very sad place. Because Jesus wouldn't live in people's hearts, and they wouldn't love one another the way they should."

"We wouldn't have a Christmas tree," Johnny added.

"Or presents, or Easter."

The young boy's eyes grew wide. "Not even Easter?"

"Nope."

Johnny sat quietly for a minute. "Then the best gift of all at Christmas is Jesus."

A rush of tenderness warmed Ashley's heart. "You said it beautifully."

Scotty squirmed out of her arms and onto the thick carpet, crawling with all his might toward the Christmas tree. Ashley hurriedly intercepted him and, with a laugh, swept him from the carpet and into the air high above her head.

Scotty gurgled with delight. "You like this funny looking tree, don't you?" she asked him, laughing. "I bet if you got the opportunity, every present here would be torn to shreds."

The front door closed, and she turned with Scotty in her arms to find Cooper shaking the rain from his hat.

"Hi."

He didn't see her immediately, and as he turned a surprised look crossed his dark features. Almost as quickly the look was replaced with one of welcome that sent her heart beating at an erratic pace.

"Claudia and Seth left you to the mercies of these two again?"

"No, they're wrapping presents. My duty is to keep the boys out of trouble."

He hung his coat in the hall closet and joined her, lifting Johnny into his arms. The boy squeezed Cooper's neck and gave him a moist kiss on the cheek.

"You know what Auntie Ash said?" John leaned back to look at his uncle.

"I can only guess," Cooper replied, his eyes brightening with a smile. Lovingly he searched her face.

"She said if Jesus hadn't been born, we wouldn't have Christmas."

"No, we wouldn't," Cooper agreed.

"I know something else we wouldn't have," she murmured and moistened her lips.

Johnny's gaze followed hers, and he shouted excitedly, "Mistletoe."

Cooper's eyes hadn't left hers, although his narrowed slightly as if he couldn't take them off her.

"Mistletoe," she repeated, her invitation blatant.

Motionless, Cooper held her look, but gave her no indication of what he was thinking.

Two quick strides carried him to her side. Her senses whirled as he placed Johnny on the ground and gathered her in his arms. Half of her pleasure came from the fact that he didn't look around to see if anyone was watching.

Cooper's gaze skidded to the baby she was still holding between them, and he let out a long exaggerated sigh. "No help for this. I can't kiss you properly while you're holding the baby."

"I'll take a rain check," she teased.

"But I won't," he announced, then removed Scotty from her arms and gently set him on the floor.

Ashley started to protest, but before she could utter a sound, Cooper's mouth was over hers. Winding her arms around his neck, she reveled in the feel of him as his hands gripped her narrow waist.

The sound of someone clearing their throat had barely registered with her when he abruptly broke off the kiss and breathed in deeply.

"You two forget something?" Claudia demanded, hands on her hips as she watched them with a teasing smile.

"Forget?" Ashley was still caught in the rapture; clear thinking was almost impossible. Cooper's warm breath continued to caress her cheek, and she knew he was as affected as she was.

"Like Scotty and John?"

"Oh." Ashley gasped and looked around, remembering how the baby had been enthralled with the Christmas tree.

Seth had lifted the baby by the seat of his pants and was holding him several inches off the ground.

"I think we've been found out," Ashley whispered to Cooper.

"Looks that way," he said releasing her.

Seth handed his wife the baby, who cooed happily, and the two men left the room.

"I've been meaning to ask you all day what you're wearing tomorrow," Claudia said, tucking her son close to her side.

"Wearing tomorrow?" Ashley echoed. "I don't understand?"

"To the party." Claudia looked at her as if she had suddenly developed amnesia.

"The party?"

"Cooper's dinner party tomorrow night, of course," Claudia said, laughing lightly.

The world suddenly seemed to come to an abrupt stop. Ashley's heart pounded frantically; the blood rushed to her face. In that instant she knew what it must feel like to be hit in the stomach. Claudia continued to elaborate, giving her the details of the formal dinner party. But Ashley was only half listening; the words drifted off into nothingness. The only sound that penetrated the cloud of hurt and disappointment were the words *family . . . friends*. She was neither. She was the cook's daughter, nothing more.

She heard footsteps, and her breathing became actively painful as her gaze shifted to meet Cooper's eyes. Standing there, Ashley prayed she would find something in his look that could explain why she had been excluded from the party. But all she saw was regret. He hadn't wanted her to know.

"Ashley, are those tears?" Claudia asked in a shocked whisper. "What did I say? What's wrong?"

In a haze, Ashley looked beyond the concerned face of her friend. Seth was standing with Johnny at his side, a troubled look on his face. Everyone she loved was there to witness her humiliation. Without a word, she turned and walked out of the house.

"Ashley." There was a pleading quality in Cooper's voice as he followed her out of the house. She quickened her pace, ignoring his demand that she wait. By the time he reached her, she was inside her car, the key in the ignition.

"Will you stop?" he shouted, his mouth tight. "At least give me the chance to explain."

Nothing was worth her staying and listening; he'd said everything without having uttered a word. She wanted to tell him that, but it was all she could do to swallow back the tears.

When she started the engine, Cooper tried to yank open the car door, but she was quicker and hit the lock. Jerking the car into reverse, she pulled out of the driveway. One last glance in Cooper's direction showed him standing alone, watching her leave. His shoulders were hunched in defeat.

Her cell phone was ringing even before she reached her small apartment. She knew without looking that it was Cooper. She also knew he would refuse to give up, so finally, in exasperation, she answered.

"Yes," she snapped.

A slight pause followed. "Miss Robbins?"

"Yes?" Some of the impatience left her voice.

"This is Larry Marshall, of Marshall's Antiques. You talked to me this morning about that china saucer you were looking for."

"Did you find one?"

"A friend of mine has the piece you're looking for," he told her.

"How soon can I pick it up?"

"Tomorrow, if you like. There's only one problem," he continued.

"What's that?"

"My friend's shop is in Victoria, Canada."

Ashley wouldn't have cared if it was in Alaska. Replacing Cooper's china saucer was of the utmost importance. He need never know it had come from her. She could give it to Claudia. After writing down the dealer's name and address, she thanked the man and told him she would put a check in the mail to cover his finder's fee.

Immediately after she replaced the receiver, the phone rang again. She stared at it dumbfounded, unable to move as Cooper's name came up on the screen. She stared at it for a long moment, unwilling to deal with him. After several rings she muted the phone and stuck it back inside her purse.

Silence followed, and she exhaled, unaware until then that she'd been holding her breath. Her palms hurt, and she turned her hand over and saw that her long nails had made deep indentations in the sensitive skin of her palm.

For weeks she'd tried to convince herself that Cooper wasn't ashamed to be seen with her, but the love she felt had blinded her to the truth. Even what Claudia had explained to her over lunch couldn't refute the fact that he hadn't invited her to the dinner party.

Twenty minutes later the doorbell chimed.

"Ashley!" Cooper shouted and pounded on the door. "At least let me explain."

What could he possibly say that hadn't already been said more clearly by his action?

Her heart was crying out, demanding that she listen, but she'd been foolish in the past and had learned from her mistakes. She'd been too easily swayed by her love, but not again.

"Please don't do this," he said.

Her resolve weakened. Cooper had never sounded more sincere. She jerked open the hall closet door and whipped her faux fur jacket off the hanger, put it on and zipped it up all the way to her neck. Then she threw open the front door, crossed her arms and stared at a shocked Cooper with defiance flashing from her blue eyes.

"You have three minutes." Unable to look at him, she held up her wrist and pretended an acute interest in her watch.

"Where are you going?" he demanded.

"Two minutes and fifty seconds," she answered stiffly. "But if you must know, I'm going to see Webber. He happens to like me. It doesn't matter to him that my mother's some rich man's cook, or that my father's a laborer."

"It's Webb."

"Dear heaven," she said, and laughed almost hysterically. "You've got me doing it now."

"Ashley," he said, his voice softening. "It doesn't matter to me who your mother is or where your father works.

I'm sorry about the party. I wouldn't want to hurt you for the world."

She bit into the soft skin of her inner lip to keep from letting herself be affected by his words. Her back rigid, she glared at the face of the watch, her body frozen. "Two minutes even," she murmured.

"I didn't think you'd want to come," he began again. "Mostly it's business associates—"

"Don't make excuses. I understand, believe me," she interrupted.

"I'm sure you don't," he countered sharply.

"But I do. I'm the kind of girl who enjoys pizza on the floor in front of a fireplace. I wouldn't fit in, that's what you're saying isn't it? It would be terribly embarrassing for all involved if I showed up wearing red cowboy boots. I might even break a piece of china or, worse yet, use the wrong spoon. No, I understand. I understand all too well." Her eyes and throat burned with the effort of suppressing tears. "Your time's up. Now, if you'll excuse me . . ." She stepped outside and closed the door.

"I want you to be there tomorrow night," he told her as she turned her key in the lock.

"I don't see any reason to make an issue over it. I couldn't have come anyway, I'm working tomorrow night."

"That's not true," he said harshly.

"You don't stop, do you? Does it give you pleasure to say these things to me . . . to call me a liar?" she whispered. "I suppose I should have learned how stubborn you are when I was forced to accept the car." She turned her stricken eyes to his. "I'm not lying."

"You told me school's out," he said with calculated anger.

"It is," she said. "This is my second job, the menial one. I'm a waitress, remember?"

Frustration marked his features as he followed her into the parking lot. "Ashley . . ."

"I'd like to stay and chat, but I have to be on my way." She paused and laughed mirthlessly. "I appreciate what you're trying to do, but you're the last person on God's green earth I ever want to see again. Goodbye, Cooper."

"Try to understand." The glimpse of pain she witnessed in his eyes couldn't be disguised. Despite what he'd done, she hadn't meant to hurt him, but in her own anguish she had lashed back at him. It was better that she leave now, before they said more hurtful things to one another.

A tight smile lingered on her mouth as she stared into his hard features. "I do understand," she whispered in defeat.

"I doubt that," he mumbled, as he opened the car door for her and stepped back.

She could see him in the side mirror, standing stiff and proud, his look angry, arrogant. He almost fooled her, until he lifted a hand and wiped it across his face. When he dropped his arm, she noted the pain and frustration that glittered from his eyes. The sight made her ache inside, but she wouldn't let herself be influenced, not after what he'd done.

Ashley pulled out of the parking lot, intent on doing as she'd said. Webb would know what to say to comfort her. He was her friend, and she needed him. Tears blinded her vision, and she had to wipe them aside at every traffic signal. Tears would shock Webb; he'd never seen her cry.

Webb's car was in the driveway as she pulled in. He must have seen her arrive, because he opened the front door before she'd had time to ring the bell.

"Ashley." He sounded surprised, but his amazement quickly turned to apprehension. "Are you all right? You look upset. You're not crying, are you?"

All she could do was nod. "Oh, Webb," she sobbed, and walked into his arms.

He hugged her and patted her back like a comforting big brother, which was just what she needed. "I don't suppose this has anything to do with that Cooper character, does it?"

Miserably, she nodded. "How'd you know?"

He led her into the house and closed the door. "Because he just pulled up and parked across the street."

Ashley's head snapped up. "You're kidding! You mean he followed me here?" She took a tissue from her purse and blew her nose. "He probably followed me to find out if I was telling the truth."

"The truth?"

"I told him I was coming to see you. Do you mind?" She glanced up at him anxiously.

"Of course I don't mind." Webb's enthusiasm sounded forced. "Cooper's only four inches taller than I am and outweighs me by fifty pounds. Do you think he'll give me a choice of weapons?"

"You're being silly." She laughed, and then, to her supreme embarrassment, she hiccupped.

"Hang on," he said, and disappeared into the kitchen.

A moment later he was back. "Here, drink this." He handed her a bottle of water.

She accepted because it gave her something to do with her hands. Tipping her head back, she took a large swallow.

"You're in love with him, aren't you?"

"Don't be ridiculous. I thoroughly dislike the man," she countered quickly.

"Now that's a sure sign. I wasn't positive before, but that clinched it."

"Webb, don't tease," she pleaded.

"Who's joking?" He led her to a chair, then sat across the room from her. "I've seen it coming on for the last couple of weeks. Other than the fact that he thinks I'm his arch rival and can't seem to get my name right, I like your Cooper."

"He's not mine," she said, more forcefully than she'd meant to.

"Okay, I won't argue. But if you love each other and really want things to work out, then whatever's wrong can be cleared up. If it doesn't, then you have to believe God has other plans for you."

Ashley closed her eyes for a long moment, then opened them and released a weary sigh. "You know, one of the worst things about you is that you're so darn logical. I can't stand it. I've always said an organized desk is the sign of a sick mind."

"And that, my friend, is one of the nicest things you've ever said to me."

They talked for a bit longer, and Webb did his best to raise her spirits. He joked with her, coaxing her to smile. Later they ordered pizza and played a game of Scrabble.

He won royally and refused to discount the fact that her mind wasn't on the game. When he walked her to the car, he kissed her lightly and waved as she backed out of the driveway.

Ashley slept fitfully, her heart heavy. The alarm went off at four-thirty, and she doubted that she'd gotten any rest. Cold water took the sleep out of her eyes, but she looked wan and felt worse. Connecting with the early ferry still meant a five-hour ride across Puget Sound to Victoria, British Columbia. The schedule gave her an hour to locate the antiques shop, buy the saucer and connect with the ferry home. The trip would be tiring, and she would barely have enough time to shower and change clothes before leaving for her job at Lindo's Mexican Restaurant.

She had visited the Victorian seaport many times, and its beauty had never failed to enthrall her. Usually she came in summer when the Butchart Gardens were in full bloom. She found it amazing how a city tucked in the corner of the Pacific Northwest could have the feel, the flavor and the flair of England. Even the accent was decidedly British.

Without difficulty she located the small antiques shop off one of the many side streets that catered to the tourists. When Larry Marshall phoned she'd been so pleased to have found the saucer that she'd forgotten to ask about the price. She paled visibly when the proprietor cheerfully informed her how fortunate she was to have found this rare piece and she read the sticker. Her mind balked, but her pride made two hundred dollars for one small saucer sound like a bargain.

On the return trip, she stood at the rail. A demon wind whipped her hair across her face and numbed her with its cold. But she didn't leave, her eyes following the narrow strip of land until it gradually disappeared. Only when a freezing rain began to pelt the deck did she move inside. Surprisingly, she fell asleep until the foghorn blast of the ferry woke her as they eased into the dock in Seattle.

An hour later she smiled at Manuel, Lindo's manager, as she stepped in the back door. After hanging her coat on a hook in the kitchen, she paused long enough to tie an apron around her waist.

"There's someone to see you," Manuel told her in a heavy Spanish accent.

She looked up, perplexed.

"Out front," he added.

She peered around the corner to see a stern-faced Cooper sitting alone at a table. His steel-hard eyes met and trapped her as effectively as a vice.

Nine

Carrying ice water and the menu, Ashley approached Cooper. What was he doing here? What about the party?

Dark, angry sparks flashed from his gaze, and a muscle twitched along the side of his jaw as his eyes followed her. "Where have you been all day?" he asked coldly.

Ashley ignored the question. "The daily special is chili verde." She pointed it out on the menu with the tip of her pencil. "I'll be back to take your order in a few minutes." Her voice contained a breathless tremor that betrayed what seeing him was doing to her. She hated herself for the weakness.

"Don't walk away from me," he warned. The lack of emotion in his voice was almost frightening.

"Are you ready to order now?" She took out the small pad from the apron pocket. Her fingers trembled slightly as she paused, ready to write down his choice.

"Ashley." His look was tight and grim. "Where were you?"

"I could say I was with Webb," she said, and swallowed tightly at the implication she was trying to give.

"Then you'd be lying," he added flatly.

"Yes, I would."

"Okay, we'll do this your way. It doesn't matter where you were or what sick game you've been playing with me . . ."

"Sick game?" she echoed, remarkably calm. A sad smile touched her mouth as she averted her gaze.

"I didn't mean that," he muttered.

"It doesn't matter." She lowered her chin. "You'd think by now that we could accept the fact that we're wrong for one another. Forcing the issue is only going to hurt us." She paused and swallowed past the growing tightness in her throat. "I'm not willing to be hurt anymore."

His narrowed eyes searched hers. "I want you to come to the party with me."

Sadly, she hung her head. "No."

"I've already talked to the manager. He says he doesn't think tonight's going to be all that busy anyway."

"I won't go," she repeated insistently.

"Then I'm not leaving. I'll sit here all night if that's what it takes." The tight set of his mouth convinced her the threat wasn't idle.

"But you can't, your guests . . ." She stopped, angry at how easily she'd fallen into his plan. "I won't be black-mailed, Cooper. Sit here all night if you like." Her pulse raced wildly.

"All right." His head shifted slightly to one side as he studied the menu. "I'll take a plate of nachos and the special you mentioned."

Furiously, she wrote down the order.

"You stay?" Manuel asked after she called Cooper's order into the kitchen. "I already call my cousin to come in and work for you. You can go to this important party."

"I'm here to work, Manuel," she explained in a patient tone. "I'm sure there will be enough work for both your cousin and me."

Nothing seemed to be going right. Cooper watched

her every action like a hawk studying its prey before the kill. By seven o'clock Manuel's cousin had served nearly every customer. Only two customers were seated in her section. Ashley was convinced Cooper had somehow arranged that. She wanted to cry in frustration.

"Cooper," she pleaded, "won't you please leave? It's almost seven."

"I won't go without you," he told her calmly.

"Talk about sick games," she lashed back, and to her consternation a sensuous smile curved his mouth.

"I'm not playing games," he stated firmly.

"Then if you miss your own party it's your problem." She tried to sound nonchalant.

By seven-fifteen she was pacing the floor, her resolve weakening. Cooper couldn't offend his associates this way. It could hurt him and his business.

Using the need to refill his coffee cup as an excuse, she avoided his gaze as she said, "I don't have anything to wear."

"Cowboy boots are fine. I'll wear mine, if you like." Her hand was suddenly captured between his. "Nothing in the world means more to me than having you at my side tonight."

"Oh, Cooper," she moaned. "I don't know. I don't belong there."

He studied her slowly, his eyes focused on her soft mouth. "You belong with me."

She felt the determination to defy him drain out of her. "All right," she whispered in defeat.

"Thank God." As he hurried out of the booth he added, "I'll meet you at your place."

Numbly she nodded. As it worked out, he pulled into the apartment parking lot directly behind her.

"While you change, I'll phone Claudia."

Ashley wanted to kick herself for being so weak. Examining the contents of her closet, she pulled out a wool blend dress with a Victorian flair. The antique lace inserts around the neck, bodice and cuffs gave the white dress a formal look. The glittering gold belt matched the high heels she chose.

Her fingers shook as she applied a light layer of makeup. After a moment of hurried effort, she gripped the edge of the small bathroom sink as she stopped to pray. It wasn't the first time today that she'd turned to God. She'd tried to pray standing on the deck of the ferry, the wind whipping at her, but somehow the words wouldn't come. The pain of Cooper's rejection had been too sharp to voice, even to God. Now, having finished, she lifted her head and released a shuddering breath. More confident, she added a dab of perfume to the pulse points at her wrists and neck, and stepped out to meet Cooper.

He turned around as she entered the room. A shocked look entered his eyes. "You're beautiful."

"Don't sound so surprised. I can dress up every now and then."

"You're a little pale. Come here, I can change that." Before she was aware of what he was doing, he pulled her into his arms and kissed her. The demand of his mouth tilted her head back. His hand pressed against her back, arching her against him.

Ashley's breath caught in her lungs at the unexpectedness of his action. Her hands were poised on the broad expanse of his chest, his heartbeat hammering against her palm.

"There." He tilted his face to study her. "Plenty of color now." Releasing her, he held her coat open so she could easily slip her arms inside. "I'm afraid we're going to make something of a grand entrance. Everyone's arrived. Claudia sounded frantic. She said the hors d'oeuvres ran out fifteen minutes ago."

"Is my mother . . . ?" She let the rest of the question fade, sure Cooper would know what she was asking.

"No, it's being catered." With a hand at the back of her waist, he urged her out the door.

"Oh, Cooper." She hurried back inside. "I almost forgot." Her heels made funny little noises against the floor as she rushed into her bedroom and came out with the wrapped package. "Here." She gave it to him.

"Do I have to wait for Christmas?"

"No. It's a replacement for the saucer I broke, the one from your grandmother's service."

"I can't believe . . . Where did you ever find it?"

"Don't ask."

"Ashley . . ." He set his hands on her shoulders and turned her around so she was facing him. "Is this what you were up to today?"

She nodded silently.

His mouth thinned as his look became distant. "I think I went a little crazy looking for you." He slipped an arm around her waist. "We'll talk about that later. If we keep Claudia waiting another minute, she's likely to disown us both."

The street and driveway outside Cooper's house

looked like a high performance car showroom. Ashley felt her nerves tense as she clenched her hands in her lap.

"Ashley, stop."

"Stop?"

"I can feel you tightening up like a coiled spring. Every man here is going to be envious of me. Just be yourself."

The front door flew open before they were halfway up the walk. Claudia stood there like an avenging warlord, waving her arms and glaring at them.

"Thank goodness you're here!" she exclaimed forcefully. "If you ever do this to me again, I swear I'll . . ." Her voice drifted away. "Don't stand out here listening to me, get inside. Everyone's waiting." Her gaze narrowed on Cooper. "And I do mean everyone."

Ashley didn't need to be reminded that some of the most important people in Seattle would be there.

Claudia gave her an encouraging smile, winked and took her coat.

His hand at her elbow, Cooper led Ashley into the living room. The low conversational hum rose as a few guests called out his name. Apparently the champagne had been flowing freely, because no one seemed to mind that Cooper was late to his own party.

He introduced her to several couples, though she knew she couldn't hope to remember all the names. After twenty minutes the smile felt frozen on her face. Some one handed her a glass of what she assumed was wine, but she didn't drink it. Tonight she would need to keep her wits about her in a room full of intimidating people. There was hardly room to maneuver, and she felt as if the walls were closing in around her.

"Is this the little lady who kept us waiting?" A distinguished, middle-aged man with silver streaks at his temples asked Cooper for an introduction.

"I am," she admitted with a weak smile. "I hope you'll forgive me."

"I find it very easy to forgive someone as pretty as you. Maybe we could get together later, so I can listen to your excuse."

"Whoa, Tom," Cooper teased, but his voice contained an underlying warning. "The lady's with me."

With a good-natured chuckle, Tom slapped him across the shoulder. "Anything you say."

Ashley spotted Claudia at the far side of the room. "If you'll both excuse me a minute . . . ?" she whispered.

Claudia caught her eye and arched her delicate brows.

"Boy, am I glad to see a familiar face," Ashley said, and released a slow sigh as she leaned against the wall for support.

"What took you two so long?" Claudia demanded. "I was frantic. You wouldn't believe some of the excuses I gave. Dear heavens, Ash, where were you today? I thought Cooper was going to go mad."

"Canada."

"Canada?" Claudia shot back. "Well, I must admit, that was one place he didn't look. Have you talked to your mother yet? I don't know what he said to her, but he was closed up in his den for an hour afterward. Believe me, he didn't look happy. No one, not even the boys, could get near him."

"I know he feels miserable about the whole thing, but I understand better than he realizes. I wouldn't have invited me to this party, either. Look at me. I stick out like a sore thumb."

"If you do, it's because you're the prettiest woman here."

Ashley's light laugh was forced. "You're a better friend than I thought."

"I *am* your friend, but don't underestimate yourself." A hush came over the room as someone in a caterer's apron made the announcement that dinner was ready. "I don't know why Cooper wouldn't invite you tonight. He wasn't overly pleased with me for letting the cat out of the bag, I can tell you that."

"No, I imagine he wasn't." How much simpler things would have been if she'd stayed innocently unaware. "But I'm glad you did," she murmured, and hung her head. "Very glad." When she glanced up she saw the object of their conversation weaving his way toward her. Progress was slow, as people stopped to chat or ask him a question. Although he smiled and chatted, his probing gaze didn't leave her for more than a moment.

"I don't want you hiding in a corner," he muttered when he finally got to her, and gripped her elbow, then led her toward the huge dining room.

"I'm not hiding," she defended herself. "I just wanted to talk to Claudia for a minute."

"It was far longer than a minute," he said between clenched teeth.

"Honestly, Cooper, are you going to start an argument now? I'm here under protest as it is."

"You're here because I want you here. It's where you belong." His control over his temper seemed fragile.

Rather than say anything she would regret later, Ashley pinched her mouth tightly closed.

The dining room table had been extended to accommodate forty guests. Ashley looked at the china and sparkling crystal, and the fir and candle centerpiece that extended the full length of the table. Everything was exquisite, and she was filled with a sense of awe. She didn't belong here. What was she doing fooling herself?

Cooper sat at the head of the table, with Ashley at his right side. Under normal circumstances she would have enjoyed the meal. The caterers had also supplied four waitresses, and she found herself watching their movements instead of involving herself in idle conversation with Cooper or the white-haired man on her right. Once the salad plates were removed, they were served prime rib, fresh green beans and new potatoes. Every bite and swallow was calculated, measured, to be sure she would do nothing that would call attention to herself. For dessert a cake in the shape of a yule log was carried into the room. She only took one bite, afraid she would end up spilling frosting on her white dress. Once, when she glanced up, she found Cooper watching her, his look both foreboding and thoughtful. If this was a test, she was certain she was failing miserably, and his look did nothing to boost her confidence.

When the meal was finished, she couldn't recall ever being more relieved.

Cooper's hand was pressed to her waist, keeping her at his side, as they moved into the living room. She didn't join the conversation, only smiled and nodded at the appropriate times. An hour later, her face felt frozen into a permanent smile.

A few people started to leave. Grateful for the opportunity to slip away, she murmured a friendly farewell and left Cooper to deal with his guests.

"I don't know how much more of this I can take," she whispered to Claudia.

"Don't worry, you're doing great. Not much longer now."

"Where's Seth?"

"Checking the boys. He's not much for this kind of thing, either. Haven't you noticed the way he keeps loosening his tie? By the time the evening's over, the whole thing will be missing."

"What time is it?" Ashley muttered.

"Just after eleven."

"How much longer?"

"I don't know. Don't look now, but Cooper's headed our way."

His stern expression hadn't relaxed. He was obviously displeased about something. "I want to talk to you in my den when everyone's gone." His look was ominous as he turned and left.

Primly, Ashley clasped her hands together in front of her. "Heavens, what did I do now?" she asked Claudia.

Claudia shrugged. "I don't know, but for heaven's sake, humor him. Another day like today, and Seth and I are packing our bags and finding a hotel."

By the time the last couple had left, Ashley's stomach was coiled into a hard lump.

The caterers were clearing away glasses and the last of the dishes from the living room when Cooper found her in the corner talking to Seth and Claudia. As Claudia had predicted, Seth's tie had mysteriously disappeared. His arm was draped across his wife's shoulders.

Seth looked over to Cooper. "You don't mind if we head upstairs, do you?"

"No, no, go ahead." Cooper's answer sounded preoccupied. He gestured toward his den. "We'll be more comfortable in there," he said to Ashley.

She tossed Claudia a puzzled look. Cooper didn't look upset anymore, and she didn't know what to think. His face was tight and drawn, but not with anger. She couldn't recall ever seeing him quite like this.

"Oh!" Claudia paused halfway up the stairs and turned around. "Don't forget tomorrow morning. We'll pick you up around ten. The boys are looking forward to it."

"I am, too," Ashley replied.

They entered the familiar den, and he closed the door, leaning against the heavy wood momentarily. He gestured toward a chair, and she sat down, her back straight.

Again he paused. He rubbed the back of his neck, and when he glanced up, it struck Ashley that she couldn't remember ever having seen him look more tired.

"Cooper, are you feeling all right? You're not sick, are you?"

"Sick?" he repeated slowly. "No."

"What's wrong, then? You look like you've lost your best friend."

"In some ways, I think I have." He moved across the room to his desk, rearranging the few items that littered the top.

Impatiently, Ashley watched him. He'd said he wanted to talk to her, yet he seemed hesitant.

"How do you feel about the way things went tonight?" he asked finally.

"What do you mean? Was the food good? It was excellent. Do I like your friends? I found them to be cordial, if a bit overwhelming. Cooper, you have to remember I'm just an ordinary schoolteacher."

The pencil he'd just picked up snapped in two. "You know, I think I'm sick of hearing how ordinary you are."

"What do you mean?" She watched as his mouth formed a brittle line.

"You ran to a corner to hide every chance you got. You wouldn't so much as lift a fork until you'd examined the way three other people were holding theirs to be sure you did it the same way."

"Is that so bad?" she flared. "I felt safe in a corner."

"And not with me?"

"No!"

"I think that tells me everything I want to know."

"You forced me into coming tonight," she accused him.

"It was a no-win situation. You understand that, don't you?"

She stood and moved to the far side of the room. Cooper was talking down to her as if she was a disobedient child, and she hated it. "No, I don't. But there's very little I understand about you anymore."

"I didn't invite you tonight for a reason!" he shouted.

"Do you think I don't already know that?" she flashed bitterly. "I don't fit in with this crowd."

"That's not why," he insisted loudly.

"If you raise your voice to me one more time, I'm leaving." Tears welled in her eyes. How she hated to cry. Her eyes stung, and her throat ached. "It's not the first time, either, is it?"

"What are you talking about?" He tossed her a puzzled look.

"For a while I thought it was just my overactive imagination. That I was thinking like an insecure schoolgirl. But it's true."

"What are you talking about?" What little patience he had was quickly evaporating.

"The first time we went out, you chose a small Italian restaurant, and I thought you didn't want to be seen with me."

"You can't honestly believe that?" His eyes filled with disbelief.

"Then Claudia phoned on Thanksgiving Day and I was there, but you didn't say a word." She paused long enough to swallow back a sob. "I knew you didn't want Claudia or Seth or anyone else to know I was with you. Even in church when you held my hand, it was done secretively and only when there wasn't a possibility of anyone seeing us."

A tense silence enclosed them.

"You've thought that all this time?" The dark, troubled look was back on his face.

She nodded. "I don't know about you, but I'm tired. I want to go home."

His dark eyes searched her face. She noted the weariness that wrinkled his brow and the indomitable pride in his stern jaw.

He opened the door wordlessly and retrieved her coat. He didn't say a word until he pulled up in front of her apartment building. "I find it amazing that you could think all those things, yet continue to see me."

"Now that you mention it, so do I," she returned bitterly.

His mouth thinned, but he didn't retaliate.

She handed him her apartment key, and he unlocked the door. She held out her hand, waiting for him to return the key. He didn't seem to notice, his look a thousand miles away.

When he did glance up, their eyes met and held. The troubled look remained, but with flecks of something she couldn't quite decipher. A softness entered as he lowered his gaze to her soft mouth. "It's not true, Ashley, none of it." With that he turned and left.

Stunned, she stood watching him until he was out of sight.

Her room was dark and still when she turned out the light. She hadn't behaved well tonight. That was what had originally upset Cooper. But she'd been frightened, out of her element. Those people were important, and she was nothing. The four walls surrounding her seemed to close in. Why had he left that way? For once, couldn't he have stayed and explained himself? Tomorrow she would make sure everything was cleared up between them. No more misunderstandings, her heart couldn't take it.

"Are you ready, Auntie Ash?" Johnny asked as he bounded into her apartment excitedly the next morning.

"You bet." She bent over to give her godson a big hug.

"You should hurry, 'cause Daddy's driving Uncle Cooper's car," John added.

Ashley straightened. "Where's Cooper?"

"He decided at the last minute not to come. What happened with you two last night?" Claudia asked.

"Why?"

Claudia glanced at her son, who was impatiently pacing the floor. "We'll talk about it later."

"Uncle Cooper bought the car seat just for Scotty," Johnny told her proudly when she climbed in the back seat. "He said I was a big boy and could use a special one with a real seat belt. Watch." He pulled the belt across his small body, and after several tries the lock clicked into place. "See? I can do it all by myself."

"Good for you." Ashley looped an arm around his shoulders.

"You should put yours on, too," Johnny insisted. "Uncle Cooper does."

"I think you're right," she agreed with a wry smile.

It was all Ashley could do not to quiz her friend about Cooper's absence as Seth maneuvered in and out of the heavy traffic.

"Christmas Eve Day," Johnny said as he looked around eagerly. "It's Jesus's birthday tomorrow, and we get to open all our gifts. Scotty's never opened presents."

"I don't think he'll have any problem getting the hang of it," Seth teased from the front seat.

"You're coming tonight, aren't you, Ash?" Claudia half turned to glance into the rear seat.

"I don't know," Ashley said, trying to ignore the heaviness that weighted her heart.

"But I thought it was already settled. Christmas Eve with us and Christmas with your parents."

Ashley pretended an inordinate amount of interest in the scenery flashing past outside her window. "I thought it was, too." Cooper was saying several things with his absence today. One of them was crystal clear. "Maybe I'll come for a little while. I want to see the boys open the presents from Cooper and me."

"Do I get to open a present tonight?" Johnny demanded.

Claudia threw Ashley a disgruntled look. "We'll see," she answered her son.

The downtown Seattle area was crowded with last-minute shoppers. Amazingly, Seth found a parking place on the street. While Ashley and Claudia dug through the bottoms of their purses for the correct change for the meter, Seth opened the trunk and retrieved the stroller for Scotty.

"Can I put the money in?" Johnny wanted to know.

Ashley handed him the coins and lifted him up so he could insert them into the slot.

"Good boy," Ashley said, and he beamed proudly.

"Now tell me what happened," Claudia insisted in a low voice. "I'm dying to know."

"Nothing, really. He wasn't pleased with the way the party turned out. Mainly, he was disappointed in me."

"In *you?*" Claudia looked surprised. "What did you do? I thought you were fine."

"I don't understand him, Claudia." She couldn't conceal a sigh of regret. "First, he pointedly doesn't invite me and openly admits he didn't want me there. Then he forcefully insists that I attend. And to make matters worse, he doesn't approve of the way I acted."

"If you ask me, I think he's got a lot of nerve," Claudia admitted. "I hardly spoke to him this morning. But something's wrong. He's miserable. He loves you, I'd bet my life on it. It would be a terrible shame if you two didn't get together."

"I suppose."

"You suppose?" Claudia drawled the word slowly. "If you love one another, then nothing should keep you apart."

"Spoken like a true optimist. But I'm not right for Cooper," Ashley announced sadly. "He needs someone with a little more—I hate to use this word, but . . . finesse."

"And you need someone more easy-going and fun-loving. Like Webb," Claudia finished for her.

"No, not at all." Ashley's cool blue eyes turned questioningly toward her friend. "I'm surprised you'd even suggest that. Webb's a friend, nothing more."

Clearly pleased, Claudia shook her head knowingly. "I don't think you realize that you bring out the best in Cooper, or that he does the same for you. I don't think I've seen a couple who belong together more than you two."

"Oh, Claudia, I hope we do, because I love him so much."

"Have you ever thought about letting *him* know that?"

A blustery wind whipped Ashley's coat around her, preventing her from answering.

"I think we should catch the monorail," Seth suggested. "It's getting windy out here. Agreed?"

The two women had been so caught up in their conversation they'd hardly noticed.

"Fine." Ashley nodded her head.

"Sure," Claudia said, looking a little guilty as Seth handled both boys so she could talk.

For a nominal fee they were able to catch the transport that had been built as part of the Seattle World's Fair in

1962. The rail delivered them to the heart of the Seattle Center, only a few blocks from the Food Circus.

The boys squealed with delight the minute they spied the Enchanted Forest. Scotty clapped his hands gleefully and pointed to the kiddy-size train that traveled between artificial trees.

"Are you hungry?" Seth wanted to know.

"Not me." Ashley's thoughts were on other things.

"I wouldn't object to cotton candy," Claudia confessed.

"I had to ask," Seth teased, and lovingly brushed his lips over his wife's cheek.

Ashley viewed the tender scene with building despair. Someday, she wanted Cooper to look at her like that. More than anything else, she wanted to share her life with him, have his children.

"Ash, are you all right?" Claudia asked.

Quickly, she shook her head. "Of course. What made you ask?"

"You looked so sad."

"I am, I . . ."

"My goodness, Ash, look, Cooper's here."

"Cooper?" Her spirits soared. "Where?"

"Across the room." Claudia pointed, then waved when he saw them.

His level gaze crossed the crowded room to hold Ashley's, his look discouraging.

"I'm going to do it," Ashley said, straightening. Claudia gave her a funny look, but didn't question her as she started toward him.

They met halfway. He looked tired, but just as determined as she felt.

"Ashley."

"I want to talk to you," she said sternly.

"I want to talk to *you*, too."

"Wonderful. Let me go first."

He looked at her blankly. "All right," he agreed.

"You asked me last night why I continued to see you if I believed all those things I confessed. I'll tell you why. Simply. Honestly. I love you, Cooper Masters, and if you don't love me, I think I'll die."

Ten

"That's not the kind of thing you say to a man in a public place." He studied her face for a tantalizing moment, gradually softening.

"I know, and I apologize, but I couldn't hold it in any longer."

"Why couldn't you have told me that last night?"

Oblivious to the crowds milling around, they stared at one another with only a small space separating them.

"Because I was afraid, and you were so . . ."

Cooper rubbed a hand across his eyes. "Don't say it. I know how I was."

"When you weren't with Claudia this morning, I didn't know what to think."

"I couldn't come. Not when you believed that I didn't want to be seen with you—that I was ashamed of you. You've carried that inside all these weeks, and not once did you question me."

Her teeth bit tightly into her lower lip. "I was afraid. Sounds silly, doesn't it?" She didn't wait for him to answer. "Afraid if I brought my fears into the open and forced you to admit it, that I wouldn't see you again. I couldn't face the truth if it meant losing you."

"The day you started ranting about your mother being my cook and your father being a steelworker . . . Was that the reason?"

She looked away and nodded.

Slowly he shook his head. "I can understand how you came to that conclusion, but you couldn't be more wrong. I love you, Ashley, I—"

"Cooper, oh, Cooper," she cried excitedly and threw her arms around him, spreading happy kisses over his face.

His mouth intercepted her as he hungrily devoured her lips. Although she could hear the people around them, she wouldn't have cared if they were in New York City at Grand Central Station. Cooper loved her. She'd prayed to hear those words, and nothing, not even a Christmas crowd in a public place, was going to ruin her pleasure.

When he dragged his mouth from hers, his husky voice breathed against her ear, "Do you promise to do that every time I admit I love you?"

"Yes, oh, yes," she said with a joyous smile.

He cleared his throat self-consciously. "In case you hadn't noticed, we have an audience."

She was too contented to care. A searing happiness was bubbling within her. "I want the whole world to know how I feel."

"You seem to have gotten a good start," he teased with an easy laugh, and kissed the top of her head. "Don't look now, but Claudia and company are headed our way."

Reluctantly, Ashley dropped her arms and stepped back. Cooper pulled her close to his side, cradling her waist.

"Is everything okay with you two, or do you need more time?" Claudia's gaze went from one of them to the other. "If that embrace was anything to go by, I'd say things are looking much better."

"You could say that," Cooper agreed, his eyes holding Ashley's. The look he gave her was so warm and loving that it seemed to burst free and touch her heart and soul.

"But there are several things we need to discuss," Cooper continued. "If you don't mind, I'm going to take Ashley with me. We'll all meet back at the house later."

Claudia and Seth exchanged knowing looks. "We don't mind," Seth answered for them.

"But . . . Seth has your car," Ashley said, confused. "How will we . . . ?"

He smiled. "I have a second car, since I can't afford to be without transportation. We'll be fine."

"Do I still get to open a present tonight? Because Auntie Ash said we could," Johnny quizzed anxiously, not the least bit interested in the logistics of the grown-ups' plans.

Cooper's eyes met Claudia's, and she shrugged.

"I think that will be fine, if that's what your Auntie Ash said," Seth interrupted.

"Uncle Cooper?" John's head tilted up at an inquiring angle.

"Yes?" He squatted down so that he was eye level with his godson.

"Is there mistletoe here, too?"

Briefly Cooper scanned the interior of the huge building. "I don't see any, why?"

"'Cause you were kissing Auntie Ash again."

"Sometime I like to kiss her even when there isn't any reason."

"You mean like Daddy and Mommy?"

"Exactly," he said, and smiled as his eyes caught Ashley's.

"I think it's time we left and let these two talk. We'll meet you later," Seth announced. Claudia lifted Johnny into her arms and turned around, then looked back and winked.

"Are you hungry?" Cooper asked.

She hadn't eaten all day. "Starved. I hardly touched dinner last night."

"I noticed." His tone was dry.

She ignored it. "And then this morning I was too miserable to think about food. But now I could eat a cow."

"We're at the right place. Choose what you want, and while you find us a table, I'll go get it."

The Food Circus had a large variety of booths that sold every imaginable cuisine. The toughest decision was making a choice from everything that was available.

They hardly spoke as they ate their chicken. Ashley licked her fingers. Cooper carefully unfolded one of the moistened towelettes that had been provided with their meal and carefully cleaned his own hands.

He glanced up and found her watching him. A tiny smile twitched at the corner of her mouth. "What's so funny?" he asked.

"Us." She opened her own towelette and followed his example. "Claudia told me she didn't know any two people more meant for each other."

Cooper acknowledged the statement with a curt nod. "I know I love you, whether we're right or wrong for each other doesn't seem to be the question." He reached across the table and captured her hand. "But then, you're an easy person to love. You're warm and alive, and so unique you make my heart sing just watching you."

"And you're so calm and dignified. Nothing rattles you, and so many times I've wished I could be like that."

"We balance one another." His eyes searched hers in a room that seemed filled with only them.

A burst of applause diverted Cooper's attention to the antics of a clown. "Let's get out of here."

Ashley happily agreed.

They stood, dumped their garbage in the proper receptacles and linked their arms around one another's waists as they strolled outside.

A chill raced over her forearms, and she shivered.

Cooper brought her closer to his side. "Cold?"

"Only when you close me out," she whispered truthfully. "If you hadn't admitted to loving me, I don't know that I could have withstood the cold."

He drank deeply from her eyes, perhaps realizing for the first time how strong her emotions rang. "We need to talk," he murmured, and quickened his pace.

A half hour later he pulled into the driveway of his home.

"Coffee?" he suggested as he hung her coat in the hall closet.

"Yes." She nodded eagerly. "But, Cooper, could I have it in a mug? I'd feel safer."

His mouth thinned slightly, and she knew her request had troubled him. "I'm not the dainty teacup type," she said more forcefully than she wanted to. "What I mean is . . ."

"I know what you mean." Lightly he pressed a kiss on her cheek, then against the hollow of her throat. "Do you have any idea how difficult it's been this week to keep my hands off you?"

"Not half as difficult as it's been not to encourage you to touch me," she admitted, and felt color suffuse her cheeks.

A few minutes later he carried two ceramic mugs into the den on a silver platter.

A soft smile danced from Ashley's eyes. "Compromise?"

"Compromise," he agreed, handing her one of the mugs.

She held it with both hands and stared into its depths. "I have a feeling I know what you're going to say."

"I doubt that very much, but go ahead."

"No." She shook her head, then nervously tugged a strand of hair around her ear. "I've put my foot in my mouth so many times that for once I'm content to let you do the talking."

"We seem to have a penchant for saying the wrong things to each other, don't we?" His gaze searched hers, and the silence was broken only by an occasional snap and pop from the logs in the fireplace.

His look was thoughtful as he straightened in his chair. Nervously, she glanced around the den she had come to love—the books and desk, the chess set. One of the most ostentatious rooms in the house and, strangely, the one in which she felt the most comfortable. Maybe it was because this was the room Cooper used most often.

"I think it's important to clear away any misunderstandings, especially about the party. Ashley, when I saw how hurt you were to be excluded, well . . . I can't remember ever feeling worse. Believe this, because it's the truth. I wanted you there from the first. But I felt you would be uncomfortable. Those people are a lot like me."

"But I love you," she said, keeping her gaze on her coffee.

"I didn't know that at the time. I didn't want to do anything that was going to make you feel ill-at-ease. Thrusting you into my world could have destroyed our promising relationship, and that was far more important to me. Now I realize what a terrible mistake that was."

"And the other things?" She had to know, had to clear away any reasons for doubt.

"Thinking over everything you've told me, your point of view makes perfect sense." He set his cup aside and sat on the ottoman in front of her chair. Holding her face with both hands, he tilted her gaze to meet his. Ashley couldn't doubt the sincerity of his look. "I did those things because I thought you wouldn't want to be associated with me. I didn't let Claudia know you were here on Thanksgiving when she phoned to protect you from speculation and embarrassing questions. The same with what happened in church."

"Oh, Cooper . . ." She groaned at her own stupidity. "I was so miserable. I know it was stupid not to say anything, but I was afraid of the truth."

His kiss was sweet and filled with the awe of the discovery of her love. "Things being what they are, maybe you should open your Christmas gift now."

"Oh, could I?"

"I think you'd better." He opened the closet and brought out a large, beautifully wrapped box.

Much bigger than an engagement ring, Ashley mused thoughtfully, fighting to overcome her disappointment. Cowboy boots? She'd tried on a couple of pairs when they'd bought his, but she'd decided against them because of the expense. But if her present was cowboy boots, why would Cooper feel it was important to give it to her now?

He placed it on her lap, and she untied the red velvet bow, then hesitated. "My gift to you is at home." It was important that he know he'd meant enough to her to buy him something special. "But I'm making you wait until Christmas."

"Maybe I should make *you* wait, too," he teased, ready to take back the gaily wrapped present.

"No you don't," she objected, and gripped the package tightly.

"Actually," he said, and the teasing light left his eyes, "it's important that you open this now." He smiled huskily and kissed her. His lips were a light caress across her brow.

Ashley's fingers shook as she pulled back the paper and lifted the lid of the box. Inside, nestled in white tissue, was a large family Bible. Her heart was thumping so loudly she could barely hear Cooper speaking above the hammering beat.

"A Bible," she murmured and looked up at him, her gaze probing his.

"I've thought about what you said about your relationship with Christ, and how important it was to you. I wanted to have a strong faith for you, because of my love. But that wasn't good enough. There were so many things I didn't understand. If Christ paid the price for my salvation with His life, then how can my faith be of value if all I have to do is ask for it?" He stood and walked across the room, pausing once to run his hand through his hair. "I talked to Seth about it several times. He always had the answers, but I wasn't convinced. Last Sunday I was in church, sitting in the sanctuary waiting for the service to begin, and I asked God to help me. On the way out of church after the service I saw the car I had given you in the parking lot. Suddenly I knew."

Ashley had been at church, but she had taught Sunday School and then helped in the nursery during the worship service. She had talked only briefly to Claudia and hadn't seen Cooper at all.

"My car? How did my car help?"

"It sounds crazy, I know," he admitted wryly. "But I gave it to you because I love you. Freely, without seeking reimbursement, knowing that you couldn't afford a car. It was my gift to you, because I love you. It suddenly occurred to me that was exactly why Christ died for me. He paid the price because I couldn't."

Unabashed tears of happiness clouded her eyes as her hands lovingly traced the gilded print on the cover of the Bible.

"I've made my commitment to Christ," he told her, his voice rich and vibrant. "He's my Savior."

"Oh, Cooper." She wiped a tear from her cheek and smiled up at him.

"That's not all."

An overwhelming happiness stole through her. She couldn't imagine anything more wonderful than what he'd just finished explaining.

"Do you recall the first Sunday Claudia and Seth arrived?"

Ashley nodded.

"I stepped into your Sunday School class." He looked

away as a glossy shine came over his dark eyes. "You were on the floor with a little girl sitting in your lap."

"I remember. You turned around and walked out. I thought I'd done something to upset you."

"Upset me?" he repeated incredulously. "No. Never that. You looked up, and your blue eyes softened, and in that moment I imagined you holding another child. Ours. Never have I felt an emotion so strong. It nearly choked me, I could hardly think. If I hadn't turned around and walked away, I don't know what I would have done."

Ashley thought her heart would burst with unrestrained joy. "Our child."

"Yes." Cooper knelt on the floor beside her, took the Bible out of its box and set the box on the floor. Reverently, he opened the first pages of the holy book. "I got this one for a reason. I've written our names here, and I'm asking that we fill the rest out together."

Ashley looked down at the page, which had been set aside to record a family history. Both their names were entered under "Marriage," the date left blank.

"Will you marry me, Ashley?" he asked, an unfamiliar humble quality in his voice.

The lump of joy in her throat prevented her from doing anything but nodding her head. "Yes," she finally managed. "Yes, Cooper, yes." She flung her arms around his neck and spread kisses over his face. She laughed with breathless joy as the tears slid down her cheeks.

His arms went around her as he pulled her closer. His mouth found hers in a lingering kiss that cast away all doubts and misgivings.

She lovingly caressed the side of his face. "I don't

know how you can love me. I always seem to think the worst of you."

"Not anymore you won't," he whispered against her temple as he continued to stroke her back. "I won't ever give you reason to doubt again. I love you, Ashley."

She linked her hands behind his neck and smiled contentedly into his eyes. "I do want children. Just being with Johnny and Scott has shown me how much I want babies of my own."

"We'll fill the house. I can't wait to tuck them into bed at night and listen to their prayers."

"What about horsey rides?"

"Those, too."

"Cooper . . ." She paused and swallowed tightly. "Why were you so angry with me after the party?" She wanted everything to be right and needed to know what she'd done to displease him.

Some of the happiness left his face. "I love you so much, Ashley. It hurt me to see you so uncomfortable, afraid to make a move. Your fun-loving, outgoing nature had been completely squelched. I wanted you to be yourself. Later—" He sat on the ottoman and took both her hands in his. "—I had already gotten the Bible with the hope of asking you to marry me, and you listed off all the things I had done to make you believe I was ashamed to be seen with you. I don't mind telling you that it shook me up. I was on the verge of asking you to be my wife, and you didn't even know how much I loved you."

"I won't have that problem again," she told him softly.

"I know you won't, because you'll never have reason to doubt again. I promise you that, my love."

The sound of footsteps in the hall brought their attention to the world outside the door.

Cooper stood, and extended a hand toward her. "I don't think either Claudia or Seth will be surprised by our announcement. Or your family, for that matter."

"My family?"

"I talked to your mother and father yesterday. They've given us their blessing. I was determined to have you, Ash. I wouldn't want to live my life without you now." He hugged her tightly and curved an arm around her waist. "Christmas. It's almost too wonderful to believe. God gave His Son in love. And now He's given me you."

While on a solo holiday trip,
one woman rediscovers her passion for music,
reconciles with her family, and falls in love in
this inspiring novel from #1 *New York Times*
bestselling author Debbie Macomber.

A Christmas Duet

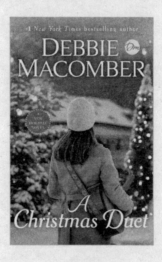

Read on for a special sneak peek!
Available soon from Ballantine Books

One

Hailey Morgan's doorbell chimed, and she hurried to answer, eager for her best friend to arrive. This was the last day of school before the holiday break and Hailey was more than ready to celebrate. As teachers at George Washington High School, Hailey and Katherine were set for a girl's night. They'd debated about going out but in the end decided simply relaxing at home sounded like a far better idea. Hailey had offered to host. She had heavily spiked eggnog at the ready and would follow up with popcorn later for the Christmas movie. Katherine was ordering the pizza.

Throwing open her apartment door, Hailey greeted her friend with a hug. "Free at last," she squealed. "Has any school day ever seemed so long?"

"It lasted forever," Katherine groaned, as she removed her hat and coat and tossed them over the arm of the chair.

The two had worked at the high school for three years. They'd been hired at the same time and quickly become fast friends.

"You got the eggnog?" Katherine asked.

"All counted for," Hailey assured her.

"The pizza is ordered for delivery," she paused and glanced at the time. "At any minute."

Just then the doorbell chimed. Katherine opened it,

took the pizza box from the teenage driver and passed along a generous tip. "Thank you," she said and promptly closed the door.

Hailey got out the paper plates and red pepper flakes. Like so many other similarities, they both shared a love of spicy food.

Slouching down on the sofa side by side, they indulged in the Hawaiian pizza, too busy enjoying their dinner to talk.

After a few moments, Katherine paused between bites. "I take it your day was as hectic as mine."

"As bad or worse," Hailey said with a heavy sigh.

The music students had their minds on anything but schoolwork. Even her band class had been chaotic, with everyone anxious for the school day to end. The teens had been watching the clock, counting down the minutes, which was exactly what Hailey had done.

Katherine taught American history, and Hailey could well imagine her friend's day. In the best of times, it was hard to control the classroom full of hormone enhanced teenagers, glued to their cell phones and posting on social media. With vacation looming and Christmas in the air, it had become nearly impossible for a teacher to hold their attention. It'd become especially hard for Hailey after the band's holiday performance earlier in the week.

"We survived," Hailey reminded Katherine.

"Barely," Katherine added.

When they finished, Hailey took their dirty plates into the kitchen.

Katherine followed her, opened the refrigerator, and brought out the rum enhanced eggnog. "What those little hellions didn't realize was that I was as anxious to get out of school as they were."

"Amen, sister."

The two returned to the sofa and Hailey relaxed, bringing up her knees and bracing her feet against the edge of the coffee table. She brushed a strand of her long brown hair behind her ear.

"Which movie do you want to watch first?" she asked.

"You pick," Katherine said with a wave of her hand. "I'm too exhausted to think."

"How about *Love Actually*?" That was one of Hailey's all-time favorites.

"Sure." Katherine settled into the sofa as she sampled the eggnog.

Reaching for the remote, Hailey cued up the movie. Mentally exhausted as she was, her thoughts went every which direction. Her day had been nothing but drama with her students. The only thing that had kept her sane was this silly melody that had been bouncing around in her head. The tune wouldn't leave her alone for several days now to the point where it was all she could hear. This was the way it'd been from the time she'd been in grade school. Music was the language of her heart, and composing it gave her a sense of joy unlike anything else.

Even as a child Hailey had gone to sleep only to dream up melodies and then the lyrics. Writing songs was as much a part of her as breathing. She'd started piano lessons in first grade after her mother had been unable to tear her away from the keyboard at church. In all, she played six instruments, some better than others. Each one filled a need in her, a desire to create. She'd loved her piano teacher and hated it when the family had moved a year later. Her father's job, working as a pharmaceutical salesman had required several moves during Hailey and her sister, Daisy's childhood.

As the assistant band director, Hailey enjoyed sharing her enthusiasm with her students. They inspired her. Her dream, however, was to one day support herself as a song-writer.

Halfway through the movie, Katherine reached for the remote and paused it. "Did I mention my parents arranged a ski vacation for the entire family at Whistler?" she asked, her eyes dancing with delight.

Hailey grinned. "Only about twenty times."

"It's going to be incredible. And the best part is that Shawn will be joining us on the twenty-sixth."

Shawn was Katherine's current love interest. Over the three years Hailey had known her, she'd watched her friend drift in and out of relationships. This time though was different. Shawn had lasted longer than any of Katherine's previous relationships. Hailey was pleased for her friend and wished her every happiness.

"He's spending Christmas with his family and then driving up to Whistler."

"I didn't know he skied," Hailey commented.

"He hasn't since high school. It says a lot that he's willing to take it up so he can spend time with me and my family."

"That it does," Hailey agreed.

"Is Zach still bugging you?" Katherine asked.

Hailey wanted to grind her teeth in frustration. She'd dated Zach all through college and Hailey, and her parents, too, had assumed Zach would propose following graduation. Instead of a wedding proposal, he'd dumped her. Three years later, out of the blue, he'd reached out, wanting to reconnect. Hailey wasn't interested. Zach, however, didn't seem to be getting the message. "Can you believe this? He sent a text suggesting he join my family for Christmas."

"What?" Katherine was as shocked as Hailey. "After what he did to you, he has the audacity to invite himself to your family Christmas."

To be fair, Zach hadn't technically dumped her, although he might as well have. Following graduation, when she was expecting a marriage proposal, they'd had the *talk*.

Before he was willing to make a commitment, the ever-practical Zach wanted to be sure they both were on the same page regarding the future and wanted the same things. That made sense, and Hailey had been pleased he'd taken the idea of marriage seriously.

Instead, their discussion turned out to be a kick in the gut. Zach wanted Hailey to be realistic about her career choice. It was all fine and good that she liked to write music, according to Zach, but there wasn't a glimmer of hope that she had what it took to make it big. He pointed out that while she had a pleasant singing voice, it wasn't good enough to garner her the attention she would need. Too many others were far more talented than she could ever hope to be.

Hailey accepted the fact that she wasn't another P!NK or Taylor Swift and that was fine. It was the songs she wrote and intended to sell. Songwriting was her gift. Not performing.

She didn't argue, which only fed the flames of Zach's speech. He'd gone on to say, because she was an introvert, she simply didn't have the personality to face the highly competitive professional world of music. Zach reminded her that she'd never been one to stand out in a crowd or to make sure she was noticed. Another truth that had eaten away at her hopes of ever succeeding. He insisted that if they were to consider marrying, she would need to put aside her fanciful dreams, be practical and find employment that would help build their financial future. He needed a wife who would support and encourage him and his career and didn't want one who would be distracted with fanciful, impractical dreams of her own. The bottom line was that she had to choose; it was either him, or her music.

The decision had been easy. She'd loved Zach, but she couldn't change who she was or deny the gift she had been given. With tears in her eyes and her heart breaking, she told Zach that no matter what the future held, she felt she had to write her songs. Without the smallest hesitation, Zach had accepted her decision and walked out of her life.

Even now, three years later, his discouragement and lack of faith hurt. What pained her most was the fact that he'd never really known her heart. For nearly two years, her creativity had been stymied. She hadn't been able to release the hold his negativity had branded on her soul. Every effort she'd made to write ended up in the wastebasket. Only in the last several months had she found her mojo again. She'd composed a few songs, even sold one to a radio station for an advertisement. Lately this charming Christmas ditty had been playing in her mind day and night. She was anxious to pick up her guitar and get the notes and lyrics down on paper over the holiday break.

And now, shockingly after three long years, Zach was back.

Well, sort of.

It started in November with a text message asking Hailey how she was doing. To say she was surprised to hear from him would be an understatement. He made no reference to their split, as if the years since they'd parted had never happened. Not one word of regret or a single anything of what had transpired. Even now, nearly a month later, Hailey didn't know what to make of this sudden change of heart, or if it even was one.

Her initial response had been polite, but she made it perfectly clear she had no desire for a reconciliation. More text messages followed. She answered the next couple with short one or two words, letting him know she wasn't willing to engage in this conversation. Then she stopped answering. That hadn't dissuaded him.

Zach continued with texts and emails, telling her about his job with Microsoft, which was what he'd always wanted. He was well on his way to another promotion and pay raise and had purchased a home in Kirkland close to the job site. His life seemed to be perfect in every way.

Most conversations and texts revolved around him and his nearly perfect life. Hailey found it all rather confusing, unsure what to make of this sudden interest. He hinted that he missed her and wished for them to get together again. Not once did he ask about her songwriting as if it was a moot point.

"Zach wants to join your family for Christmas?" Katherine repeated. "You've got to be kidding."

"I wish. I let him know that wasn't going to happen. I

don't know what more I can say to convince him I'm not interested. He seems to feel if he keeps contacting me that eventually he'll wear me down and I'll change my mind. That isn't going to happen."

"I should think not, after what he did."

Hailey treasured Katherine's friendship her support and encouragement.

"Did he get the message this time?" her friend asked.

"I can only hope. Part of the problem is my mom," Hailey said, thinking out loud. If her mother got wind of Zach reaching out, she'd be thrilled with the possibility of the two of them getting back together.

"Mom was always Zach's biggest champion. She was devastated when we split. My mother would do everything she could to get us back together."

"Does she know he's reached out."

"I certainly haven't said anything, and I won't. What she doesn't know can't encourage her."

"What if Zach contacts her?"

Hailey didn't want to consider the possibility. Dread filled her. It would be just like Zach to go behind Hailey's back.

A sinking feeling swept over her. Hailey was convinced that reaching out to her mother was likely Zach's backup plan to win her over.

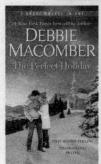
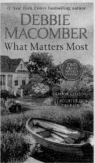
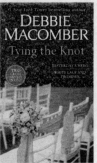
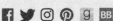